FARSIDE

ISBN-13: 978-1518837418
ISBN-10: 1518837417

Cover design by JT Lindroos.
Book design and layout by Fresh Ink Foundry.
CreateSpace Independent Publishing.

For Matthew:

Who at the tender age of five informed his parents that when he grew up he was going to ride a motorcycle on the Moon and smoke cigarettes. We're still not sure what to think about that.

Luna

Keep breathing.

Human nature deceives us into taking our body's routine exchange of oxygen for granted, until that fundamental task becomes impossible.

Simon Poole could barely think of anything else now, despite having spent much of his adult life at the mercy of machinery that protected his fragile body and provided for its every need. He'd learned how to escape from a crippled submarine and to survive rapid decompressions in space, but throughout it all the simple act of breathing had always been something that just was.

Until now.

His skin stung from a million needle pricks, a warning from his capillaries of the rapidly evacuating air. His lungs strained to absorb the pitifully scarce oxygen molecules, and soon the ambient pressure would be so low that reflexively holding his breath would rupture them like overinflated balloons. He forced himself to exhale, an act of will against the animal panic that would come before hypoxia and delirium set in.

He just hoped his eyeballs didn't freeze first.

Simon pulled at release clamps surrounding the airlock hatch and cursed the engineers who made them so overcomplicated. What a damned stupid place to store the emergency patch kits in the first place. More items for his flight debrief when (if?) they returned to Denver.

Sidewalls fluttered behind him as the supporting air escaped. Built around a central utility tunnel, the hab module was essentially a big cylindrical Kevlar balloon which now threatened to deflate like a worn party favor. The cylinder walls began to collapse inward, something his vacuum-addled brain oddly welcomed. It was getting awfully cold in here. A blanket would be nice.

Keep breathing.

His focus returned along with a sudden, piercing headache. Simon braced himself against the hatch rim and gave the lever a final, frantic pull. He recoiled from a stinging blow as the stubborn portal flew open and connected with his forearm. With higher air pressure on the other side, the simple act of breaking the seal had been enough to spring the hatch as if it had been kicked open by some invisible giant. Simon ignored the pain to push ahead, inhaling deeply as the compartment emptied into the void behind him. The near-blinding migraine mercifully disappeared with it.

Thinking clearly again, he moved to shut the hatch with his good arm. It was much harder now, having to work against the torrent of air. Grunting from the strain, he finally felt the door seat itself against the rim. There was a satisfying whistle as the pressure stabilized.

Peering back through a small porthole, he watched helplessly as the hab collapsed around its core. Now fully exposed to space, its once-rigid fabric hung like loose sails in doldrum seas.

Simon turned away to numbly take stock of his surroundings: emergency rations, first aid kit...and the caulk gun from the emergency patch kit. Fat lot of good that'd do now.

He took another luxurious lungful of air and exhaled with a sigh as he realized this tiny compartment was likely to become his sarcophagus. As the ancient Egyptian kings had once commanded their servants to face eternity buried with them beneath the great pyramids, so would he spend it in this small aluminum cylinder, doomed to forever circle the Moon.

Keep breathing.

1

Polaris AeroSpace Lines
Denver, Colorado
Two hours earlier

Audrey Wilkes could have sworn her watch was running backwards. Hadn't it already been two a.m. an hour ago?

The Omega Speedmaster on her wrist, a feminine version of the classic astronaut model, had been the one indulgence she'd permitted herself when Arthur Hammond hired her away from NASA. From the moment she'd removed it from the box, Audrey had kept it meticulously synchronized with the Naval Observatory's atomic clock and never took it off, save for her habitual trail runs through the foothills after work.

Night shift in the flight control center threatened to become a permanent fixture of her existence. The boss still wanted his lead flight director on duty during the critical phases of each mission—*cruise,* she corrected herself—but those always seemed to happen after the sun had gone down. Driven by physics and the needs of their customers, at times it was hard to tell which was the more exacting.

In this case, taking paying passengers into lunar orbit had been a constant balancing act between the two competing needs and her presence was probably the only reason Grant, or even Hammond himself, hadn't been hovering around the control center in the middle of the night. Which was a real shame, as they usually brought plenty of food for the night crew.

Hammond had practically lived here during the first proving flights into lunar orbit, at least until the Federal Aviation Administration's new Office of Space Transportation was satisfied that they could reliably run something more than a simple free-return trajectory. That Art had also managed to keep up with the rest of the business throughout all of that

FAA micro-management convinced her to stay in Flight Ops. Rocket science was a lot more straightforward.

This trip, however, had become as demanding as all of their previous flights together. A multinational expedition bankrolled by Middle Eastern oil concerns, it was led by a celebrity scientist who'd been keenly interested in surveying the lunar surface from orbit. They were 21st century prospectors loaded out with optical telescopes, laser interferometers and even a compact magnetic mass driver instead of pans and pickaxes.

It made sense, she thought. As OPEC's grip on the world's oil supply weakened, a whole new economy was opening up beyond Earth orbit. And wherever humans went, the need for resources followed. Water and its base elements, oxygen and hydrogen, would be more precious up there than petroleum had ever been down here. And if the Moon held the vast stores of Helium-3 that many believed, the potential for a new clean energy economy would be staggering. Hammond's engineers wouldn't be the only ones building landers if that came to pass.

Audrey impatiently tapped a pencil along the edge of her desk as she studied the big wall screens. Behind her, rows of flight controllers and technicians monitored the company's fleet of suborbital Clippers. Having placed most of the world's major cities within two hour's reach, the spaceplanes had become as close to routine as they would probably ever be—not that "routine" carried much meaning around here. Art always had another big idea waiting in the wings; she'd decided his life's goal must have been to amass enough wealth to build all of the fantastic machines he'd imagined since childhood.

Industry pundits had assumed the "Block II" orbital Clippers would be his last venture. Sharing the original model's same general form, their upgraded engines and external drop tanks allowed regular flights to orbit from the old shuttle landing strip at Cape Canaveral. But instead of ending there, Hammond had sown the profits into his next venture: cruise liners known as "Cyclers" that continually flew on a long-period orbit between Earth and Moon.

The Cyclers were actually less complicated than the Clippers that serviced them. A barrel-shaped inflatable module held enough living space for up to a dozen people. It was capped at either end by docking ports: one was surrounded by a cluster of tanks, antennae and solar panels. On its own this could host people in orbit for weeks, but when joined with a separate propulsion module it could be pushed out to the Moon. This "flight module" was a fat cylinder of carbon fiber and aluminum festooned with tanks, thrusters, and a bulky cluster of rocket engines at its rear. Its tapered front end featured two large oval windows above a nose-mounted docking port, which made it look for all the world like a hound dog's snout. It was no coincidence they'd quickly nicknamed the two flight modules *Snoopy I* and *II*.

Audrey had been skeptical of sending a big Kevlar balloon full of people off into the void, but enough ground tests with various projectiles fired from a high pressure cannon finally convinced her the stack could survive several micro-meteor strikes. The first Cycler, *Shepard*, had been circling back and forth from the Moon for almost a year now with barely a hiccup. Once the second ship, *Grissom*, had finished its checkouts there would be a constant stream of new travelers coming and going around the Moon.

Her mental meanderings were interrupted by the trajectory officer: "Loss of Signal in five, Aud."

As "Big Al" fell tail-first around of the Moon, its main engines would slow them down enough to let gravity capture it. Taking a Cycler out of its permanent free return orbit for the first time was eventful enough; that it would all happen after they'd slipped behind the far side and into radio blackout didn't make it any easier for Audrey to project calm.

"Copy that," she said, irritated that she'd let her mind wander again. She had to get off the graveyard shift one of these days.

• • •

SS Shepard

Simon Poole had been around the world many times over, though the depths he'd navigated as a submariner had kept him from enjoying much of a view. Or for that matter, most of the world's exotic ports.

His second career as an astronaut made up for it. Similar as spaceflight could be to life on his beloved nuke boats, he relished the differences: windows, mainly. Though everyone asked about weightlessness, which had always mystified him: who wouldn't want to come up here just for the view?

A perk of being Captain was having lots of opportunities to enjoy that view. Besides the flight module's forward windows, a small observation dome was mounted in the overhead behind them. Its unobstructed view of the entire Earth-Moon system offered a stunning demonstration of the distances they traveled and of the yawning gulf beyond.

Simon stole a glance over the pilot's shoulder to get his bearings before floating up into the dome. The darkened Moon loomed like a hole in the roof of stars, threatening to swallow Earth's tiny crescent before leaving them in the far side's shadow.

He turned at a rustling sound beneath him to find a stocky man in a passenger's jumpsuit. Their lead client was recognizable right away by his neatly trimmed goatee. "Good evening, Dr. Varza. Trouble sleeping again?"

Kamran Varza was uncharacteristically sheepish. "I'm afraid so," he admitted. "I find it difficult to get used to, and I'm afraid Doctor DeCarlo is too excited for everyone's sake. He's forever fretting over his instruments and muttering to himself."

"Not much we can do about the latter problem, but we stock plenty of sleep aids for the former." Adjusting to long term microgravity could be harder than most people expected, and having to deal with someone else's noise made finding rest that much harder. There was much to be said for having a soft bed in a quiet room at the end of a long day.

"They're narcotics, if I'm not mistaken?" Varza looked disappointed. "If so, I must decline."

"Of course, Doctor," Simon apologized, forgetting his passengers' strict religious preferences. "My apologies."

Varza flashed the disarming smile that had become his trademark. "Think nothing of it, Captain. The truth be known, sleep is doubtful. There's much to be anxious about."

"No need to worry. We've practiced this several times." *In the simulators*, he didn't add. Worrisome as it could be to fall tail-first past a giant ball of rock at five thousand kilometers per hour, slowing down just enough to get flung into orbit without crashing into the surface, Simon's bigger fear was getting out of orbit when they were done. *With my luck, the engines will work fine the first time and go tits up the second.* Which was when it really counted. Otherwise, there would be no return trip home—at least not until they could send the other Cycler out to meet them. And depending on where they were in relation to each other, that trip could easily take a month. The Cycler's usual "free return" trajectory had ensured there was no way they wouldn't emerge from blackout.

"I do appreciate your confidence," Varza said. "But tell me, are you certain it would not be possible to observe from up here? The view is so much better than from my room."

He was tempted to oblige but their safety rules were strict: no passengers on the control deck during critical phases of flight. "I'm afraid not. This is one of those times when we have to insist everyone buckle down in their cabins."

Varza almost looked relieved. "Of course," he said, his eyes studying the control deck. "Why isn't your entire crew up for this?"

"Mister Brandt is off duty in his quarters." Either Simon or his First Officer was always at work in the control deck or resting in the crew compartment.

Varza appeared pleased. "Then I shall leave these matters in your capable hands. Good night, Captain."

Simon nodded politely as Varza flew back into the connecting tunnel. Once the cabin was clear, he floated forward to settle into the observer's seat behind the pilots. It had been turned into a de facto Captain's chair, not entirely by accident as Simon had overseen the cabin layout. "Sorry for the distraction, fellas. Have to play nice with the payload."

"We'd get that a lot on the Clippers," one said, "but the passengers didn't have as much time in zero g. Tended to keep their wanderings to a minimum."

"Hardened cockpit doors didn't hurt either," Simon pointed out. He unlocked a flat screen from overhead and rotated it down to face him. "Looks like I'm just in time," he said, studying the situation display. "Anything change?"

"Negative," the senior pilot said, not turning away from his own instruments. "Just finished the LOI checklist. Loss of signal in thirty seconds, burn still at plus two minutes."

Simon grunted his approval as he finished snapping himself into the seat's four-point harness. He pulled his headset microphone in close and thumbed the intercom switch. "This is the Captain," he announced quietly, mindful of their light sleepers. "We are two minutes from lunar orbit insertion. You'll feel mostly normal gravity for about five minutes while we're braking, so please strap in and secure any loose items in your sleeping berths."

The copilot finished their final checklist with Denver just as Earth slipped beneath the horizon. Their radio's reassuring buzz stuttered into silence, their tenuous link to home replaced by an eerie hiss: the background noise of the universe.

Simon tuned out that audible reminder of their isolation, preferring to study the two pilots as they did their jobs. Satisfied that the ship's orientation was on target, he reached up to kill the volume. The cabin was utterly silent but for the hum of air circulation fans. "You guys mind if I switch to low light?"

"Go for it."

He flipped a selector switch and turned the cabin from cool blue-white to red, preserving their night vision. As their eyes adjusted, the black sky exploded with stars. One arm of the Milky Way slashed across the void as if it had torn the fabric of the universe, exposing a treasure trove of delicate jewels.

"Nice job, skipper."

"I can't take credit for that," he said, "but you're welcome anyway." If the far side was going to cut them off from the rest of humanity, they might as well enjoy the view.

"Retro burn in ten," the copilot announced.

Simon switched his panel to mirror the pilot's primary flight display. A computer generated Moon rotated past as they followed a narrow corridor around it. A pulsating dot floated just ahead, a graphic depiction of an empty point in space which represented the culmination of all their efforts. The ship's big orbital engines fired as they crossed it, pushing them into their seats and filling the ship with the reassuring thunder of properly functioning rockets.

The command pilot had to raise his voice over the new noise. "LOI on target. Nominal chamber pressure and propellant flow—"

Crack.

Simon whipped his head around. He'd long ago become familiar with Big Al's odd creaks and shimmies, random noises that eventually settled into familiar patterns and could tell a man more about the condition of his vessel than instruments ever could.

This sounded more ominous, like the snap of a tree branch in still woods.

A draft tickled the hair on his arms: air movement.

A *bang* reverberated up the connecting tunnel. The lead pilot turned, his face a silent alarm as one hand hovered over the throttles. "Not yet," Simon ordered after a quick mental calculation. "There's still time until Abort One condition." He punched the quick-release buckle on his harness and slipped out of his seat, twisting down for the access ladder embedded in the deck.

The draft became noticeably stronger as he approached the tunnel. A klaxon blared to life and the pilot shouted to him over the noise: "Pressurization alarm! Cabin differential's dropping fast!"

2

Denver

"One minute to Acquisition of Signal."

Audrey rubbed tired eyes with the heel of one hand. "Understood," she said, stifling a yawn. "AOS in one. Keep an eye on their residuals." If the braking burn wasn't spot on, they'd have to waste propellant correcting the orbit later. She didn't expect that to be any more necessary than it had been to remind her team about it in the first place. It was amazing how much better they got at this stuff when the vehicles weren't expendable, a lesson only partially learned by her former colleagues in Houston.

Thirty seconds. Her status board lit up as each controller checked in: gray boxes from guidance, environmental, propulsion all quickly turned green.

What about comm? She wondered.

Ten seconds.

And there was comm, checking in after a short delay in pinging the network of relay satellites.

Board is green, all systems go.

Time.

"*Shepard,* Denver; comm check." Her comm tech was answered by the same empty hiss of background static they'd tuned out for the past hour.

"*Shepard,* this is flight control," he repeated, this time with a more authoritative timbre. "Please acknowledge." Despite the two second delay between radio signals bouncing back from the Moon, the crew always answered on the first hail if they didn't beat her team to it. It was often a contest to see who could time it better. While no less hazardous than any other point in the journey, radio blackout on the far side had a way of mercilessly highlighting their isolation.

Comm was unusually strident on the third call. "*Shepard*, Denver; please respond. Over."

Audrey shot an anxious glance at the mission clock: AOS plus twenty, and it felt like a lifetime. They could tolerate a little slop in their numbers, maybe a second or two. Nowhere near this much. "Nav, what's their telemetry telling you?"

The navigation and guidance tech answered immediately. "A big fat nothing, Aud. Our screens are dead. They're just looping the last data set."

A chill shot through her as if someone had torn away a warm blanket during a deep sleep. Audrey sucked in her breath and closed her eyes before methodically pushing away from the console. She was painfully aware of the need to project absolute calm in spite of the cry welling up inside her: *Where's our spacecraft?*

• • •

An early riser by habit, Arthur Hammond was still surprised that the control center was calling at this hour. Not that he ever really shut himself off: a laptop tucked away in the alcove of their master bedroom was continuously linked to the company network with the status of their entire route system. His wife insisted that he at least keep the thing turned away from their bed with the screen off.

"Hammond," he whispered gruffly. A call at this time of night was rarely good news.

"Good. You're up." If there'd been any sleep left in him, the worried hitch in Audrey's voice wrenched him free of it. "I'm calling to report an overdue spacecraft. *Shepard* entered radio blackout as planned at 1142 Zulu," she said with a forced efficiency that only amplified his dread. "Planned signal acquisition at 1243Z was unsuccessful. We have no comm with the crew and no telemetry from *Shepard*."

"I understand." Hammond settled back onto the bed, scratching his words out. "And there've been no mayday calls on the guard frequency?" Not that the fledgling Space Guard could offer much help; they were still confined to low Earth orbit, mostly clearing debris hazards with drone satellites.

"Nothing, and we've pinged the relay sats twice," she said. "The network's fine, there's just nothing on it. The comm techs are combing through their logs for anything that might explain this, but so far they've got nothing."

"Except for a hole in space where our Cycler should be," he sighed. There was a telling silence as Audrey hesitated to take the next step.

"That's affirmative," she said, choking on the words. "We have to declare a missing vessel."

He knew it was coming, but...*damn.* "Then I concur. Activate the emergency response plans and I'll notify the Feds."

"Thank you, Art." There was relief in her voice; he'd just saved her from a flood of unwelcome distractions. "I'm also going to make some calls to our friends in Houston...at least the ones who'll still talk to us," she offered. "Maybe they can find something with a Lidar sweep."

"Good thinking." A laser-ranging scan worked much like radar but was more precise over long distances, provided they knew where to look. "We're not going to just sit on our thumbs and let this play out," he said, as much a command as it was a query.

"Way ahead of you. The midnight flight planners are already working out high energy trajectories to send *Grissom* up there."

"What's your plan, Aud?"

"Let you know as soon as I come up with one, boss."

...

Penny Stratton awoke with a start when the buzzing telephone landed on her stomach.

"We really need to move that thing to your side of the bed," her husband grumbled. Joe could be a little testy when the company called this early.

"Wuss," she yawned, and thumbed the receiver. "Go ahead," she grunted, hoping that made her sound fully awake. It wouldn't do for the chief pilot to sound groggy, even if it was just a scheduler reporting another crew trying to get out of a trip. She really hated the games they played when contracts were up for negotiation...

If only it were that mundane.

"*Missing?*" Penny fell back into the pillows, massaging her temples. "Have you called Charlie? Okay...I'm on the way." She set the phone on the bed and lay still, lost in thought. Silently praying. For what, she didn't yet know. Part of her brain registered Joe's voice asking *what's wrong* but she might as well have been underwater.

She looked down to find herself robotically twirling a strand of loose hair. Joe always said it was the signal that something was bothering her. If he only knew. It had been what, five years since the last major incident? She shuddered at the memory of it and of the good friend they had lost.

She finally slid out of bed and padded into the bathroom without a word, heading straight for the shower without bothering to turn on a light. She emerged soon after in jeans and a sweater, blonde hair pulled back into her customary loose ponytail. Her emergency "go bag" was slung over one shoulder: a sixty liter backpack filled with the essentials she'd need for a short notice trip to unpredictable locations. The apologetic look she gave her husband conveyed more than words could: this was really bad, and he shouldn't expect to see her for a few days.

Joe lifted a curtain to peek outside. An early spring snowfall had begun while they were asleep. "I'll put some coffee on," he said groggily, and headed for the kitchen.

...

The control center was quiet when Penny arrived thirty minutes later. Still early, activity would swell in another hour or so when the morning shift arrived and would really start jumping when word got out about the missing Cycler. Crisis response teams would be crowding the War Room and they were sure to be set upon by people from all over the company.

She brushed the snow from her hair and made a beeline for the Emergency Operations Center in the far corner. A guard had already been posted at the entrance, which meant the situation was about as grave as expected. Peeking through the frosted glass door, she made out several figures huddled over a network terminal. She nodded a silent greeting at the guard, swept her badge over the latch, and stepped inside.

Audrey was briefing a handful of executives. It was amazing how quickly they could show up when there was a hint of blood in the water.

Once Hammond arrived, Aud could at least count on him to keep them off of her back. For the time being, it was her job to mollify them.

"...it's been over an hour since the expected acquisition of signal," Audrey was explaining. "That's long enough to have completed another orbit."

"Assuming that's where they are," one somnolent reed of a man yawned. "How certain can you be?"

She half expected Aud to tear the poor guy's head off. "Certain enough to drag all of you in here at four a.m.," she explained coolly. "This is as serious as it gets. Best case is that they've had a total radio failure, including telemetry."

"And the worst case?"

Audrey knew more about cislunar orbital mechanics and spacecraft operations than anyone in the company, but too many of the suits wouldn't listen to anyone who didn't hold the title *pilot*. Penny used that opening to step in. "There's actually a couple of worst cases," she interjected. "Either they burned too long, which means they slowed down too much and crashed into the surface, or they didn't burn long enough and have been shot out into deep space. In which case we'd certainly be hearing from them. Pick your poison." She turned to Audrey. "Did I miss anything?"

"I think they've heard enough bad news for now," Audrey said. "Any other questions?"

Penny's lecture had the desired effect: there were none.

...

SS Shepard

Simon thought his arm felt pretty good until he tried to actually do anything with it; then it hurt like hell. Just gingerly lifting it to check the time sent shooting pains clear through his shoulder. Clenching his teeth, he unzipped his flight suit with his other hand and slipped the injured arm inside. Better, if only a little. At least it wasn't flopping around freely anymore.

He pushed away for the other end of the compartment and its first aid kit. Inside, he found a sling and inflatable splints. It also held a fair amount of painkillers, everything from ibuprofen to something that looked like it could put down a horse. Probably best to stay away from that one for now.

He pulled the splint over his arm and opened its self-inflating valve. The sleeve expanded slowly, exerting some welcome uniform pressure around his forearm. He slipped it into the sling and drew it tight against his body with a relieved sigh; it began to feel halfway normal again. Immobility might be inconvenient but it sure felt good.

Simon closed his eyes and floated against the sidewall, clearing his head. What the hell had just happened in the last two hours?

Everything had really gone down the crapper in the first two minutes. He peered through the inner hatch's tiny porthole: emergency LEDs still illuminated the tunnel, the end of which was now open to empty space. Not long ago it had been safely docked to the flight module, *Snoopy I.* No light at the end of this tunnel.

Now that's a lovely metaphor. You should be a friggin' poet.

Now that he was freed from the distraction of constant pain, he took another look around. The airlock was only a couple of meters across in any direction, just big enough for two people in full EVA suits. It resembled the inside of a dive chamber – essentially what it was – made of brushed aluminum and composites painted gloss white. A half-dozen LEDs produced a cool bluish tint, the only contrast coming from the touchscreen set in a panel by the tunnel door.

It was a claustrophobic's nightmare, and his only shelter for the next couple of weeks. Any longer and it would become something else…

No time for that. He shut the thought out of his mind and continued his inspection.

Emergency rations. Ten liters of water. A flashlight. An EVA suit, with repair kit for said suit. A patch kit for the hab – *too late, bubba* – with a few basic tools. Extra CO2 filters. The intercom panel…

Intercom. If someone were on the other side of that wall it might be useful. Now it just taunted him. It sure would be nice to push a button and talk to somebody. As it was, it could only communicate with the suit radio. So he could talk to himself from the other side of the room. *Whoop-dee-doo.*

He reached down into his hip pocket and found his tablet. About two-thirds of a charge left, a full day's use if he wasn't stupid about it...so no movies to pass the time. He secured it to one of several Velcro strips along the bulkhead and tapped the icon for Big Al's wiring diagrams. Time to get to work.

3

Denver

The corporate crisis teams failed to notice when a lanky man with a salt-and-pepper crewcut slipped inside, as Charlie Grant's near-ubiquitous presence in flight control was taken for granted. The operations director practically lived in the control center, having been known to keep a cot and fresh clothes in his office "just in case."

"Morning, Charlie," Penny said. "Surprised you didn't beat me here."

Grant lifted a mug of black coffee in salute, signaling that he'd in fact been here for hours. He conspicuously ignored the throng of executives, wading through them straight to her. "I've been down in the server farm with the IT guys," he explained, just loudly enough for her to understand it was for the benefit of the gathered outsiders. Left unsaid was that he'd wanted to be absolutely certain they had locked down all of *Shepard*'s flight data on a secure off-network server. He leaned in close. "Anything new?"

"Called some friends at Johnson on my way here," she said, referring to the manned spaceflight center in Houston. "They're going to run it up the flagpole with the Deep Space Network in Pasadena."

"DSN can cover a wider spectrum, that's for sure. Let's hope they don't have to take it all the way up to NASA headquarters." The agency's new administrator was notoriously hostile towards the private space industry, Hammond in particular. "Pictures would be even better. They have anything that can see that far?"

She stared at a projection of the Moon on the far wall, as if brooding over it might tease out some lost detail. "National Recon Office might, but you need serious juice to re-task a spy sat." It was something she could have made happen back when she worked for the agency.

Grant led her to his console and tapped at the screen. *Shepard*'s vital signs began playing out before flat-lining like a terminal hospital patient.

"That's Big Al's last info dump, right up to LOS. About three thousand channels of information hiding in there, and probably not a damned thing we can do with any of it."

Penny brooded over that. An earlier deal they'd reached with the Feds to lease frequencies from a relay satellite in lunar orbit had been inexplicably canceled, with no explanation offered except the boilerplate "needs of the government." The irony was that no matter how this turned out, that same government was certain to *require* uninterrupted contact for any future trips despite having denied them access in the first place. "Art's going to have to find a way to get our own comsat up there sooner."

"Forget it," Hammond's voice piped up behind her. "Same reason you can't make a baby in a month by putting nine women on the job. It takes what it takes."

"Sorry, Arthur."

Hammond waved it away. "I pay you to call it like you see it," he said through his frustration. "Let me worry about the politics. But I agree: a missing ship would be a whole lot easier to find if they could've spared some bandwidth."

"Might never have lost it in the first place," Grant said sourly. "We don't even have enough to put together a half-assed TLE." A Two-Line Element described all of the variables they needed to model the ship's orbit and predict where it would appear at any given time. Without it, they were stabbing in the dark. "But Audrey's made a couple of swags at their next position out of blackout."

Hammond leaned in expectantly. "And those would be?"

Grant swiped at one of the big wall monitors. The Moon zoomed into focus, encircled by a scattering of orbits depicted in different colors. "We considered two scenarios to narrow our search pattern: either they burned just long enough to make orbit before everything went to hell," he said, "or they were on target but somehow lost comm and are exactly where they're supposed to be."

"Nice thought, but not likely." It didn't escape Hammond's notice that they'd left out the other option: a wrecked spacecraft on the far side of the Moon. Perhaps it didn't need saying, or maybe they just didn't want to. "In the meantime, I want a status report on *Grissom* and a crew roster for the search party."

...

John F. Kennedy National Spaceport
Cape Canaveral, Florida

Ryan Hunter cinched a worn Virginia Tech ball cap down over his head, shielding his eyes from the hazy sun climbing above the marsh. Not yet eight in the morning, and it was already turning steamy. He looked up and down the line of technicians strung along the pavement's edge and motioned them forward.

While the Clipper spaceplanes were still earthbound, foreign object damage was their number one worry. The daily FOD walk was a painstaking ritual of combing over the parking apron for any stray bits that might otherwise get sucked down an intake and destroy some very expensive engines. As the launch hub's manager, Ryan saw to it that everyone took personal ownership in preventing that. As their group slowly walked across the tarmac, people began to bend down at random and pick up small bits of debris. One took a folding knife from his belt, fished something out of a seam in the concrete, and pocketed it with evident satisfaction. No doubt whatever he'd found would be entered in a running competition for the most ridiculous piece of flotsam, the winners of which were ignominiously displayed in a trophy case tucked away in the maintenance office safely out of public view.

Ryan's concentration was broken by the phone jangling in his hip pocket. He waved the others on without him as he fished it out. The line had just reached the front of the hangar, so he ducked inside beneath its shade. The building sat on an expansive new apron alongside the old Shuttle Landing Facility, a three-mile-long runway that had fallen out of use until Polaris leased it as the launch site for their orbital Clippers.

"Hunter," he answered, not even looking at the caller ID.

"It's Penny," came the equally brusque reply. "Need you to drop whatever you're doing for a minute, okay?"

"Already did," he said with a hint of curiosity. Whenever she was that abrupt, it meant something was up.

"Can you confirm the status of your hot spare? Any maintenance gripes that we wouldn't know about yet?"

Ryan faced the plane in question, a silver and black arrowhead sequestered in a corner of the hangar behind two other Clippers. "It's clean," he said. "Ready to go."

"Keep it that way. If one of your other birds breaks, cancel the launch. The hot spare's off limits until we say otherwise."

Now that was weird. Denver typically left those decisions up to the manager on site. "Even if that causes us to miss a launch window?"

"Nobody gets that plane without me or Charlie approving it."

Ryan frowned and made for his office. "Understood. So is this the part where you tell me what's up?"

He could sense her caution over the phone. "We lost contact with Big Al about three hours ago. Just up and disappeared behind the far side," she said, and laid out everything that had happened since.

He stopped in mid-stride and nearly dropped the phone. His head swam as a host of wild scenarios played out; none ended well.

"You still there?"

"Yeah," he stammered. "How could it just *disappear*?" He felt ridiculous for asking. Whatever it was, things must have really gone to hell up there. Finally reaching his office, Ryan closed the door behind him and slid into the chair at his desk. He tapped at a keyboard and their flight plan appeared on his wall monitor. "That's Simon's crew, isn't it—the one for that resource survey?"

"That's the one," she said. "The big question is what we do about it. *Grissom*'s not ready to carry paying passengers, but we're not too worried about creature comforts. We can have it ready to break orbit in five days."

Ryan barely heard her. His mind raced through the possible scenarios and their implications, and always at the center of them was Simon. For as much as they valued him for his expertise as a former space station astronaut, he owed him a deep personal debt…

"Ryan?"

After all, the man had saved his skin and sacrificed his career in the process…

"Ryan."

"Sorry," he muttered, like a schoolboy caught daydreaming. "It's a lot to process. I let it get personal."

"Figured as much," she said. "You can think it over on the way out here. Art's already sent the Gulfstream."

4

SS Shepard

Simon took a halting sip from the water supply, fighting the urge to chug the entire bladder. His body wanted more, but there was no telling how long he'd have to make this last and he wasn't in much of a position to bargain with nature. After combing through every nook and cranny of the airlock he hadn't been able to find anything beyond the standard equipment. Perhaps it was divine punishment for running a tight ship. He always suspected that God had a peculiar sense of humor.

It could have been worse. At least the rations were stocked per the manifest: enough to sustain two people for two days on the outside chance that it would ever be necessary. Like right now. The problem was, he figured it would take the better part of a week for them to prep *Grissom* and start burning moonward.

He was confident that Art was already working on it. Simon had seen the man's commitment first hand while he was on the International Space Station, helping Ryan Hunter rescue the marooned *Austral Clipper*. If he hadn't essentially stolen it in defiance of a government impound order and flown it home at the ragged edge of its envelope...well, chances were they wouldn't be in business right now. It had sickened him to learn some people high up in the space agency would've been happy to see that. *In hindsight, maybe I shouldn't have helped him out. I'd be sitting on my porch in San Diego on top of a nice fat government pension.*

He clipped the water hose back into its mount, pulled on the rubberized spacesuit gloves, and floated over to an open maintenance panel. Fishing out two exposed wires, he held one in each hand and waited for Earth to reappear in the window. As his home planet rose above the lunar horizon, Simon began rhythmically tapping the stripped ends together.

...

Denver

The kink in Audrey's back reminded her of just how long she'd been hunched over her workstation, awkwardly balancing a phone on her shoulder while talking to JPL's deep space network. Her eyes kept returning to a timer above the wall screen as it counted down to the next predicted end of radio blackout. She felt a surge of anticipation as it reached zero, and looked over at the comm tech. He answered with a disappointed shrug, just more of the same mocking hiss of a dead frequency.

All of a sudden she shot upright, pressing her headset tight while contorting to balance the phone by her other ear. "Say again...where is it?" She scribbled some coordinates on a notepad and threw it at the comm tech. "Frequency change! Align the antennas here," she shouted, "quickly!"

He punched up the antenna controls on a separate monitor and began shifting the high-gain receivers. A wildly oscillating pattern burst to life on screen. "I've got something! Static, but it's not background. Sounds like carrier wave, Aud."

Hammond pushed through the crowd with Penny and Grant trailing behind. He leaned in beside her while Penny hurriedly slipped on a spare headset, shutting out the ambient noise. "Can you talk to them?"

"Not yet," she said, switching the feed to her desktop speakers. "Sounds like a stuck mic or something." The tantalizing noise ended abruptly, then started again. Audrey frantically fine-tuned her own receiver only to have the buzz disappear once more. She lifted her hands plaintively; it wasn't affected by anything they were doing.

"So maybe this really is just a radio failure?" he asked hopefully.

There was an abrupt shushing from Penny, who had been sitting in a near trance with the spare headset snugged down tight. "Listen. There's a pattern here." She gestured for Audrey to turn up the volume. "Hear that?" She looked out at a room full of blank stares. "Come on, nobody here remembers Morse code?"

They'd caught the last transmission in midstream so it took a moment to comprehend: three long bursts, a brief silence, then three more short bursts. The intervening gap had felt like an eternity until the pattern repeated a few more times: three short, three long, three short.

Hammond's face lit up like a kid on Christmas. "Is that what I think it is?"

They leaned in closer, not quite believing their ears as the signal repeated: S.O.S.

...

Melbourne, Florida

Ryan dumped his go bag onto the bed, hurriedly separating the field gear that he wouldn't need from the warmer clothing he would need. "Any luck yet?" he called in the general direction of their closet.

Marcy emerged with a winter jacket that hadn't seen much use. As she brushed off the dust, their son trundled out in his dad's boots and looked quite satisfied with himself. They easily came up to his knees.

"Marshall Thomas Hunter," Ryan said with mock severity. "Where exactly do you think you're going with those?"

"To the mountains," he answered seriously. "With you."

Marcy gave Ryan a nervous smile and laid his coat on the bed before bending down to lift Marshall out of his father's boots. "No hon," she said gently. "Daddy's got to leave in a hurry to go help his friends."

He flopped onto the bed with a disappointed frown. Having Daddy home early in the day usually meant something special. "I can help. Please?" He begged. "I want to see snow."

Ryan sat beside him and laid a gentle hand on his shoulder. "Sorry pal. I'll be at work the whole time. It wouldn't be any fun for you at all." *Or for anyone else*, he left unsaid.

"Rockets look like fun. Why aren't they fun for you?"

It was the kind of sucker punch only a little kid could throw. "They *are* fun," he said defensively. "Grownups just have a way of making stuff boring sometimes." He looked to Marcy, his eyes pleading for support. "Right, babe?"

She made it a point to distract their son with a toy before responding the way any wife would: as if she'd read his mind.

"Missing?" she whispered sharply as her mind ran through the possible outcomes. She had worked with or trained most of their cabin crew until Marshall came along, but their relationship with Simon Poole was on a whole different level. "There's no way to pinpoint their orbit?"

"There's ways," Ryan said as he dug through the back of a drawer. "None of them are quick. Our antenna farms can't sweep that wide of an area without everything turning into background noise. They have to have a pretty good idea of where it'll show up first."

She began to appreciate the circular riddle. "So you can't find it without already knowing where it's likely to be…"

"Right. But DSN can, eventually." NASA's Deep Space Network could find the proverbial needle in a haystack from a million miles away. "Penny's greasing those wheels for us right now."

"Sounds familiar. You think they'd be on to us by now." They were both watching Marshall, who was vigorously leaping about the bed after discovering it could make Daddy's duffel bag bounce. She turned back to face Ryan. "Find them. Find Simon. We owe him a lot."

"We owe him everything," Ryan said, and lifted the pack onto his shoulder.

…

SS Shepard

Simon let loose with a frustrated curse. He was confident that his improvised telegraph key had worked, but he couldn't know if it had gotten their attention. He needed something better than one-way comm. Art's machinists had done too good of a job mounting the intercom, probably without any thought that someone out here might need to actually remove it one day. And why would they? Who could possibly foresee the need to jury rig the airlock intercom into the high-gain antennas?

The torque-absorbing electric screwdriver he was currently struggling with could apparently only do half of its job: it kept him from spinning in the opposite direction but it couldn't unseat the panel's mounting screws.

He clipped it back into the tool kit and unfolded a screwdriver from the multi-tool that he habitually carried in his jumpsuit. This wasn't going to be easy. His body had to both impart enough force to do the job and counteract it at the same time. Twisting hard one way would spin his body the opposite way.

Simon braced his legs against opposite bulkheads in a ridiculous ballerina stance that strained him in some decidedly unpleasant ways. Twist one way, push the opposite way. Twist and push. Again. He grunted with the strain, imagining the hernia he was probably inflicting on himself.

One more time.

The stubborn screw finally moved under the blade. Only a quarter turn, but it was enough to finish off with the fancy space tool. One more addition to a growing list of gripes for his debrief log.

Keep telling yourself that, hoss. Maybe you'll actually find a way out of here.

After a blessedly easier time with the remaining fasteners, he was finally able to open the panel and get a good look inside. It was crowded in there, a tangle of conduits and cable harnesses. He poked in with the blade of his tool, pushing a bundle aside…

The airlock went dark.

Power failure? No. Far as he could tell the ship was still drawing from the solar cells and charging the standby batteries while they were in sunlight.

What the hell could've shorted out? He regarded the tool in his hand and questioned his own memory of first buying it – the thing was supposed to have nonconductive blades. Sure it did. It's not like anything had been cut in there…which meant he must have nicked something earlier when he hotwired the high gain antenna. Whatever he'd moved had to have pushed against whatever else he'd cut earlier without realizing it. Now he'd have to troubleshoot *that* before he could finish cobbling together his makeshift radio. It would be easier to trace the lines if he could see their tags and color coding.

As his eyes adjusted to the darkness, shapes began to resolve themselves and the compartment turned a bluish gray from weak starlight. He felt around in the emergency kit for the flashlight he knew would be there, and carefully set it floating in place above the open panel. It was enough, even though it'd be like working with a bare light bulb swinging above his head.

And here I was wondering how to keep myself busy.

5

Denver

The operations center was as Ryan remembered: a high tech amphitheater filled with semicircular rows of computer workstations, all facing a bank of wall-sized monitors that showed the company's route system and the airspace around their launch and reentry corridors. The graphics were filled with little blue triangles, each representing a Clipper in flight.

He blinked as his eyes adjusted to the low light. No matter what time of day it was, it always looked like the dead of night in here. The indirect lighting had a subtle psychological effect, which helped tamp down the noise that always threatened to erupt. People tended to keep quiet when it felt like they might wake somebody up.

The weather overlays always drew his attention: a deep low pressure system had settled over the northeast United States and was wreaking havoc on most of their routes. An outsider would have barely detected the heightened activity, but the swell of background noise and movement told the real story: phones ringing incessantly, supervisors pacing behind rows of flight controllers, a dispatcher gesturing wildly across the room seeking some unseen person's attention. A few had the haggard look of a midnight crew that should have been long gone by now. He waved at Charlie Grant over by the fleet manager's station, who nodded in recognition while rubbing the sleep from his eyes. He noticed a few key desks were empty; no doubt he'd find their occupants at the next stop.

He slipped into the EOC and quietly dropped his bag by the door, barely noticed by the controllers and engineers hunched over consoles or huddled in small groups. Penny looked up from a chart table and met him with a tired smile and warm embrace. "Welcome to the party," she said. "How's the family?"

"Marcy's worried sick and Marshall begged to come with me. We have firm orders to find Simon and bring everybody home."

"I'll make sure Art knows his former cabin safety instructor is still keeping our feet to the fire." Her smile turned apologetic. "I haven't seen either of you in forever. Hate that we have to meet like this."

"You're the chief pilot, lady. Maybe you should spend more time out there flying the line. I keep waiting for you to come down to the Cape for a check ride."

"I put you in charge down there precisely because I'm scared to death of flying with you," she said with her customary punch on the arm. "Come on, let's get you briefed in."

The chart table was a large touchscreen framed in ordinary laminate desktop, ostensibly to keep harried controllers from spilling coffee or marking it up with notes. Audrey was leaning against it, idly turning her glasses in one hand as she scrolled through a plot of the Earth-Moon system. When he'd learned of the influence she'd wielded behind the scenes at NASA when he'd been stranded in orbit aboard the *Austral Clipper*, it immediately put her at the top of his list of favorite flight controllers. And right now, she looked exhausted.

"Hey Aud," Ryan said, giving her shoulders a quick rub. "I hear you're getting transmissions?"

"We were," she sighed, "up until a few hours ago. Haven't heard squat since. Not even carrier wave static."

"Any chance whoever it is might just be getting some sleep?"

"That's what we're hoping."

"Were they coming in a reliable pattern before that? Anything other than a distress code?"

Audrey shook her head.

"I'm not used to uncertainty from you."

That at least got a grin out of her, probably her first of the day. "Something's not adding up, either the weights or their final delta-v. It's possible that whatever we heard from is roughly half of Big Al's mass."

"You're kidding?" He shook his head. *Of course she wasn't.* "So you think they had to detach?"

"That's our operating theory for now," Penny cut in. She laid a diagram of the spacecraft over the chart projection, pointing out the control cabin and rocket stage docked to the big inflatable passenger module.

Each sported pairs of long solar panels. "Remember, the flight module is able to maneuver independently. The hab doesn't go anywhere that we don't drag it."

Ryan's eyes grew wide. "So you think half the ship may be somewhere out of comm range?" he asked, shuddering to think about what *somewhere* could mean.

"Given what we know? Not much else makes sense. If there was a problem with the hab while they were on the far side, they would've evacuated everyone into the control cabin. If necessary they'd have ditched the hab and started burning for home."

"But all of the primary comm gear is in the control cabin." Ryan scratched at his head, mussing an already unruly tangle of black hair. "So we ought to have heard from them."

"That's why we think the problem was with the flight module, so they bugged out to the hab."

"But that has its own radios…so why wouldn't they just use them?" He stared at the blueprints, struggling to visualize what might be left. He slowly traced a finger down the diagram. "The S-band antenna's right here, mounted to the tank support truss."

"Correct," Penny said, "and all the conduits run through the docking node. Makes it easier to fix things when they break."

"So whoever's left behind just hot-wired the antennas from the airlock?"

"Wouldn't be that hard to do," Audrey said, "at least for someone who understood the systems."

"That narrows down which end of the ship we're looking for, and who we're looking for," he thought aloud. There had to be at least one crewmember in there. "So when does the search team need to be wheels up?"

"Three days," Penny said. "Launch window's tighter than a…well, let's just say we're gonna be in a hurry."

Ryan didn't want to sow doubts, but he had to ask. "Will that even get you there in time to do any good?" He assumed Penny would be flying the other Cycler.

"No way to know," she said. "Primary food and water storage is all in the hab. There's emergency stores in the docking node that could possibly be stretched out for a week or so, but eventually they'll run out."

Been there, done that. Ryan's mind wandered to whoever might be up there and what they must be going through right now. Which was worse: to be stranded as your home planet slipped past just a hundred miles outside your window, or to have it a quarter-million miles away and hopelessly beyond reach?

"Okay then," he finally said. "We turn and burn. Cape ops can strip the standby bird of everything it doesn't need and start fitting it with extra propellant tanks for Gus. I'll work out the mission plan with Charlie, just tell me what you need to take up there."

Penny's eyes bored into him. "You, for starters."

. . .

Hammond might have otherwise been startled when the heavy door to his office swung open suddenly; maybe it was slow reaction times from fatigue. He looked up from his desk in a calculated "son, did *you* just screw up" expression. Charlie Grant had been working in the opposite corner and rose up to meet them when they both recognized Ed Bentley, the Federal Aviation Administration's chief inspector assigned to Polaris. Normally even tempered and agreeable for being in such a nitpicky job, he looked uncharacteristically sheepish. Before Hammond could even think to ask why, the answer became obvious.

A husky man with a clean-shaven head dressed in a government-plain navy blue suit barged past Ed, sweeping around to make a beeline for Hammond as his flustered secretary rushed up behind them. "The gentleman wouldn't wait," she said apologetically, heaping a particularly caustic emphasis on *gentleman*.

The man threw a disinterested glance at them, then flipped open a black ID case from his breast pocket and flashed his badge. "Special Agent Kruger, Department of Homeland Security," he said gruffly.

Hammond waved his secretary out. "It's all right," he told her while keeping a wary eye on their visitor. "Everyone's a little high strung right now." If this Agent Kruger of Homeland Security sympathized with them at all, it didn't register. The guy looked like he probably spent his spare time clubbing baby seals.

"Hello Charlie," Bentley said, hoping to break the ice. Grant acknowledged him with a silent nod and regarded the new visitor with concern. Bentley appeared relieved to not be the one on the receiving end of his gimlet eye.

"To what do we owe the pleasure?" Hammond asked cautiously, returning the badge and gesturing them toward two empty chairs.

Grant was less accommodating, being in no mood for small talk with strangers. "Ed must have briefed you on our situation already. We have a lot to do and not much time to do it, Mister Kruger. I'm not sure why DHS would have any interest in a private search-and-rescue operation."

"And you are?"

"Charlie Grant. Director of Operations."

"We understand completely, Mister Grant," Kruger said, telegraphing that he wasn't the only interested party inside the government. "Considering the unique nature of your enterprise, Homeland Security thought it wise to look into this matter."

"We deal with unique problems all the time," he said. "It's kind of our thing. What we don't have are eyeballs on our spacecraft. Perhaps you can help us out?"

Kruger arched an eyebrow. "You've located it?"

That's not what he said, Hammond thought. By the look on Charlie's face, he'd caught that too. "We've picked up what sounds like an SOS. The timing helped us rough out the orbital period."

Kruger slid forward in his chair. "You're certain?"

"As certain as we can be without better data or direct imagery," he said, now more relaxed. It was always good to be the one holding the info with these types. He lifted a pair of thin glasses to his nose while flipping through a notebook. "Bear with me. The more dependent we get on technology, the more I revert to pen and paper." Not to mention they'd had no time to put together anything more sophisticated. "Our flight director worked up the most likely deviations, and sure enough it started right about when she expected it to emerge from radio blackout. Based on our limited observations, we think there's a possibility that a sizeable portion of the ship is gone." He found the marked page and handed the notebook to Kruger and Bentley.

Intrigued, Kruger paged through their notes while Bentley simply gazed at his shoes uncomfortably. "That's...quite interesting," he said haltingly. "In this case, I think we can convince the right people to get some imagery of this target."

The turn of phrase made Hammond more uncomfortable than it probably should have, but he couldn't ignore the chill that crept up his neck. *Target?*

"For pictures, of course," Bentley explained.

Kruger glared at him. "We only want to help find your ship and eliminate any potential threats it may present. Isn't that right, Ed?" Bentley nodded obediently and cleared his throat.

Interesting point of view, Hammond thought. Solicitous bureaucrats had a way of making him apprehensive, especially the ones with badges and guns. "And we just want to get our people back."

"We understand," Kruger said. He stiffly buttoned his suit jacket as he rose. "But to help you, we're going to need access to some information. Starting with crew records and a complete manifest of passengers, cargo, and baggage."

"I believe you'll find that Ed here has all of that in his office right now," Grant said with a nod towards the FAA man. They had no doubt Kruger already knew.

Kruger continued as if he'd been invisible. "Plus the maintenance history, flight planning, telemetry records, and personnel files of every individual who could've touched it."

Hammond whistled. "That'll take some time." *And a warrant.*

"We'll also need dedicated, secure office space," he continued without missing a beat. "I believe that's customary for accident investigations?"

"It would be for an NTSB go team, but this isn't an accident," Hammond objected. "It's a search and rescue operation. Why are the Feds always in such a big damned hurry to assume the worst?"

Bentley finally intervened. "Arthur, their first thought was to set up a mobile command post in your parking lot."

"Which Bentley here convinced me would be counterproductive. For now," Kruger interrupted. "Let us know when we can set up shop, otherwise we'll be in touch as soon as there's anything worth contacting you about," Kruger said. "We don't wish to take up any more of your time." He tipped his head in parting and left with Bentley shuffling behind.

Hammond perched on the edge of his desk, glowering at the still-open doorway. "What in the flaming hell was that all about?"

"I was about to ask you the same thing. That goon sure acted like he had bigger things on his mind."

"As he damned well should," Hammond snorted. They didn't have time for being caught up in some bureaucratic power play. "This isn't exactly in their wheelhouse. Could be he was ordered here to keep a few well-connected big shots happy." It was more speculation than an observation.

"Looks like that's what he wants us to think. And did you get a load of Ed? He's rattled. I don't think he made eye contact with us once."

"That's what has me worried." They normally had as good of a relationship with the FAA as anyone could ask for. "This is plenty serious on its own. So why all the intrigue?"

Grant frowned and kicked at the floor as he thought. "We're looking at this from the wrong angle," he said. "You said it yourself: this isn't their thing. Maybe it's time we got Posey involved?"

Hammond stared quietly out the window, idly turning over his phone in his hands as he considered his suggestion. "It is," he finally said, and tapped out a message to his security chief: PAX MANIFEST...START DIGGING.

6

Golden, Colorado

Hammond stepped onto his back patio and lifted a beer out of a cooler built into the stone retaining wall. He downed half the bottle before he was caught in his wife's disapproving glare, and flopped into a lounge chair with an exhausted sigh. "Relax, Abby. I'm not going on a bender." But it was tempting. He couldn't recall the last time he'd had more than two in a single day. Though he couldn't recall much about the times he'd had more, either.

"That's right, you're not," Abigail Hammond said sharply. "Your head needs to remain thoroughly uncluttered, my dear."

"A little less browbeating, please," he said tiredly. "Afraid it's too late anyway. My head's already cluttered to hell and gone."

Normally they would sit quietly and enjoy the sunset silhouetting the Front Range. Tonight it felt pointless: the crescent moon overhead might as well have been sent by fate itself to mock him.

Abigail settled in by his side and spread a blanket over them anyway. "Sorry. You must be exhausted." They'd not had time to speak since he'd left in a rush early that morning. She laid her head on his chest and remained still until she could wait no longer.

"This is bad, isn't it?"

He screwed his eyes shut as if simply thinking about it brought physical pain. Before he could answer, the doorbell rang from inside the house.

Abigail squeezed his hand. "I'll get it. You stay here and try to relax."

Hammond's expression settled into one of grim detachment. "It'll take a lot more of these," he muttered, lifting the bottle as she walked away.

. . .

Abigail returned a few minutes later, escorting an olive-skinned man whose beard matched the charcoal of his impeccably tailored suit. Well north of six feet, he towered before Hammond and deliberately bowed his head in deference to his host.

"Please forgive my intrusion, but it is important that we speak. My name is Ibrahim al-Aqsa."

Hammond was too weary to conceal his surprise. "Have a seat, please. Can I offer you anything?"

Their guest was likewise not very good at hiding his distaste, assuming Hammond meant alcohol. "I'm afraid not."

"Suit yourself. We have plenty of other refreshments." He polished off the beer for effect.

Al-Aqsa settled onto one of the cedar chairs beside Hammond. "Impressive architecture. I've always found the Victorian style appealing."

"Abby didn't want anything bigger. She refuses to hire housekeepers."

"An honorable woman, then," Al-Aqsa offered, as if that were a rarity. They stood quietly and admired the distant mountains, now purple in the retreating sunset.

"I must say, you have the perfect setting for appreciating nature's spectacle. The view is stunning, Mr. Hammond."

"Thanks. I put the patio in myself."

"A man of your resources who still works with his hands? There are too few like that in this world."

"It's a good way to blow off steam. Keeps you grounded." Hammond turned to face his guest. "No need to lay it on so thick, Mr. al-Aqsa. And I'm tired as hell so let's dispense with the small talk. What brings you here?"

The man didn't miss a beat. "Your missing spacecraft, of course. I once worshiped with one of your passengers, Kam Varza."

"I see." *Now we can get down to business.* "Rest assured we are doing everything we can to locate your friend and our ship," he said. "Solving intractable problems seems to be our specialty."

"Indeed," Al-Aqsa said through a thin smile. "You reference prior events, of course. The saboteur who almost destroyed one of your Clipper planes in orbit? Tell me, how does a foreign operative find his way into an organization this complex? And how can we know you're able to prevent it from happening again?"

"That's not exactly something that turns up in our employee background checks. Counterespionage is more of the FBI's purview," he explained. "Let's just say it was a complicated situation and leave it at that." And not all of it had made the news, thanks to a government gag order in the name of national security. He knew they just didn't want the embarrassment.

"A common problem when the FBI gets involved," al-Aqsa observed sourly, then shifted gears. "Your business model is unusual to say the least, Mr. Hammond. And please forgive me, but it is fraught with risk."

Hammond waved it away. "There's nothing to forgive...I'm sorry, is it *Mister* Al-Aqsa? Reverend? Grand Poobah? I'm not too clear on titles."

"Our community calls me 'Imam,' but 'Ibrahim' is fine."

"Ibrahim," he said. "To your point...yes, our profession is inherently hazardous. Flying is in general, but the airlines have managed the risks down to the point where the average passenger barely gives it a second thought. Spaceflight, however, still has some way to go."

"I'm not particularly well versed in these matters, but it seems obvious that the environment would be much less forgiving."

"Correct again," Hammond agreed. "The distances and speeds involved are too great. That's why we build so many redundant systems into these vehicles, particularly things like pressurization and life support." In other words, the stuff that could kill you fastest.

"And is that what you believe happened here?" he asked anxiously. "How could anyone survive such a thing?"

"We have no way to know yet. Please don't take my comments as anything but speculation."

"Nevertheless," he said calmly, "Varza and his associates were on one of your ships. Now it is missing, though it may not be entirely lost."

And how would you know that, Ibrahim al-Aqsa? Absent your prophet announcing it to you in a dream or something. Hammond fought to appear unimpressed while carefully considering his answer. "We got a signal for about twenty minutes. Someone's still alive up there and in orbit, judging by the Doppler shift."

Al-Aqsa's eyes were wide. "Signals?" he finally asked. "What sort of signals?"

"Old-fashioned Morse code," Hammond said. "S.O.S."

The Imam turned away, slowly stroking his beard. Clearly this was not what he'd expected to hear. He stood, smoothed down his suit, and once again bowed slightly. "Mr. Hammond, you've been most gracious. I will not take up any more of your time," he said, and offered a business card. "I trust you will notify me as soon as you learn of anything else?"

• • •

Hammond waved politely as Al-Aqsa's car pulled away. Abigail emerged from the front portico a moment later. "What was *that* about?"

Hammond frowned while studiously turning over al-Aqsa's business card. "Pretty sure I don't know." He pulled his phone from his pocket, scrolled through the contact list, and thumbed a number. The phone rang once: Hammond could always count on his security chief to pick up quickly. "Tony, I'm about to send you a scan. Stand by," he said, and swiped the card across the phone.

• • •

Hammond turned in bed, exhausted yet maddeningly unable to sleep as his mind wound through any number of increasingly implausible scenarios. His phone rang as if answering his own silent plea for a distraction: Posey. He thumbed the speaker. "What do you have, Tony?"

Posey answered in his stately baritone. "Interesting character, Arthur. How do you know this guy?"

"Old drinking buddies," Hammond joked. "He dropped by my house a few hours ago, felt like he was pumping me for information." He described their brief visit. "He knows the lead pax on *Shepard*."

"Then we just blew right past 'interesting,' boss. This guy showed up on watch lists under a couple different aliases, then went dark about ten years ago. Near as I can tell, he gave you his real name."

"So he turned legit without attracting attention to himself?" That in itself wasn't particularly surprising. Nor was it especially comforting. He could sense Posey's suspicions. "And we've never been ones to believe in coincidence, have we?"

"As my kids say, 'true dat,'" Posey said. "It gets worse. The Feds haven't exactly been encouraging my newfound interest in our load manifest."

"That's too damned bad," Hammond said testily. "They're quick to forget it's *our* property. Just because we had to hand over the master copy doesn't mean they own it."

"Agreed, but they can sure tie things up if their lawyers get involved. When Kruger got wind that I was cross-referencing the manifest against possible aliases the same way I did with your boy Ibrahim, he promptly told me to not concern myself. He says they're on top of it." Posey's sarcasm at that last point practically dripped from the phone.

"Don't I feel better," Hammond fumed. He looked up at the Moon, imagining their missing ship and wondering if there'd been any more cryptic transmissions. None of this added up to begin with, and new variables kept getting added to the equation. Kruger was a meathead, running around their property like he owned the place. The types of law enforcement assigned to work alongside NTSB were usually a lot more tuned-in than that, at least in the airline world.

Nobody else is flying cruise liners around the moon, genius. There wasn't a lot of resident expertise out there. "I've had just about enough of us being someone else's political football. I need to know exactly what this Kruger character does."

"Thought you might," Posey said, "so I shook a few trees. It didn't take long for stuff to fall out. He works for Homeland Security's counter-terror branch."

That revelation hung heavily as Hammond processed this latest surprise: why had this particular agent been assigned to an accident team? "You don't suppose he's been transferred out of that recently?"

"Doesn't sound like it," Posey said. "He's actually pretty far up in the Fed's food chain. His field work is...*selective,* I'd say." Which meant DHS only let this guy off the leash for the really high-profile cases.

"That actually helps make sense of this," Hammond said, considering the many unknowns that had roiled his mind. "But what we're left with just got a hell of a lot harder."

"Maybe not. We have another interested visitor that you need to know about."

7

Denver

"This way, please."

Hammond waved their latest government guest around a cordoned-off area beneath a Clipper, which looked for all the world as if its skin had been peeled off. Which was about right, as the thermal protective coatings had to be stripped and replaced on a regular basis and the underlying structure thoroughly inspected. The spaceplane sat on enormous jacks with its landing gear folded up as technicians in protective coveralls combed over every inch of exposed structure beneath.

Penny wrinkled her nose at the stinging odor of industrial epoxies and delaminated carbon fiber as they wound their way past the grounded spacecraft. The boss had made it clear that he would escort this delegation himself, though she trailed close behind to field the inevitable questions. She found it interesting that so far there'd been none.

Beyond cursory introductions (where he had oddly skipped any first name), the gentleman she knew only as Quinn hadn't uttered a word beyond an occasional murmur in recognition of some point of interest as he toured the cavernous hangar. Surrounded by machines that represented bleeding-edge technology, he seemed indifferent. As if he'd seen it all before.

Penny watched closely. If Quinn was gawking around his head movements sure weren't giving anything away. He looked older than she suspected he was, his weathered face speaking to a life spent largely outdoors. He appeared to habitually check the corners every time they entered a new room. His gait was purposeful and precise. Self-controlled, almost predatory. And as a healthy female, she couldn't help but notice what had to be a well-muscled physique filling out a casual suit that looked like it rarely saw the light of day. Precisely pressed slacks, polo shirt, sport jacket…no, these weren't his normal work clothes. She suspected dressing up for a day's work entailed lots of rip-stop fabric and nylon webbing.

Special Ops...in our hangar? Whatever for, Arthur? She intended to corner him at the first opportunity if he didn't give up some info soon.

Quinn showed a telling hint of curiosity as their tour wrapped up in the control center: the big screens that charted Polaris' route system impressed him enough that he actually turned his head. A map of the lunar surface visible through the glass partitions of the EOC seemed to be of particular interest.

Their tour ended in the executive boardroom, itself somewhat of a museum and Hammond's single personal indulgence. The paintings on its walls presented a chronology of aeronautical feats, from Lindbergh to Armstrong. Interspersed among the artwork were pedestals holding mementos and artifacts that Hammond had collected over his lifetime: a combustion cylinder from an old Wright Cyclone radial engine, an Apollo guidance computer, a wind tunnel model of the first Clipper.

It was designed to spark conversation and reflection, a reminder of their contribution to a long heritage, open for anyone to roam whenever the boss didn't need the room. It was perhaps because of this that Penny was most surprised when Quinn didn't even blink, instead heading straight for his seat on one side of the room's massive conference table.

Audrey and Ryan had been waiting patiently and remained standing on the other side while Kruger stalked the perimeter with a thin black wand, waving it over every nook and cranny. He ignored their arrival, his attention fixed on a small tablet in his other hand. No doubt he was scanning for bugs while the rest of them engaged in the usual introductions and formalities. This promised to be interesting.

After everyone had taken their seats, Hammond leaned against the back of his chair. "This gentleman's been sent here as a representative of the Defense Department. It's been explained to me that he may be able to help us."

Quinn looked for some kind of confirmation from Kruger.

"It's clean. Go ahead."

As Quinn plugged his tablet into the projector, his posture confirmed Penny's instincts: ramrod straight and precise movements with no fumbling around. Definitely an operator. The only question was which service branch.

"As Mr. Hammond said, I've been authorized to share some information that you'll want to see. I must point out it is extremely sensitive, classified Top Secret-codeword. Normally we'd have to bring you to a secure vault so it *must not leave this room*," he said sternly. "I had to vouch for each one of you personally. If there's even a hint of blowback, after I'm assigned to a cell in Leavenworth you'll all be next in line for a Justice Department rectal exam."

Hammond stared down his team with his best *do not screw this up* look, then signaled his agreement. "We'll accept that risk. But we trust you to have some solid data on our spacecraft. Please don't stick our heads on the chopping block for some analyst's wild goose chase."

"You won't be disappointed," he said. "It goes without saying – so I'm saying it anyway – that we can't divulge the source of this imagery. The quality is limited by the extreme distances, but the base image—"

Imagery? They were just expecting radio signals...

Penny's throat tightened, her senses barely registering the chorus of stunned gasps that erupted around the room. Though fuzzy, it was unmistakable: a fat cylinder of loose reflective fabric, attached to an octagonal truss that encased a half-dozen spherical tanks. An array of antenna masts and solar panels fanned out from behind.

Without a word, Quinn clicked through more pictures of the same vessel. Each came from a slightly different angle, as if it had passed by overhead: the remains of *Shepard*, crippled but apparently in a stable orbit.

"The hab's depressurized," Audrey said with alarm. The hull fabric had collapsed around its core and the flight module was nowhere to be seen. "How did you find it this quickly?"

"The math weenies at the Joint Space Ops Center used your predictions to narrow the search band." He pushed a folder across the table, bordered with red tape and stamped TOP SECRET. Audrey snatched it and began poring over their data.

"A comforting thought," Hammond said as he glared at Kruger. "But I suspect we're not getting the full story, and frankly your presence makes me even more suspicious. The government's showing an alarmingly high degree of interest in our problems."

As usual, Penny thought.

Kruger made a show of adjusting his tie and cleared his throat. "Homeland Security," he said officiously, "is always interested in probable hijackings."

The implication hung like a storm cloud. Penny noticed that Hammond remained surprisingly composed, so it hadn't taken him entirely by surprise.

She, however, felt decidedly less reserved. "*Hijacked?* Mind sharing your basis for that theory?"

The agent was unflappable. "We're not at liberty to discuss that yet," he said with a glance in Quinn's direction.

Quinn shot back an annoyed look, which Penny decided was a clue they could probably trust him. "Not at liberty..." she said. "You bring us pictures of our missing ship and then tell us its a secret? It's *our* ship, and we're going up there in three days no matter what. So if you know something about where the rest of it is, now's the time to share with the class."

Hammond had likewise run out of patience. "I've had about enough of this hide-the-salami game, Kruger. You've stonewalled us every time we've gotten close enough to actually learn something useful. We have a badly damaged ship with a missing control module, way the hell out at the Moon, and now you're suggesting our passengers are behind it...all of whom made it through preflight screening," he said, letting the implication hang. "Did I miss anything?"

"You're assuming that only your passengers are behind this," Kruger said.

Hammond glowered at the agent. "Now just one damned minute..."

Penny was incredulous. "You're actually going to suggest that one of our own crewmembers was involved?" She saw Ryan also bristle at the implication while Audrey was strangely detached from it all, instead rifling through Quinn's briefing papers while they argued with this pinhead.

"I need you people to step back and take an objective look at this," Kruger began defensively. "We're talking about a *spaceship*. The cross section of people who can both afford a ticket and be competent enough to fly it is exceedingly small."

"Same for most old-fashioned hijackings," she argued. "D.B. Cooper didn't know anything about flying a 727. All he needed was to get the crew to do what he wanted."

"And how many airliners have been commandeered by a psychotic crewmember?" Kruger countered.

Quinn cleared his throat. "Agent Kruger, we have some information that concerns you as well." He turned to Penny. "Ma'am, our intelligence services are extremely compartmentalized. There are good reasons for that but it does make sharing information difficult. This is one of those times."

"I flew strategic bombers before I was an astronaut," Penny explained. "B-1's with live nukes plus various and sundry other brands of nastiness. We practically needed an Executive Order just to get new toilet paper for the women's john. So what else do you have for us?"

Quinn looked to Kruger, who reluctantly nodded his approval. "Two of your passengers are of particular interest to the counter-terror community: Kamran Varza and Omar Hassani. They've both popped up on our threat boards under different names over the last year, but were never tied closely enough to rate any professional attention."

"By 'professional attention', you mean..."

"Snatch-and-grab operation," Quinn said. "No ma'am. Until now there's been nothing to warrant committing the assets. We didn't even know they were aboard until yesterday."

"Little late now," Penny said. "How'd these two make it past the security screening?"

Kruger shifted uncomfortably. "Everyone cleared the no-fly list. They were flagged as 'selectees' until we could correlate all the different aliases." A step down from the no-fly roster, being on the "selectee" list meant they had nonetheless pinged Homeland Security's radar.

Hammond had heard enough. "And you didn't *tell* us?" he thundered. "You people could screw up a one-car parade, you know that?" Penny rested a hand on his arm and squeezed until she felt his tension subside.

"Our screeners followed their normal procedure," Kruger said. "They were under instructions to monitor and record the subject's movements. Apparently no one considered a trip like this to be an immediate threat. That will change."

That drew a scornful hoot from Ryan. "Closing the barn door after the horse is already out? Beautiful. Is TSA just too busy feeling up all those grandmas flying back from Miami for the winter?"

"Polaris wasn't the only organization to get that information after it was too late," Kruger said, briefly dropping his aloof façade. "I've been in law enforcement too long to be sandbagged by a bunch of half-assed mall cops."

"So what can you tell us about them that we don't already know?" Hammond asked, more calmly this time. "Since we don't have access to Washington's omniscient data mine."

"Dr. Varza is well known to anyone who owns a TV, so pretty much everybody. He's become quite wealthy as a science popularizer and environmental advocate. His business partner, Omar Hassani, is the one who initially flagged the no-fly database under a different name. Varza seemed more like guilt by association, but his Iranian family connections roused some suspicion. We were more concerned about his involvement with environmental extremist groups."

"The 'earth firsters?' Great," Hammond said. "So he's been dealing under the table with a bunch of eco-terrorists and his partner's working for the Islamic Caliphate. I can't wait to hear about the others."

No one had said anything about that, Penny realized. So Arthur did have his own sources.

"I understand you met Imam al-Aqsa." So it hadn't escaped Kruger's notice either. "The others aren't that surprising for this kind of expedition: Dr. Joseph DeCarlo is an expert on free-electron lasers and remote sensing. He's worked with Varza in the past. The others are relative nobodies: Jonathan Briggs is a mechanical engineer, Ernest Hadley is a software coder. Both have experience working for a handful of other spacecraft manufacturers. Individually they wouldn't ping our radars," he explained, "but taken together they make a formidable team. Especially when two of them have some unsavory acquaintances."

“Wouldn’t be the first time we have bad actors monkeying around with our spacecraft,” Hammond said. “So what are we going to do about this?”

“We?” Quinn asked. “Interesting that you would frame it that way.” He checked his watch. “It’s time we took you on a road trip.”

8

Colorado Springs, CO

It had been an uncomfortably silent trip down Interstate 25, small talk being difficult when everything is classified. Quinn took their black government SUV onto a side road that meandered into the hills around Cheyenne Mountain, winding their way past nondescript suburbs up to the mountainside entrance to NORAD, the North American Aerospace Defense command.

They drove past a parking lot that was notable for its complete lack of any cars, having been transformed into a hasty landing pad filled with heavy-lift helicopters and tiltrotors. A camouflaged military policeman kept one hand wrapped around the pistol grip of his M4 carbine as he checked ID's and waved them through the open blast doors. The massive steel slabs were designed to shield the underground base from every conceivable threat, up to and including a nuclear strike.

Ryan had always harbored doubts about that, but then again the men who'd built it had presumably known what they were doing. Or so everyone had hoped. Walking through the corridors and anterooms as they descended deeper into the facility, he was struck by its Cold War anachronisms – the place might have been updated over the years, but there was no escaping its original purpose. For decades, America had been prepared to wage World War III from this location while fully expecting to have been directly targeted by multiple Soviet warheads. What a thing to know that somewhere in the world sat a nuclear bunker-buster with your name on it.

As they continued down into the mountain he came to appreciate exactly how big of a bomb they'd have needed, with plenty more coming after it. Supposedly the entire underground complex rested on gigantic shock absorbers; he could only imagine how that ride would feel as successive nukes plowed into the mountainside.

His thoughts turned to the neighborhoods they'd driven through on the way up. Nearly all were base housing, filled with the families of the people who worked here. And the city not far away – all civilians, all living under the threat of unspeakable destruction that could have been visited upon them within twenty minutes of Ivan pushing the proverbial big red button.

Ryan shuddered involuntarily. Simply having a family continued to turn his perspectives inside-out. Every experience was now weighed against its effects on his wife and son, and he found himself going through life with his head on a swivel. Turning into his father wasn't necessarily a bad thing, though he dreaded the day when he'd inevitably blurt out "Because I said so!" in exasperation.

Ryan realized he'd barely paid attention during their quick courtesy tour. Once again he'd allowed his mind to wander, another byproduct of being a rookie parent.

• • •

Penny was caught up in her own meanderings. As they went deeper into the complex, she couldn't escape noticing that a tremendous number of collapsible shipping boxes had been stacked up along the corridors. NORAD had supposedly been relocated to more civilized facilities at the base in town years ago while the mountain had been kept as a fallback site.

Obviously, someone had decided it was time to fall back.

As they passed a hallway with a "crew ready room" sign hanging above it, she sidled up to one of their escorts and gently grasped his elbow. "I'll catch up in a second," she whispered, flashing an embarrassed smile. It was all too easy for an attractive woman to throw a young man off guard, middle-aged or not. "I need to find the ladies' room. Too much coffee on the way down."

The sentry caught the attention of one of his partners and pointed down a side hallway. They soon found a restroom – *latrine,* she corrected herself – and she paused at the door. "You're not following me in, are you?"

The young airman's face flushed red. "No, ma'am. But I'll have to wait out here for you."

"Thanks. Sorry for the trouble," she said, and pulled the door shut behind her. After a quick look around she found another door across the room. Fortunately things hadn't changed much: it seemed like every facility was designed the same way. She pressed an ear against the metal door, listening for any noise on the other side. Hearing none, she inched it open into a locker room that was blessedly empty. She poked her head inside and quickly found what she was looking for: a good old-fashioned message board hanging on the wall.

She ducked inside and rapidly scanned the postings for anything about unit deployments or other mass movements. As expected, there were lots of references to Cheyenne: schedules, pickup times, planning meetings...so this had in fact been a recent move.

NORAD wasn't the only command going to ground. There were references to other strategic sites being reactivated: she recognized the names of old underground missile facilities in Montana and the Dakotas, silos that had been mothballed for decades. Nothing about disposition of warheads or missiles, which she wouldn't expect to find on an unclassified board anyway. But an awful lot of logistics and headquarters squadrons were on the move. Lots of big shots and all of their stuff.

Penny flipped over another stack of papers and found a penciled-in reference to coordinate something with Greenbrier. *Greenbrier?* In the bad old days it had been Washington's fallback bunker, a duplication of Capitol Hill offices constructed beneath a mountain resort in West Virginia.

So the whole national command structure was digging in?

Raucous voices erupted from the other end of the room; another door opened as an outbound Osprey crew entered from the adjacent ready room. *Crap.* She spun around and found two solid rows of lockers between them and her. She stepped quietly back to the latrine door and slipped through with her back to them, just another chick in a blue uniform.

Safely on the other side, Penny leaned against the door and caught her breath. What did they have to do with any of this? She quickly straightened her hair then flushed the toilet and ran the sink for effect before stepping back out. She almost ran into her escort, who was standing squarely in the doorway about to knock.

"We have to hurry, ma'am. Briefing starts in five. The President doesn't take kindly to stragglers."

• • •

"At ease. Take your seats."

They had been escorted into a small auditorium where a barrel-chested man in Air Force blues stood at a lectern in one corner of the stage. Ryan noted three stars on his shoulders and leafed through the briefing notes they'd given him at the door: that would be Lieutenant General Sam Nichols, Pentagon J2: the Defense Department's chief intelligence officer. More brass was gathered behind him and most of them wore stars. There was a full-bird colonel in Marine green, and an Air Force major who was no doubt the general's aide.

Nichols motioned to the major, who proceeded to boot up two of three widescreen monitors hanging behind them. One displayed a chart of the Earth-Moon system superimposed with different trajectories, which unsurprisingly looked to be exactly what Audrey had been working on. Another was a closed-circuit feed, showing a crowded conference table cluttered with tablet computers and surrounded by men in uniforms and suits. The seat at the head of the table was conspicuously empty.

A door closed quietly behind him and he turned to see Penny slip inside with a flustered junior officer escort in tow. She eased into the seat next to him. "That would be the White House situation room," she whispered.

His eyes popped when he recognized who was taking the head seat just now. "You know something I don't?" he asked under his breath.

"Not anymore."

Ryan cast a furtive glance around the hall, sizing up the rest of the audience as they streamed in. Like the men up on stage, those in uniform all sported Colonel's eagles or General's stars. There wasn't a low-level aide in sight. The few not in uniform looked deadly serious. Like Quinn, they moved with a quiet grace on athletic frames that their suits barely disguised. "More spooks," Ryan muttered, "and you can't swing a dead cat in here without hitting a three-star. This is *big*."

"You're more right than you know."

Ryan could see the wheels turning behind her eyes. Before he could press her for details, they were cut short by a gruff voice from one of the monitors. "We're ready when you are, General." It sounded vaguely familiar, until he recognized it as the Secretary of Defense.

"Thank you, Mr. Secretary." Nichols looked directly at Hammond and their small group. "The security council has agreed to let us take the time to brief you in before we begin."

The third screen flickered to life. An ungainly assembly of metal cylinders, insulating foil, and reflective panels appeared. Spacecraft held a different aesthetic than ships or airplanes, but this was by far the most unusual they'd ever seen.

It was like a mechanical butterfly. At its center were two cylinders joined to a central hub, which itself sported immense circular solar panels. What resembled an enormous, partially-folded umbrella sprouted from the opposite end: sunshields for insulating propellant tanks, he guessed. The picture was remarkably clear for something that must have been taken from a great distance.

"What you're looking at is Gateway Station," the general explained, "a manned complex at Earth-Moon Lagrange point two." A region of deep space where Earth and Moon's gravity essentially canceled each other out, space-exploration advocates had been begging NASA to build an outpost there for decades. The idea made sense: being out of a gravity well, EML-2 was a perfect location for a fuel depot and waystation for operations beyond Earth. It also explained all of the heavy-lift launches that had been wreaking havoc on their flight schedule for the last year or so. About every six weeks a new Jupiter III or Vulcan Heavy had gone up, shutting down the airspace along with it for hours.

Gateway had even taken Hammond by surprise. Whatever else the boss may have learned on his own, he hadn't counted on this. "An outpost?" he asked. "You have people up there?"

"Not many, but yes," the General said. "Four men, for about six months now." So at least one of those boosters had been crewed – and keeping that under wraps would've been no mean feat. Too many external visual clues for a manned rocket, like the escape tower. Which meant they'd risked going without it.

They had been very busy...and very quiet.

"So this is a military outpost?" Hammond asked hopefully. Ryan could feel the anticipation animating him. Maybe there was already a rescue mission underway?

"Not quite, Mr. Hammond. Technically this is a National Science Foundation project."

More details emerged as the station slowly turned on its axis. An Orion crew capsule rotated past, docked to the main hub. Penny leaned in and whispered impatiently: "so they changed their mind about canning that program? Why didn't we hear about it?"

An ungainly craft appeared next, an assembly of foil-wrapped tanks with four spindly legs. From this angle, it took a minute before they recognized it as an Altair lunar lander. He nudged Penny back. "Didn't they whack the budget for that thing a long time ago?"

"Not before they finished building one, apparently." The deep-space exploration vehicles had supposedly died along with her first husband in the *Orion I* disaster years ago. This wouldn't have been the first time a NASA project had been resurrected by the Air Force.

A third module slowly rotated into view: a gleaming silver and white cylinder sporting two long solar wings with its squat conical nose docked to the station. A blue POLARIS logo dominated one side.

Their missing flight module. His arm hurt from the squeeze Penny gave it.

Was this a live shot? If so, these guys could see a whole lot more than they'd let on. The image drifted slowly across the screen before shifting back to center. Ryan looked around the room for any telling reactions and found none. The government types had no doubt seen this before.

General Nichols gave them little time to absorb it. "Twenty-one hours after your vessel was declared missing, we lost contact with Gateway."

9

North American Aerospace Defense Command (NORAD)
Cheyenne Mountain, CO

"Let's back up, General," Hammond said as he glared at Kruger and Quinn. "Your people knew the rest of our ship was up there, and you're only telling us this now?"

"Mr. Hammond, your escorts had orders to hold that information close. There are extremely sensitive security issues at play..."

"Which we're reminded of every time we do business with the Pentagon," Hammond said. "We sold you an entire squadron of Block I Clippers outfitted to your specs. I think we've earned the right to be treated as equals."

"And that's exactly why you're here," the General reminded him. "But this had to wait until we could bring you to a secure location. Gateway and everything associated with it is part of a larger project codenamed FIREWALL, a word which is not to be repeated in this context. Ever."

"Let's get on with it, Sam," the Defense Secretary interrupted. "I think they'll figure it out soon enough."

"Yes, Mister Secretary." Nichols turned back to his briefing notes, obviously used to being cut off by impatient higher-ups. "Space Guard received the first report that S.S. *Shepard* was missing at 1303 Zulu time the day before yesterday. Approximately sixteen hours later Gateway made contact with its command and service module, which was broadcasting in the blind and declaring an emergency. It was a weak signal, VHF line-of-sight. We thought it damned lucky that our people heard them in the first place. They reported a catastrophic failure with their habitation module, which took out their primary O2 tanks and disabled their long-range comm."

Penny suspected that no one here any longer believed luck had anything to do with it. "Which we could've told you was probably a load of crap," she said. "When you get right down to it, the hab is for comfort. The flight module carries enough O2 to sustain everyone for an emergency burn back to Earth."

"We certainly know that now," Nichols said. "The situation deteriorated quickly from there. Hell, our crew didn't even let us know what they were doing until your module was already inside the hazard zone. By the time we knew about it, they'd berthed it with the station's grappling arm and reported a successful hard dock. That was the last we heard from them."

"Any more EVAs since the last pass?" someone asked from the White House feed.

"Negative, sir," Nichols said. "No one has emerged from the outpost since yesterday's activity." The image blurred out of focus briefly as he changed views. It reappeared in the infrared spectrum. "However, these increased heat signatures are recent developments," he said, pointing to the heat exchangers and their radiators which fanned out atop the complex. "It suggests a substantial increase in power output."

"And the reflectors?" someone asked from the Situation Room. It sounded like Donald Abbot, the new NASA administrator. Already apprehensive, Penny got a sinking feeling in her gut. The farther away he was from them, the better.

"What about the capacitors?" another urgent voice asked, before Nichols could answer. "Are they building up a charge?"

"That would be a valid assumption, gentlemen. Judging by the heat signature, they're running at full output. All that energy has to go somewhere."

"They're charging the laser," the Secretary opined, then turned to Abbot. "So to answer your question, we can at least presume they didn't destroy the emitter."

She thought Ryan was going to choke on his coffee. *Laser?*

"That would be my first conclusion, sir," Nichols said. "Or they're intentionally burning out the capacitors."

SecDef frowned and drummed his fingers. "Not likely. There are much easier ways to disable the outpost if that's their play. So far they've taken great care to keep everything else working."

A more familiar voice cut in. "So have *any* shots gone off as scheduled since yesterday?"

Nichols' normally sober countenance turned sour. "Negative, Madam President."

Groans erupted both on-screen and around the room. Whatever that news meant, it had hit them like a punch in the gut. "We've tasked two KH-12 satellites on this and neither of them have detected any new emissions."

The grim silence that followed told her a great deal: something vitally important had been interrupted and it had the brass scared, all the way up to and including the White House. That it seemed to involve their company's missing ship was of secondary concern to them.

The President broke the silence. "Next steps, General? Assuming there's still time."

Nichols turned to one of the officers seated behind him. "Colonel Flagg?"

The Marine colonel stood and tugged smartly at the bottom of his olive-drab dress tunic before taking the podium. "A warning order from Joint Special Operations Command was issued to our Trans-Atmospheric Combat unit at 1900 yesterday, ma'am. Gunnery Sergeant Quinn's alert team is now in pre-deployment lockdown at Camp Lejeune."

Trans-Atmospheric Combat...what the hell was that? So at least she knew they were military operators and not undercover spooks, which gave Penny some small comfort. Nevertheless, her teeth clenched in frustration. They'd really been played this time: their ship hijacked so the bad guys could gain access to some top-secret facility which in turn was part of some equally top-secret weapons program.

Flagg called up a diagram of the Gateway outpost and its position relative to the Moon, more than fifty thousand kilometers above the far side. "Madam President," he said, "Given these recent developments we now believe direct action is required. We only need your order to execute."

The President gave her defense secretary a curt nod. "Operation VALIANT ARROW is approved," he said on her behalf. "Please summarize your latest operational plan for our new team members."

She exchanged uneasy glances with Ryan. New team members?

"Very well, sir." The colonel lifted a remote from the podium and began walking the stage, pausing by each screen as new information appeared. He remained focused on Hammond, which suggested the gathered brass already knew the big picture and that this was for the civilian's benefit. The President wouldn't have so readily given it her thumbs-up otherwise. "The TAC alert team will arrive at your Cape facility tomorrow evening for transport up to your spacecraft *Grissom* the following morning. A full itinerary will be provided after this briefing. Our intent is for your ship to depart Earth orbit at the earliest opportunity and execute a maximum-energy translunar burn, allowing for payload of course."

They hadn't counted on this becoming a military operation, and the news dropped like a bomb. It would be cute to hear what they had in mind for payload...

Flagg continued. "...entering a low-stability halo orbit at L2. Once the team has the objective in sight, they'll advance on Gateway along its X axis to minimize exposure." A crude animation showed *Grissom* sneaking up on Gateway, hidden from view behind the complex's massive insulating umbrella.

Penny was ready to jump out of her seat and climb the stage. "Pardon my manners, gentlemen, but since I'll be flying this thing I have a few pertinent questions." They'd already budgeted propellant for a crew of spacewalkers with a couple metric tons of rescue equipment. How the Marines thought they could just throw on more crap was the least of her concerns. "Namely, what about that laser?"

"That's why you'll keep station behind the sunshield. Once we're in close proximity, you'll maintain position while we conduct an EVA to board the complex. Your number one job is to remain undetected."

"Excuse me," she said tartly, "but our number one job is to rescue our missing people."

"Not anymore, ma'am."

...

Audrey barely listened to the erupting squabble, instead scribbling on a notepad while struggling to remember her undergrad optical physics classes. She'd found the subject mildly interesting, though it had largely gotten lost among the plethora of other difficult concepts she'd had to master along the way.

A free-electron laser, undoubtedly a weapon, parked way out beyond the moon and safe from any prying eyes. Besides the massive photovoltaic panels, she'd counted at least a half-dozen nuclear-thermal generators mounted around a hexagonal truss. So what was their combined output? The size of the radiator panels suggested it was quite high. It all depended on the isotopes and whatever materials they'd used for the thermocouples that turned nuclear heat into electricity. They worked a lot like solar cells: that is, not terribly efficient. The best she'd heard of had been around 30% and that was with the heat really cranked up. Out of those six generators, she figured the beam could transmit the energy of maybe two running at full tilt. More than enough if you're just roasting a turkey, but so what?

She'd have to dig up old notebooks out of her attic, maybe look up some professors back in Alabama if she could figure out how to frame the questions without bringing down the FBI on their heads. So scratch that – besides, they might tell her *how* but the real mystery was *why*. A secret crash program to orbit a weaponized space station on the other side of the Moon was no small feat. A directed-energy weapon from out there wouldn't be very effective against targets in Earth orbit. They'd gone to an awful lot of trouble to build something that could've easily been placed in geostationary orbit. Or even at L1, permanently between Earth and Moon instead of being hidden on the opposite side. For that matter, build it all on the ground.

So again: why go to all that trouble?

Lasers and telescopes were famously sensitive to atmospheric distortion. Adaptive optics had advanced to the point where atmospheric disturbances could be compensated for well enough that newer ground-based telescopes now rivaled the Hubble. But that for was passively gathering light over a long period to create an image of something light-years away. Projecting energy through a focused beam of light over a few seconds was different. It was one thing to build a ground station that could blind a spysat in orbit; they'd been doing that since the Eighties. Zapping them out of existence entirely was still the domain of science fiction. Maybe.

From Gateway's point of view any spy birds would've had their sensor packages pointed towards Earth, not the Moon. And that was when they weren't masked entirely by either body. So dazzling them wasn't the point, since they wouldn't have direct line of sight. And that worked both ways, thus the need for having people aboard. Besides needing the ability to precisely focus a lot of energy over a significant distance, they needed positive control. Power, range, control…what else would the military care about?

Stealth, she realized. Second law of thermodynamics dictated that nothing giving off heat could be hidden in space. And *everything* gave off heat, especially big-ass lasers powered by nuclear generators.

L2 made sense as a fuel depot, not a military base. Again, why put it way out there behind the far side? Audrey could have smacked herself for avoiding the obvious answer: *because they didn't want it to be found.*

…

General Nichols interrupted Penny's interrogation. "When your missing vessel report first popped, it was flagged by a junior signals analyst who connected the dots immediately," he said with a hint of amusement. "I'm told the kid's a bit of a space nerd and couldn't help himself. Turned out he was on to something."

"Glad to know someone in the Puzzle Palace is paying attention," she said caustically.

Nichols ignored the barb. "More than you know." He motioned to his aide, who opened a sealed envelope and stepped offstage, giving the contents to Hammond. "By the direction of National Command Authority," he said, meaning the President, "Polaris Aerospace Lines' Civil Reserve Air Fleet agreement is hereby activated."

Hammond looked up in disbelief. CRAF allowed the military to essentially commandeer airliners in the event of war or some other national emergency.

"None of your suborbital routes will be affected," Nichols explained, "but we will need you to commit at least one orbit-capable Clipper to this operation along with the lunar vehicle *Grissom*. We'll provide whatever additional support you require, including a Vulcan upper stage which can be docked with *Grissom* for additional delta-v."

Perhaps Art had to take it with a smile, but he counted on Penny to be his bulldog when necessary. "We appreciate the help, but something isn't adding up," she said. "If you were able to set up an outpost way out there at L2, then what exactly do you need us for? Can't NASA get you there?"

"Not in enough time." Nichols pointed to the image of Gateway Station and its attached crew capsules. "What you see here is the sum total of our nation's lunar architecture," he said with barely concealed frustration. "It took almost eighteen months just to set up a four man outpost. Even if another crew vehicle was available, those heavy boosters attract way too much attention. Half the damned state of Florida shows up whenever we launch one."

On the White House monitor, Don Abbot's porcine face flushed at the general's pointed critique. Maybe she could get along with this three-star after all. "We, on the other hand, have Clippers taking off from that location almost daily," she observed. "Except when the Eastern Range is closed for a short notice military launch. This project really played hell with our route system, you know that?"

General Nichols smiled in a way that she found vaguely unsettling, like he still knew something she didn't. "We understand your frustration. But your instincts are correct, Colonel Stratton." Now why would he use her old Air Force rank?

He looked at Ryan next. "This situation presents a thorny dilemma: we need to regain control of our station, and you need to reclaim your spacecraft." There was a telling failure to mention anything about the *people* aboard it. "We don't have any pilots qualified on your Block II Clippers and we know even less about your moonliner. There's no time to get our people properly trained, yet this operation must remain under military control. And you require access to information we can't give to civilians."

Penny's heart raced as she realized where he was going, just as the President spoke: "Getting our TAC team up there takes precedence over your search and rescue mission, for reasons which will be made clear soon enough. I am sorry, but you'll have to trust us."

Ryan rose to stand beside her in nervous anticipation. "You don't just need us for transportation," he said. "You need us for cover. No one will think twice about us heading moonward after one of our own ships."

"Also correct," Nichols said, stepping down from the podium. "Though I'm doing it anyway, I'm certain you don't need reminding that your commissions as regular officers in the Air Force and Marine Corps are held in reserve status and can be reactivated in times of national emergency by the President or Secretary of Defense."

He handed each of them a leather document holder. "Penelope Lynn Stratton, Ryan David Hunter: by authority of the Commander in Chief, you are hereby reactivated for assignment to the US Special Operations Command at your rank last held on active duty. Your commissions will return to inactive status upon completion of this operation." He shook their hands. "Lieutenant Colonel Stratton, Captain Hunter…welcome back."

Penny felt as if she'd been swept up in a whirlwind and was grasping for a way out. "General, I can't…" She caught herself and looked up at the monitor. "Madam President, we're going there whatever the circumstances. Putting us back in uniform doesn't do anything but complicate matters."

"On the contrary," she replied, "I think you'll find SOCOM to be pretty nimble. They've certainly surprised me at times. When they need something, they get it."

Like right now, Penny thought.

"Captain Hunter was right," the President continued. "You need information and we need cover. This is the best way to get you fully briefed in and to get our men to Gateway. This operation is as black as it gets: no uniforms, no haircuts, and no talking about it."

Ryan studied his fresh orders and eyed Penny dubiously. "This doesn't mean I'm calling you 'ma'am'…"

She cut him off quickly. "Stow it, jarhead."

A satisfied grin finally cracked the General's face as he clapped them each on the shoulder. "See? It didn't take long for you two to get back in the groove."

10

Washington

Don Abbot had never been one to hide his emotions well; that he had been able to rise this far within the Administration was widely seen as a testament to his technical abilities and organizational acumen. That it had just as much to do with his knowledge of whose skeletons were hidden in which closets was not as widely known.

As the President and her cabinet filed out of the situation room, Abbot conspicuously remained seated. Tapping his pen against the table, his tense posture and pursed lips broadcast to anyone who bothered to notice exactly how much he was stewing over this latest development.

"Don, you really have to learn to play closer to the vest."

He looked up to find Defense Secretary Horner lingering by the doorway. He tossed his pen onto the table and pushed himself away. "What's your point, Hal?" he sighed, knowing full well what the old man meant. "I hardly got a word in edgewise, not that they seemed interested in anything I had to say in the first place."

"That, my friend, is the point," SecDef said as he pulled up a chair and grabbed the pen Abbot had been tapping away with. "You don't play poker, do you?"

"Never had the patience," he admitted. "I didn't care to digest the rules: which hand beats which, et cetera." Though the few hands he'd played had taught him it was remarkably easy to bluff when you really didn't know what you were doing.

"Yet you literally wrote the book on spacecraft design," Horner pointed out. "You're damn near a genius, Don."

Near? Abbot thought, realizing too late that he'd just been baited to prove a point.

"See?" Horner smiled. "I just insulted you. The look on your face gave it away. Don't be so prickly. This is one time the President needs everyone to set aside their personal agendas to do what's necessary for the country."

"What 'personal agenda' would you be referring to?" Was Hal really that kind of gung-ho idealist? It was an easy way for a man to get rolled in this town.

"Art Hammond," Horner said flatly. "Maybe I'm more attuned to past history than the others because I bought some of his planes, but the fact is he's been peeling away talent from your agency for years. It happens, Don. That's business. Don't let yourself get so pissed off over it. At least don't wear it on your sleeve."

Abbot smiled thinly. The old guy almost understood. This wasn't "just business" and he didn't care about the people as much as the institutional power they represented. Individuals could be replaced. In fact he'd found organizational control to be much easier when there was a steady churn among the middle managers. The really motivated ones tended to have agendas that didn't mesh with his own; it was best to keep them off balance.

No, what really had incensed Don Abbot was the collapse of the human spaceflight program. Having risen through the ranks back when a government ride was the only possible way into orbit, he'd never been able to adjust to the new reality: corporate hucksters and dotcom billionaires peddling rides into space like so many hayseed barnstormers. What were their standards? And to what purpose? Shouldn't space exploration be something nobler...more nationalistic? Shouldn't somebody be in charge of it all?

Of course, as Hammond and his ilk saw it, each was in charge of their own domain which meant that nobody was in charge. It was a recipe for disaster, at the very least a wholesale cheapening of the exploration ideal.

Cheap. That was it. They had cheapened the whole experience as they drove towards the lowest common denominator. Hammond's spaceplanes could barely get a dozen people into orbit at once; that they claimed to make up for it in daily volume was irrelevant. Yet because of that, the ruthless budget slashers who had overrun Washington with the arrival of this simpleton President had seen an easy target in the space agency. And those other fools with their absurd "reusable" boosters...it was a neat trick, being able to fly a rocket back to land right next to its launch pad. Real 1950's sci-fi stuff. But so what? If they could only get a dozen launches out of the same machine, how much money were they really saving? It wasn't like you could pull off such a stunt with a serious heavy lifter anyway. The thought of one of his heavies falling back to the Cape and hovering on its thrust over a concrete platform gave him nightmares.

"Hammond's bunch can screw around in low orbit all they want," he said dismissively. "If you want to get anywhere beyond Earth, it's go big or go home."

"Sure about that?" Horner asked pointedly. "They managed to get a couple of moon-orbiting vehicles up there. Kind of the point of this whole problem, Don."

Abbot's face flashed red with anger. "And they couldn't even do *that* on their own! They had to hire their own competitors just to get the major structures into orbit."

"So what? They're serving completely different markets. That's how it works. When I was at Lockheed we'd contract with Airbus all the time. They were the only ones with freighters big enough to move an entire fuselage."

"Yet *none* of these yokels could've launched Gateway in one shot," Abbot argued, stabbing a finger into the air for emphasis. "Or for that matter, had the spare ISS modules on hand to build it. *We* did that."

"For which you'll have the eternal thanks of a grateful nation... someday," Horner said. "I have to admit it's a good thing you had a couple of those big bastards sitting idle in the VAB."

What Horner had just offered as conciliation instead had the opposite effect. "And if they'd given us the budget I'd asked for, we could've had a whole fleet of them at the ready," he fumed, "instead of cobbling together some damned fool escapade on a slapdash 'spaceliner.' We wouldn't be having this conversation if Hammond hadn't been selling rides around the moon in the first place."

Horner's expression darkened. "You're not the first to voice that opinion," he said. "I wouldn't want to be in Art's shoes once this is over with. Dollar to a doughnut says Homeland Security will be three feet up his ass the minute our guys land. They've already got an agent on site, and from what my contacts tell me the guy's already been reeled in a couple times just to keep this operation on schedule."

Contacts, Abbot realized. That's how an idealistic ninny like Horner thrived in this town. Information was power, an asset he'd played well in Houston but had yet to develop in DC. "Mark my words," he grumbled, "Hammond is going to get people killed, on a scale even I couldn't have imagined."

SecDef stretched with an exhausted groan as he considered Abbot's prediction. "I hope to God you're wrong, for all of our sakes."

• • •

Gateway

Omar Hassani silently cursed the persistent fog inside of his faceplate. With each successive breath it threatened to spread until it blocked his vision, something Varza had warned him about. He ground his teeth against rapidly mounting anxiety, struggling to recall what he'd been told to do about it. Something to do with the regulator, which he couldn't see. How was he supposed to adjust his air flow if he couldn't see the blasted controls? How were they expected to keep anything straight when surrounded by certain death in hard vacuum?

His newfound appreciation for the actual hard work of being an astronaut was interrupted by a gloved hand tapping his visor. "Hang on, buddy," Briggs' voice rattled in his earphones. The tinny radio only amplified the man's grating northeast accent. Hassani had spent enough time in America to become well acquainted with most of its regional dialects and had come to especially hate this one. "We need to dial down the temperature and get more air moving across your faceplate. Hold still and breathe easy for me, okay?"

Hassani nodded hurriedly and gave his spacewalk partner a quick thumbs-up once he realized the man probably couldn't see his face. He resented being coddled like a child but played along for now. A cool breeze soon caressed his face and the fog on his visor began to clear.

"Wow," Briggs said. "You're really sweating there, buddy. Remember, there's a microfiber towel sewn inside your helmet liner."

Helpful advice, but if Briggs called him "buddy" one more time the fool was likely to find his suit sliced open. All in due course, as Varza would have reminded him. Hassani turned his head and pressed it into the padded microfiber. "Thank you," he said with sincerity that was only partially forced. "Good to go now." The casual lingo felt equally stiff, though it had been effective at placating their companions. "Shall we continue?"

"Absolutely," Briggs said. "Not quite the same as floating around in the vomit comet, is it?" Before leaving Earth they had chartered several training sessions in a converted airliner, flying endless stomach-turning parabolas high above the Gulf of Mexico. They might have been better served practicing in a neutral buoyancy simulator, though a scarcity of the giant swimming pools ensured they would have attracted too much unwelcome attention.

"It certainly isn't," Hassani agreed, finally able to see clearly. They were tethered outside of Gateway's antenna masts, awaiting word from Varza to physically disconnect the system. It would be their final piece of insurance against earthbound interference.

...

Varza floated behind his own partner, an annoyingly chatty Midwesterner who spoke constantly of the farm country he'd grown up in. It appeared this pig had taken one too many turns at the feed trough himself, no doubt at all the church potlucks his parents had forced him to attend. Just one more thing Ernest Hadley wouldn't shut up about.

"Almost done," the programmer said. "Easier than my last girlfriend, and I don't even need shots afterward."

Varza found that surprising – this troll was able to maintain functioning relationships with actual women? The man was a brilliant engineer, but he'd come off as a social zero. "Is that your secret to success? Treat machines like women?" he asked, amused at the idea.

"More like make 'em my bitch," he chortled as he tapped away at the keyboard. "About the same, I reckon. Once you understand what makes 'em tick, it's all a matter of knowing which buttons to push." He ended with a grating cackle that Varza forced himself to remain smiling through.

Finishing this job would be a pleasure, of that there could be no doubt. Varza checked his watch – he'd spent weeks building a precise schedule and any delays threatened to begin a cascade with no time to correct. "And will you be able to bring this one to heel in time? If we miss the first emission…"

"You said 'emission.' Heh," Hadley snorted. "Believe me, I don't want to have to re-sequence this any more than you do."

Varza was in no mood for making light. "That won't be the problem. If we miss this window," he said, really meaning Hadley, "there's only one way to correct it. I don't believe either of us wants to think about that."

"Far be it for me to interfere with the grand scheme of the universe," the programmer said, and folded the keyboard back into its tray with a flourish. "Done."

Varza smiled with almost genuine appreciation as he braced himself against a foothold in the deck. "After all this time, our work is finally done?"

"See for yourself," Hadley said, and turned back to the fire control station.

"I would be delighted," Varza said as he dug into his hip pocket. He moved with surprising speed, sliding the dagger from its sheath and driving it into the base of the programmer's skull. Hadley's frame jerked once and went limp. A trickle of blood leaked out, pooling up on the skin at the hilt. The last one hadn't been nearly as clean. This time, Varza made certain to leave the blade inside and keep the wound sealed. Too bad; it was one of his favorite knives. Nevertheless, he gave thanks for the time they had invested in those training flights, and especially for bringing the others in only after he and Omar had become comfortable with their zero gravity fighting skills.

He grabbed the body by its feet and pushed it towards an open storage locker, being careful to avoid passing any portholes visible from outside. Waste disposal complete, he thumbed the radio to signal Omar. "Interior work is complete. The targeting routine has been reprogrammed. You are cleared to proceed."

…

"Understand we are go to proceed," Hassani answered, closely watching his spacewalk partner. "Disconnect the relays."

Briggs gave him a clumsy thumbs-up as his fingers were barely able to close in the stiff gloves. "Heard him the first time," he said cheerfully, and began methodically dismantling every physical connection between Gateway's control module and its comm array. Not only would it be impossible to reconfigure or bypass from the ground, it would require considerable effort to reset even if they sent a crew up here.

Hassani watched with envy as Briggs functioned effortlessly in this frustrating environment. When finished, the maddeningly enthusiastic engineer secured his tools in the beta cloth pouch clipped to his waist. "Done and done," he said. "Ready to get back inside?"

"You don't want to linger and enjoy the view?" Hassani asked with uncharacteristic cheer. It was always good for people to let their guard down after a big job.

"Love to," Briggs said. "I was just looking out for you, big guy. Maybe you're finally getting the hang of this."

"There is indeed much to appreciate out here," Hassani agreed. He made a circling motion above his stomach. "But nature makes other demands that are not as appealing."

"Ah. Motion sickness," the engineer smirked. "Curse of the space age. Wouldn't do for you to puke in your helmet. Well my friend, let's get you inside and out of that suit." He pointed to the airlock and began pulling them along a safety tether towards the open hatch. Briggs slipped in first and pushed off for the inner door. Hassani followed silently and dogged down the hatch. As the tiny compartment pressurized, he noted with satisfaction that their engineer was completely focused on the atmosphere controls. As expected.

"Pressure differential coming up nicely," Briggs said as the gauge climbed past 6 pounds per square inch, the same as their suits. "I'm getting this helmet off." Briggs was unlocking the neck ring before he even finished his sentence and set his helmet floating free.

Hassani watched with amusement as the engineer took a long breath. It wasn't as if he couldn't do that with the helmet on. He began theatrically fumbling with his own neck seal. "Just a moment. This bothersome lock ring..."

"Sit tight, buddy. Let's have a look."

Hassani turned and hooked one arm in a handhold. When he lifted his sun visor, his sunken eyes flared with malevolence. "I am not your buddy," he said darkly, spinning the outer door seals free. The hatch flew open, blinding them in a sudden whiteout as the air exploded in a fog of ice crystals. The roar of escaping gases quickly fell silent as the last molecules vented into space.

Multiple alarm strobes flashed angrily in impotent silence. Hassani floated up to the open hatch and was rewarded with the sight he'd longed for: Jonathan Briggs' face contorted into a mute scream of horror as the vacuum claimed his life. Seeing his mouth agape like a hooked fish as he tumbled into the void made enduring the man's insipid blathering almost worth it.

• • •

SS Shepard

After a few hours of carefully poking around with a flashlight clenched between his teeth, Simon had finally located the conduit he'd nicked while pulling apart the intercom. It looked frayed, like it had been worn down by some unanticipated movements – yet another debrief item.

You're an engineer, he scolded himself. *It shouldn't be this easy to short out the lights*. He considered the multi-tool that had lived on his side for so long, then regretfully zipped it into a hip pocket safely out of reach. Only "approved for space" non-conductive blades from now on.

"Screw this," he finally said aloud. "I'll be damned if I gonna die cold and dark." He spliced the wiring back together and wrapped it with electrical tape. He sniffed the air, on guard for any wisps of smoke or telltale scent of ozone. Doubtful with a blown breaker, but now was the time for caution.

He carefully inspected the open comm panel: there was a lot more going on in there than just a microphone, so maybe it was best that he quit using his ersatz telegraph key for now anyway. He fastened his tablet to the bulkhead and zoomed in on the schematics until they matched what he saw. He was in *Shepard*'s central node: power, water, air…everything came through here. Putting the circuit breakers on the opposite side of the bulkhead had been a necessary design choice, but that didn't make it any less of a pain right now.

The hab could function unattended for weeks, even though it couldn't maneuver without being docked to a flight module. So power and water weren't a problem, barring some unseen damage.

Breathing air would be a different story. The hab used carbon dioxide scrubbers based on molecular sieves of the type he'd been familiar with on the ISS. The airlock, however, was intended only for short-term use and therefore relied on a separate system: the same type of lithium hydroxide filters NASA had employed since the Sixties. The spares gave him about three more days of clean air, which he could extend by maybe eight or ten hours by sealing himself up in a spare EVA suit. After that he'd begin to slowly poison himself with each breath.

He pulled himself over to the hatch and shone his flashlight through its little window. Down the darkened tunnel he could see the air ducts had sealed, so the emergency systems had worked as designed. The ducts had closed as soon as the system recognized an uncontrolled decompression, preserving precious oxygen. All he needed was a way to seal off the tunnel and redirect that air into his compartment.

Assuming he could also get the lights back on.

He stared at the spacesuit, then down at his almost certainly broken arm. This was really going to suck.

11

Denver

The simulator cabin was illuminated by little more than the glow of instrument screens. A three-dimensional image of the lunar surface hovered just beyond the windows. Penny and Ryan sat in the pilot's seats with Audrey buckled up behind them in the instructor's chair. "Everybody set?" Penny asked.

Audrey turned to the instructor's panel. "Sim is locked down, walkway's retracted." They were isolated inside of an exact replica of the Cycler's flight deck, itself supported by a complex arrangement of hydraulic pistons underneath. An amber warning beacon began flashing outside, signaling anyone in the sim bay that the beast could start lurching unpredictably at any minute. Not far away a Clipper simulator bucked atop its own hissing hydraulics.

"Let's go dark."

Audrey reached above the console and opened the voice and video recorder's circuit breakers, blinding any potential outside observers. It was the most isolated place they could find on company property. "We're secure."

"So what do ya'll think we're getting ourselves into now?" Ryan drawled. "I still haven't figured out how to tell Marcy I've been drafted."

Penny realized she hadn't even talked to her husband yet. "A big fat hairy mess is what we've gotten into," she griped, with a nod toward the computer-generated moon outside. "Anyone else almost forget what we were supposed to be going up there for in the first place?"

"They made it easy enough to forget, what with all that secret mission talk," Audrey agreed. Which had been quite a feat, considering they still hadn't heard from *Shepard* since yesterday. "Soon as we find out our ship's been hijacked, the Pentagon hijacks us. And here's what really worries me: have you seen anything about us on the news?"

What should have been irresistible round-the-clock news bait hadn't been mentioned at all on any outlet. Not a missing spacecraft, certainly not a hijacking. It was clear that the government had been leaning on newsrooms all over the country, no doubt feeding the networks some carefully crafted misinformation.

"Good point, not that we want the attention," Penny said. She turned to Ryan. "What's your gut tell you about our new friends?"

Ryan was uncharacteristically quiet. He fiddled with the pitch control, shifting the image of the moon outside. He eventually stretched back, folded his arms behind his head, and blew out a sigh. "There you go again," he said. "Just because I wore the same uniform, I'm supposed to be all up in their business."

"Exactly right. You know their world better than we and you were Art's liaison for our Pentagon sale. That leads me to believe you have some insight as to what they're about."

"Funny thing about the Corps was they really meant that 'every Marine an infantryman' stuff. So we were expected to spend a tour with the grunts, coordinating air support and stuff like that. When my number came up, dummy me volunteered to go with Recon battalion. I wanted something adventurous."

"That's what, Special Forces?" Audrey asked. "Like the SEALs?"

"Special Operations. Different purpose." It was a minor but important distinction. "But yeah, something like that. Let's just say they gave me what I signed up for in spades," he said acerbically. "Even back then there were some forward thinkers figuring out ways to take advantage of all these newfangled suborbital spacecraft."

"I remember that – global rapid response," Penny said. "Space drop a squad of Marines anywhere in the world on a couple hours' notice. They were on to something, but it nearly got them laughed out of the Pentagon." She wondered if the men who'd advocated for it even knew that their ideas had been put into practice. Something told her probably not.

"Just like Billy Mitchell," Ryan said. The legendary pilot had nearly been drummed out of the service after demonstrating that it was possible to sink a capital ship with only aerial bombardment. In an ironic twist, the Army Air Corps had eventually named a bomber after him.

"At least these guys didn't get court-martialed for their trouble," Penny said. Now, it was much easier to wreck a troublesome officer's career through innuendo and a few carefully worded comments in a fitness report. "So they actually went ahead with the 'Space Marine' idea?"

"Sure looks like it. But I didn't hear a peep about it when I was delivering those Clippers to the Air Force. I figured they wanted them for rapid transport but they didn't say a thing about troop drops." The idea was perhaps too crazy for him to have taken seriously: leaping out of a suborbital vehicle over hostile territory, diving from space and hitting the atmosphere as a supersonic projectile. The concept had been proven from high-altitude balloons, but the thought of doing it in an armored spacesuit with a combat load? Nuts.

"Actually it's not that surprising," Audrey interposed. "Why else would they have wanted a separate airlock system for the pax cabin?"

The pilots stared at her until Ryan broke the silence. "Leave it to her to figure it all out before the rest of us."

"That still doesn't tell us anything about our present situation," Penny reminded them. "They're awfully interested in that outpost."

Ryan tapped impatiently on the glare shield. "That's what I can't get my head around. What's that contraption for in the first place? There have to be easier ways to get the job done."

Audrey was eager to finally give voice to the thought experiments that had consumed her all day. "Depends on what you think the job is," she said. "Think about it: deep space, and on the wrong side of the Moon. No consistent line of sight with Earth, so it's next to useless as an anti-satellite weapon and worthless against ballistic missiles."

"Could be a proof of concept," Ryan mused. "Keep it out of sight so they can blast away without attracting attention. Because I'm pretty sure this thing violates about a half dozen treaties."

"Speaking of line of sight," Penny said, "we'll be in blackout for a good portion of the flight. And they're installing encrypted radios, which is going to seriously limit bandwidth. Any open comm is going to have to go through some kind of code, which we won't have time for."

"We'll be out of contact right about the time you guys will need the most help," Audrey agreed.

Penny exchanged a knowing look with Ryan. "You're right," she said. "That's why you're going with us."

. . .

Melbourne

"What's that?"

Marshall Hunter had pulled his mother by her hand into the back yard, which was becoming a habit of late. The night sky above their home exploded with stars and while they'd always encouraged his natural inquisitiveness, this latest fixation had a suspicious way of interfering with bedtime. He was beginning to recognize patterns and was immediately drawn to anything new or out of place. What his mother didn't yet realize was that he'd also begun to connect it with his daddy's work and was intently searching for him up there. He was particularly eager tonight, since they'd just learned Ryan would be home tomorrow.

"It's a comet, dear," Marcy said patiently. She wondered if he actually expected Ryan to leap down from the sky.

"What's a comet?"

Marcy carefully considered his question, searching for an explanation that would fit a toddler's understanding. She thought of their trip to see Aunt Penny in Colorado last winter. "It's like a big snowball," she said. "A really big snowball."

"Big as me?"

"Much bigger," she smiled.

He was getting excited now. "Big as daddy's planes?"

"Even bigger."

His eyes grew wide. "Big as our house?"

"No, hon," she said gently. "Big as the whole town."

He stared at the white smudge hovering above the ocean, then looked back past their neighborhood as he considered his mother's words. "Is it going to land here?"

"No, baby," she said. "But it is going to fly right by us in a few weeks." The networks had been chattering about it breathlessly, in fact. And to be fair, it was hard to overstate. The closest pass by any comet in known history promised to be spectacular.

He sounded disappointed. "Okay." The boy took one last look and turned back to their house. He was satisfied with his mother's explanation, as the big flying snowball had been steadily getting bigger.

• • •

Denver

Audrey sat by her bedroom window, staring in disbelief at the crescent moon as it rose into the orange sky above the eastern plains. She tried to imagine what it was going to be like spending almost a month up there, completely confined to their spacecraft and utterly dependent on it functioning properly. Being confronted so personally with the inherent risks sharpened her outlook in ways she hadn't counted on. This should have been exciting, after all.

Trying to imagine what whomever up there might be enduring at this moment made her shudder. There'd been no signal from the hab in two days. If anyone held out hope that somebody might still be alive up there, they'd not had the courage to say so.

But still. Simon was the most tenacious person she'd ever known, which was the word she used when she was feeling kind. He could also be exceptionally bullheaded. He always kept things light, but in the end the man had a talent for getting things done his way.

Audrey had pushed aside any thoughts of his probable fate as she struggled to comprehend this latest turn. She was about to finally embark on a childhood fantasy. *You're going to the Moon, girl. So what's your problem?*

Reality was the problem: a good friend was missing, his passengers were probably terrorists, and the President of the freaking United States has decided it's serious enough to send in the Marines. Yes, that about covers it.

It had already been a brutally long couple of days. With plans changing, her team would be in for another all-nighter creating mission rules and running simulations, now with Charlie personally at the helm. She'd rapidly been crushed by competing demands, but being tapped for the crew had made one thing easier: she'd had no choice but to go home and pack.

And what a joke that had been. How does one pack for the trip of a lifetime when the circumstances are so grim? All she'd been able to think of were workout clothes, of which she had plenty: running shoes, pullovers, zip-off pants...she'd tossed in a quarter-zip fleece and a pair of jeans just for good measure and reconsidered it twice. *Too much*, she thought. *Gotta keep the weight down.* Her bag sat atop the bathroom scale while she debated over the last gram. Out went the jeans, but she'd kept the fleece as she'd have no control over the temperature aboard Gus.

A whimper drew her attention to her feet, where a small dachshund bounced up and down by her knee. "Wernher, here." She held out her hands and the dog happily jumped into her lap. "Gotta leave soon. Wish I could take you with me," she said haltingly. "I'd probably feel a lot better about this."

He looked at her in that quizzical way dogs have, before indulging his nightly habit of licking her hand until he fell asleep.

"Quit looking at me like that."

12

Melbourne

Marcy struggled to process what her husband had just told her, while their son's raucous delight over his daddy being home wasn't making it any easier. Given his news, dashing home just long enough to get a few hours' sleep before running back to the Cape was worse. Seeing him remove his old service pistol from a hidden lockbox in the garage to slip inside his flight bag would've been intolerable.

"Run that by me again?" she demanded, in the singularly menacing tone of a wife who'd just been given some very unwelcome news. "You've been *what*?"

"Activated," Ryan sighed, defensively crossing his arms as he leaned against their kitchen counter. "Penny too. Our commissions were still held in ready reserve, so –"

"I know what that means," she said impatiently. "But we never expected them to actually *need* you." They'd both forgotten about it, especially after the interminable Middle East conflicts had died down. They'd been spared the threat of a sudden activation that might send him on an open-ended deployment to some faraway hellhole. "You couldn't have told me about this any sooner?"

"Not without a scrambled phone or encrypted email," he explained. "It had to wait until we could talk in person."

"Why are you whispering? You afraid someone's listening?" she asked, perhaps a bit too harshly.

"Old habits. This isn't supposed to be widely known, babe. It's part of their cover story."

"Cover story…what's there to cover? You're still going, right?"

He stared at the ceiling, carefully considering what to say next. "Yes…and no. We're still launching day after tomorrow. But our manifest has changed a bit," he said, and explained the very few details of the plan he'd been allowed to share. And as with most military couples – they were both having a hard time thinking of themselves that way – he probably shared too much.

After turning it over in her mind, Marcy let her guard down and leaned into her husband's side. "So Penny outranks you?" she asked, fussing with his shirt collar. "At least there'll be some adult leadership up there."

...

SS Shepard

Simon taped his forearm to a makeshift splint made of some plastic ribbing he'd liberated from behind the intercom panel. His bad arm would have to be the first into his suit; he'd have to keep his good arm free to manipulate everything else. He'd already tried getting the inflatable splint over his cooling garment but found no way it would fit. Thank goodness it zipped in front, designed for a person to suit up unassisted. He'd never aspired to be a contortionist and being crippled made him downright clumsy, despite the lack of gravity. It might have even made it worse.

He studied the setup one last time and ran through the backwards procedure he'd cobbled together. The suits could be adjusted for nearly universal fit with minimum bulk. Dressing out for EVA was meant to be as simple as possible, given that this garment was all that stood between the wearer and certain death. For that reason, the suiting-up process had been carefully crafted to ensure proper fit and function. Stick to the checklist and everything would be fine.

Too bad there was no way in hell he'd be able to do this by the checklist.

He took a deep breath and gingerly slipped his injured arm through the opening. Not bad, compared to the compression and cooling undergarment first. Getting into that had been so unpleasant that he was considering staying in it after this job was done.

The helmet was typically the last item to go on, but in this case he'd secured it to the neck ring ahead of time as it would've been impossible to get a good seal one-handed from inside the suit. He carefully twisted the rest of his body into the open shell and snaked his head up into the helmet, double-checked the locking ring, and took a test sip from the hydration tube by his cheek. So far, so good.

Now for his busted arm...he tucked it in and extended it through the sleeve into the already attached glove. Once his hand was pushed through the wrist ring he began fishing for the zippers by his waist: inner seal first, then the diagonal outer seal across his chest. Next came the other glove, which was going to be a real trick. This one had been saved for last, keeping his good hand unencumbered for as long as possible. The glove had to be slipped onto his hand and over his wrist before it could be locked into place. He'd wedged it into a seam between bulkhead panels, not counting on any mobility from his other arm. He pushed his hand through, felt the rings seat against each other, and gingerly braced himself with his other hand. Pain shot through his arm as he pushed off, twisting his body clockwise to lock the rings.

When the locks finally clicked in place, Simon heaved out a sigh and finished with a curse. That had sucked about as much as expected.

• • •

Kennedy Spaceport

Ryan squinted into the distance at the sound of an approaching jet, focusing on a smudge that emerged from the gray afternoon sky. The shape soon resolved itself into twin-engine airliner, which he guessed to be an older model Boeing. As it settled in on final, trailing condensation vortices in the humidity, the alternately flashing landing lights that shone through the haze confirmed his guess.

Tires barely chirped as its main gear kissed the pavement, hinting at a lightly loaded aircraft and a pilot with an exceptionally smooth touch. The old bird continued down the runway with its nose still in the air, bleeding off speed. As its nose wheel finally settled onto the pavement, he heard the rumble of thrust reversers. With nearly three miles to touch down and roll out, the unmarked 737 easily reached the turnoff for the Polaris apron without once having to tap brakes. As its engines spun down, the plane's main door opened and a ground crewman rolled out air stairs to meet it. Notably absent were any flight attendants in the doorway.

Passengers emerged soon after, men who would have been unremarkable except for their uncanny similarities: all were dressed in casual khakis with polo shirts and sporting uniformly close haircuts. Despite their best efforts to appear incognito, there was no mistaking that the Marines had landed.

Another door opened along the plane's belly. Not waiting for ground crews – specifically instructing them to stay away ahead of time, in fact – four of the men gathered around a belt loader parked alongside the jet's cargo pit. Two of them hopped up to clamber inside, and soon pallets laden with worn olive-drab duffel bags and rugged shipping containers began rolling out.

Quinn came down last. Ryan extended his arms dramatically, as if he were greeting a fresh load of tourists. "Gentlemen," he said, "welcome to the Cape."

"Wish it were under different circumstances," Quinn said as he took in the subtropical scenery. He settled on the massive Vehicle Assembly Building and the service gantries that rose up in the distance beyond the mangrove trees. "Always wanted to see this place, but could never convince the ex-wife to cut me loose when we took our kids to Disney."

"Guess that command authority only went so far," Ryan observed wryly.

"The price for being away from home too much," Quinn said, showing his bare ring finger. "You know what they say: if the Corps wanted me to have a wife…"

"They'd have issued you one in boot camp," Ryan finished for him. "Just as well, because if they did we can only imagine what she'd look like."

"Ever the comedian, Captain," Quinn said. He unslung a backpack, which was heavily padded and clearly not government issue. "Is there somewhere I could set up a telescope later on tonight? Little hobby of mine."

Ryan thought for a moment, then pointed around the corner of their compound. "Out back, behind the visiting crew quarters. There's a concrete patio and picnic tables."

Quinn studied the surroundings. He seemed especially interested in the lighting.

"The skies aren't too bad here," Ryan said. "Most of the lights are concentrated over there around the VAB and whatever launch pads are being prepped. Our ramp lighting is minimal unless we need it," he explained. "The Cape's a wildlife preserve. We have to avoid disturbing the native critters as much as possible. Just keep an eye out for gators." He'd once stumbled into one sunning itself along a service road, and the guttural belching of its extended family lurking in the marsh was a constant reminder of what had been a close call.

Quinn lifted his sport jacket to reveal a custom 1911 pistol with tritium sights, not the standard-issue service sidearm. "No problem there. Nice thing about Special Ops is being able to carry your own weaponry."

Ryan studied it appreciatively as he ran a thumb behind his shirt to the diminutive .380 auto holstered inside his waistband. It felt shamefully inadequate by comparison. It would stop a gator with a head shot, which was just as likely to mean the creature would already be latched onto him. He also kept a magazine of birdshot-filled snake rounds on hand for the Cape's other dangerous critters.

He decided to steer the conversation towards more serious weaponry. "So what's in those containers?" he asked with a nod towards the stack of green shipping boxes. "Anything we should be worried about?" Various brightly colored stickers indicated they were chock full of all manner of hazardous materials that required special handling.

Quinn hesitated, apparently having to decide for himself if the pilot deserved to know what they were carrying. "Lots of grownup toys designed for vacuum and zero gravity," he finally said. "M55-A1 low-recoil rifles, flash-bang grenades, man-portable magnetic rail gun, targeting lasers..."

Ryan whistled. "All the toys a young man could want." The high-tech stuff was impressive, though he was more concerned about the damage from a simple flash-bang going off accidentally inside of a pressurized spacecraft.

Quinn opened a nearby case to lift out a boxy, mean-looking rifle. It was a compact bullpup design, which kept the magazine and action behind the grip and trigger group, close to the shooter's shoulder. "The M55's built special for us space cadets. It's reliable but not as accurate as an M4 or SCAR," he explained. "We figured out pretty quick they couldn't build them with tight enough tolerances and still leave room for thermal expansion." When temperatures in space could change 200 degrees just by moving from shadow to sunlight, materials could behave in surprising ways. "On the other hand, we load frangible rounds so they don't blow holes in our spacecraft." Quinn cycled the action, making certain the chamber was clear before handing it over. It would have been in no other condition for transport, but such discipline was the only thing that prevented otherwise inevitable accidents and was therefore ruthlessly enforced.

The pistol grip and trigger stood out right away: oversized and chunky, like a kid's toy. More like a paddle, meant for operating with spacesuit gloves. He immediately pointed the rifle away from the ramp and towards empty swampland, which Quinn noted approvingly. Ryan suspected he was sizing up his habits and trigger discipline. He turned it over appreciatively, then shouldered the empty weapon and sighted through its low-magnification scope. A holographic reticle appeared to hover steadily over the marsh. "Nice balance. So how much recoil does it really absorb?"

"Most of it," Quinn said. While the butt was still firmly in Ryan's shoulder, he reached around and gave the weapon a gentle tap. "About that much here on the ground, like shooting a rimfire. It gets weird in zero-g, almost feels like it's pulling you forward. If you stay snapped in, the closed-gas action keeps you from spinning too far off target."

Ryan arched an eyebrow at him, taking his eyes off the sight picture. "You're kidding. You guys have actually fired this in space?" He wondered exactly how they'd managed it – and at what?

Quinn shrugged. "Part of the training. We start with a high suborbital space jump from an S-20," he said, meaning the Air Force's militarized Clippers. "They boost a reflective target ahead of us, then we drop just after apogee and shoot the hell out of it on our way down before we have to deploy the re-entry ballutes."

"Those heat shield balloons? The ones that turn you into a human meteor?" Ryan was incredulous, though he'd suspected that was just one of several crazy ideas they'd indulged after the Air Force bought their own Clippers.

"It's sporty," Quinn said drily. "You have about six minutes to shoot, inflate the shield and assume the position. If not, you'll land with a few appendages missing."

...

The rest of the TAC team had stacked their remaining crates in a secure area at Penny's direction and shouldered their personal gear, ostensibly heading for the visitor's dorms. No one seemed too interested in settling down yet; this bunch was too amped up and eager. The four lingered around the hangar, studying the vehicle they'd be riding into orbit tomorrow.

"Looks different," one said. "Same, but smaller. Meaner looking." He shook his head, thinking that couldn't be right. It was still quite long, easily bigger than the old Concorde he'd once seen at the National Air & Space museum. But with a lot fewer windows. And it did look menacing head-on: the sloping nose, delta wings, canted tailfins, and bulging engine contours gave it the appearance of a predator waiting to pounce.

"Won't change the ride none," his partner drawled laconically. "Strap in, get shook up like you're in a damn paint mixer and hope you don't blow chunks before we get to the drop zone."

"Your friend's about right," Penny interjected as she walked up with Audrey close behind. "It's the same basic airframe as you guys are used to riding, just stripped down and souped up to make orbit. We made room for a fourth engine and drop tanks, which changed the outside shape a little. It costs some payload, but it's still cheaper than expendables."

Another peeked up the stairs that led to the cabin. "Think we could get a look inside, Staff Sergeant?" They turned towards a hulking man who Penny assumed was their ranking NCO.

"Fine by me," he said with a nod in her direction, "if this lady's okay with it."

"Be our guests. Audrey here can show you around, including showing you what not to touch."

The others bounded up the stairs, barely waiting for her to finish. "Thanks," the sergeant said. He had ruddy skin and black hair like a wire brush. Native American, Penny figured.

"This looks like a big improvement over what we're used to riding in. Even makes the Air Force look cheap. And that's hard to do," he said with grudging admiration.

Penny smiled. "They do like their creature comforts."

"That's no joke. We spend a lot of time on their bases, and let me tell you..." he trailed off, hinting at tales of untold excess. "Sorry, I didn't get your name before?"

"Stratton. Penny Stratton. I'm one of the pilots taking you up tomorrow. And you are...?"

His back straightened, suddenly realizing he'd been speaking rather casually with a Lieutenant Colonel while cracking on her service branch. "Staff Sergeant Breedlow, ma'am," he said, ill at ease. "My teammates up there are Sergeants Haggerty and Goode. The young guy is Corporal Voss."

"Relax," she said cheerfully. "I've been out of uniform too long to care about that. Think you can keep your buddies from rolling an old zoomie like me too hard?"

He laughed. "I doubt you'll need my help, ma'am. Word is you're high speed, low drag. No BS. We like that."

"Then we read each other just fine, Sergeant," she said, giving him a stiff clap on the shoulder. "Come on up, I'll show you guys around if you can promise not to drool all over my plane."

13

Kennedy Spaceport

The gathered team waited patiently in Ryan's office as Quinn completed the now-familiar routine of scanning the room for bugs. "Let us know if you find anything," he said. "The union's already convinced Art's hidden cameras and mics all over the place."

"That won't be a problem," Quinn said as he collapsed the wand. "Your office is clean."

Ryan watched as he fiddled with the window shades. "Closing the shutters not enough?"

Quinn placed a small cube on the sill, which appeared to do precisely nothing. "White noise generator," he explained. "That glass will vibrate with every word we speak. A clever person could eavesdrop if he aimed the right equipment at it. This'll skunk anybody with bad enough manners to try that."

"So is it safe for us to finally get down to business?" Penny asked. "Because you guys have given us just enough information to let our imaginations run wild. It's turning into a distraction. We don't like distractions."

Quinn leaned by the door and stared at Audrey, who sat quietly by Ryan's desk. "I'm afraid this brief is for the operating crew only. Sorry ma'am."

"She is crew," Penny said. "Aud's our lead flight director and we're going to be cut off from the ground, which is decidedly *not* how we prefer to operate. And it won't change the fact that we'll still need her help. Think of her as a flight engineer or navigator."

"Which one?"

"Either, depending on the need. Trust me, you don't want to leave this up to a couple of dumbass rocket jockeys."

"Never said that, ma'am. But is it possible to reproduce all that computing power we saw in Denver aboard your ship?"

"It's not like we need to carry a server farm with us. What we really need is an objective set of eyeballs. We pilots tend to get task-saturated at critical junctures; ground control is there to tell us the things we don't have time to figure out. Spaceflight's like a chess game: if you're not thinking a dozen moves ahead you'll run out of options in a hurry."

"And she's the chess master?"

"I'm actually not too bad," Audrey spoke up, giving Quinn a look. "Hadn't really connected the two before, but I'll take it."

"Miss Wilkes, I don't question your abilities but there's a very short list of people who are cleared for this operation."

"And I'm not one of them?"

He answered with a curt nod.

"That's going to make things difficult whether I do my job down here or up there."

"Gunnery Sergeant Quinn," Penny continued, "the funny thing is I outrank you. I'll take full responsibility for clearing Audrey."

"I'm afraid it doesn't work like that, ma'am." Quinn may have been talking to Penny, but he was looking at Audrey. Sizing her up. "Miss Wilkes, you had a colorful history at NASA. Ever run any classified missions?"

This guy had done his homework. To her credit, Audrey remained unflappable. "I spent a year helping transfer the X-37 project to the Air Force." The military had rescued the drone spaceplanes from NASA purgatory and had been quite pleased with the results. "Interesting work."

"No doubt it was," he said, baiting the hook. "Operating it so close to that Russian beast took some real skill."

She didn't blink. "I'm afraid I don't know what you're talking about." Which meant she knew exactly what he was talking about.

"ARKON-III? You must have heard of it. The Kremlin sank a lot of rubles into that bird. Word is it had been working perfectly until it suddenly died. Only telemetry they could recover indicated it was tumbling ass over teakettle and blind as a bat."

"Sucks for them," Audrey shrugged. "Spaceflight can be a risky business."

Quinn relaxed. "Very well, then. Miss Wilkes, consider yourself briefed in." He turned to a diagram of Gateway's potential approach vectors and zoomed in on the immense sunshield umbrella. "I expect your 'passengers' will object to our arrival, which is why we'll approach from the station's blind spot. Next steps are rather limited: board the complex, or disable it from outside."

"And what happens if they're holding hostages?" Penny asked.

The dark expression that crossed his face told her he'd been thinking the same thing. "Not like we can just kick the door in anyway. The element of surprise is gone the moment we start cranking open that airlock. We may have to starve them out, cut off the oxygen and water tanks."

"Not a bad idea. Look here," Audrey said, tracing a finger along the station's main axis. "These are all surplus ISS modules. The oxygen tanks can be disconnected externally, but all of their breathing air is recycled through a Sabatier reactor. It'll be a while before they start noticing. Your best option is to cut their power, including the emergency batteries." She zoomed in on the station's service module. "Which are all safely contained inside."

"Going in cold isn't a good way to run an op. That tends to get messy." A wave of grim nods from the rest of the team underscored his point.

"We still haven't talked about the elephant in the room," Audrey said haltingly. "With all this talk about Gateway, there hasn't been any mention of *Shepard*. We haven't heard from them in three days."

• • •

SS Shepard

The astringent odor of canned air was a constant reminder of the carefully engineered nature of Simon Poole's existence. Over the hum of circulation fans in his life support backpack, he listened for any telltale whistle of escaping air and watched the suit controls on his chest as the airlock slowly depressurized. It would be apparent soon enough if he'd missed a step. Just as carefully, he made certain the compartment's mixture of oxygen and nitrogen vented into their recovery bottles instead of being wasted outside. Every gram was precious, and if this worked he'd be able to add the tunnel's supply to the mix.

If it didn't work...well, better not dwell on that. There'd been a popular myth about the first astronauts being supplied with cyanide pills in case they ever became hopelessly stranded. He'd been amused to find that old urban legend still alive and well in Houston – shouldn't they of all people know better, that it was a lot simpler to just blow open the hatch and be done?

Then again, after his experience with the rapidly venting hab the prospect had become downright horrifying. Maybe there was something to the rumors after all.

It looked as if he'd be spared that fate for now: compartment pressure zero, suit pressure steady at 5.2 psi. Ten solid hours in the suit, pre-breathing the pure oxygen environment to prevent an embolism. *No scary death for me today. Once again, I've found a way to drop trou and show the Grim Reaper my ass.*

He slipped his boots into the molded floor restraints, reached for the inner hatch and twisted the lever.

Nothing.

He pushed again, as hard as he could stand. *Simon says: Open!*

Still nothing. He pressed his faceplate against the tiny porthole, looking for whatever out there in the hab tunnel was blocking the airlock. The latches were definitely disengaged; he could sense the play through his gloves. Was there any metal-on-metal contact that might cold weld in vacuum? It was one of countless otherwise trivial details that had combined to make spacecraft so complicated over the years. They'd gotten around the problem (and saved precious weight) by relying on composites, to the point where parts of the ship made it feel like they were living inside of a big plastic model kit.

He spun about to face the outer door and considered his options. One: go outside in an impromptu EVA and make his way across ten meters of wrecked hull with who knew what kinds of surprises. Or two: stay put, eventually run out of scrub filters, and choke to death on his own breath.

He sighed and began unpacking the safety tether, wondering if they'd stashed any cyanide in the med kit. Just in case.

...

Kennedy Spaceport

Quinn had managed to find the darkest possible spot that didn't involve wading out into the marsh itself. He swept the area with a red-lensed flashlight to preserve his night vision and rested one hand on his sidearm. *Here, gator.*

There were no demonic eyes reflecting his light, no guttural croaking. *So, no giant toothy reptiles lurking around tonight.*

He wondered what else might be out there. There were stories of fearsome beasts being released into the swamps, exotic pets that had grown much bigger and become more troublesome than their owners had bargained for. If the hype was to be believed, Florida was in imminent danger of being overrun by giant man-eating pythons. The idea that such a creature could be slithering around out there in the sawgrass gave him the creeps. An ornery rattlesnake would stand its ground and a cottonmouth might even give chase, but neither would actively *stalk* him.

He shook off that thought to settle down behind a compact catadioptric telescope and selected a wide-field eyepiece. He adjusted the mount to its new latitude, ensuring it would track his target as Earth rotated beneath the sky. After tapping in the object's designation, the scope quickly began tracking into position. When it came to a stop, he sighted down its smaller finder scope and found his quarry centered in the crosshairs: a fuzzy white blotch, low on the horizon but distinct against the emerging stars.

He leaned into the main eyepiece and relaxed his vision. The fuzzy white blotch bloomed with exquisite detail, its bright coma and diaphanous tail centered perfectly in the eyepiece. The coma even had a shock front, not unlike the bow wave ahead of a ship. The object had only recently been catalogued with a soulless alphanumeric code that would tell astronomers the order in which it had been discovered, a decidedly unglamorous method that diminished the spectacular in favor of the mundane. Nature demanded a little more respect.

Just as well, Quinn thought. Perhaps it was better that it remain popularly known for the gentleman who was credited with discovering it, Niall Weatherby of Christchurch, New Zealand. It was less well known that his discovery had first been detected nearly two years earlier by an astronomer wintering over at the Amundsen/Scott Antarctic research station, who'd quickly realized the significance of his find and had possessed the good sense to keep quiet about it. As a result, a very few select astronomers had been watching this object for much longer than its official scientific designation would've led anyone to believe.

Now he was finally able to see it in person. He turned away from the eyepiece to check that his tablet was synched with the Naval Observatory's atomic clock before opening an astronomy app. His thumb hovered over a "record" button on the little screen as he settled back behind the eyepiece. He waited perfectly still, breathing shallow in the way he might have observed a hostile objective from afar through a rifle scope.

There. A bright flash erupted from the comet's nucleus. Quinn thumbed the screen as soon as it appeared. In a few moments he was rewarded with another flash. Both its celestial coordinates and event times were now part of the International Astronomical Union's database on C/22 P1, otherwise known as Comet Weatherby.

14

Kennedy Spaceport

Audrey had always been meticulous but today she felt pickier than usual. She sat at a terminal in the darkened crew ready room, poring over the mission plans from Denver and hoping that the work might settle the butterflies in her stomach.

It hadn't. Today would be her first launch into orbit. Tomorrow, she'd go even farther. That had to be it. Maybe. The other implications she preferred not to think about.

"Nice accommodations."

Audrey jumped at the voice that seemed to come out of nowhere. She spun away from the terminal to find Quinn ensconced in an overstuffed recliner in a corner. Her first reaction was to ask exactly how long he'd been there watching her, but all she could get out was a surprised "excuse me?"

"I meant this place is comfy. Relaxing. You guys have a nice little operation here." He was apparently sincere.

"Thanks," she said warily. "This is actually the first time I've been here. The pilots turned this place into a crash pad to use in between flights."

"You haven't flown on your own planes before?" It sounded almost like a challenge.

"We all have to do cockpit rides to stay qualified. I've been on the suborbital routes plenty of times but the mass fractions on orbital flights are too small," she explained. "No unnecessary payload."

"I doubt that 'unnecessary payload' is a term they apply to you very often."

Audrey hoped she hadn't blushed at that, which meant that she probably had. "I meant they're weight-sensitive. An extra rider means one less passenger or paid freight."

"Got it," he said with a wry smile, and changed the subject. "So, that maglev catapult. Are we still gonna need it?"

Was he actually nervous about that? She stifled a grin. "Sure. Every little bit helps. The less fuel we use down here, the more we have left in the tanks up there. Never know when that might be useful."

• • •

The hangar glowed beneath a halo of floodlights as an early morning fog settled in. The sun lurked just beyond the eastern horizon, heralded by a melodic croaking from the marsh. Two Clippers were perched on the ramp outside, dripping wet with dew. The lone Clipper inside was surrounded by a throng of technicians quietly immersed in their final preflight checks.

Penny had wandered in from the crew quarters with an empty coffee mug, wondering if it would be more effective out of an IV drip. It had been a restless night for her and there was still a long day ahead. This would be her last chance to have real brew for the next few weeks and she savored the feeling that came from the very first pour. Instant java sucked through a plastic tube just didn't have the same flavor.

Penny cracked open Ryan's office door, knowing him to be a like-minded coffee snob and therefore expecting him to have the best in the building. As she reached for the light switch, she was stopped by a soft rumble. She slipped inside and gave her eyes a second to adjust: there he was, asleep on a sofa and sawing logs. So, coffee later then.

She pulled the door shut and flipped over a meeting-notice card above his nameplate. Hopefully the bright red "do not enter" sign would keep him undisturbed for a couple more precious hours.

As much as they ripped on each other, she cared after Ryan and his young family like a mother hen. When she'd been promoted to chief pilot, it had been a surprisingly tough choice to put him in charge of their Cape operations. She and Joe hadn't been in Colorado all that long but had quickly become surrogate grandparents to Ryan and Marcy's newborn son. Or maybe an aunt and uncle. She wasn't that old yet.

Seeing them leave had been harder than she'd wanted to admit but it had been the right call. Ryan was energetic, creative, and had earned his reputation as a "hot stick" among the other pilots after bringing *Austral*

Clipper back from orbit in a stunt that had probably saved all of their jobs. And as much as Ryan was a proud Southerner, Marcy was even more so. Penny smiled to herself, knowing full well how that deal always worked: if Mama wasn't happy, then nobody was. Off to Florida it had been.

As she walked the ramp, marinating in the fragrant predawn dew, Penny understood their zeal to move closer to home. She'd always appreciated the Space Coast's brand of heat more than Houston's: one enveloped you like a warm blanket while the other threatened to smother you, soak you in gasoline and set you on fire.

She turned past the hangar and stared at the massive VAB in the distance. Shining under a bank of floodlights, it loomed as a stark monument to great endeavors. For being so blocky and functional it remained iconic; the space age's Taj Mahal. Red strobe lights blinked silently atop its corners to ward off any stray aircraft, not that any were likely.

Maybe? A discordant thrumming echoed off of the steel walls behind her, tricking her sense of direction in the way helicopters did. If the noise came from one direction, then the bird was probably…there. A new set of blinking lights appeared in the northwest: red left, green right, a flashing strobe in the middle. An airplane, not a chopper. Sure sounded like one though. That was when she realized it was a little of both.

Penny actually hadn't seen too many V-22 Ospreys as the services were just starting to pick them up when she'd mustered out. The beast roared overhead before turning upwind and slowing dramatically as the giant wingtip propellers pivoted vertical. The big tiltrotor quickly transitioned from level flight into a noisy hover at the end of the taxiway. At least its pilots had the good sense not to land too close to the parked Clippers; the last thing they needed was a bunch of dirt blown all over the ramp.

The machine was painted in mottled gray with Air Force roundels on its fuselage. It settled onto its gear and a loading ramp opened just long enough for a squad of camouflaged military police to storm off. They crouched low, bracing against the battering rotor wash while the giant tiltrotor climbed back into the fog. As the Osprey's lights faded into the overcast, one stood and approached her while the squad fanned out into a defensive perimeter around the parking apron. He showed a flash of recognition, matching her face to a picture on whatever report he was checking as he walked up. He came to a halt a few feet away and saluted.

"Colonel Stratton? Lieutenant Mendez, 41st Air Security Squadron. We've been tasked with guarding your air…spacecraft."

She reluctantly returned his salute, being out of uniform and supposedly covert. "You'll pardon my surprise, Lieutenant, but couldn't they have just brought you guys in on the back of a truck?"

The young officer looked apologetic. "We received orders to come here an hour ago, ma'am. Normally we'd mount up on armored Humvees, but somebody up the chain must be feeling dramatic. We'd have preferred some lead time and a nice quiet entrance. They were pretty fired up to get us on scene ASAP."

He was chatty enough. "Guess it's too late to keep a low profile."

"Low profile?" he smirked. "Ma'am, all that does is attract staff officers trying make names for themselves, like flies to – well, you know. Somebody somewhere decided all of a sudden that whatever you're doing is awfully important." He looked around the complex, dumbstruck by the bustle of a spacecraft being prepped for launch. "Our orders are to make certain that whatever you're doing here goes off without any interference."

"Thank you for having our backs, Lieutenant. But I'm more concerned about what happens after we take off."

• • •

FV Elena Mireles
North of Grand Bahama

Orlando Cardenas had seen enough of his new "crew" and their outlandish demands. Five times each day, all activity on his ship came to a halt as they dropped everything to face east, throw down their ratty little rugs, and kneel down in prayer. The day had barely begun, the sun just beginning to peek over the horizon as they sped north only to have their progress interrupted by the unnerving prayer call of the group's appointed *muezzin.*

It was all the more galling that he had to keep the ship oriented so as to keep them facing the proper direction each time. The sun rose in the east each day, just as it had since the beginning of time. Could the damned fools not deduce that for themselves?

Raised by strict Catholic parents, Cardenas knew a thing or two about forced rituals but his patience with this bunch had quickly worn thin. Perhaps it came from the knowledge that it was every bit a sham, as he'd readily accepted the central truth about all religions: the traditions and liturgies only served to corral individuals into a manageable herd. His instructors back in Caracas had seen to that. That the Marxists had simply replaced one religious framework with another had not occurred to him at the time, having still been young enough to be consumed by a desire to seek justice for the oppressed.

All in service to the state, of course.

It was that same motivation which had led him to this very place on this day. That fate – God, Jehovah, Allah (all interchangeable and irrelevant in his mind) – may have somehow played a hand did not enter into his thinking. He thought no more of any particular deity than he did of any other philosopher or movement leader, certainly none more so than he thought of Marx, Guevara or Castro. In the end all that mattered was for one to be in the service of progress: Cardenas had a mission, and he would carry it out. It was that simple, and it had to remain that simple if he were to maintain cover. He and the *Mireles'* small permanent crew had become skilled at catching just enough fish to conceal their real game: eavesdropping on the signal traffic of their enemies. That typically involved steaming up and down the western Atlantic, tuning into American radio frequencies.

They'd occasionally loiter off of Florida to monitor a space launch if the suspected payload had been deemed worthy of attention. That was where they were headed now, after a midnight rendezvous with an Iranian tanker the day prior. There was quite a scramble to board their cargo and secure it in the main hold before dawn; fortunately the men they'd taken on with it had known what they were doing. He was happy to let them manage that aspect of this mission under the watchful eye of his first officer.

Otherwise, they annoyed him to the point of distraction. It wasn't their obvious fanaticism that galled him as much as their arrogant insistence that everyone else on his crew defer to their idiotic customs. "Opiate of the masses," indeed. The insufferable Catholics may have been masters of guilt projection but at least they allowed unbelievers to mostly go about their business. Cardenas looked past his annoyance and took comfort in the knowledge that their common enemy would eventually collapse under its own weight. Perhaps with a little push in the right direction, like felling an ancient tree. They would have to sort out the differences with their putative allies in this historic struggle later, a spat he suspected would not end politely. The barbarians were too intent on bending the world to their will.

His meditation was interrupted by a polite cough from the watch officer. "We are ready to resume course at your command, *Capitán*."

Cardenas stepped out of the wheelhouse to look over the railing. The apes had finally rolled up their rugs and returned to work below decks and he'd completely missed it. He brushed it off with a muted grumble. "I have let our visitors distract me." He leaned over the old chart table to check their position. "Very well. Resume course, *Señor* Reyes. Best speed. We have an appointment to keep."

• • •

SS Shepard

Simon gave his safety line a reassuring tug and pulled himself up through the outer hatch. His EVA suit held four hours of breathable air, precious time which could slip away in a hurry. He'd done a couple of spacewalks during his tour on the Station, but earth orbit simply couldn't compare to this: he floated above an utterly hostile world nearly a quarter of a million miles from home. For being a lifeless ball of dusty gray rock, the Moon's thoroughly alien nature made it all the more compelling.

He turned to find Earth: there was home, just over his shoulder. The sight was literally breathtaking; he felt himself choke up when it came into view. Remarkable enough when seen from inside the observation dome, out here in the open it was beyond his capacity for words.

It brought to mind the stories he'd heard of the final Apollo missions, when the Command Module pilots – who'd stayed behind in lunar orbit while their crewmates hogged all the glory down on the surface – were given the consolation prize of a deep space EVA during the flight home to recover film canisters nestled deep inside the service module. He'd met one and from the old guy's telling it sounded like he thought they'd gotten the better end of the deal. A few days of solitude above the moon followed by a life-changing interplanetary spacewalk did sound like a pretty good deal. Out here, he could finally appreciate what they'd experienced. For the first time in his life, Simon Poole felt like a real spaceman.

He looked up at the hab's solar panels, which fanned out like petals of a giant sunflower. He grabbed the nearest support truss and began climbing it for a better view of his ship.

Big Al was well and truly wrecked. The reflective coating dazzled him as its wrinkles and folds reflected the sun like ripples on a pond. What had been taut under pressure was now slack, clinging loosely to its internal frame. It no longer resembled a spaceship so much as it did a sad, deflated balloon.

Anger welled up inside; there was a flush of heat in his face as his heart hammered in his chest. Frustration suddenly threatened to boil over to rage as he surveyed the disaster from his perch. *Not an accident. No way in hell.* The destructive test cells had simulated just about every conceivable deep space impact or potential human screw-up and the hull fabric had held up every time. Even a high powered rifle bullet hadn't been able to put a dent in it. Of course that had been the material's first intended use but it wasn't like anyone was up here with elephant guns. It took one hell of a lot of concentrated energy to penetrate all of that Kevlar…something with a high ballistic coefficient, like an especially dense micro-meteoroid. But a meteor dense enough to breach the hull would've also been big enough to destroy the ship, with no time for them to even realize what had happened.

The windows were a different story. Structurally they are the weakest point of any pressurized vessel, be it an airliner or a spaceship. He pushed away from his makeshift perch and floated forward, counting portholes along the way. It didn't take long to find his first officer's compartment: it was the only one with a gaping hole in it. He lingered above it, searching for any other outward signs of damage, then reached for the fire extinguisher he'd brought with him. Pointing away from the hull, he gave the trigger a gentle tap and was rewarded by a quick spurt of compressed

CO2. The makeshift maneuvering jet slowly pushed him toward the window.

The inside pane of triple layer polycarbonate had been punctured clean through, nearly a three-centimeter hole so clean it looked like it was meant to be there. The middle layer was less so: not a perfect circle, as if whatever had punctured the first layer had begun to wobble. By the time it had hit the outer pane, the projectile was in full tumble. The hole it left behind was ragged and oblong. He was looking at *Shepard*'s exit wound.

A bullet? Couldn't be. They inspected every person and piece of equipment.

Equipment...damn. *What's the difference between a mass driver and a rail gun?* It all depended on where it was pointed. The gauss accelerator Varza's crew had brought to shoot titanium slugs into the lunar surface from orbit, ostensibly to observe and record the types of volatiles released on impact, had been fired from inside his ship. The magnetic gun had been disassembled and secured in the cargo compartment; it was to have been assembled and mounted outside with the rest of the survey package once they were safely in lunar orbit.

It wasn't all that big. Didn't have to be. Conceivably a single person could handle the thing. But it had to draw from the ship's power, and it couldn't be fired like a rifle. The controls were remote.

So two people, then: one had aimed while the other played trigger man. Aimed at *my* first officer, inside of *my* ship, in his own quarters. No doubt by complete surprise, because why the hell would anyone hijack a spacecraft? What would they do with it, become pirates?

He angrily sucked the inside of his cheek and pushed away, forgetting the action/reaction equation. After a frustrating tumble out to the end of his tether, he recovered and climbed more deliberately towards the open docking collar. He pulled himself inside of the tunnel and disconnected his tether, lest it get tangled outside. If this worked, he wouldn't need it again. He reached out to pull the hatch down and felt it seat against the rim as a thud echoed dully through his suit.

His helmet lamp shone down the ten-meter tunnel as he drifted along, shadows dancing away at odd angles from the light beam. The forward deck was closest to the flight module when docked and so was dedicated to crew quarters and equipment storage. He dialed open the latch and the door slid out easily, there being no pressure left to work against it. The spares locker was right by the entry so finding the extra filters was simple. Next trip, he'd be sure to relocate them back by the 'lock where they were most needed.

He pushed back through the door and floated into the tunnel with a sack full of new filters. The panel closed just as easily as it had opened. Its simple barber-pole indicator popped back into place as he dogged down the seal, gratified to finally have something work as intended.

Simon moved on, inspecting the tunnel as he passed the other two decks. The mid deck was subdivided into six closet-sized passenger berths with two lavatories. The aft level was a common area for dining and recreation, which generally involved hanging out by the windows or cavorting around in zero g.

At each deck, he stopped to check that the access doors were all properly sealed. He was happy to see they were, and probably would've held pressure if the damned front door hadn't been left open. Could he keep the tunnel sealed and pressurize the space to use its oxygen? That airlock was getting awfully cramped.

He shook his head angrily. Too risky. The tunnel wasn't meant to hold pressure against hard vacuum indefinitely, especially without knowing what other damage it sustained. Even if the vents and hatches had sealed as designed, each one of them was a potential failure point.

It was another strong hint that the remaining crew hadn't been in control when everything went sideways: no way would Russell undock Snoopy without closing Big Al up first.

He checked his suit controls: two hours. Halfway spent. Damn but time flew by out here. He'd dwell on this mess later; at least it'd give him something else to occupy his mind while waiting for *Grissom* to show up. Assuming it did, of course. *Keep telling yourself that, big guy. Nothing like a little hopeless optimism.*

He finally made it back to his safe haven, the aft airlock. While it was useful for accessing all of the Cycler's critical plumbing, it also gave them room for expansion later: add a storage module, maybe an upgraded powerplant and they could take this stack halfway across the solar system if they ever got serious about it. As a wise man once said, Earth orbit was halfway to anywhere.

For now, he just needed to get serious about getting across the next couple of meters. Tracing a hand around the inner hatch, his headlamp beam showed him an otherwise normal seal. Except...there. Lower left quadrant, a structural support from the floor webbing had bent back on itself and was now wedged against the door. It ought to be quick work.

He planted his feet in a pair of floor stirrups, pried at the support with his good arm, and snapped the reinforced polymer rib free. Satisfied that he'd cleared the entry, Simon turned the release. This time the hatch opened slowly beneath his gloved fingers, not having any pressure behind it to smack into him like before. He caught himself unconsciously rubbing his arm beneath the bulky spacesuit, suddenly remembering how much the sonofabitch hurt.

Next came the lights. He snapped the breaker panel open and easily found the culprit; fortunately the lights were the only system that popped. He pressed the switch back in, felt it lock in place beneath his glove, and was rewarded with a flicker of LEDs coming to life on the other side of the hatch.

He made another check of his suit controls. Ninety minutes, which meant there was enough time for his secondary goal: food. He pushed up and reached for the third level's hatch, opening up into the galley deck.

The experience was not unlike scuba diving inside of a shipwreck. That it was his boat – spacecraft, whatever, he liked the term *boat* – which now reluctantly gave up its treasures to him was hard to swallow. His headlamp danced over crumpled bulkheads and rippling sidewalls, an occasional loose piece of tooling or personal gear reflected back from midair.

Fortunately the galley locker wasn't blocked, so he hurriedly filled the satchel with anything that didn't require cooking or rehydrating.

Simon left his feet inside the portal and reached back out into the tunnel. He gave the sack of food and filters a gentle push and sent it floating safely into the airlock.

He searched the galley and recovered more loose bottles of water. They were frozen solid, but that problem would take care of itself after a few hours. He tossed them through the open portal as well, followed by more packets of food. A diet of beef jerky and dried fruit was better than starving. This little treasure hunt might actually require a couple of trips. *Surrender the booty!*

Damn but that would've been funny in any other context.

15

Kennedy Spaceport

"Definitely better seats than the S-20," Voss said as he flopped into the wide, leather trimmed seat and fiddled with a personal entertainment system recessed in the sidewall.

"It's like your own little personal space," Breedlow agreed. "I'm surprised they don't have drink service built in."

Haggerty rooted through the small compartment by his seat. "We'll see about that. I ain't done yet, bro."

"Don't get too used to the creature comforts," Quinn growled as he stalked the center aisle, inconspicuously inspecting each man. "We're not here for vacation, gents."

"Kinda hard to forget, Gunny," Voss muttered sullenly. He'd succeeded in getting Quinn's attention.

"Your point?"

"Long time to spend putzing around en route, and in full view of that Gateway place most of the way. I don't like it."

Quinn frowned. "You don't have to like it, Voss. Think of all the grunts we shipped to Europe on ocean liners back in WWII. How many weeks did they spend dodging U-boats? Same thing."

"Except they had destroyer escorts," Voss argued. "We've got precisely dick."

"Embrace the Suck, brother," Haggerty chimed in. "If your number's up it might as well be here, enjoying the lifestyle of the rich and famous."

"I'm content to remain anonymous and barely solvent," Voss snorted as he lifted a mini-bottle capped with a spill proof zero gravity nozzle.

Quinn unceremoniously swiped it out of his hand. "Drink service is not provided on this flight, gents."

"Hell, Gunny," Haggerty said as he cinched down the harness, "my next question was 'where's the hot stewardess?' I guess you're it."

Quinn leaned over his seat. "Look into my eyes," he said caustically, "and you'll find the depths to which I care about your sorry ass." He always delivered his harshest lines with the hint of a crooked smile, part of their ritual pre-mission haggling. "Never forget your real chain of command: God, the Commandant, and me, and not necessarily in that order."

"Would you please tell my mom that?" Haggerty shot back. "Because she still thinks she's in there somewhere."

"Your dear old mother had damned well better think you're still sunning yourself on some beach and not about to blast into orbit," Quinn cautioned him. "Now stow the grab-ass and buckle up."

"Watch it bro," Voss interjected. "Gunny's always looking for a new ex-Mrs. Quinn. That'd make him your daddy."

They laughed as Quinn headed forward to the flight deck. "Right now I *am* your daddy," he growled. "Now shut the hell up and enjoy your flight."

• • •

Above South Florida

"Shamrock Flight," a pair of Navy F-35s out of Key West, traced a long oval in the sky high above the hazy muck of the Everglades. A voice sounded in the flight leader's helmet: "Sham Three One, SEALORD; stand by for new tasking. Eastern range is closing for a space launch."

"Copy SEALORD, Sham flight standing by," the pilot, Commander "Thor" Gunnarson, replied. SEALORD was the radio callsign for Jacksonville's Fleet Area Control and Surveillance Facility (otherwise known by a typically dense Navy acronym, FACSFAC-JAX), which managed a long swath of Atlantic airspace that continuously buzzed with military aircraft. Shamrock's mission had been a scheduled live fire exercise, so both aircraft were loaded with 25-millimeter cannon rounds and air-to-air missiles with pilots who'd been looking forward to a rare opportunity to unleash live ordnance against a host of target drones.

Thor's headset erupted with complaints from his wingman. "Whiskey-Tango-Foxtrot, over?" he piped up. "They handed us this op a month ago and now the range is cold? Awful damn early to get up for nothing."

"Relax, Spock." The Navy had a long tradition of nicknaming its aviators in creative ways, typically a play on names or recognition of some feat the individual would've just as soon forgotten. The more inappropriate the better: while his wingman's prominent ears gave him a passing resemblance to the iconic *Star Trek* character, his excitable personality was exactly the opposite. "They didn't recall us to base, either, so just play the game."

As if making his flight leader's point, Jacksonville answered their question soon enough. "Sham flight, SEALORD; you're south sector CAP for this launch. Stand by for coordinates," the controller said, sounding frustrated himself. Instead of vectoring aircraft with live weapons onto maneuvering targets, he'd get to watch them burn holes in the sky on Combat Air Patrol. Maybe they'd get lucky and some schmuck in a Cessna would wander into their airspace, which would at least let them practice intercepting something even if they couldn't shoot it.

"Sham flight copies," Thor answered. "Heading to our sector now. ETA twelve minutes." He switched over to his wingman's frequency and turned northeast. "Let's turn and burn. At least we'll have a good show."

• • •

FV Elena Mireles

Cardenas hovered over the worn chart table and carefully traced a precise circle around their position with an antique set of dividers, then projected their course with a grease pencil along an equally old-fashioned plotter. He stroked his goatee while working out the trigonometry problem in his head. According to their cargo's technical adviser – a Russian, and therefore the only one who wasn't a babbling fanatic – Cardenas had to center his ship inside of a circle with a two-hundred-fifty kilometer radius. He called it the "PK" range, something Cardenas understood would ensure their desired outcome.

His problem was centering that circle where it would be most effective also brought the *Mireles* uncomfortably close to the American launch exclusion zone. The skies around it would be protected by barely visible aircraft while armed frigates prowled the horizon. Guaranteeing their mission's success likewise guaranteed they would receive a great deal of unwelcome attention.

He made one last check against the ship's clock, snapped the dividers shut, and slipped them into a worn leather pouch. "Reyes."

The watch officer turned from the conn. "*Si, Capitán*?"

"I think it best that we prepare the dinghies…just in case," he said quietly. "It promises to be an exciting morning."

Reyes knew the harder he had to listen for his Captain's voice, the more serious the man was. "*Si*," he acknowledged, and reached for the intercom that would be heard by their shipmates below.

…

Kennedy Spaceport

"Clipper Six-One-Eight Heavy; ready to taxi."

Ryan didn't have to wait long for a response, being the only traffic for the spaceport's single runway. "618 heavy, taxi into position at runway 11 and hold. Maglev rails are on standby."

Penny read back their clearance and returned to her half of their launch checklist. "I always forget how much easier this place is than Denver."

"And I keep telling you to get out here more often, but *no*," Ryan taunted. "The chief pilot's too important for us rednecks down here in the swamps."

She almost looked hurt. "That's it. You just put your finger on it: I can feel my brain cells dying already. We'd better get airborne before I end up short a few IQ points."

"Lady, you lived in *Texas*," he chortled. "Seems like you came out of that just fine." He'd long ago had to accept the fact that Southerners were probably the last population group on Earth that was acceptable to make fun of. "You might've even come out smarter for the experience."

"All those brainiacs at Johnson made it bearable," she said as they spun up the engines. "So yeah, it's a good thing you never showed up there."

Ryan had to raise his voice over the guttural roar rising behind them. Even at idle, the combined cycle turbines felt like primeval beasts straining at their chains. "A tragedy, I'll admit. It just might have saved the whole program. We'd probably be on Mars by now."

"*One* of us would be. They'd have happily sent you on a one-way trip. I'd have helped you pack."

Audrey sat dumbfounded at the observer's station. "I know this might be asking a lot, but can we focus here? Our launch window opens in ten minutes." She caught an amused look from Quinn in the opposite jumpseat. She had never flown with these two together, but he'd obviously spent plenty of time at the mercy of wisecracking pilots.

They suddenly went quiet, both turning to stare her down until Ryan broke their silence. "What are you talking about? This *is* serious. You should see us when we're screwing around." He turned to his side window and made a jerking motion with his thumbs, signaling the ground crew they were about to get moving. "Let's roll."

16

FV Elena Mireles

Cardenas reluctantly placed a portable GPS on the chart table, leaving his prized antique sextant to sit idle in its worn pine case. He was justifiably proud of his ability to ply the Atlantic guided by little more than the stars and a good watch, but sailing this close to the American launch corridor demanded a greater degree of precision than he could manage alone.

They idled just shy of 28 degrees north latitude, thirty miles off of Cocoa Beach along the southern edge of the exclusion zone. Satisfied with their position, he turned back to the navigation board behind Reyes. Both displays matched. Cardenas checked the ship's clock: their prey would be appearing soon, as predicted by their passenger's intelligence services and confirmed by the Notice to Mariners that was just broadcast. Kennedy's eastern range was closed to all traffic for the next hour.

He stood by his watch officer, surveying the weather deck below and the gray Atlantic beyond. He knew it might be his last chance to enjoy this view, despite the assurances from their handlers in Caracas. Their cover story would soon disappear in a trail of smoke.

"Arturo," he called, using his watch officer's first name in a rare display of comradeship. "Please activate the search radar and open the main hold."

"Aye, *Capitán*," Reyes said dutifully. An old cathode-ray monitor flickered to life as an antenna blade above the wheelhouse began spinning lazily. The stench of rotted fish wafted over them as two doors on the forward deck rolled open to expose the main hold.

Inside were two squat tubes painted in earth tones that had long ago been bleached pinkish-white by the merciless desert sun. As their protective covers opened, a menacing growl could be heard over the hastily installed fire control station in *Mireles'* wheelhouse.

"Missiles are active," Reyes said. "Searching for targets." He craned his neck to scan the sky, then paused, hesitant to show any doubts in front of the Captain. "Sir, is there any chance we..."

Cardenas anticipated the question and cut him off gently. "There is always a chance, *compañero*," he said, "but there will be no mistaking. We could probably target them just with our eyes and ears." He looked to the eastern horizon, from where any naval interference would be most likely to appear. "And they, us."

...

Kennedy Space Center

Polaris flight 618, the *Gemini Clipper*, sat at the end of Kennedy's three-mile-long runway, engines growling at idle as it settled onto the centerline. "Two green bars," Penny reported. If there was any doubt that the magnetic rails embedded in the pavement beneath them were less than fully functional, they'd have to resort to an old-fashioned takeoff roll. It would get them to orbit, but with most of their reserve propellant lost in the trade.

"I show same. Positive lift," Ryan said mechanically as he cross checked his display against hers. He turned to their guest in the observer's seat next to Audrey. "Pax cabin's secure. How about you, Gunny?"

He replied with a stiff thumbs-up and stole a glance out the window, which didn't escape Penny's notice. "Everything all right?" she asked innocently.

"Fine, ma'am," he said warily. "Haven't flown like this before."

"Meaning you're waiting to see what happens when we retract the gear," she said. "It takes getting used to. For someone who spacedives for a living, I figured you'd be kind of unimpressed. I sure couldn't do your job."

"Space drops don't seem like that big of a deal once you've done a couple of extreme altitude jumps," he said, more comfortable with the subject. "Especially when we use the reentry ballutes."

"How many jumps?" Ryan asked as he manipulated switches.

"A few."

"And you managed to keep all your limbs attached?"

"If you want the full experience, it's the only way to go. Push off, enjoy the view for a minute, then its knees to the breeze."

"Still not something I ever wanted to do," Penny said as she nonchalantly pulled a lever in the center panel, turning some lights green. "They couldn't get me to try skydiving at the Academy. Never saw the appeal of jumping out of a perfectly good airplane."

"Might be why so many jumpers I know hate flying. Maybe we just can't wait to get out. So when do you guys go wheels up?"

"A few seconds ago," she smiled. "While we were chatting."

Quinn did a double take: the plane's long morning shadow was missing three telltale stems where the landing gear should have been. Almost half a million kilos of mass was now sitting atop a magnetic cushion.

"Clipper 618 Heavy; launch window is open. You are cleared for takeoff, climb direct as filed to transition for launch corridor Bravo. Maglev standing by for your count."

"618 Heavy copies Launch Bravo; we're moving in three, two, one..." Ryan said as he wrapped his hands over the throttle levers. The steady rumble behind them quickly grew into a thundering roar as the four air-breathing rockets quickly reached full thrust. The air itself seemed to shake as they were catapulted down the runway into a thin morning fog which instantly vaporized behind them. Ahead lay nothing but blue sky.

...

"Sham flight; new bogey, designate Charlie-One," Jacksonville reported. "Civilian launch out of the Cape, callsign Clipper 618 Heavy."

"Roger bogey. We're painting him too," Gunnarson said, indicating he could see it on his own radar. "No visual yet."

His wingman chimed in almost immediately. "Thor, tally on that Clipper. Nine o'clock, climbing like a bat out of hell."

Thor strained to see any change in the perpetual gray funk that hung over coastal Florida. Finally, a bright shining ember rose atop a white contrail in the distance. "SEALORD, Sham flight has visual on Charlie One." He switched back to his wingman's frequency. "Quite a show, ain't it?"

"Meh," the younger pilot grumbled. "Still more fun to shoot something."

Jacksonville broke in again. "Sham flight; new surface contact, southern edge of the exclusion zone, designated target Sierra-Two," he said tersely as a new symbol appeared on their tactical screens. As he twisted to look over his shoulder a red diamond began pulsing in his helmet display, superimposed over the ship's exact spot on the water. "Nearest friendly vessel is twenty klicks out. Need you to get eyeballs on this guy."

"Copy that SEALORD. Leaving angels two-five for angels ten." Thor waved at his wingman to signal a turn, then quickly peeled off to reverse course and head west as they dove to ten thousand feet. "Time to scare off the rubberneckers."

...

Denver

"They're off," Grant said, pushing away from his console. "Only six seconds into the launch window, too."

Hammond hovered behind him in the EOC, transfixed by the plot on the big screen. On one side was flight 618, just another tourist ferry to catch SS *Grissom*, now passing by three hundred kilometers overhead the Cape. "And Gus?" he asked. "No surprises please."

Grant leaned over an adjacent terminal. "We're pinging the Cycler team now, Art," he said with a nod toward the flight controllers out on the main floor. "Okay…setup crew on *Grissom* reports all systems go, ready for transfer."

"Don't jinx us, Charlie," he warned. "It's bad luck for management to make pronouncements like that." Hammond relaxed and let himself enjoy watching them work. "How's their climb profile?"

Grant held up one finger and pressed his headset to his ear as he queried their flight dynamics controller. "Right up the middle, Art. Hunter's nailing it."

...

FV Elena Mireles

Reyes put down the intercom handset. "Acquisition crew confirms target is airborne, bearing three-one-zero and accelerating along heading one-one-zero."

Cardenas acknowledged the report with a grunt and returned to his plot. The American spaceplane would enter the Probability Kill circle around his ship in a matter of seconds, tracking directly across their bow. Once committed, there would be no undoing it. He and his crew would have to deal with whatever consequences befell them. "Any other airborne or surface targets?"

Reyes leaned over their radar. "One surface vessel, to the east," he confirmed. "Bearing zero-nine-four, sixteen nautical miles. No other aircraft." Which was not entirely unusual for a civilian space launch.

"Very well," Cardenas finally said. "Sound general quarters." An unheard-of command aboard a commercial fishing vessel, it was entirely appropriate for a warship preparing to engage the enemy.

...

Gemini Clipper

Quinn was engrossed in the rapid crosstalk between the pilots as the Clipper climbed higher and faster. It shook even more than he'd expected, probably because of those big fuel tanks slung beneath the wings. His understanding of aerodynamics was limited to the wildly varying effects on the human body during a space drop, but figured their drag was a major contributor to the unpleasant sensation of being inside a giant paint mixer.

"Left and right side heat exchangers are live," Penny – Colonel Stratton – said. "O2 tanks are filling up." Their engine intakes were diverting some of the outside air into rapid precoolers for storage as liquid oxygen to use above the atmosphere, filling up at roughly half the rate they were burning fuel out of the drop tanks. "Full tanks in two minutes."

"Got it." Hunter appeared to be cemented in his seat and focused on the heads-up display in his windshield, whereas both ladies' heads seemed to be on a swivel as the acceleration load settled down. "How are we looking for stage separation?" The expendable tanks made them a "stage and a half" launcher, letting them dump unnecessary weight as soon as their fuel had been used up.

"Max Q in ten seconds," Audrey said. That was when the Clipper would be at maximum aerodynamic stress.

"So we're ahead of the energy curve," Penny said. Quinn had decided to follow her closely, knowing she'd flown profiles similar to this several times on the old Space Shuttle. Probably while Hunter was still in flight school. He didn't want to think about what Audrey was doing at that time. Maybe college, probably high school. *Same as me*, he realized.

Audrey was grunting against the acceleration. They were pulling, what, two gees? Less than at takeoff but still half of what they'd reach after they dropped tanks, when the ride really started. "Denver says go for orbit." So she was their relay to Polaris mission control. He was surprised they weren't as autonomous as military aviators; perhaps because it was a good idea to have a roomful of detached experts looking ahead for them. Not that he'd ever want a similar arrangement in the field.

"A wise man once said: 'Don't get cocky, kid.' I think it was Plato. Or Aristotle, whoever," Penny said.

"I thought it was John Wayne," Audrey replied.

"Negative," Ryan said. "The Duke said 'life is tough, but it's tougher if you're stupid.' You guys are hopeless. Ain't that right, Gunny?"

Quinn tried to smile, preferring that they put aside the verbal grabassery and pay attention to the freaking controlled explosion currently propelling them into orbit. *Pilots.*

...

FV Elena Mireles

Clipper 618 crossed the range circle Cardenas had illuminated over their radar plot. Just as he grabbed the microphone to alert his crew, a crackling roar shook the bridge. The ship shuddered once, then twice, as twin fountains of flame erupted from the tubes in the forward hold and a thick curtain of smog swept over them. As the acrid cloud dissipated, he watched two columns of white smoke climb into the morning sky and begin tracing an arc to the north.

...

Shamrock 31

Gunnarson's headset exploded with radio chatter just as he spotted the same two pillars of smoke climbing up from the gray ocean almost directly ahead. "*Vampire! Vampire!* Sham flight, missiles in the air! At your ten, angels six and climbing!" His defensive system screeched its own recognition.

"Shit just got real, boys." This was no longer a training evolution. Instead of frantically twisting away to evade, his first reaction had been to follow their path to see if they were tracking him. Some things could still be discerned with the old Mark One eyeball faster than his onboard computers could ever manage. If they'd been intended for his flight, they'd better be infrared because both stealth jets would be invisible to any fire-control radar. Probably.

The smoke trails were climbing steadily northeast. Satisfied that neither he nor his wingman were in immediate danger, he tapped a thumbwheel on the control stick in his right hand. Two diamonds, fresh target designators, appeared at the top of each contrail. He'd often worried that air combat was turning into one big video game, but damned if this didn't make it easier.

"SEALORD, Sham lead has tally on both bogies. They're targeting that civilian." He tossed a hand signal to his wingman to prepare for action.

"Sham lead, roger that. Both originated from surface bogey Sierra Two. Radar signatures look like SA-21's." Radar guided, they could cover a two-hundred mile effective range at Mach 5. They'd be in a whole different zip code soon.

"SEALORD, Sham lead is going after the SAMs. Dash Two will engage the surface bogey."

Jacksonville didn't hesitate, though it was a different voice this time. Must be the watch officer. "Sham flight, SEALORD concurs. Killbox is active, weapons tight. Happy hunting, gentlemen."

Gunnarson looked at his wingman and stabbed a finger at the ship, just a speck on the water at the end of a rapidly dissipating smoke trail: *waste them*. He then shoved his throttle to its forward stop and felt the kick of the afterburner roaring to life behind him. The jet leapt ahead as he desperately raced to cut off both missiles before they sped out of reach. The airspeed numbers in his visor ticked over furiously as he maintained a shallow climb, setting himself up to put the jet into a maximum speed dive to close the distance. He pointed the jet's nose ahead of the missiles, aiming for a point in space dead center between them and the Clipper. In a steady climb with no countermeasures, it was the proverbial sitting duck.

His wingman's voice crackled over the radio. "Thor, I'll be on the surface bogey in thirty seconds. Can you even keep lock on those SAMs?"

"We'll find out," he said brusquely as zigzag lines and boxes danced in his visor while a warbling tone sounded in his ear. "Fox three!" With that quick warning, he thumbed a red button on the stick twice. Weapons bay doors snapped open along the jet's belly and two missiles leapt from their rails.

...

FV Elena Mireles

"Target! Aircraft just appeared on radar...ten miles, bearing two-seven-six!" Reyes paused as the display recycled, following the sweep of its antenna. "Wait...now it's gone." It was a question more than a report.

Cardenas ran out to the railing and looked west. There: two smoke trails, streaking toward their missiles still climbing away in the distance. "Those aren't for us," he said calmly. The next ones most certainly would be.

"Yes sir," Reyes confirmed. "They're active; radar signature consistent with American AMRAAM's." The advanced medium-range air-to-air missile was mercilessly accurate and the newest model was nearly hypersonic. Whether they could intercept two SA-21s remained to be seen, though he suspected the pilot had been desperate. That he presumably hadn't maneuvered to avoid them meant he'd deduced their target.

A sudden radar contact which just as suddenly disappeared: a stealth fighter, dropping its mask long enough for its weapons bays to open. He knew as a matter of doctrine that fighter pilots never flew alone, which meant another one would be out there somewhere. Cardenas continued searching the sky for what had to be at least two interceptors. "What about infrared?"

"One heat signature, headed north at high speed." No doubt the first jet, racing to where the missiles would converge. "Nothing else."

Which meant his partner had already dived to a low altitude and was undoubtedly headed their way. His heat signature would be lost in the surface clutter, indistinguishable until he was already on top of them. "Alert the air-defense team," Cardenas barked. "I want both archers on the stern, *now*!"

...

Gemini Clipper

Penny pressed her headset against her ear, not believing what she'd just heard over the emergency frequency. "Say again, SEALORD?"

Ryan immediately recognized the callsign. "What's up?"

Penny's eyes widened. "Two SAMs inbound," she blurted out, "both active homing."

"*What?*" The nose pitched down briefly as Ryan fought his instinct to release their external tanks and start jinking, throwing the plane into a series of violent turns and dives. While standard evasive procedure in a fighter, doing that in a rapidly accelerating spaceplane would tear it apart. At the very least it would waste precious energy needed to reach *Grissom* in orbit.

Their only option was to outrun them. "How long until we can punch tanks?"

Penny tapped an instrument display and checked their fuel flow. "Twenty seconds."

...

Shamrock 31

Gunnarson leaned into his shoulder harness, unconsciously willing his jet between the Clipper and the two approaching missiles. He was racing to place himself at the apex of a rapidly shrinking triangle. He swore in despair as his own missiles fell away harmlessly, unable to track their small targets.

That left him one option. "No joy, SEALORD, repeat no joy. Sham lead is moving to intercept. Out."

His wingman sounded grim. "Figured as much, skipper. Need me in trail?"

"Negative," Gunnarson shot back. "Just put the fear of God into those bastards."

"Roger that," he said. "Bravo Zulu." *Good job.*

Gunnarson quickly reversed his zoom-climb, throttling the engine back as he rolled over and pulled the nose through the vertical. As the horizon spun overhead, he shoved the throttle back into full afterburner. The jet shuddered as it passed Mach 2 in his dive between the missiles and their target, well beyond the jet's certified maximum speed. He thumbed the radio button on his throttle for the universal emergency channel.

"Polaris flight, this is Shamrock Three-One on Guard," he announced, in the calmest voice he could muster. "Be advised: you have been fired upon and are being tracked by two surface-to-air missiles."

A deadpan female voice answered. "We noticed that, Shamrock. Any suggestions?"

Gunnarson smiled behind his oxygen mask. Whoever this lady was, she sounded ice cold. Sometimes the chicks really did sport the biggest pair. "Shut down your transponder and radar. I'm closing from your two o'clock."

He dipped a wing to present his plane's belly to the oncoming missiles and said a quick prayer as he opened the weapons bays, shut off his electronic jamming, and flipped on his radar transponder. The little stealth fighter had just become a much juicier target.

He chopped the throttle to idle and threw out the speed brakes, the sudden deceleration violently shaking his jet. He was rewarded with an angry warning tone: at least one had locked onto him.

. . .

Gemini Clipper

Penny jumped as an alarm rang and a flashing red diamond appeared on the collision avoidance display. "That was quick," she said. "It's an F-35, just lit up like Vegas. Closing at twelve hundred knots."

Ryan was tense, not his usual laconic self. "You flew Lancers. Ever outrun a SAM?"

"Not in that thing," she said. "It redlined at Mach 2." The supersonic B-1 bomber had been her first high-performance jet, and was a fair approximation in size and shape of the Clipper. "And we had two guys in back dedicated to spoofing radar."

"What's our fuel state?"

She noticed he'd kept them level, building speed instead of climbing. The annoying skin temperature alerts made it hard to ignore. "A few more seconds," she said calmly, guessing his plan. "Stay cool. Make it count."

...

Shamrock 31

Gunnarson was beginning to wish that Jacksonville would just leave him alone. "Sham lead, you've been spiked. One of the bogies is locked!"

Damn. Only one? "I know!" he shot back. "Mark my position. Sham 31 is ejecting. Out!"

He threw his head back against the seat, tucked in his elbows and yanked at the yellow handle between his knees. He was battered by a hurricane of air as his canopy tumbled away, and dazzled by the ignition of solid rockets beneath his seat. His world turned gray, as if someone had suddenly dropped a few hundred pounds of sandbags into his lap.

Gunnarson blacked out as he was rocketed away from the stalling fighter only to be shocked into consciousness by the concussion of a missile exploding into his aircraft. He prayed the 'chute would hold off just a couple of seconds until he'd fallen clear of the expanding fireball. After all this trouble, it wouldn't do to end up plummeting to his certain death beneath a burning parachute.

...

Gemini Clipper

Penny was still looking out for the fighter that had called them when she saw the explosion, and quickly found the other missile's smoke trail against the overcast. Constant bearing, decreasing range: they were boresighted, with maybe ten seconds before it found its mark.

Quinn had managed to keep quiet until now. "Can you outmaneuver it?"

She kept her eyes locked on the missile. "No. If it didn't tear the plane apart it'd still blow our climb schedule."

"So the mission's shot. Can we outrun…"

"Drop tanks purged," she shouted and slammed down the tank release levers. "Punch it!"

Ryan shoved the throttles forward and pulled into a steep climb. The plane bucked like a wild horse, liberated from the drag of the empty tanks now falling away from them. "We are outta here!"

…

Gunnarson swung beneath his chute, watching the spectacle play out overhead. Even through his noise dampening helmet that Clipper roared like Satan's own trumpets. Maybe two miles away, four pillars of flame erupted from the spaceplane as it thundered away. The SAM attempted to follow, but a telltale squiggle in the smoke trail signaled that its homing radar had suddenly become confused. It began spiraling west, away from its target and straight towards the two enormous aluminum cylinders tumbling away in the plane's wake.

He smiled under his mask. Each tank was easily as big as his destroyed fighter and were perfect decoys; to a dumb radar they were infinitely more tempting than a spaceplane built mostly of carbon composites. Gunnarson twisted in his harness, straining to follow the missile as it screamed high overhead before diving after the tanks. He laughed out loud and pumped his fists as it connected with one and exploded harmlessly. He suddenly thought of his impatient wingman: maybe he'd quit acting like junior-officer scum and listen to his superiors a bit more from now on. *I told him there'd be a good show today.*

…

Shamrock 32

"Copy SEALORD, understand Sham lead has punched out. Dash two is rolling on target." Spock was righteously pissed off. As the rundown trawler became visible, he made certain his HUD camera was recording. The intel weenies might find it useful since he didn't plan on leaving much physical evidence.

He made it a point to light his afterburner for maximum effect as he screamed overhead, clearing the ship's mast by less than twenty feet. An alarm blared in his ears, accompanied by a telltale angry warbling: missile lock. Heat seekers.

He pulled the jet into a violent, twisting climb while spraying a trail of white phosphorous flares in his wake. He twisted to see behind him and cursed the flush rear canopy rail. It supposedly made the jet stealthier but it also made it nearly impossible to clear his six without relying on a balky rear-view camera. He had better situational awareness in his wife's Honda.

The warning tones disappeared, so he must have defeated the older shoulder-fired antiaircraft missiles. Obsolete didn't mean much if one of those things flew right up his tailpipe.

So now they'd gone and made it personal. Settling into an altitude that made it easier to keep an eye on the boat, he charged the fighter's internal Gatling gun. A target pipper began dancing in his visor.

"Sham three two." It was SEALORD, interrupting again. "You are cleared hot on target Sierra-Two. Smoke the sonofabitch."

At least they were keeping it simple this time. Good thing, as he was taking the shot anyway and wasn't in the mood to wait for permission. "Dash two is going guns," he said and angrily shut off the radio. He'd let them know how it turned out once he was finished with these tools.

He rolled in at three hundred feet and lined up on the trawler with a careful eye on his altitude. Judging height above water was hard enough; strafing a surface target made it dangerously easy to "scope lock" and fixate on it to the exclusion of all else. A lot of otherwise good pilots had plowed into the ground that way.

The rangefinder painted concentric rings around the trawler: it was in gun range. He tightened his grip on the control stick, dipped the nose to set the glowing pipper just beneath the superstructure, and gently squeezed the trigger beneath his index finger. A staccato *brrapp* ripped through the air just outside his canopy.

The sea ahead erupted in spray as he walked the glowing rounds onto his target. The ship's bridge flew apart in a cloud of burning shrapnel as Sham 32 screamed past overhead. The trawler's hull began listing hard to port, belching oily black smoke from every open hatch and porthole. Not sinking, but certainly not going anywhere. More importantly, not lobbing any more missiles into the sky. The Coast Guard could handle the rest.

"Shacked!" he exclaimed, pulling the fighter into a steep climb above the burning vessel before finishing off with a classic victory roll. He switched back to the ground controller's frequency: "SEALORD, target Sierra Two is toast," he said, then rolled inverted to look down on his quarry. Men were leaping away from the smoking hulk and into the sea. "Have a nice day, assholes."

17

Gemini Clipper
Flight Day Zero

Quinn was pleasantly surprised at how well his new pilots had kept their cool, despite having two radar-guided missiles bearing down on them. He'd fully expected them to punch tanks and evade the moment their radios lit up with frantic warnings. Though altogether satisfied with how they'd handled an immediate threat, he now had to contend with an even more troubling fact: their cover had been blown.

The whole episode had taken perhaps a minute: sixty seconds during which they were already locked on to what needed to happen in the next minute, and the next, and so on. He knew enough to understand that if they missed an altitude or velocity target in one phase, it would be that much harder to make up for it in the next. Freaking out would have only guaranteed failure, so maybe it was a good thing that this happened so soon. Get the kinks out now.

And whether or not these two conscripted pilots liked it, it had demonstrated the brass' wisdom in reactivating them. At the very least it had put them in the right mindset. This would not have gone well with a couple of civilians at the wheel.

Not too chatty either, despite the earlier trash talk. Both were "heads down," continuing to fly their ship into low orbit while Audrey calmly related the whole event to their control center.

"Aud," Stratton called, "our velocity's off. What's our new cutoff point?"

"Waiting on Denver," she grunted, struggling against the merciless four-g pull. The incessant vibration wasn't helping either. He couldn't make out a damned thing on his own wristwatch; he had no idea how they read anything useful from their instruments in this environment without going cross-eyed. The thought made him nauseous – he hoped that was the cause.

"Here comes," she announced in a burbling voice. "Lost…two hundred…meters per second." She took a breath. "Nothing we…can't fix."

Quinn smiled to himself. *Tough chick*. Good.

It looked like Hunter was nodding in response, though it could've just as easily been from the vibration. "Sorry guys. First instinct…drop the nose."

"No sweat," Stratton said. "Aud's fault. Rookie jinx."

"Pilots," the tough little redhead groused. "Redundant…components."

He closed his eyes, shrugging off the stress of a fight that had been entirely out of his control. The ride into a hot landing zone could be more frightening than the battle itself. He took some deep breaths and relaxed as the g's pressed against him like a heavy blanket. When he opened his eyes, the cobalt sky had already surrendered to infinite black.

…

Denver

"MECO," Grant announced. "Messy, but we'll have numbers for a new intercept before the first correction burn."

"That's in about a half hour," Hammond said. His eyes followed the sine waves of both orbits as they wrapped around the map projection. "Not bad, considering the circumstances. Ryan kept his cool."

"I'd get awful testy if someone was shooting at me," Grant said, "especially if I thought somebody might have been able to warn me about it." He looked over Hammond's shoulder at Kruger, who was lurking over some poor controller across the room.

"Wouldn't be the first time," Hammond said sourly. He stormed out of the control room, gesturing for Grant to follow. "Mister Kruger," he bellowed, "my office. We need to chat."

…

Gemini Clipper

Quinn reflexively held his stomach as they coasted past apogee and into orbit. He'd never experienced the sensation of going over the top of a roller coaster without coming down. The butterflies went away after a few minutes on the suborbital birds, now he'd have to get used to it being permanent. He'd just noticed how badly his sinuses were plugging up when he realized Stratton was talking at him. "Say again?"

"I said, our cover's blown. If we ever had it to begin with."

Quinn choked back the nausea. "My money's on the 'never had it' part." They couldn't have just been some random target of opportunity. "Whoever that was didn't just show up with actively guided SAMs. They were waiting for us."

"I started getting worried when that security detail showed up," she said. Sometimes the lack of visible protection was its own best insurance.

"I expect surprises from the bad guys," Quinn agreed. "It's worse when they come from our side."

"Amen to that. Guarantee you some staff puke got wind of this and just had to go put his personal stamp on it."

"You sound pretty certain, ma'am."

"One year of Pentagon duty," she said with mock vanity. "Put otherwise good officers into staff jobs and they crap their brains into their shorts."

True, but there had to be more to it. "This would've taken time to organize," he said, "probably longer than we've been planning this mission."

Her face darkened. "Somebody doesn't want us going up there in a bad way. I think your target list might've gotten a whole lot bigger."

...

Denver

Hammond hadn't uttered a syllable since leaving the ops center. For that matter, neither had Kruger. The men sat opposite each other in Hammond's office as Grant leaned protectively against the door. "Well, then. That was lively," Hammond said, having waited long enough. "Anything you'd like to share with us?"

"Not particularly," Kruger said stiffly.

"Somebody just fired on one of our planes," Grant reminded him. "We take that kind of personally, Mr. Kruger."

He remained maddeningly aloof. "There was always a risk of interference."

"Interference?" Hammond's fuse was burning short. "Is that what we're calling it now when someone tries to shoot down a civilian aircraft? Not 'act of war?'"

"Enemy action, then," Kruger said. "Until now, we were more afraid of this happening to your garden-variety airliner."

"Perhaps you should be. But nice try anyway," Grant said. "Did you have specific…what's the phrase…'actionable intelligence' that there might be a credible threat?"

Kruger wouldn't answer and his expression gave no clues, a monument to obstinate diffidence.

"You blow in here and start throwing your weight around, claiming 'national security' to shoehorn yourself into my company," Hammond fumed, "yet you don't see a need to point out the possibility that somebody might start *shooting at our planes*." He let the accusation hang.

"Technically it's a military operation," Kruger reminded him. "There was always the danger of some kind of counter move from the enemy."

"And who might that be?" Hammond demanded. "These aren't – what do you call them – rogue actors?"

"That's for Washington to figure out," he said coolly, "especially if someone just started a war. Kam Varza is deeply embedded in the global depopulation movement but that doesn't necessarily make him an eco-terrorist. And Hassani's connections to the Caliphate were tenuous at best."

"I'd say they just became a hell of a lot less tenuous. So we're talking about space-age Islamist hijackers now?" It was a prospect he had never considered. Until now he'd been more afraid of some crackpot hijacking a Clipper and plowing it into an unsuspecting city at hypersonic speed. It seemed like they would always be reacting to the last threat, unable to predict the next one.

"Hassani's a gulf Arab. Everybody in that part of the world has ties to some radical group," Kruger said. "So you see our problem connecting the dots: relationships are convoluted by design. The hardcore Gaia freaks and the Islamofascists both want to take society back to the dark ages for different reasons. They'll fight over who's in charge when the dust settles."

...

Washington

Contacts. Don Abbot had scarcely been able to think about anything else after Hal Horner's friendly rebuke days earlier.

Maintaining control over a single center like Johnson had at first seemed a monumental task, but it had quickly become second nature to him. He'd been quite familiar with the goings-on of each directorate under his thumb, and being able to pop in unannounced whenever he felt the need had kept his people on their toes.

Running a large organization was about controlling the motivations and proclivities of its people. To do that, you had to intuitively understand what motivated them. At Johnson Space Center the astronaut corps had inserted themselves into just about every function, whether they were actually needed or not. Ultimately they reported to him, and Don Abbot knew exactly what they wanted: flight assignments.

It had been remarkably easy, actually. He controlled the available seats, which in turn meant he controlled the people who wanted them. And if the rest of the Center responded to those people, in the end all he'd had to do was manage a few dozen personalities.

The difference in Washington had been jarring. For one, NASA was a huge organization, with independent centers scattered all over the country. Each had its own focus and its own set of priorities, an autonomy he'd cherished as JSC director. Back in Houston, he could issue a directive and be certain it was carried out. Here, he might get one or two centers to play ball if it served their interests. The others would assign some functionary to an office with a title that maintained the appearance of doing work while its real purpose was to ignore him completely. In the end, each center catered to the whims of their congressmen.

If money made the world go 'round, then D.C. was its polar axis. NASA was competing for a puny slice of a shrinking federal pie, and Abbot had even less insight into his competing agencies than he did the various space centers under his control. He'd been skunked on the Gateway project, and would be damned if he'd let that happen again.

Contacts. Hal was right, much as Abbot hated to admit it. If he couldn't stay close enough to exert pressure where he needed it, then he needed insight. He needed to find those pressure points.

Abbot leafed through the personnel folders on his desk, though he'd already settled on his target: Blaine Fitzgerald Winston, the executive assistant assigned to him when he'd first arrived in Washington. In the year since, Abbot hadn't found any reason to replace the young man. He supposed he didn't need one, and the kid had proven to be tremendously efficient. More importantly, he knew his way around the Hill.

He took one last look at the dossier: Georgetown grad with stints at EPA, State, Defense…Winston had been marinating in this town since his teens. No doubt he'd come here to help change the world like everybody else. It was time to see what he could do to help change their little corner of it.

18

Gemini Clipper
Flight Day One

Ryan eavesdropped on Audrey as she helped the Marines find their way around in back of the cargo hold. The boisterous chatter of men tooling up for a mission carried through the cabin as they began liberating their gear from the storage lockers. The smells of gun oil and canvas completed his mental picture: it was funny how even the most advanced military equipment eventually smelled like the inside of a sea bag.

The old familiar sensations were distracting: he hadn't noticed the main engines had finished pulsing, kicking them into a transfer orbit to intercept *Grissom.*

"Insertion on target," Penny said, interrupting his wandering thoughts. "We'll be in position for rendezvous in twelve orbits."

"Better part of a day," Ryan yawned. "I'll take first watch."

"Bad idea. I'll take it. I'm too wound up to sleep and you look like hell."

"Only because I did all the flying. It's hard work staying this cool with two SAMs sniffing up your backside."

She rolled her eyes. "I've ditched more than you can count. You just didn't want a chick showing you up."

"I'm pacing myself. Besides, the only reason you're still awake is because you're epically pissed off. Right?"

"You always could read me like a book."

"It's easy reading," he said. "Especially when we both know we're being mushroomed."

"Kept in the dark and fed a load of crap," she agreed bitterly. "This really did turn into a military op, didn't it?" She scrolled their flight plan across her tablet, checking it against the onboard computer. Ryan decided not to point out that she'd done so twice already, letting the pantomime of work sooth her nerves.

As too often happened, the need for secrecy had been perverted into a crippling information embargo, an already messy package gift-wrapped by the obligation to follow orders. It absolutely made sense from the military's perspective: reactivating their commissions was a handy way to give them what they needed to know but prevent them from asking too many uncomfortable questions. An altogether unpleasant reminder of why Ryan had left the service in the first place and of the conflicting loyalties he'd felt at the time. "Quinn's no happier than we are," he finally concluded.

"That's all?"

Ryan shrugged, not offering anything more. Maybe his mind just didn't want to go there.

"You're my friend," Penny said hesitantly, "practically my little brother. Once we break orbit there's no turning back, so don't hold it against me if I get all uppity and start pulling rank."

"Wouldn't blame you." In fact, he was hoping she would. Having Penny Stratton outrank the actual on-scene commander was a sign that maybe the Pentagon hadn't entirely thought this through.

Sunlight flashed across them as they emerged from night above the eastern Pacific. Ryan fiddled with the sunshade above his window as he considered the weight of her words. She wasn't easily rattled, and too many coincidences were piling up. "Have you noticed," he wondered, with a nod towards the passenger cabin, "those guys don't harbor many doubts about getting the job done."

Her normally bright eyes turned cold as she realized what he'd left unsaid. "They're more afraid of *not* getting it done."

. . .

Denver

"Maybe there's no connection," Hammond said around a mouthful of sandwich. The company cafeteria had become about the only place where he had time to indulge his appetite; otherwise he was left with the unsatisfying healthy stuff Abigail had been forcing on him lately. "And if there is, there's still not a damned thing we can do about it except wait around and listen for phantom signals from deep space."

Posey pushed his own plate aside and eased back into Hammond's well-worn sofa. "Doubtful. Too many open questions, with all of the likely answers pointing to something nasty. The Caliphate isn't known for tolerating dissent. They're harder on their own agnostics than they are Jews or Christians."

Hammond wondered how broadly a bunch of apocalyptic radicals might define 'agnostic.' Anyone insufficiently enthusiastic for the cause would be suspect. "Like a jailhouse code of honor?"

Posey nodded. "It's even worse if you're one of them and switch teams," he said darkly, and drew a finger across his throat for effect. He'd seen the leftovers of men found to be traitors to the cause, long ago and far away. "Which makes Varza and Hassani even bigger enigmas."

Hammond recoiled at the thought. "So what about the others? Are they just drones – part of a cover story?"

"Been wondering that myself," Posey said. The remaining hijackers – assuming that's what they were – had solid histories. Not one invented backstory. "Why would a hardcore Islamist take them on a bus trip to Detroit, much less the Moon?"

"We think too much alike, Tony. I don't see how a radical like Hassani ends up playing second fiddle to a lesser radical like Varza. So you don't believe he's seen the light and reformed his ways, singing 'Kumbaya' and holding hands with the radical Greens?"

Posey smiled. "My teenage daughter would say 'Oh *hell* to the no.' They know we're suckers for a good story if it comes off as sincere enough."

"Some of us," Hammond groused. "I'd have never let the bastards anywhere near us if we'd known who he really was."

"Thus all the prior aliases," Posey said. "The serious operators create multiple layers of elaborate back-stories to cover their tracks. And once they've made you a target, the only way you can win is by playing even dirtier than they do. They count on us being too civilized for that."

"And if we'd gotten suspicious and refused service, his cronies would've slapped us with a big fat discrimination suit just for kicks."

"That's precisely how they operate: conceal what they're all about in order to worm their way inside of whatever organization they're trying to penetrate. They'll wait decades, if that's what it takes."

"Which made us easy marks," Hammond concluded in disgust. "We only had to be fooled long enough to get them into lunar orbit."

...

Gateway Station

Hassani had to remain calm for only a little longer. For being so instrumental in a long and complicated operation, the big man had a great deal to learn about the virtues of patience under pressure. He also knew the others had seen him as their requisite muscle to enable Varza's grand designs. That he'd been able to assemble all of it through legitimate business ventures without attracting any unwanted attention had been masterful work, perhaps even more than the relatively low body count he'd achieved thus far. And out here in cislunar space, disposing of the evidence was as simple as opening an airlock.

Varza called from the control node. "Is our associate ready to board?"

Hassani took a deep breath before looking back up through the open hatchway, lest he telegraph his frustration. "A bit more effort than anticipated, but we are ready." He tipped his head backward, hinting that their remaining conspirator was getting cold feet.

"Not quite, my friend. In preparing your partner, it appears you've neglected yourself," Varza said kindly, pointing to Hassani's missing helmet. They were dressed in full-mobility EVA gear, spacesuits fitted with extended life-support packs and maneuvering jets. Dr. DeCarlo had generally been quite enthusiastic about their mission but had become reluctant when the time came to leave the confines of the spacecraft. The physicist was brilliant but notoriously erratic, convinced that humans had been relentlessly destroying their environment like a virus. The planet must somehow be restored to its natural state, which Hassani didn't altogether disagree with. To Hassani, he was nothing more than a modern-day Druid who worshipped the planet as Supreme Being instead of the One who created it.

How one could embrace the former while scoffing at the latter confounded him to no end. How was one worldview more intellectually acceptable than the other? DeCarlo's impressive credentials were most certainly the source of the man's erratic nature: as the Americans Hassani had lived among would say, he was a man who'd had the common sense educated right out of him.

He pushed his helmet down through the docking tunnel. "If you could be so kind. The remaining cargo is bulky. It will be easier to load if I can see all the way around."

"Of course." Varza caught the helmet and secured it on the opposite side of the Orion command module. Just big enough to hold four suited astronauts, it also worked for three men with cargo. "Please have the doctor come in. He should be willing to help you load his equipment, I would think." With some luck their hectic schedule would force the man to stay focused. If not, they would have to extract his expertise in other ways.

. . .

Varza had anticipated personality conflicts, but even he was becoming increasingly frustrated at how much time he'd had to waste settling disagreements and soothing egos. Perhaps he should have known better. Scientific collaboration often involved stroking tender egos as much as doing the actual work. It had gotten particularly bad once he became involved with the climate movement, though it had been easier to accept – better than anyone, they understood the irreparable harm mankind was inflicting on its only home.

Time was running out. Humanity's options for reversing course would only become more radical as time progressed, eventually running out as a runaway greenhouse effect rendered Earth uninhabitable. Depopulation and deindustrialization were coming, the only question was if humans would be able to choose how before Nature restored the balance on her terms. That so few were able to see it clearly had both stoked their anger and strengthened their resolve to act on this unique opportunity. If that entailed a few personality conflicts, it wasn't entirely without precedent when working at the frontiers of science.

Hassani was of a different breed, though. Being of Iranian descent himself, Varza had assumed Omar would to be easier to manage if only because of a shared belief system. But then he'd never spent this much time with someone so comparatively uneducated. With only a bachelor's degree from some second-rate university, their "fixer" might as well have been a dropout though he'd had to admit the puissant Arab had been both a gifted intelligence source and master logistician.

It wasn't enough that he'd brought Varza the first hints of Gateway's existence; the speed with which he'd been able to secure funding and materials had been breathtaking. If Omar had appreciated the demand for such abilities in the research sector, he'd be able to command a generous salary from any university or foundation upon their return – or at least those left standing who remained sympathetic to the cause. They would soon find out which ones were serious and which ones had only attached themselves to whatever fashionable causes attracted the most grant money. He suspected quite a few of the latter.

Varza took comfort in the knowledge that Nature and Allah – one and the same to him, actually – had ways of weeding out the superfluous. It was his life's highest privilege to be so instrumental in restoring the balance which had been suppressed for too long. It was that same faith that allowed him to accept that balance might also result in a frustratingly large number of brutes like Hassani, at least for a time. The unfortunate rule of ignorance through violence would eventually come to an end, even if it wasn't settled in his lifetime. Being blessed with setting the final reckoning in motion would have to do. If there were to be future history books, Kamran Malik Varzavani, Ph.D., would figure prominently in the planet's Great Rebalancing.

He pushed away from the fire-control station and flew down the length of the module to find DeCarlo at the primary reflector controls. This entire module was dedicated to directing the tremendous amounts of energy being generated for it. The physicist looked perturbed, which Varza was coming to learn was his normal state. "Problems, Doctor?" He'd also learned DeCarlo took great comfort in the formalities of academia.

"Not sure…not sure," he mumbled. "Throughput is in excess of one hundred megawatts, as expected. But output…" he trailed off, tapping his chin as he fell deeper into thought. Hassani floated behind him, glowering. The longer they were up here, the more the big man seethed with impatience.

"What matters is the final energy placed on target, which is more than sufficient," Varza said, pulling DeCarlo back into the present while shooting a cautionary glare at Hassani. *Not now.*

"But not optimal," he argued. "Not even close. This is a remarkable system for being so compact. It's capable of so much more—"

Varza cut him off, gently laying a hand on his shoulder to soften the rebuke. "It more than meets our needs, Joseph. Your work has been exemplary but we are bound to a very tight schedule, my friend."

DeCarlo's mouth tightened in exasperation. "Of course," he muttered. "It's easy to overlook. I even forgot about my nausea for a time."

Varza remained fixed on the erratic scientist. "Then we are glad that it helped you in that regard. Omar and I still have much to do on the secondary systems. Do you require any further assistance?"

"For now, no," DeCarlo conceded. "You know, their—"

"We need your full attention at the missile control station," Hassani interrupted, tiring of their wordplay. "Your duty comes first, then you can play with toys. We are required outside," he said, pointing at himself and Varza. "You must be ready to bypass the safeties immediately upon our signal."

"Of course," DeCarlo sighed. "The warheads."

19

Gemini Clipper
Flight Day Two

Penny worked from the small docking compartment behind the cockpit, talking Ryan into position as they drew closer to *Grissom*. A small control panel embedded in the ceiling let her guide them into position, presenting a view of the target alongside *Grissom*'s berthing. Columns of numbers scrolled down either side of the screen. "Eighty meters, closing at point five," she said calmly as their ships raced together, high above the equator.

"Affirmative, *Gemini Clipper* holding at Proximity A," Ryan announced into his headset mic, responding to a query from Denver. There was a long mechanical thrumming as their docking port's overhead doors retracted into the fuselage.

Penny switched her radio to the hab's frequency. "Gus, our docking target's clear. Light 'em up." A warbling tone chimed from the speakers. "Lidar's locked," she called.

"Riding the beam," Ryan confirmed, and removed his hands from the controls. *Grissom*'s setup crew had locked their ship's laser rangefinder onto a target by the Clipper's exposed dorsal hatch, which would direct the spaceplane straight onto the open berth. After a full day of chasing them down and making careful adjustments after each orbit, all he had left was to make certain the automated system worked. In practice that had been about half the time, which he didn't really mind as no self-respecting pilot was content to let the machines do all of the work.

The completed stack was easily a hundred meters long and looked for all the world like a flying potato masher. Beginning with the bulbous hab module and its spread of solar panels, the vessel was completed by its cylindrical flight module and throwaway lunar injection "kick stage" at its far end.

Ryan squinted through a small overhead window and dialed up its polarization against the dazzling sunlight. "I need to have a talk with Art about his color schemes when we get back," he said, shielding his eyes. "Might as well have covered the damned thing in mirrors."

"Where are you going to find a paint shop up here?" Audrey asked. She'd been glued to the windows all day, enjoying their reliance on Denver's guidance while she still could. Once the injection burn for the Moon was finished, they would "go dark." That made today the only free time she'd have for the next couple of weeks.

"Be glad for it. It'll make Big Al that much easier to find," Penny said.

Ryan tapped a multifunction display in the center of the instrument panel, bringing up the docking camera with *Grissom*'s main port centered in the crosshairs. Thrusters thudded around the nose in rapid succession, spitting icy vapor as *Gemini Clipper* fine-tuned its approach in response to some unknowable command from *Grissom*'s alignment beam.

Penny continued announcing the vital signs. "Ten meters, closing at point two. Dumping velocity on schedule." The spaceplane crept towards it target at less than a quarter of a meter per second. "Five meters…three…"

A shudder reverberated through the Clipper, followed by a rhythmic knocking as docking rings locked together. A single amber light in the center panel turned green. "Hard dock."

…

Washington

"Yes, Doctor Abbot?"

Blaine Winston looked every inch a product of Washington: young and thin, with angular features and meticulously sculpted brown hair. His clothing hinted at resources far beyond his GS-8 salary, something Abbot had found intriguing. It suggested connections.

"Shut the door," Abbot said. "Have a seat, please."

"Of course, sir," Winston replied obsequiously as he slid into a chair. He sat quietly as his boss mimed tending to business at his desk. Abbot was, of course, using the increasingly awkward silence to size up the young man. No signs of impatience, no fidgeting or slipping a look at his watch. He had to give credit where it was due: the kid didn't budge.

He ceremoniously shoved some files into a drawer and locked it shut, then leaned back comfortably. "Thank you for your patience. I'm afraid the work never really ends around here, does it?"

"I suppose not, sir." He did like to keep up the formalities, waiting for his superior to get to the point instead of trying to improvise a conversation. That could be useful, too.

Abbot tapped his meaty fingers on his desk, signaling that he was considering matters of importance. "We have a problem, Mr. Winston." It was meant to be off-putting, but to his credit the kid didn't seem fazed.

"Whatever it is, sir, I'm confident we can find a solution."

Short, solicitous, and just vague enough to suggest he'd do anything required of him. The earnest look on his face sealed it. Abbot smiled. "I'll be blunt with you," he finally opened up. "I'm an engineer at heart. A rocket scientist, in popular parlance. Solving complex problems is as second-nature to me as filling out a grocery list." Bombastic, though not entirely inaccurate.

"Engineers are not generally recognized for their people skills," Winston offered carefully, hazarding a guess at where he was going. "Though I must admit you're the first I've worked for, sir."

Interesting choice of qualifiers: *for*, not *with*. "I appreciate that, Winston. Yet I am still left at a disadvantage. I may understand NASA and its people, but negotiating the political swamps of this town has been difficult." It was an honest admission. "Which is why I brought you in here."

"My background with the other agencies," Winston surmised. "You believe that could help you, sir?"

"The obvious conclusion, you have to admit."

"Yes sir, I suppose so. Of course, you know I requested to be assigned to your office..."

"And that's unusual, isn't it?"

"At least having the request approved is unusual," Winston said. "Most executives at your level bring someone they know with them." More like someone they trusted, but the point was valid.

"I couldn't talk Martha into leaving Houston, which left me at the mercy of the system."

"Perhaps it was fortuitous then, sir. I have professional relationships all over the Hill. If that can help you, then by all means I'm at your service."

Abbot smiled. "What do you know about something called project called FIREWALL?"

20

SS Grissom
Flight Day Two

Audrey had learned some hard lessons about the realities of spaceflight: her face felt like a water balloon, and her hair went everywhere if she didn't keep it tied back. Without it, her mane would fan out like a halo of fire. Quinn had already taken to calling her Red, which she still couldn't decide if it pissed her off or not. But the man had a talent for it.

The other thing she'd learned was how easily distracted she could be, and it wasn't just the view. Running a mission from the flight director's console, she had every conceivable bit of information in front of her with a small army of technicians constantly feeding her advice. And she commanded it all like an orchestra conductor.

Out here was different. Everything happened insanely fast. What looked like a pretty reasonable plan on the ground could get seriously backed up in orbit. There being so many events which had to happen at precise moments, so many deadlines, that a phenomenon they called "time compression" took over every aspect of their lives. She'd heard about it from every crew she'd ever worked with, and believed them, but it was something that had to be experienced to truly understand. "Space time" carried a whole different meaning to an astronaut than it did an astrophysicist.

After a full day's work of moving their gear from *Gemini Clipper* and topping off *Grissom*'s propellant, Trans-Lunar Injection had come up quickly. Even Ryan showed signs of the pressure, but she realized that perhaps it shouldn't have been surprising: this was his first trip beyond Earth orbit too. It would be Penny's third, after running the first two test flights with Simon. They were nearing the end of what had become a rapid-fire checklist, which Audrey could barely follow now despite knowing it by heart. There was an urge to jump into the middle of things, but she forced herself to remain content observing while Charlie ran the show from Denver.

His voice already sounded far away. "*Grissom*, checklists complete. You are go for TLI in one minute."

"Copy go for TLI," Penny answered in the measured "pilot voice" Audrey was used to hearing from hundreds of miles away. She could see now that while partly for clarity's sake, it came more from having so much going on at once. Penny's head barely moved but her eyes darted about. Ryan was much busier, configuring systems for her. His hands seemed to be flying everywhere. "Aud, confirm pax cabin's secure."

"On it." She switched to the intercom. "Quinn, confirm your team is secure." She'd personally checked back there ten minutes ago but that was a long time to forget instructions.

"We're belted in, Red. But Haggerty has a request..."

Before she could ask, he jumped right in. "Can I use the head while we're doing this? That zero-g crapper is for the birds. Sure would be nice to take a dump in gravity again."

Audrey shook her head. These guys reveled in finding your comfort zone and stepping all over it. "Negative on the waste dump, hoss. You'll have to hold it."

Penny had only heard her half of the conversation. "Seriously?" She shot an accusing look at Ryan, who held up his hands in protest.

"How is this *my* problem?"

"Your tribe, jarhead."

They were like squabbling siblings, which forced Audrey back into her flight director's persona. "Thirty seconds, guys," she said firmly.

"Thirty seconds," Professional Penny answered. The flight deck remained quiet until the main engines roared back to life, the acceleration pressing against them at twice the normal gravity.

...

Twenty minutes later they were back in freefall after jettisoning the spent kick stage. Technically still in Earth's influence, they would continue outward for almost a week until crossing the invisible boundary of the Moon's gravity well. Audrey was shocked at how fast Earth had already receded in the window.

"We copy your shutdown, final numbers coming up." Charlie's voice had taken a hollow quality that was disconcerting. Were they already seeing the effects of distance? A minute later: "Good gimbals, no residuals; velocity 10,800 meters per second. Next burn on schedule for PC minus two." A long pause telegraphed how reluctant he was to finish. "Denver out."

It would be their last contact with home for what was beginning to feel like forever. Any more comm would be through an encrypted burst transmitter supplied by Quinn's team. It was now on her to navigate them through to lunar orbit, five days from now.

One final transmission from Charlie appeared in her message window: GO AUD. ROLL TIDE.

...

Vandenberg AFB, California

The S-20 Starlifter II had already been on alert when the launch order came from Special Operations Command. It had taken longer to fly the Marines' west coast TAC team up from Camp Pendleton than it had for the Starlifter's crew to preflight the militarized Clipper.

From outside the Starlifter looked no different than a Polaris Clipper except for the mottled gray and black camouflage, though someone with an eye for detail would have recognized the radar-absorbing paint's unique texture. Closer inspection would reveal more differences, such as the chaff and flare dispensers mounted below the tail for confusing enemy missiles.

Inside, the differences were more pronounced. Though not as spartan as a conventional military cargo plane, its interior was nowhere close to the corporate jet quality of a Clipper. Fewer windows allowed less natural lighting, and gray sidewall insulation replaced the spaceliner's more aesthetically pleasing fabrics. Exposed ductwork made maintenance tasks easier, and a bare metal floor with adjustable cargo rails allowed them to configure the cabin for whatever might have to be carried. For this mission, it held six high-g acceleration couches with quick-release five-point harnesses.

The cabin was perhaps half the size of its civilian counterpart, needing more room dedicated to the airlock, which separated it from the unpressurized cargo bay. The bay would have been indistinguishable from the passenger cabin but for the lack of seating and an overhead clear of any wiring or plumbing. A seam ran down the middle of the ceiling, if one followed its panels down to where they joined the sidewalls it became obvious that they were designed to open in flight.

Directly beneath the big cargo doors was more of the same railed flooring, which held six odd contraptions shaped like turtle shells mounted atop bulky spring-loaded platforms. The Marines carefully loaded their weapons and gear into foam cutouts inside the shells before proceeding into the cabin. Already dressed out in quick-donning EVA suits, they were greeted by life support technicians who waited by each seat. As the Marines settled in, the technicians carefully buckled them in and connected them to the Starlifter's life support.

The entire process took less than an hour. After a painstaking round of preflight checks, the command pilot called "faceplates down" and taxied the craft to the end of Vandenberg's long runway. As it thundered into the early-morning sky, the spaceplane turned west. It would be over its target in less than an hour.

• • •

After a few minutes of punishing acceleration – the other aspect of flying a military spaceplane that was markedly different from its civilian cousin – the Marines switched to their personal life-support packs and disconnected from the Starlifter's air supply. An Air Force jumpmaster in an orange vacuum suit "stood" at the airlock behind them.

"Port side, release," he called, and the three men on the left side of the spacecraft smacked their quick-release harnesses in unison. They floated out of their couches and pushed back for the airlock. Upon hearing "Starboard side, release," the men on the right did the same.

The jumpmaster followed them through the airlock and into the cargo bay, locking down the hatches on either end. As he checked that each Marine had secured himself in one of the turtle-shell Personal Ablative Reentry System (PARS), the jumpmaster reported "cabin secure, depress" to the pilots. Green lights around the bay turned from amber, then red, signaling that they were now in vacuum.

The jumpmaster attached himself to a harness along the sidewall. "One minute," he called.

"One minute!" the Marines answered. Above them, the seam cracked open as the cargo doors began to move silently on their hinges. Instead of seeing black sky and stars, the pilots had already rolled the spaceplane belly up. As it coasted over the top of its suborbital arc, Asia slipped by two hundred kilometers below.

"Thirty seconds!" The green jungles and azure seas of Southeast Asia turned to the snowy peaks of the Himalayas, shining orange and yellow in the morning sun. "Armed!" the jumpmaster called as he activated the ejection mechanisms beneath each Marine's reentry shell.

"Stand by!" Mottled brown deserts began to appear overhead before slipping into the predawn darkness below.

"Go!"

The Marines ejected in sequence, a ripple of gray and black tortoise shells flying out of the cargo bay and into space over Iran.

• • •

"Raiders, this is Six. Check in!" The team leader would not open his own reentry shell until he knew the rest of his men were safe. After a rapid reply of call signs from each Marine, he pulled a D-link and waited for the balloon on his back to inflate.

Raider Six began rocking gently side-to-side, the first hint that his shell had opened in the tenuous atmosphere. Falling from space on his back, all he could see was black sky above. Blinking directional cues projected in his faceplate told him they were on track to their landing zone. Grip controls in either hand gave him the ability to keep the reentry shell upright, which was all the directional control they needed at this point. Anything more robust risked someone upending and falling back from space unprotected.

The team soon became a cluster of human meteors. The PARS shells had inflated to over two meters across, around and over them to where each Marine rode inside of a heat-resistant shuttlecock. With his shell's tail end open to space, Raider Six had an unlimited view of the plasma sheath that raged around him during his plunge into the atmosphere.

• • •

The reentry itself had only taken two minutes. At one hundred thousand feet, the men were still falling at well over the speed of sound. At a time cue that flashed in their helmet displays, each man pulled another D-ring that disconnected them from their PARS shields. Still forty miles from their actual landing zone, the men held out their arms and legs in a flying squirrel pose, opening the wingsuits that were integrated with their EVA gear. They would glide this way until passing through a thousand feet above ground, only then would they open their parachutes to drift onto the rocky desert south of Tehran.

...

The firefight had been surprisingly one-sided. The Iranian military police had been an easy target for a predawn raid. The Marines had waited in the hills surrounding the facility until their first objective, a squad of Russian Spetsnaz commandos, had appeared during a routine perimeter patrol. Though just as capable as any American operators, months of patrolling empty desert to protect this tiny Iranian facility had weakened their senses. They'd become complacent, and as such were picked off one by one with silenced weapons as they moved down a dry riverbed.

The remainder of the security force was readily dispatched. Other than a few sentries caught in the open, most of the Iranian and Russian platoons were still asleep in their barracks. The Marines posted two guards at each exit in case anyone got any funny ideas while the two men on the entry team made their run. No sense picking a fight just yet. By the time they figured out just how badly they'd been owned, the Raiders would be hundreds of miles away.

If they'd been there to "eliminate high-value targets," the operation would have involved a lot more men. But this was about intelligence gathering, SOCOM having been tipped off to this facility by a captured Venezuelan ship's captain.

The camp held a number of ramshackle cinderblock buildings, all looked to be hastily constructed around the same time. None looked more than a couple of years old. The largest building in the complex was also the best maintained, with enormous air conditioners and two separate backup generators. Probably had a lot to do with the cluster of antennas atop its roof. Whatever was in here, they didn't want it losing power. Ever.

Getting in was simple, using a swipe card lifted from a recently deceased sentry. Raider Six swept the first darkened room with the infrared sight mounted on his helmet. It held two blocky pods on hydraulic stilts, each fed with hoses and electrical cables. Those would be the flight simulators he'd been told to expect. He pointed to his companion and signaled him to keep cover while he got pictures inside each sim.

Next they moved onto a partially-lit hallway, risking the absence of cover for their main target at the end. Silently padding down the corridor, they paused by a set of double doors and switched off the lights, satisfied no one was milling about to notice. He snaked an optical cable beneath the door as Six watched the feed through a screen on his wrist. "Right," he whispered, and his partner turned the cable.

"Sweep left." The cable turned slightly, moving the camera at its end to pan across the room. Six watched as their primary target moved steadily across his screen. The space was dark but for the glow of computer monitors along three rows of consoles, with one big floor-to-ceiling screen at the end of the room. Each console had at least one person working at it, all of them apparently answering to a director in back. Most of them looked Iranian; the Russian boss seemed to rely heavily on a couple of translators.

As the big screen centered in his view, he ordered One-one to stop. "Zoom…okay, stop. Focus. Hold it."

The screen was divided into three sections, one a cascade of numbers and symbols in both Persian and Cyrillic, another showed the Moon with what looked like the orbits of two or three vehicles overlaid on it. The third depicted some kind of space station, one like nothing he'd ever seen. So this dump was their mission control center, apparently built with a lot of help from Moscow...*what the hell were these guys up to*?

21

SS Grissom
Flight Day Four

Ryan watched from the tunnel in fascination as Quinn's men wrapped up a martial arts workout in the open common area. While their ship may have been hastily outfitted for this trip and missing most of the storage lockers and creature comforts, the Marines were happy to have so much open space and free time. Until a couple of hours ago, they'd all had to stay holed up inside the tunnel's natural radiation shelter as the ship crossed the Van Allen belts.

Watching them bound around the toroidal compartment, he reflexively ran a finger along his bottom lip, a reminder of the only physical altercation he'd had up here. It hadn't even been a proper fight, just a wild kick from a panicked passenger that split his lip wide open. Marcy's hasty stitch job with some medical adhesive and butterfly bandages had left a scar that suggested something worse than the actual injury.

It was a misadventure that had gnawed at him ever since. There had to be a better way of dealing with unruly passengers besides zapping them with a Taser. Or worse, having to subdue some adrenaline-charged brute immune to fifty thousand volts. Wealthy clientele didn't guarantee good manners; there was always somebody's cousin Bubba along for the ride who might not behave once he got a few drinks in him.

As the men streamed past and flew up the tunnel, he floated into the open deck. It was beginning to smell like a gym. Quinn loitered by a window, dressed in a t-shirt and camo fatigues. His combat boots were noticeably missing. "Captain Hunter," he acknowledged without taking his eyes off the view outside. "Interested in going a few rounds?"

"Am I that obvious?"

Quinn turned to face him. "Like a kid watching his team practice from behind a fence."

"Can't deny that," Ryan said. "I've been wondering – how can you defend yourself if someone jumps you? Seems to me that no matter how you set it up, whoever takes the first shot wins."

"That's assuming you connect," Quinn said. This was the first time they'd ever been able to practice for more than a few minutes on a suborbital Clipper. "Martial arts work great when you can use gravity to your advantage. But how do we stand our ground when we can't stand up? We figured out real quick that you'd better not miss."

It should have occurred to him that Quinn would happily welcome him aboard as a crash-test dummy. It had almost certainly occurred to Penny right away, he realized too late, as she came down behind him but remained safely in the tunnel. He, on the other hand, was beginning to feel ridiculous.

"How can I throw a punch in zero-g if I can't plant my feet?" Quinn asked, assuming the instructor's role. "Because otherwise I'm just flailing around." He crouched in a boxer's stance and tried throwing an uppercut, which left him twisting comically in midair. He'd stayed close to a bulkhead and was able to quickly regain his footing. "Unarmed combat's been on my mind a lot," Quinn explained after righting himself. "They picked us for this mission because we're the only ones with any kind of zero-g experience. Plus we have armored spacesuits and no-recoil carbines."

"Which is cool," Ryan said.

"Yeah, it is," he smiled. "Anyway, I figure space combat won't leave much middle ground because of the speeds involved. If you don't drop your man from far away, you'll find yourself in an extremely close-quarters battle. I for one don't want to have rounds going off inside of a big metal balloon, so we should plan on dealing with these gomers the old-fashioned way."

Ryan nodded. "Everybody thinks 'zero g' really means what it says, and it doesn't. You haven't left the gravity well, you're just falling in a circle around it. We still have mass, which means we still have momentum."

"Exactly. Once you move, you're committed." Quinn launched himself across the bay at Ryan, lowering his shoulder and driving hard into his midsection to wrap him up like a linebacker. The impact drove them both into the opposite bulkhead. He finished with a forearm across Ryan's neck. "So what just happened here?"

"You just knocked the crap out of your ride home, that's what."

"Yeah, there's that. But what could you have done to me?" Quinn asked. "Imagine we're doing this in armored pressure suits."

"Your PLSS backpack's vulnerable. I could've cut a hose if you hadn't gotten the drop on me."

"True," Quinn said, not pleased with the obvious vulnerability. He smacked the padded sidewall behind them. "But once I was moving, this was the only place we were gonna stop."

Ryan floated away from the wall, rubbing his sore stomach. "Which made you vulnerable because there was nothing to grab on to. So never stray too far from a handhold or hard surface?" Like the joke about how to avoid a runaway train: just step aside.

Quinn nodded in assent and pushed off for the opposite corner. "Get out of the way if you have time. You have to be able to plant your feet to punch or grapple, which you can only do up here by using these footholds. That looks like a good way to end up with a broken knee."

Ryan cringed at the thought, remembering the torn meniscus he'd suffered years ago. That was when he'd noticed Quinn bounding back at him again. This time, Ryan simply pushed off with his toes to pirouette safely out of the way and mimed a slashing motion across Quinn's back as he passed.

"Much better. So we've established three rules for Space Fight Club," he said, and began counting on his fingers. "One: hit first. Two: Don't be a turtle." Meaning don't be stranded in the middle of open space with nothing to push against. "Three: always have a blade on you. If you get wrapped up with a bad guy, cut his hoses or suit before he gets to you."

"And here I am without a knife."

"There's a spare Ka-Bar in my bag," Quinn said. "It's yours."

...

Washington

"We have to handle this very carefully," Blaine Winston counseled his boss. "That project you asked me about is Top Secret/SCI," he said, leaning in conspiratorially. SCI – special compartmentalized information –

meant the project had been assigned a codeword which limited access to a very select few. "Just uttering the word FIREWALL around the wrong people opens you up to some very uncomfortable questioning."

Not to mention putting you on a half-dozen watch lists, Abbot thought. He'd known as much, but didn't have the authority to read anyone else into the project. It had been more useful to let Winston assume that risk on his own; if nothing else it told him exactly how deep the young man's connections went. "That does present a problem. It's not an uncommon term, after all. I'm surprised the spymasters at Langley weren't more creative."

"Sometimes hiding in plain sight is the best tactic," Winston observed, "because if everything I've learned is true…"

Abbot held up a hand to cut him off. "It is," he said. "I had to give up three Skycrane landers that were already booked for the next round of Mars rovers."

"So that's why those programs were cancelled?"

"Funding was diverted to Fire—," he caught himself, "this project, which they wouldn't even read me in on until the Pentagon decided they'd need people up there to service it."

"They do take security rather seriously," Winston said. "Do you believe it's warranted?"

The kid hadn't learned everything, otherwise he'd have known how ludicrous that question was in the first place. Abbot folded his hands atop his gut and nodded somberly. "Absolutely."

• • •

Gateway Station

The complex was empty, its critical systems now remotely controlled from within the Orion crew module barely a kilometer away. Docked to its companion Altair lander, the two vehicles' family resemblance to their Apollo forebears was obvious. Though much larger, able to hold twice as many people, Orion's gumdrop shape remained quite similar. And whereas the original lunar module might have resembled some kind of metallic origami insect, its next-generation cousin looked more like a water tank atop a flying drill platform.

Varza would have preferred they stay inside. He'd reluctantly accepted DeCarlo's judgment that the amount of energy they were about to redirect presented a real danger of turning anyone left aboard into a microwave dinner. The reflectors couldn't handle all of the energy they were about to beam to it, not over such an extended period. The waste would be regrettable but necessary.

Removing the station's secondary weapons had threatened to wreck their timetable. But now that a half-dozen W87 nuclear warheads with kick stages and guidance packages were safely nestled inside Orion's equipment bay, he felt much better about their situation. They would be useful bargaining chips when the time came.

Varza made a final check of the station-keeping settings in the spacecraft's flight computers. Satisfied it would keep them at a safe distance, he locked down the instrument panel and pushed away, floating across the module to hover over DeCarlo's shoulder.

DeCarlo, typically picky about his personal space, remained oblivious to Varza's presence. He was immersed in his own work on a backup system which exactly duplicated the primary mirror controls aboard Gateway. His fixation at least gave Varza time to check his work without hectoring the peevish physicist.

"Joseph?" He waited patiently for a response.

Perhaps a bit more pointedly this time. "Doctor."

"Yes, Kam." Apparently he was waiting for a formal greeting. Interesting how he never saw fit to return the honor. "What can I do for you?" His voice was tinged with impatience.

"Time continues its march, and our opportunities grow limited," Varza said patiently, with a nod to a countdown clock on the center panel. It was maddeningly difficult to make him understand how mercilessly time ruled their work. "Is everything to your satisfaction?" Markedly different from simply being *ready*, it was a choice of words assured to elicit a thorough reply.

"Marginal," he answered. "I need more time to calibrate the primary mirror. I estimate retransmission loss at ten to the minus six."

"Which is well within tolerance," Varza reminded him. DeCarlo was obsessed with wringing every last milliwatt out of the system, whereas Varza was far more concerned with accuracy. "What of the targeting controls?"

"Perfect, actually." He actually smirked with that comment. "A model of simplicity for the end user. Omar designated the target two hours ago and it's tracking well within the margin of error. I've confirmed the solution myself."

As the entire system had been adapted from an airborne laser weapon, it of course had been kept dirt simple. No doubt it was intended for use by some halfwit raised on video games, who put on a uniform and did his job mindlessly at the behest of his superiors. Such was the way of war, Varza realized sadly. For now.

22

SS Grissom
Flight Day Six

"Got it," Audrey said. "One o'clock, twenty clicks." She looked up from the docking monitor, expecting to see the same old unnerving view ahead. Instead it was considerably worse: the windows were filled with varying shades of gray sweeping past. Were they actually pointed straight down at the Moon now? "Will you be able to find them against all that?" she asked, hoping it disguised her anxiety. The emptiness and stark clarity really screwed up her depth perception.

"I think we already did." Penny pointed at what looked like a piece of reflective foil outside. Audrey lifted a pair of binoculars and saw it was *Shepard*'s tattered hull, right where they expected it to be. She was happy to not be the one suiting up to climb inside it.

. . .

Simon reached for the drinking tube and rolled up the hydration bladder attached to it one more time. *Just a little more,* he thought. *Squeeze out that last drop.* He was rewarded with a shimmering glob of water that floated out of the nozzle directly in front of him. He gingerly brought his mouth up to the undulating sphere and swished it around, coating his mouth in the precious moisture before swallowing it.

He checked the date on his watch: eight days since everything went to hell and he was pretty damned proud of himself to have made it this far, thank you very much. The remains of his ship had been slowly tumbling for some time now, the automated stabilizers having failed days before. Probably a reaction wheel in the guidance section…couldn't very well be anything else since that's all that was left, he told himself. Outside, black sky steadily gave way to the white glare of the lunar surface. It was still a hell of a view, despite the utterly hopeless situation Simon found himself in. What was the point anymore of distracting himself with idle sight-seeing? And yet…

And yet. Maybe there'd be some new feature he hadn't noticed before, though by now he had every knoll and pockmark permanently committed to memory. *Permanent…yeah, you're about to become a permanent fixture yourself, pal.*

He finally resolved that he at least wouldn't spend his final hours bored out of his skull, and pulled himself over to the porthole with resignation. He was shocked when the airlock was suddenly plunged back into darkness, as if it had just slipped behind the moon again. What came next was even more startling.

• • •

Shepard's remains hovered just ahead, lifeless as a shipwreck and holding just as many secrets. As they slid into position, the derelict moonliner fell into shadow as *Grissom*'s bulk eclipsed the sun. The sight gave Penny a shiver. "Looks bigger when it's falling to pieces," she said to herself, wary of so much debris in close. She switched on the exterior floodlights. "We're stable," she announced over the intercom. "EVA crew, we're waiting on your signal."

"Roger that," Ryan's voice crackled in her headset. "Five minutes."

Simon was now fully convinced he was hallucinating and therefore almost dead. Another ship, identical to his own, filled the window and its floods bathed his little compartment in brilliant light. A thud coursed up the length of the tunnel, jostling him inside the airlock, as it docked with the opposite end.

More lights now danced inside the tunnel, which he finally saw to be the helmet lamps of two spacewalkers as they drifted towards him.

The leader looked for all the world like a real life GI Joe toy. His dark spacesuit very nearly disappeared in the background, which had to be on purpose. As the mystery astronaut came closer, he could make out white block lettering stenciled on his chest: QUINN / USMC, just above the Corps' ubiquitous eagle, globe and anchor insignia.

Jarheads in space. If I'm dead, this must be Hell. Already wobbly from exhaustion, he couldn't help but laugh. The next face to appear in his window made him downright giddy.

...

"I think we found your man."

Ryan flew over to the porthole and brought his faceplate level with the window. "Simon!" he exclaimed as if they could hear each other, and knocked on the glass before giving a thumbs up and lifting his sunshade to reveal a toothy grin. Inside, Simon returned the gesture weakly. *Hunter*, he mouthed silently.

"That's the ship's captain." Ryan pressed against the glass again, straining to see farther inside the airlock. "He's the only one I see."

Simon must have known what he was thinking, as he held up one finger then pointed to himself. "He appears to be it," Quinn said, "not that there's room for anyone else." He didn't mention that their lone castaway looked like he didn't have much left in him: pallid skin, sunken eyes...markers of severe dehydration and malnourishment.

Ryan moved quickly. He pounded the glass once, gave Simon another thumbs-up, and flew back down the tunnel. Lights came on as he drew power from their flight module and began to bring the tunnel back up to pressure. The hatch release lever began moving and a gasp of air escaped as it cracked open.

...

Penny smacked the quick-release buckle on her chest and swam free of the harness that had kept her safely in the command pilot's seat. She pushed away to fly down into the docking node. "Come on," she chanted impatiently, staring at the idiot light that would tell her when the compartments had equalized. When it turned green, she hurriedly twisted the lock and flung the hatch open. "Simon!" she called, and flew up *Shepard*'s tunnel.

"You don't have to yell," he said tiredly. "I'm right here."

Penny laughed and caught him midair in a bear hug, then pulled back and wrinkled her nose. It smelled like a stale locker room in here. "You reek. I've got old underwear that smells better than you."

"Always the refined lady. I'd have cleaned up if I'd known the boss was coming." Simon's tired face beamed as he looked past her. "So that was Hunter I saw up there? You get around."

"In the flesh." Ryan was still in his EVA suit, now sans helmet. "I think this makes us even," he said, tossing a full bulb of ice water down the tunnel.

Simon caught the bottle in midair and greedily sucked it dry. "Not even close," he said between gulps. "You'll recall I did have to find a new job after saving your ass."

"Which almost got shot off on the way up here," Ryan said as he gripped him by the shoulders. "Damn, it's good to see you. Been a strange week."

Simon did a double-take when the next person drifted in. Audrey was beaming. "He's not kidding. We've got a lot of catching up to do."

• • •

"So I wasn't seeing things?" Simon asked, only half-joking. "Somebody finally decided to let the Corps play Buck Rogers?" The casualty rate for combat spacediving had to be grotesque. He wondered what stories were behind the prominent scar on Quinn's forehead. Sea stories would have to come later. "So you guys are up here to catch the bastards who hijacked my boat?"

"'Catch' may not be the right way to think of it," Quinn said before explaining the situation at Gateway. "I'll be real honest, Mr. Poole: we weren't sure about Colonel Stratton's insistence on finding you first. We're hoping the intel you might provide will be valuable enough to balance the risk."

Simon's face twisted in confusion. "Colonel?"

"Lieutenant Colonel," Ryan clarified. "She's not *that* big a deal..."

"Long story," Penny sighed. "Don't worry, I'm not going anywhere."

Quinn cleared his throat. "Sir, we need to know everything that you saw," he said.

"I was hoping you guys could fill me in, not the other way around." Simon closed his eyes and groaned at having to relive this for them. "I know they're nothing like what they seemed. Varza set us up like bowling pins. All of that survey gear on their manifest?" he scoffed. "It's not hard to make a magnetic driver into a gauss gun."

"So that's how they blew the hab?" Penny asked.

"Couldn't tell at first," he said. "Things went all to hell right after we started our LOI burn. There was a pretty loud bang from in back, so I went to investigate."

...

"Mister Brandt! Report!" He was answered by a whistle of escaping air in the distance and the blaring of alarms overhead.

"Bill!" he shouted as he clambered out of the central passage and into the open crew deck. "Report!"

With one hand firmly clasped around a handrail Simon twisted about, searching for any damage or injured passengers. He was surprised by an undulating sphere of strawberry jam slowly fall past, pulled by the thrust gravity from their still-burning engines. A few droplets trailed behind, their crimson hue and faint coppery smell signaling that this wasn't a spill from the galley. He instinctively pushed off from where the blood trail appeared to come: their sleeping compartments.

"Captain!" someone shouted at his back. It was a passenger, still down in mid deck berthing. "What's happening? Are we in trouble?"

What was your first clue? *Simon thought as the pressurization alarm continued to wail. "I don't know yet," he barked, perhaps too firmly though he didn't much care about civility at this point. "Evac procedures, just like you practiced! Everyone into the tunnel right now!"*

There was a bustle of activity behind him as the others emerged from their closet-sized cabins. He was surprised at how calm and orderly they were; he'd expected panic. Though right now he was more concerned about finding his first officer and isolating whatever had ruptured. He climbed back up to the crew berths.

There was another flurry of motion from down-ship as the passengers scrambled through the docking node and into the flight module. Simon paused and counted as each man passed, not going any farther until he was satisfied all of them had made it into the safe zone.

The air currents were getting stronger as he drew closer to the source. He clambered into the crew deck and turned upwind. It was really howling now, which meant that the hab would soon be bottoming out: there wouldn't be enough pressure to keep the structure inflated or the air breathable.

He passed his own quarters and made it to his FO's. "Bill!" He yanked at the sliding door. It was locked, a privacy feature typically left unused thanks to an informal agreement between crewmates.

The wind was especially strong here. The doorway was whistling: the breach was in Bill's compartment. Simon unfolded his multi-tool, jammed its needle-nose pliers through the thin plastic panel, and began twisting at the lock. They were still burning, so there was still a sizeable fraction of gravity to hold him in place. Thank goodness, as he wasn't sure how this would work in zero-g with nothing to brace against. The door finally gave way in a rush of air.

Each crew berth wasn't much bigger than a small walk-in closet. One wall held a couple of lockers for personal gear and a tablet linked to the ship's network, on the opposite wall was a sleeping bag. Bill hung inside it like a rag doll, lifeless and cold with an ugly quarter-inch cavity in his temple. The far wall, normally dominated by a porthole, was now covered in his blood. It rippled and swirled along the polycarbonate, streaming through a hole in the glass and into the void.

It was then that Simon noticed a telltale ripple course across the side-wall. The hab was collapsing.

He recoiled in horror and stumbled back into the door just as the engines stopped burning. Back in null gravity, Simon grasped for the door-frame and pulled himself out into the gangway. He pushed off for the stores lockers, bounding his way around the circular corridor.

Already open, the lockers appeared to have been thoroughly rummaged through. A sinking feeling settled in his gut as he twisted around to where the emergency kits should be waiting, right by the door.

Of course they weren't there. Bare strips of Velcro remained where the supplies should have been, including the hi-tech caulk gun that constituted their emergency repair kit. Besides the immediate threat, that didn't make any sense. Bill was the only crewmember in here, so who would've grabbed the patch gun?

The thought hit him like a hammer blow. With no time for anything but reaction, until now he'd assumed a freak accident: some bolide had zipped out of nowhere, through a porthole and into one of his crewmates.

The exit wound was pointed toward the window, not away from it as if something had come from outside. No, this had come from inside.

Inside.

Whoever removed the patch kits was the same sonofabitch who put the hole in Bill's window. In his head.

A quaking groan surrounded him as the outer skin, four-inch thick layers of ballistic synthetics that separated them from hard vacuum, began to flex. Simon knew instinctively the supporting pressure had passed its point of no return: the air was thinning rapidly and he'd soon succumb to hypoxia.

He placed his feet against the sidewall and pushed off for the tunnel, flying through the hatch and bouncing off its curved inner wall, pushing off again to fly towards the airlock at the other end. As the air grew thinner, a single thought crowded out all others:

Keep breathing.

23

SS Grissom
Flight Day Seven

Audrey relaxed and let gravity wash over her as they burned out of lunar orbit for EML-2, leaving the derelict *Shepard* behind. Zero g had left her with clogged sinuses for the better part of a week, even a few minutes of not feeling like she had a perpetual head cold was wonderful.

Until now she had been able to avoid thinking about what might await them on the other side of the Moon. Though she didn't have any military background, it was obvious that hijacking was just a tactic – what was their goal? This wasn't like some run-of-the mill nutball taking an airliner to Cuba. If they wanted to commandeer a spacecraft and use it as some kind of kinetic-energy weapon on an earthbound target, weren't there better ways to go about doing that?

She'd known from the beginning that couldn't be it. Spacecraft were ridiculously fragile once they hit the atmosphere at orbital speeds. If their goal was mass destruction they would've have had an easier time just stealing an old Pakistani nuke.

So of course they were after Gateway and its weapons platform, which made only slightly more sense. *It's on the far side of the freaking Moon.* What could they possibly use it against? Taking out a couple of spysats seemed like an awfully minor goal from all the way out here.

So the Pentagon – scratch that, the President and her entire cabinet felt it important enough to cobble together an insanely high powered laser weapon that was permanently hidden from view? Notwithstanding the flagrant treaty violations, what exactly was it targeting if the only place it could aim was at empty space? The UFO conspiracy kooks would wet their pants if they ever found out.

Empty space. "Empty" wasn't entirely accurate, now was it? There were lots of odd things out here, all of them moving pretty fast. They might seem few and far between to us puny humans, but on a cosmic scale the solar system could be an awfully crowded place. There was the random space junk like old boosters and dead satellites. Micrometeorites were a constant hazard in orbit, but asteroids and comets tended to draw more popular attention...

Comets.

Her eyes snapped open with a start. The shoulder harness dug into her neck as she strained for the small window by her seat.

"Everything all right?" Penny asked sharply. She instinctively did a quick instrument scan, reacting to Audrey's sudden flinch. "Something I need to know?"

"No," she said. There was nothing to see from this angle, being pointed nose-first away from the moon. It should come into view as they slipped around.

Ryan watched her with concern from the corner of an eye. "You okay, Aud?"

"Fine." They continued in silence but for the main engines' steady rumble. She stared into the depths, marveling at how small and remote Earth seemed from here. God or whoever – she still had trouble getting her head around the idea – had placed humanity's only home right smack in the sweet spot of the Sun's habitable zone, protected by a nice sized moon and gigantic outer planets to divert any wayward leftovers of creation away from their little blue ball. For the most part it was an arrangement that had worked out nicely over the millennia of human history.

On the other hand, it hadn't worked out so well for the dinosaurs.

Lots of odd things, and they all move pretty fast...

Ryan interrupted her train of thought. "MECO."

She'd daydreamed her way right through main engine cutoff. Audrey looked down to find herself floating again. She unbuckled and pushed off to land between the pilots, checking her bearings against the attitude ball. "Can we turn? Forty degrees starboard yaw...pitch minus ten."

Ryan and Penny exchanged a quick look, wondering where she was going. He shrugged his shoulders and tapped the joystick to slew the nose right. The Moon's limb slipped back into view. Beyond it hung a bright white smudge in the sky, its glow washing out the background stars.

"Have a good look," she said, pointing at Comet Weatherby. "Because that's why we're here."

• • •

Denver

Charlie Grant, for his part, had not wasted much time ruminating on the purpose behind Gateway. Between managing the fleet, keeping up with *Grissom* and their daily struggle to maintain contact with *Shepard*, it was all he could do to remember to sleep at night. And so it was that the encrypted text message from Audrey took some time to digest.

It was a string of alphanumeric code, starting with a time stamp and followed by another set of numbers labeled "RA" and "DEC": Right Ascension and Declination, the precise coordinates in the sky for some unnamed object at a specific time. After that came a string of what looked to be orbital elements, but nothing like the two-liners he'd seen so many times for artificial satellites. This was a very long-period orbit, heliocentric or maybe even hyperbolic. It described something passing through the solar system and grazing the sun. Something like a comet.

That new one, Weatherby, was supposed to put on a real show next month. Now why would Aud feel the need to dig up that information, much less send it here? It's not like they weren't busy up there – which meant she'd had a pretty good reason.

Grant stretched out the kinks in his back and began rooting around beneath the chart table for a celestial almanac and star atlas. He could've looked up the same information on his computer, but doing things the hard way served to clear the mental cobwebs. It took a few minutes to pinpoint the location, which he checked against some recent information about Weatherby on his tablet.

Sure enough, that was it. So what? That was when he noticed Kruger looming over his shoulder.

"Something I can help you with?" the agent asked.

Grant eyed him suspiciously as he reached for a phone and punched in Hammond's office. "That'd be a nice change."

• • •

"I can neither confirm nor deny your hypothesis," Kruger said with stiff decorum. His body language alone told them Audrey had nailed it.

"I think we need to dismiss with the charade," Hammond said, and made a sweeping gesture around his office. "Take a look. We are the only ones here, and we're not talking. Somebody already has ears inside your operation, otherwise Hunter and Stratton wouldn't still be prying seat cushions out of their asses from dodging those SAMs back at the Cape."

Kruger's face remained a blank slate. Perhaps that was a desirable trait in a counter-intel operative, but right now it was just pissing Hammond off.

"My boss means 'let's cut the crap,'" Grant said, moving to stand next to him. "You've already told us what's up there, so figuring out what it's for isn't too much of a stretch. This ain't rocket science."

"Puns aside, it's even bigger than you think," Kruger said. He pointed to the computer-animated map of *Grissom*'s path on Hammond's wall. "They may well be a quarter-million miles away, but you can obviously still communicate."

"Who do you think they're going to tell?" Hammond argued. "The encryption gear you people installed has scrambled everything between here and L2. Do you have any idea what a pain in the ass that is for us?" Encrypted radios added another layer of attenuation to what were already fussy signals. "Besides, I can guarantee you Audrey figured it out all by herself. She didn't need any help from us."

"And you'd know that how?"

"Because it doesn't take much for her put things together once she has time to sit and think it through. That's a luxury we haven't had of late."

"He's right," Grant said. "I put more faith in her guesses than I do most other people's facts."

"Why we need to take back Gateway shouldn't matter," Kruger argued, "it is U.S. government property, after all."

Hammond wasn't letting up. "If this were a salvage mission, we might agree. But you guys made clear it wasn't, so I think more background is in order. You don't even have to say anything. Charlie will do the talking."

"My job tends to get complicated, Mister Kruger, so I like it when things fit into nice little mental boxes. And for the life of me I couldn't figure out why anyone would be in such a hurry to put a directed-energy weapon out where it couldn't be used on any useful targets. I ruled out the whole alien invasion angle pretty quickly."

"Glad to hear that," he said. "I'm certain your boss doesn't want anyone that nuts working here."

Grant ignored him. "But without little green men or invading Klingons, that didn't leave much. So what else might cause somebody to park a megawatt blaster out there?" he asked, then swept at Hammond's wall monitor to bring Weatherby dead center in the map. Kruger looked unmoved, as if his façade could deflect the truth.

"Crafty arrangement," Hammond conceded. "Controlling it from L2 makes good sense. The location hides it from prying eyes, but gives you almost unlimited visibility of anything approaching off plane." Weatherby was making its closest pass to Earth from well south of the ecliptic, the plane upon which all of the major planets orbited the Sun. "Are there any other complexes out there?"

"I can neither confirm—"

"Nor deny, yada yada, I get it." Hammond went to the heart of Audrey's theory. "So it's being used to flash the comet's nucleus, isn't it? You guys have been creating those gas plumes to shift its orbit."

Grant whistled. "You have to admit that is pretty slick. Anybody paying attention thinks it's a naturally occurring phenomenon. Heat the nucleus enough to create a gas vent and gradually change its orbit. If you can do it early enough, it doesn't take a lot of energy."

"So they created a natural thruster out of the existing material," Hammond concluded.

"And if that were correct, which is not to imply that it *is*," Kruger backtracked, "what are you going to do about it?"

"Keep it the hell quiet," Hammond said to Kruger's evident relief. "Close as that comet's going to pass, I'm assuming they didn't go to all this trouble just to prove a concept." He had avoided following Audrey's theory to its logical conclusion. "It's going to hit Earth, isn't it?"

"If Varza's gang keeps control of Gateway? Yes."

24

Farside

Tsiolkovskiy crater is perhaps the most identifiable feature of the lunar far side. Named for the man whose foundational rocket equation had made the trip possible, it was first discovered by a Russian probe during the Cold War moon race. One hundred and eighty kilometers across, the crater's floor is a smooth bed of solidified lava made all the more prominent by the far side's otherwise jagged surface. Except for crater's central peak, thought to rise as high as 3,000 meters, it is considered one of the few hospitable landing sites on the entire pockmarked hemisphere. It was this combination of stability, ease of access, and natural camouflage that made it the perfect site for a high-energy laser.

What the Air Force had nicknamed "Fire Base Farside" had been delivered over three separate missions by autonomous landers hastily repurposed from delivering future Mars rovers. The final landing brought a small crew of military astronauts to assemble the system. The first two components, a compact nuclear reactor and the particle accelerator it would power, both remained atop their landing stages. The assembly team had only to connect the power and attach the optical turret to its mount on the accelerator before calibrating the system.

The turret itself was lifted from a mothballed YAL-2 airborne laser mounted in the nose of an Air Force 747. Together, the entire system could deliver nearly a full gigawatt of focused energy up to Gateway Station. Its beams had never pulsed for more than two or three seconds at a time, and never at full power. Anything more would have overwhelmed Gateway's targeting mirrors and its electronics while cooking its occupants with infrared energy.

Until now, it hadn't been asked to operate at its full potential, as no one in control had any desire to undo a years' worth of carefully targeted lasing of Comet Weatherby.

Until now.

...

SS Grissom
Flight Day Eight

Quinn took Audrey by the elbow, her reflex to pull back tempered by the warmth in his gesture. "Could we go somewhere private?"

"Excuse me?"

"Secure," he said seriously. "Where nobody's listening."

"Sure," she said warily, looking around the open mid deck. "We could use the tunnel, I guess." She led him down through an open hatch and pulled it closed behind them. "We'd planned on this being the smoking area," she joked.

Quinn smiled. "Figures. You're from Colorado, right? Where they legalize pot but damn near criminalize cigarettes. Hell of a place."

"Not your cup of tea, then?"

"Hardly," he said. "I'm from Montana. Despite what you must hear from the hippies down there, we're a little more civilized."

"Actually I'd believe that," she said. "I'm originally a 'Bama girl. But you didn't pull me out here to socialize, did you?" She hoped that didn't make her sound disappointed.

"Suppose not," he conceded. "You're the kind of person who asks all the right questions. You deserve some answers."

Audrey was whipsawed between excitement and dread as he confirmed everything she'd deduced about Weatherby and Gateway's purpose. Her mind raced to visualize the comet's relative position, possible trajectories, impact zones...The event that astronomers agreed would eventually happen had in truth been just months away, barring human intervention. How close had they actually come to extinction? She unconsciously began chewing a thumbnail, her mind drifting into unpleasant directions.

"You okay?"

"This puts us in an impossible position," she said. "You can't expect us to keep this secret. Weatherby's one of those comet-of-the-century events. The amateur astronomers are all over this. They're posting observational data on the Web in real time. And all those doctoral candidates out there competing for attention? How'd they all keep quiet?"

"Because the higher-ups made it look benign. You're right, a bunch of scientists scattered all over the world would never be able to keep a lid on this. We got lucky in that they didn't *have* to. The guy it's named for wasn't the first one to see it. We just let him take the credit."

"We?" she asked.

"Sorry...by 'we' I mean the government. I like to believe that occasionally we're still all on the same team," he said, self-conscious in his idealism. "Yes, we got lucky. It was a rogue object out of the southern sky. The first observations were actually made from the South Pole."

"That would certainly make it easier to keep quiet."

"The guy wasn't even looking for it. But when the same glitch showed up repeatedly over a bunch of different images, it wasn't hard for him to figure out what he'd found."

"That tends to happen when you're looking for something else. So it was just one guy?"

"He was wintered over at Amundsen-Scott about three years ago," Quinn explained, "the only astronomer left on station. It bothered him enough to drop whatever he was doing to track the thing full time. Not much else to do down there in the winter except work math problems, I reckon."

Her eyes widened. "*Three years*? They've known about it that long?"

"He was literally the only man on Earth looking at that piece of sky long enough. The big shots kept it quiet until they could decide what to do."

"Averting a worldwide panic?"

"Secrecy has its purpose," Quinn said. "Sometimes society is better off not knowing the whole truth. I don't always like it, but it works."

That was when Audrey realized he'd already figured out what she'd transmitted to Charlie, and this little chat was about putting everything into context for her. She studied him approvingly. "That's not a sentiment I'd expect from someone like, well..."

"Like me? Just doing my job," he said with a playful *aw-shucks* smile. "I'm a dumb cowboy at heart. What you see is what you get."

She was finding him to be a good deal more complicated than that.

...

Farside

A casual observer would have been disappointed. Instead of unleashing a thunderbolt of brilliant light, Farside's laser was silent and invisible, there being no atmosphere to either transmit sound or reflect light.

Though had anyone been left aboard Gateway, it might well have been the last thing they saw. When nearly one million watts of focused energy hit the directional mirrors, they could only absorb so much. The rest was transmitted as heat throughout the complex. Designed to tolerate temperature swings of a few hundred degrees – a normal space environment – the station's thermal insulation was overwhelmed by several thousand degrees of "spillover" energy. Outside, fragile Mylar blankets began to wrinkle around the base of the complex, nearest the targeting mirrors. Inside, plastic surfaces began to bubble and the air became filled with smoke, triggering the automated fire suppression system. It would eventually shut the complex down and begin venting its atmosphere into space, working on the assumption that conditions had become so bad that its human occupants had either abandoned ship or were already dead.

Such a disaster would eventually render the targeting controls useless, which wouldn't matter for the few seconds Varza needed it to function. By the time shutdown protocols had engaged, their beam had already been focused on its target.

Three hundred thousand kilometers distant, Comet Weatherby began to vent a dazzling plume of vapor, bigger than anything seen before. And though not rivaling its tail in brilliance, the sudden appearance of a powerful new geyser spouting from "Old Faithful" was sure to excite astronomers around the world.

They would quickly find this venting was different – whereas the earlier phenomena had been short, regular fountains of gas, this was a tremendously long burst from the opposite side of the nucleus. Until now, it had been utterly quiet.

Even after Farside's laser had done its job, the geyser continued just as Varza and DeCarlo had predicted. The beam had imparted a staggering amount of heat onto a relatively small area, which would take time to cool down. This heat had also liberated a considerable volume of gases that had until recently been frozen deep within the comet's nucleus. Their venting continued apace, creating a natural thruster that subtly began shifting the comet's orbit back to where Nature had intended it to be. Humanity would finally have to deal with the consequences as Earth rebalanced herself.

What no one could see, even from *Orion*'s telescopic camera, were the fissures that appeared around the molten hole they'd just bored into Weatherby. As more avenues appeared for escaping vapor, the more cracks spread as new ruptures appeared. The reaction was not unlike asphalt fracturing in a winter thaw.

With a final burst of venting gas, a particularly large crevasse raced down a ridge along Weatherby's surface until there was no more surface to split. The bulbous nucleus, invisible beneath the coma, shattered in two. The outcropping nearest to this new artificial geyser was flung loose, a half-kilometer slice of cometary debris slowly moving into its own orbit.

25

SS Grissom
Flight Day Ten

Even from ten kilometers away, Gateway sparkled like a jeweled ornament against the black. Ryan thought it faintly angelic, like something he'd have used to top their Christmas tree. Its layers of reflective shielding were wrapped like a skirt around the propellant tanks, attached to a hub of polished metal cylinders topped with wings of radiators and solar panels. They were directly behind the massive propellant tanks and their insulating umbrella.

Ryan couldn't believe they'd been able to do something so audacious in such secrecy. Hardly anyone heard about the good things done in the name of national security, only the screw-ups or outright betrayals. It was counterintuitive, which was how the spooks preferred it. Let the rest of the world think America couldn't get out of its own way; it becomes that much easier to read the bad guy's mail.

"Phase burn coming up," Penny said. They were entering a halo orbit, tracing an ellipse around an empty point in space where the gravity of Earth and Moon cancelled each other out.

"I just hope they didn't spot us during the approach."

"I think we're okay," Quinn said, gripping a handhold in the ceiling and peering at their target. "We're looking right up their skirt. That thing only has a couple of windows and no sensor suite except for the docking radar and laser ranging. If they spotted us, we'd have known it by now."

"You mean they'd have turned that laser on us by now," Ryan said in a cold statement of fact that belied enormous dread. Though it grew more remote with each passing minute, there was always the possibility of an invisible beam of focused energy carving a hole in their pressure hull or blasting open a tank of liquid methane. And they wouldn't know it until the depressurization alarm sounded or a fuel tank exploded.

"It's what I'd have done. Use what you've got."

"I was thinking the same thing. Makes my skin crawl," Penny said. She turned to Quinn. "Tell your boarding team to stand by."

...

"We ought to be real pros after this, Breed. Maybe Colonel Stratton can get you a gig with NASA."

"Why the hell would I want to do that?" Breedlow asked, tugging at the locking rings around his EVA gloves. "Let them stick me on the space station for a year just so I can go out and fix coolant leaks or replace a busted antenna? No thanks."

"Reckon you're right," Goode said laconically. "This is about to beat that all to hell, ain't it?"

"Depends. At least on the Station there's nobody waiting to booby-trap us." He clicked on the team frequency. "Raiders, confirm HUDs are up." Breedlow's own faceplate dimmed while he checked over his men; ghostly projections of his suit's vitals floated at the corner of his vision. "Weapons check."

Goode, Voss, and Haggerty cleared the action and magazine wells of their M55 before shouldering the weapons, each carefully placing gloved fingers alongside the grip and not on the chunky trigger paddle. When they depressed the oversized safeties, a red target reticle appeared in each man's faceplate, moving with the weapon as they shifted aim. "Weapons safe...good sights."

Breedlow repeated the same check for himself, then gave each man's helmet a final swat. "Raider Six, Raider One-Five. We're go for EVA."

Quinn's voice answered. "Raiders, this is Six. Colonel Stratton says get the hell out of her airlock."

Breedlow smiled and saw the same reaction from the others. "We'll try not to leave too much of a mess. Egressing now." With that, he snapped the butt of his carbine into a harness by his shoulder and pushed the outer door open. After fastening his safety tether to an outside trunnion he cleared the hatch, waving them on.

Goode's head and shoulders emerged first, his hands firmly on the hatch rim. Breedlow watched as he slowly turned around to take in the full view. "Damn. We really are out there."

Being some thirty thousand miles beyond the Moon's orbit, the view from L2 showed them the full expanse of the inner solar system. The entire Moon was visible, as was Earth beyond. The Sun's glare was almost painful but he could make out the shining disc of Venus at western elongation. What looked like the rusty pinprick of Mars was far off in the other direction. With no atmosphere to bend the light, nothing twinkled. As he finished turning, a ghostly light came into view: Comet Weatherby, an unwelcome and malevolent visitor in their tidy little cosmic neighborhood.

Breedlow shook his head to clear the cobwebs. *Focus. One threat at a time.* "Make sure you're tethered before checking your jets. Radio silence from here."

Each man waved to signal he'd heard the command, then tugged at his harness before pulsing his maneuvering pack. Clouds of compressed gas burst from around their shoulders as they spun about.

Gateway loomed barely 100 meters ahead, dominated by the enormous reflective skirt shielded its tanks of methane and oxygen. A floating gas station, attached to a comparatively puny cluster of metal cylinders. Unless there were surveillance cameras mounted somewhere on the skirt, there was no way anyone aboard could have identified them.

He surveyed the skirt's rim and found nothing resembling optics pointed in their direction. Clearly, DARPA or NASA or whatever other alphabet agency that claimed responsibility for this place hadn't figured on encountering hostiles. If they had, the assumption must have been that they could take care of themselves just fine with the weapons on hand.

Breedlow waved an arm forward in the "go" signal, and they unhooked the safety tethers to push off for the complex. With a few minor pulses from their thruster packs, they were aimed squarely at the skirt's rim. He flipped over and deftly landed feet first in the skirt's inner toehold bar, letting his knees absorb the momentum. *Stuck the landing – ten points.* If a man couldn't enjoy his work, then what was the point?

He waved his hand flat, signaling them to stay put, and grabbed the skirt's framework to pull level with the rim. He slowly poked his head over the side, halfway expecting to get it shot off for the trouble. Unlikely, but it was something he'd have done if he was the other guy.

Breedlow took a deep breath, satisfied his face wasn't about to be split open by a projectile or melted by some kind of damned death ray. He'd just as soon not be remembered as the first dumb SOB to get fragged by a laser weapon in deep space. Looking up towards the complex's main hub, he quickly got his bearings and recognized all the major features: hab module, service module, radiator panels, docking portals…

Aw hell.

…

Quinn flew past Ryan into the observation dome. "Say again, One Five?" That he'd broken silence this soon was not a sign things were going well.

"No joy, Six," Breedlow's voice answered. "Tell Polaris their ship is still docked, but the *Orion* and *Altair* are long gone. Lots of heat damage around the mirror farm and lower modules. Looks like they've bugged out."

He muttered a few choice obscenities. "Copy that," he grumbled, then asked the question on all of their minds. "Any reason for us to do the same? Those propellant tanks could create one hell of a bang."

"Negative, Gunny. We're already halfway up the sunshield and can't see any evidence of tampering. Still no line of sight from their windows."

"Understand."

"So there's several hundred tons of liquid propellant sitting right in front of us," Ryan said. "Big deal. We fly around with explodey stuff all the time. What about the missing vehicles?"

"Could be Gateway's crew escaped," Audrey suggested. "But then we'd have heard from them, right? Maybe Varza and Hassani killed them and used the capsules to dispose of the bodies."

"Not a bad theory," Quinn agreed, "but it's a lot easier to just toss them outside." He thought about it more and shook his head, factoring something else into his mental calculus. "No. The spacecraft are gone because *they're* gone." He swiped at his tablet and handed it to Penny, which displayed an after action report from the other TAC squad.

"Farside Base," she read. "So they generate the beam on the surface and use Gateway to redirect it." She skimmed the report before handing it to Ryan, her face a mask of anger. "This deal just keeps getting better."

Ryan scrolled down into the details. "At least they found out who was shooting at us."

"Venezuelan spy trawler, equipped with Russian SAMs, transferred via Caliphate operatives aboard an Iranian-flagged tanker. The 'Axis of Weasels,'" Quinn said. "More third world throwbacks playing with the big kid's toys."

Ryan scrolled farther down the report. "The ship's captain 'fessed up rather quickly."

"That'll happen when you're floating in open water with sharks nosing around. The skipper of that Coast Guard frigate wouldn't bring him aboard until he started talking. Too bad about his foot."

Ryan whistled and handed the tablet back to Penny. "Look at this – full motion cockpit sims and a mission control center."

"They also found a bunch of Russian eggheads hiding in a server room," Quinn explained. "Instructors, translators, network technicians... all of them became pretty agreeable once they figured out their protective detail wasn't coming."

Penny talked over her shoulder as she flew back to the pilot's station. "So they're like the 9/11 hijackers? Learn to operate the equipment just enough to turn them into weapons?"

"No," Audrey said. "Use them to turn other things into weapons."

...

The space-suited Marines floated along the insulation skirt to arrive at the station's central hub. "Glad that's done," Goode said, reattaching his tether to the first available bracket. "That's a hell of a long way."

"Helps if you don't look down," Breedlow said as he pulled himself to the nearest porthole.

"Ain't no up or down out here," Voss chimed in. "Focus on what's in front of you."

Breedlow planted his faceplate against the glass and peeked inside, halfway expecting to find another dehydrated astronaut just as they had with Poole.

It would have been preferable to what he saw. He snorted in disgust and lowered his head away from the window. Goode came up alongside to see for himself. "Damn," he whispered.

The window's interior glass was glazed over with a greasy smudge, as if it had been used for a cooking surface. What little they could see of the inside likewise appeared burned.

"Damn," Goode repeated, then a question: "Still going in, right?"

"You'd better believe it," Breedlow growled. "Let's move." He pushed away from the window and hand-walked down the cylinder to the docking hub, where two portals were still wide open. "Doesn't look like we'll have to make a forced entry. Good thing," he allowed. "I still wasn't too sure how we were gonna do that in no gravity."

"Now you tell me?" Goode pointed at a red warning light by the latch. "Vacuum inside."

Breedlow waved a hand at the inner door and pointed at the junior sergeant, signaling him to prepare for entry. He grasped the oversized latch with stiff, gloved fingers and rapped Goode's helmet. *Go.*

With a quick pulse from his backpack thrusters he flew inside, instinctively turning to check the corners for any unwelcome surprises. "Clear," he radioed, then bounded away toward the opposite portal. Breedlow flew in behind him as Voss and Haggerty took covering positions by the door.

The hatch flew open easily and he tumbled through the open portal. Goode hung from a foothold by the opening, using the rifle's viewfinder projection in his faceplate to sweep the room. The control cabin was wrecked: synthetics were warped and painted surfaces were bubbled and charred, like the whole compartment had become a big microwave oven. The body of one station occupant had been consumed, hanging lifeless in a sleeping bag along one wall.

"Fire bottles are empty," Goode said, looking at the damage control systems. "Looks like it was put out autonomously by dumping atmosphere…you think this guy was still alive?"

Breedlow looked over the scene with a scowl. "I don't." He floated over to the scorched panel and swatted away a jumble of melted wiring, then tapped at a screen embedded in his suit's left wrist. A layout of Gateway Station appeared and he zoomed in on its control module. "Thought so," he grumbled, poking at the charred console with the muzzle of his rifle. "This was the life-support control."

Goode removed his wire cutters and pried a blackened metal canister from the console's underside. It had burned much hotter than anything else. "Thermal fuse," he said. "The heat tripped some kind of thermite charge and torched the place. They made sure it couldn't be used again."

Breedlow pushed down beside him and examined the charred cylinder. "Chemical oxygen generator, part of their emergency gear. Light one off without the safeties and it'll burn like hell."

"Not sure I'd like having that inside a space station in the first place."

"Same thing they use in airliners," he said. "Those little Dixie cup masks? Hundreds of these things are sitting in the overheads."

"And I'm traveling by bus from now on," Goode said. "On the bright side, if there was a booby trap they've already sprung it," he said, pointing out the mess around them. "This place ain't worth a bucket of warm piss now."

Quinn's voice interrupted. "Is that a technical term, Sergeant?"

Breedlow answered for them. "Affirmative, Gunny." He spun about to survey the compartment once more. "Control and hab modules are secure. Moving to secondary objective now," he said, referring to the still-docked Polaris spacecraft.

This time Voss and Haggerty leapfrogged ahead to fly into the docking hub, wedging themselves into a corner to cover the remaining hatch before giving Breedlow a quick thumbs-up. He nodded and pushed off to land beside them. He held up his free hand and repeated the silent three-finger countdown, then smacked it against the bright red emergency release handle.

A cloud of vapor blew past as outflow valves opened, dumping the attached ship's remaining atmosphere instead of going through the longer process of recycling it into the station's tanks. The icy white snow quickly turned to crimson. He tore the hatch open and rolled back against the adjacent bulkhead. If there was going to be any resistance, this was where they'd find it.

Goode came forward and flipped on the spotlight beneath his carbine's barrel, sweeping the flight deck. "Damn. Two more, both KIA," the sergeant finished. "Clear."

"Clear," Breedlow repeated after sweeping the control deck with his own sights. He punched the voice-activated mic back on. "Six, this is Raider One Five. Primary and secondary objectives are secure. This place is a dry hole. You're safe to dock."

. . .

Orion

Hassani had been studying the comet through their stolen spacecraft's onboard telescope when the fragment appeared. A second comet had emerged: small but distinct, and according to the tracking program now moving along a tangent to its original orbit. That explained why the parent body's new track had confounded them: most of its energy had been expended in an unanticipated direction. "Gentlemen," Hassani said, "We may have a problem."

"And what might that be?" Varza asked impatiently, not happy for the distraction. He and DeCarlo were likewise scrambling to evaluate the change they'd imparted to Weatherby.

Hassani kept his eyes against the viewfinder as he spoke. There was no judicious way to say this. "The nucleus has separated in two."

"*What?*"

"Look for yourself," he said, and moved away from the scope.

Varza bounded across the cabin and pressed his face into the twin eyepieces. "What are you talking about?" he demanded, uncharacteristically agitated. Hassani watched in amused satisfaction as the arrogant fool's jaw fell open, searching for words. "What the…did you…did you reacquire the nucleus?"

"I have ranging on both," Hassani said calmly. "The new information should be waiting in your data folders."

Varza pulled away from the telescope and glared at DeCarlo, who held up a finger without looking. "Uploading it now," he said. "Yes, Kam," he sighed after a moment's study. "Omar is correct."

"I can see that!" Varza snapped. "It's right there in the blasted eyepiece. But what did it do to the trajectory?"

DeCarlo remained professionally detached, which only angered Varza more. "It appears that most of the kinetic energy was imparted on this fragment. Angular separation is already a half degree of arc."

"So what does that mean for us?" Varza asked. "The fragment's going to impact, not the nucleus?"

"Much too soon to know, but it would seem likely."

Varza was turning frantic. "Unacceptable!" he said. "Flatly unacceptable! We are shaking a hornet's nest, Joseph – you either burn it down or leave it alone. No half measures!"

DeCarlo was unmoved, still working through his new calculations. "'Doctor,' if you please," he said irritably.

Hassani thought Varza would strangle the man right then and there; he was now in a position to rein him in. "Gentlemen, this is neither the time nor the place. It is clear we must employ our contingency plan to control the laser directly from Farside. Barring that, we have further options," he said, hinting at the warheads in *Orion*'s equipment bay. "If our landing attempt does not work, I propose we exercise them."

. . .

Shepard's command deck was intact, something which could not be said for her remaining crew. The two pilots floated lifelessly in their seats, strapped in as if they'd just arrived on station. Both had been roasted from the inside out.

Every pilot harbored fears of hijacking. Unpredictable by nature, at any moment your airplane could be taken over by psychopaths with nothing to lose. In the old days, they'd been instructed to not resist. It was believed that peaceful compliance was the best way to save themselves and their passengers. But as soon as the bad guys had shown their willingness to turn airliners into manned cruise missiles, the equation had been forever changed. No one would entertain that delusion again.

That had happened long before Ryan had started his own flying career; he'd still been a rangy kid in the Virginia foothills. He remembered his mother's horror at the burning Pentagon: not too far away from their home in Roanoke, but to his young mind seeing it on TV meant it was on the other side of the world. A field trip to Arlington National Cemetery a few years later had disabused him of that notion.

His mind raced and his stomach churned. Here they were, as far away from home as humans had ever been, faced with the same ancient depravity.

"First time?"

Ryan shook himself out of his torpor. "Say again?"

Quinn moved between him and the dead pilots. "First time you've seen it up close. Shakes everybody up, Cap. I've seen some pretty sick shit before, but this is next-level sick."

"For what it's worth, they'd been dead a while," Goode, the intel sergeant, observed. "No signs of a struggle. Varza or whoever dumped atmo and exposed them to vacuum. And just left them here—"

"So is that all this is?" Ryan demanded, his simmering rage about to boil over. "More of their damned suicide pact excuse for a religion? Slaughtering people because they want to live in the dark ages?" *Maybe it was time we accommodated them.*

"Doesn't matter why," Quinn said. "Results are the same." He looked back at the dead pilots and shook his head sadly. "They grow up in a dysfunctional culture and are taught to look for someone to blame."

"Some think we put an end to that insanity years ago," Ryan scoffed. "I always had a feeling that was wishful thinking." With Iran on the brink of deploying nuclear weapons, the Jordanians and Saudis had formed an unlikely alliance with Israel to "neutralize" them. It was a sanitized euphemism for what had been a long, messy operation, rendering large swaths of Iran uninhabitable while opening the door for the marauding Islamic State movement to overwhelm the country. What was still nominally recognized as "Iran" was now the seat of a larger Caliphate that spread from Afghanistan to Syria and caused trouble far beyond.

"All we did was abandon the places that kept showing up in the news. We're constantly sending strike teams into cesspools you never hear about. It's global whack-a-mole."

"So where does that leave us?"

"Up here?" Quinn asked. "It leaves us holding one big empty bag. Down there," he said, pointing at the Moon, "they're holding all the cards. So we've got to figure out a new game."

Ryan understood what that meant, but it would be an enormous delta-v hit. "I think we can help."

"We were kind of counting on that."

• • •

Penny was skeptical to put it mildly. She stared down Ryan with an intensity he hadn't anticipated. "Are you out of your freaking mind?"

"Possibly," he said with a cautious glance at Quinn. "But Varza's happy little band of psychos definitely are. There's no doubt they're headed for the surface. Might already be there. They cooked Gateway, so now they have to finish the job directly."

"I have to agree," Audrey said reluctantly. "Weatherby's above the local horizon at Farside now, so they don't need to redirect the beam from up here. If they just wanted to blow town and head back to Earth, they'd have taken Orion and left Altair here."

"Or cast it loose along the way," Penny argued. "Throw us off their trail so we waste propellant on a dangerous landing attempt when we could be chasing them down. And did I mention *dangerous*? We haven't tested the platform yet."

"Begging your pardon, ma'am," Quinn interjected. His insistence on protocol would've upset her more if it hadn't been so damnably effective. "You're correct that we can't rule out a diversion, but I have to take Miss Wilkes' side here. That's a lot of trouble for not much benefit to them. Control of Farside is critical, and from down there it's harder for us to interfere." He jerked a thumb out the window at the Moon. "But before we go rolling in like the cavalry, how hard is that thing to fly? Is it even likely they were able to land?"

Penny twisted a strand of hair as she considered the question. Leave it to a grunt to point out something a pilot should've immediately recognized: *Would I want that thing floating out there unpiloted in my own maneuvering area – especially if I'm at the controls of an unfamiliar ship*?

The answer was no, and apparently Varza and Hassani had found a way to make themselves quite familiar with both vehicles. They had redundant controls for a very good reason – if you could fly one, you could fly both. Being here to service Farside, the maneuver targets and approach vectors would've been constantly updated by *Altair*'s flight computers.

If anything, their flight module's guidance was even better: *Snoopy I* and *II* had been designed from the outset to eventually be capable of landing on the Moon: it's why the skids along the lower hull were there in the first place. Maybe the brass really had thought this through when they commandeered them. But there was one other person who needed to weigh in: "Audrey?"

"You're looking at the better part of a day just for descent to your initial point, not to mention the delta-v budget," their tagalong flight director warned, "but Gateway's got all the propellant we need. If we can top off here, you'll have enough for a landing and ascent. Leave the hab and utility modules in a low enough orbit and the back end of that equation gets easier."

"We'd have to go light. Essential passengers only. That leaves you and Simon behind in the hab," Penny said. "I don't like that. No control, no propulsion. I suspect Simon will like the idea even less."

Audrey began to protest, but Ryan waved her down. "I've been thinking about the mass problem," he said. "It ain't pretty, but if we've got both flight modules up here we should use them." He paused to let the idea take root, with the knowledge that there'd be a dismal cleanup job first. "We dock Big Al's flight module to the opposite end of our hab, tank up both, and *phht*...off we go."

"I can give you a couple of men to handle the unpleasant work," Quinn offered, "if that presents a problem."

They looked to Audrey, who tapped her fingers along a handhold as her mental gears turned. "The whole system's modular for a reason. Common berthing ports, primary thrust structures along the same axis...it's a kludge but it'll work."

"What about the plumbing?" Penny asked. "How do we know Gateway has common fittings? None of this works if we can't top off tanks."

"Because they bought them from Hammond Aerospace," Audrey said. "It's one of those things we tested on the X-37 that I'm not supposed to talk about." She returned a knowing smile from Quinn.

"No wonder Art didn't want to waste time testing it ourselves," Penny sighed. "I'm starting to think he's psychic." She glared at their Marines. "Very well, gentlemen. I hope your suits came with dust covers."

26

SS Grissom
Flight Day Eleven

The ship had nearly doubled in size, now sporting identical flight modules at each end and looking for all the world like a flying rolling pin. It had taken most of the day to tank them up and assemble the new vehicle; they would make up the time with a more rapid descent, using the extra module's engines to brake them into a parking orbit thirty kilometers above the surface.

Audrey had immersed herself in tweaking every bit of wasted velocity out of their flight plan while Simon worked with Quinn's men at the grim task of making *Snoopy I* functional again. She tried not to think of what that must have entailed.

The last week had been a whirlwind, and the wholly unexpected opportunity to fulfill a life's dream – flying to the Moon – had overshadowed the truth of why she was here in the first place. Audrey now realized that was probably by choice. She was well aware of the risks, being the one Art counted on to pare them down to an acceptable level. She could accept threats from decompression, meteor strikes, solar flares...those were part of the environment and she understood exactly how to deal with them.

Manmade threats were another matter, and seeing Simon's frail condition after spending over a week on the brink of dehydration and oxygen starvation was only the first hint. The grisly scene Ryan had described inside Gateway was beyond her comprehension. She had intended to go aboard, but the burned-out control modules had left nothing of value. An empty logistics module and its docking port at the top of the stack were the only usable components left, and right now they represented nothing but extra mass.

Audrey cursed herself. Here she was, thinking like an engineer again. *No wonder everyone thinks we're antisocial.* An optimist sees the glass half full, a pessimist sees the glass half empty, and an engineer wonders why they made the glass so big. So how's that work with a burned out space station full of dead people?

It doesn't. Audrey realized what she was doing: burying herself in work to avoid the truth of what lay just a few meters down that tunnel. That it was absolutely necessary work and in fact the reason they'd wanted her up here made the excuse even more convenient. She could ignore the horror for now. She could even get used to the acrid smell as long as she didn't have to face the source.

No, there was too much to do and time was too short. She could grieve later. There was always later.

...

"Docking tunnel is purged. Comm check." Penny waited for Audrey to answer. Her eyes had been glued to the array of touchscreens around her seat and she reached up to push aside all but one. In her case, the primary guidance display was the only screen left in her line of sight, giving her an unobstructed view of the lunar surface. In contrast, Ryan would be acting as her flight engineer and had loaded up his screens with every bit of information available on their combined spacecraft.

Inside *Grissom*, Audrey's makeshift flight director's station was considerably more cluttered. She had networked every tablet and laptop she could find and strapped them to every square inch of open panel space. "Good comm, *Snoopy*. You are go for separation, initiate powered descent from T-minus ten on my mark. And...mark."

"Hack," Ryan said as he synchronized the onboard chronometers.

"Undock checklist complete." Penny twisted to face their passengers. "Faceplates down, gentlemen. I need positive checks of your O2 flows. Now would also be a good time to secure your butts and safe your weapons. I don't want any sharp objects or smelly asses floating around my spacecraft."

The men tugged at their harnesses and showed her cleared weapons as Quinn gave her a thumbs-up. With an interior about the size of a small RV, the normally spacious flight module had quickly become crowded once they'd loaded up the full team. As the docking clamps released with a thud and the outboard thrusters thumped to life, it felt almost suffocating.

That sense of isolation grew as they drifted away from their mothership. Penny stole one last glance behind her to look beyond the row of faceplates and into the men behind them. Their expressions were somber. Hard. They wore the looks of men who knew they were about to visit great violence upon their enemies.

...

Snoopy raced upside down and backwards above the Moon, with Penny's judicious pulses from the main engines pushing them into a lower orbit which would end at the surface.

"Altitude ten thousand, down at five." Ryan was fixed on a monitor that continually recalculated their descent profile. He ignored the pockmarked lunar surface sweeping past outside. "Pitchover's coming up."

"Got it." The heads-up display in Penny's window showed a ghostly green line, representing the track they needed to follow above the surface. Two glowing diamonds danced along its center, each responding to her gentle pulses from their directional thrusters. If she could get them to intersect at the right point, they'd land squarely on target. "HUD's telling me we need a twenty second burn. That look right to you?"

"Stand by," Ryan said, feverishly cross-checking another display while querying Audrey. "Yeah, Aud says those numbers are solid. Just follow the bouncing ball." There was a firm push at their backs as she slid the throttles forward. He counted down the seconds and she chopped throttles as he finished, immediately tapping the control stick forward to pitch them over.

The Moon disappeared above them to be momentarily replaced by stars wheeling across the black sky. As the lunar surface crept back into view, she tapped the stick again and stopped their rotation. Straight and level, they were steadily falling toward the lunar surface.

"Stable approach," Audrey reported. "Go for powered descent."

...

"Wake up, Gunny."

"Wasn't sleeping, meathead."

"Could've fooled me," Voss said, leaning into his limited field of view.

Quinn made a mental note to remind the team that they'd have to rely on each other to clear their sixes. Turning your head didn't do a lick of good when your faceplate didn't move with it. It was too much to hope the enemy would agree to remain straight ahead. He slowly lifted an eyelid to regard the young Corporal with practiced indifference. "I'm thinking," he finally said with a crooked grin. "You should try it sometime."

"I'm trying to avoid it," the junior NCO replied cautiously. "We're landing soon, you know. Shit, Gunny…the *Moon*. Who'da thunk it?"

"A few science-fiction writers come to mind. Not to mention HQ warned us this might be a contingency," he said, reminding him of the secondary plan known as VALIANT HAMMER. The brass always picked something to sound especially motivating when they knew it meant everything had completely gone to hell.

"So now we're supposed to take op orders seriously?" he joked. "Damned if this doesn't just keep getting better. Next you'll tell me we might actually end up in a shooting war down there."

"You signed up for this gig to make history, remember?" Quinn prodded him. "Embrace the Suck."

"Semper Fi," Voss sighed. "They're gonna have to add this to the Hymn, you know: 'From the halls of Montezuma, to the…dusty lunar sea.' Yeah. Think you could put in a good word with the Commandant?"

"Next time he has me over for drinks," Quinn scoffed. "I never figured you for a poet, meathead."

"It was the only thing that rhymed with the rest of the song. Actually I think it does sound kind of stupid."

"Won't matter anyway. We pull this off and nobody is ever gonna know about it. And if we don't, there won't be anybody left to brag to."

"Anybody tell you what a ray of sunshine you are?"

"A couple of ex-wives, all the damned time."

…

"Three hundred meters, down at ten. A little hot." Ryan's voice was tense.

"I know," Penny shot back. He'd confirmed what she already sensed: they were falling too fast. At this rate they'd be on the surface in thirty seconds with crushed landing struts. She goosed the throttles to slow their descent. "Hoped I could save us some ascent fuel. Stupid."

"First time for everything," he said. "There we go…vertical velocity's down to six. Lateral velocity's back to zero. The lady's still got it, sports fans."

"I know you're not talking about my looks." She leaned into the window for a better view. "What's our distance from Farside?"

"Twenty clicks. We're below their horizon." She had flown the last leg at barely a kilometer above the surface to mask their approach. "Two hundred, down at three. Looking great."

"It'll be a long walk for your boys back there," she said. "Think it's safe to get them in closer?"

Ryan frowned as he zoomed in their map. "Safe is a pretty loose term at this point. You trying to save their air?"

"Buying them more time. I'm hoping they won't need it."

He pointed out a depression on the map. "There's a low spot in the mare about ten clicks in, looks nice and flat. Gets them in closer and keeps us in defilade. I like it." Finding cover from enemy fire should have been the farthest thing from their minds during their first Moon landing, yet it never entered into their mental calculus.

"That's our landing site. Punch it into the FMS."

• • •

"Fifty meters, down at two. Picking up dust."

"I see it." A powdery gray plume fanned out beneath them, kicked up by the descent engines at each corner of the cylindrical spacecraft. Inside, the cabin rattled and thumped as she pulsed thrusters to keep them level.

"Abort guidance on," Ryan said. "Not that we're gonna need it."

"Not going anywhere if we did," Penny said. "We're committed."

"Roger that. Thirty meters. Fuel's still in the green," Ryan said. Outside, the dust cloud began enveloping them. "It's getting murky out there. Your instrument rating current?"

"Bite me. I've forgotten more about flying blind than you ever knew, hot dog."

"Just checking. We have to watch out for you management pilots."

"Stow the grabass," Penny snapped. "I'm trying to land on the Moon here."

"Right. Fifteen meters, down at one. Lateral's still zero. Spot on."

A smile spread across her face despite the circumstances. *We're really doing this.*

His eyes were locked on the radar altimeter. "Ten meters. You're making this look too easy."

"I wrote the book on this bird, remember?"

"Not really. It was a boring book." A warning pulsed in their HUDs as thin wire probes brushed the surface. "Contact!"

"Shutdown," Penny said, and chopped the throttle. They fell the remaining two meters in the gentle one-sixth gravity and landed with an unnerving jolt.

It was perfectly silent. No one spoke – not the pilots, not the men in back. Everyone seemed to be holding their breath.

As he tended to do, Ryan broke the silence. "I'll be damned. The beagle has landed."

27

Washington

Winston stepped into Abbot's office unannounced and pulled the heavy oak door shut behind him. It was becoming perhaps too comfortable a habit, but there'd be plenty of time to bring this youngster to heel later. For now it was good to keep him feeling important.

"You have a PR problem, sir."

Abbot was nonplussed. "Excuse me?"

"A public relations problem."

"I'm aware of what it stands for. Why is it a problem?" *Especially for me personally.*

"I should be more specific," Winston backtracked. "It's a potential problem, sir. That is, with the Gateway station disabled…"

Abbot cut him off. "Our mystery site is all that's left. What's your point? How is this a NASA problem?"

"By all rights it shouldn't be, but that's not how things work here. If the worst case scenarios come to pass, everyone up to and including the President will be desperately covering their asses."

It was the closest thing to profanity he'd ever heard from the kid's highly polished Georgetown mouth, but he couldn't think of any better way to describe it either. "What do you know?"

Winston's eyes darted around the room, as if giving voice to his concerns would bring them to pass. "I'm sure you know the old saying about poker?"

Here come the poker analogies again. What was with these people? "Amuse me."

"If you're sitting at the table wondering 'who's the mark,' you're it."

Now that actually made sense. Somebody was going to get pinned with this mess, and you could bet it wouldn't be the people actually at fault. That never happened in this town. His lack of information only meant they were holding out on him for the inevitable setup when it all came crashing down. Digging any deeper would only tip an already weak hand. If they were going to be playing the blame game, then it was time to go after the root cause of the problem. The smile that spread across Abbot's smile stopped at his eyes. "Then we need a new mark."

...

Tsiolkovskiy Crater
Ten kilometers from Farside

Twenty years of wearing Marine Green had taken Marcus Quinn around the world many times over. Most were places he'd just as soon never see again, yet they were the very ones the Corps had felt the need to grace with his presence: Afghanistan. Iraq. North Africa. Afghanistan, again. Collectively known as "The Sandbox." *They might as well have permanently stationed my sorry ass there*, he'd thought.

This, however, beat everything. Even the trackless deserts of the hopelessly screwed-up Middle East had felt more welcoming than this Godforsaken place.

What must have been static electricity from their lander had pulled some of the fine powder back inside as the door slid open. Kneeling at the hatch, Quinn traced a gloved finger through the dust. It looked like charcoal he would've dumped from the grill behind his condo back in Topsail Beach. It seemed a lifetime away now, even farther than he knew it to be. Earth's blue globe barely kissed the horizon; its eternal, senseless quarreling between cultures now a quarter-million miles distant.

Or rather the quarrel was once again between modern civilization and the Dark Ages, he corrected himself.

A quarter of a million miles, and now the conflict waited just beyond that ridge. Ten kilometers distant, it looked like a quick hop away. The absence of atmospheric haze ruined all sense of perspective. With his entire adult life spent chasing bad guys from one corner of the world to the other, what does he do after landing on the damned Moon, of all places?

Mix it up with yet another gaggle of jihadis who'd gotten their hands on way too much firepower, that's what. Next they'd be chasing these peckerwoods halfway across the solar system. The towering absurdity of it all had led him to remind his team of a favorite quote from that old movie about George Patton: "Gentlemen, whatever else we do in life, we won't have to tell our grandkids, 'I spent the Great War shoveling shit in Louisiana.'"

Back at Lejeune, the briefers had told them to expect disorganized resistance if it came to this point. Quinn and Goode had listened politely, maintaining a professional demeanor while slipping each other the "we know better" look. "*Achmed didn't go all the way to the friggin' Moon to play footsie when we come kicking down the door,*" Vern had said under his breath, surreptitiously checking his watch as the MARSOC Intel officer droned on.

"*It's going to get sporty up there,*" Quinn had quietly agreed. "*If they're right, this one really is for all the marbles.*"

The irony didn't escape him, not least because Quinn was also a keen amateur astronomer. And here he was, standing in a place he'd only dreamed of seeing while the stakes for humanity exceeded anything he could have imagined.

He turned back to the team and methodically waved his left hand palm forward with the all-clear signal. They would be under strict radio silence until they closed to contact with Farside. In their armored EVA suits, he couldn't get over how much they reminded him of characters from the video games he'd played as a kid. He'd never understood why they'd used Navy ranks for what were supposed to be Marines of the future. *Master Chief, my ass.*

Tightening a gloved fist around the chunky pistol grip of his M55 carbine, Quinn lifted his free hand and crisply waved it forward: *On your feet. Move out.*

As the team scrambled out into the airless gray desert, more of that cursed dust found its way back through the hatch as Hunter emerged from the pilot's station. Pausing at the door, he noticed the old insignia patch with his rank and pilot wings hastily fixed to his civilian Polaris spacesuit. The pilot watched with fascination as the team clumsily formed a defensive perimeter around the spacecraft.

The men shook hands as best they could in the stiff gloves. Quinn leaned his helmet faceplate against Hunter's. It would allow them to talk without breaking radio discipline, though their voices were muffled by the glass.

"Nice ride. Sorry about the dirt."

"No problem. We'll just tidy up while you go take care of business," Hunter said, then turned serious. "I'll be on the emergency freq. Call if you need a dust-off."

"Appreciate that," he said, and saluted as best he could in the pressure suit. "Semper Fi." He hopped out of the open hatch, kneeling as he landed in slow motion. Fine grains of dust scattered uniformly about with each step before slowly falling back to the surface, the strange phenomenon of low gravity on an airless moon.

"One small step for man, one big assed leap for the Corps," he muttered, and shouldered his weapon.

...

Ryan watched Quinn lead his team up to the ridgeline and tried to judge the terrain ahead of them. It was taking them time to get their Moon legs. Used to shouldering a hundred pounds of gear on Earth, most of that weight was suddenly gone. But the mass remained, and so no amount of berating from Quinn could prevent them from stumbling all over themselves as their momentum carried them along.

It reminded him of toddlers learning to run, which turned his thoughts to Marshall. He just as quickly forced it aside, ignoring a pang of guilt.

They got the hang of it soon enough. As the last man disappeared over the rim, Ryan swung one leg outside to gingerly place a foot on the surface, then lifted it back. It left behind a crisp boot print in the dust, reminiscent of Buzz Aldrin's iconic photo.

He screwed up his courage and stepped out with both feet. That wasn't so hard…

Boy, if Dad could have seen this. The old man had been a real space nerd. And though Ryan had been born more than a decade after the moon landings, as a child he'd not lacked for information about that era. His father's study had been filled with books and films on the subject, and truth be told it had probably sparked Ryan's desire to fly in the first place. Dad's stories about witnessing one of those giant Saturn launches still resonated every time Ryan looked out over the massive launch gantries that still dominated the Cape. His old man had a way with words, too: *They shook you all the way to your core, son,* he'd said. *Five miles away, and it still thundered as if God Himself had reached down to smack the Earth with His fist.*

"Sorry Dad," Ryan muttered to himself. It would have dismayed the old man to see his generation's greatest achievement be transformed into a tourist attraction, with his son's help no less. Although the landing zones had been designated historic sites, and the company had strict plans to keep any future traffic at a respectful distance, they wouldn't be the only ones coming up here. It was just a matter of time before pieces of Apollo hardware began showing up on internet auctions. Or maybe Sotheby's. These were wealthy clientele, after all.

That is, if the market didn't get shut down entirely for the same reason we still had to jump through hoops to keep terrorists from turning airliners into guided missiles. Even though they'd only been successful at it once, how much more would we be forced to endure now that they had turned the damned *Moon* against us?

Okay, only part of the Moon, he reminded himself…that part with the gigawatt laser on it. He turned south – at least he thought it was south, this place was so insanely disorienting – and searched the sky. There it was: a gauzy white stain in the black, only now appreciably larger. Its apparent size would continue to increase dramatically now that it was so close.

What would Quinn's men find? Everyone assumed they wanted direct control of Farside's laser now that Weatherby was above the local horizon and Gateway was toast.

All of them had their own insane death cult motives. Whether they were Earth Firsters or apocalyptic Jihadis, he considered each to be its own form of barbaric fanaticism. It didn't matter if they were ivory tower academics who were in over their heads: at least one of their number was a cornered animal. More unpredictable. More dangerous. He turned away and stepped back into the flight module, closing the outer hatch and pressurizing the compartment.

"Your boys make it out?" Penny asked.

"Headed downrange," he said distractedly. He was staring at an olive-drab container strapped to the deck, which held spare weapons and equipment. "How long does it take to power up everything from standby?" he asked. "Charging the thrusters and all?"

"Maybe ten minutes," Penny said. "What are you thinking?"

"I'm thinking Quinn's right. Hassani and Varza didn't come all this way just to let us bag them at the last minute. They must have some kind of defense prepared."

"The S2 weenies seemed pretty confident that they wouldn't."

Ryan frowned. "Air Force intel ever let you down?"

"Occasionally," she admitted. She'd had to dodge more than one anti-aircraft site that had inconveniently showed up somewhere it wasn't supposed to be. "So what's your point?"

"Defensive positions are hard to assess without eyeballs on the ground," he pointed out. "And we just got here."

"So we can't know what they're packing until our boys get near that complex."

"This is the Hail Mary play for the whole 'let's have an apocalypse' movement," Ryan said. "All that 'survey equipment' they listed on the manifest? It wasn't hard for them to piecemeal a railgun from it. They're not going anywhere without a fight."

Penny drummed her gloved fingers on the glare shield. "Guess that makes us the cavalry," she said, and began unlocking switches in the overhead panel. "Standby batteries are good for another eight hours. Once the thrusters are warmed up, they'll light off whenever I goose the throttle. Cabin pressurization—"

"Won't need it," he interrupted. "We stay suited up and open the doors as soon as we're clear of our dust cloud." He lifted a thickly insulated loop of cable from a closet behind them. "We plug into each other and communicate through the suit umbilical. All that rad shielding ought to keep any chatter just between us."

"No sense letting the bad guys listen in," she agreed, then looked at him with disbelief. "You're not planning to be up here, are you?"

"Nope," he said, and trundled back to the open container. Inside were two more M55's with magazines and spare grappling equipment.

"You'll need an aerial spotter," he said, lifting one of the rifles from its case. "Maybe even a door gunner."

...

The TAC team had deployed into a wedge formation and was holding together better than Quinn had expected. Once they'd found their footing, each man then had to work out his own best way to manage the load he carried. Most of them hunched over into a loping gait, a few others had adopted an odd bunny hop.

He lifted his left wrist up to his faceplate and flipped open a laminated map that had come with their sealed operations order. It was maddeningly hard to find bearings out here. Looking over at Vern, it appeared he was having just as much trouble. He raised a fist, signaling them to halt.

What appeared to be another ridge lay ahead, but the stark contrast of an airless landscape made it difficult to judge. It might not even be a ridge. Could be a crater rim. He switched on the rangefinder in his rifle scope, centered it on the ridge, and waited for the solution to appear in his faceplate. Checking against his map, he cursed under his breath. *Nope. It's another friggin' crater. Where the hell are we?*

Quinn looked up into the black, hoping to find a field of stars that would give him direction. Only a few of the very brightest ones were visible; he'd forgotten that it was still daytime here and that the stars were almost as washed out as on Earth.

Giving up, he followed the directional cues projected onto his faceplate. *Okay, maybe we should've listened to S2 on that.* Ability to judge terrain was a fundamental infantry skill which had been neutralized by the unfiltered sunlight and utter lack of depth perception. The long shadows offered some relief; he didn't want to imagine how hopelessly lost one could get at "high noon" here. Or midnight. Either condition lasted for days.

There it was – maybe two more clicks and a quick jog to the east. They would advance from the south, masking their avenue of approach behind a low hillock. But there would still be a lot of open ground between it and their objective.

He looked to Sergeant Goode, who nodded back. He'd apparently come to the same conclusion. Quinn kneeled down and traced some outlines in the lunar dust. The stiff gloves made hand signals harder but they couldn't risk transmitting in the open. He pointed at Breedlow, motioning him forward. *Entry team, up front.*

He pointed at Haggerty next, making a hopping motion with one hand over the other. *Overwatch,* he signaled, *along that crater rim.* He tapped two fingers to his faceplate. *Get us some eyeballs over that ridge.* The sniper nodded inside his helmet, gave a clumsy thumbs-up, and hopped away with his spotter. The pair loped off towards a small crater to take position along the reverse slope, protecting the team's flank while hopefully staying hidden from view.

The approach didn't look this ugly on the maps. What appeared to be shallow gulches on paper might as well have been Alpine valleys here. Goode loped over and tapped the map on his wrist, shaking his head. He was apparently thinking the same thing: behind the visor, Quinn could see his brow knitted in frustration. He leaned in and pressed their faceplates together.

"I don't like it, Gunny. Not one damn bit."

"You read my mind, Vern. But I don't see any better way in there. Not with the time we have."

Both men kneeled in the dust as Goode unrolled a larger map. He drew a finger along their planned approach and pointed to the surrounding terrain, then leaned back into his faceplate. "Either these maps are FUBAR, or this place messes up your perspective that badly."

"Probably some of both," Quinn said. "Contours look even worse on the other side. You hang back here and let me scout ahead."

Goode shook his head. "Let me do the grunt work, Gunny. You're not doing command any good if you get waxed."

"Command ain't here, Vern. It's occurred to me that we're pretty much on our own."

"So then you won't mind if I politely disagree."

"You telling me to go pound sand?"

"I'd never do that. I'd just tell you to go piss up a rope," he said cynically. "Just watch your ass, Marcus."

28

Farside

Haggerty kneeled in the unwieldy spacesuit, being careful to not expose any part of himself above the crater rim. Against the stark black sky, it would be awfully easy to skyline himself and present an easy target – though for what exactly, he had no idea. He depressed a latch in his rifle's forward grip to release a pair of bipod legs and dug his knees and hips into the powdery gray dust.

As he settled into firing position, Voss plugged in their shielded communications umbilical before digging in himself. He propped up his own rifle to one side and set up the spotting camera. Settling in behind it, he cursed in frustration. "Rotten place for a hide," he said quietly.

"Crater's not that bad," Haggerty grunted. "Seen worse, brother."

"I mean the whole deal," Voss replied. "The terrain, the suits…I don't like having to rely on all this tech," he said. Traditional spotting scopes were useless, being unable to get close enough to their eyepieces. They were forced to rely on laser rangefinders and low power scopes, the latter being especially distasteful to a precision marksman.

Haggerty grinned. "Looks like you signed up for the wrong unit, dumbass. Keep your melon down and get that scope dialed in."

"I'm on it," Voss said calmly. "Just making an objective analysis of the current tactical situation, that's all."

A short *click* sounded in their headsets, Quinn signaling that new information was coming. A three-second pause, then another fast on-and-off click, followed by a short hiss of static as he held the mic open: *Objective in sight.*

…

Hidden from view atop the control platform, a solitary figure perched behind a cluster of tanks. He slowly lifted an arm to check his O2 and suit coolant, careful not to create movement that might expose him to the approaching enemy.

Squaring himself behind the viewfinder, Hassani snugged his faceplate up against the small video screen and settled its crosshairs onto the opposite ridge. He'd spied a telltale glint minutes earlier and had patiently waited for it to reappear. Fortunate, he thought, that they came during his watch outside. It must surely be Allah's will that it fell upon him and not some frail scientist.

Not quite one hundred meters away, atop Farside's particle accelerator, the bulbous turret quietly slewed to its new aim point.

...

Haggerty glassed the area around Farside for any movement. The sun was at their backs, which ordinarily would have been to their advantage, keeping his scope from reflecting any stray light and giving away their position. The harsh unfiltered sun lit up everything like they were on a movie set and threw shadows everywhere.

He was about to make a mental note of that when he heard a burst of static and noticed sudden movement to his right. *Voss*. Turning, he watched his spotter writhing in the dust, kicking the damned charcoal sand everywhere. *What the hell was he doing*?

And then he knew. As Voss flipped over, Haggerty could see his face contorted in agony as he pawed at his visor. Blisters were forming on his skin, and the inside of his helmet seemed to – what *was* it doing, anyway?

Haggerty blinked in shock. The air inside Voss's helmet was shimmering, like heat waves boiling up from a country road in summer.

He reached for his spotter and recoiled in searing pain, as if he'd just shoved his arm into a bonfire. Voss had been cooked alive by some kind of damned microwave beam. *Oh shit.*

He punched the microphone switch on his chest. *"Contact! Ambush front!"*

29

Farside

Quinn was caught in the open when the frantic call came and instinctively dropped to his belly, burrowing into the charcoal dust and hoping he wasn't next on the target list. As he stared into a faceplate that was now buried in gray powder, he immediately realized his mistake. What had been a defensive reflex on Earth was useless here, foolish at the very least and maybe deadly. Facedown in the dust and unable to see without lifting his helmet and silhouetting himself, Quinn was blind as a bat.

He lifted his head slowly, hoping to be able to see through the small oval window in the top of his helmet. He only saw more dust. Quinn cursed and chinned his radio. "Raider One Three, Raider Six. Report!"

The pause told him everything. "Six, my spotter is KIA. No rounds, repeat no rounds. Weapon appears to be directed energy," Haggerty choked. "Voss got lased."

Dammit. He quickly shut out any thoughts of what the kid must have endured. Later. "I'm pinned. No visual. HUD says I'm two hundred meters from the objective, bearing one-four-zero on your position, over."

"Copy that, Gunny. Stand by…okay, I've got you up in my HUD. Be advised you're damn near invisible down there."

So I got that going for me. "Can I move?"

Haggerty didn't take long to evaluate his situation. "Negative. I've got visual on the shooter...scratch that, the weapon. Looks like they're using the primary laser. It's slewing around, like someone's searching for a target."

"That's his ray gun all right," Quinn said. "Does he have a bead on me?"

"Negative, Marcus. But you're in his kill zone."

Great. They only used first names on the radio when everything had really gone to shit. "Stand by…Six, I've got movement. One bandit just came down off the platform." His voice was low, whispering reflexively. "Don't move. He's heading your way, looks like he's going to the lander."

"Do you have a clear shot?"

"Negative. I'm watching the feed from Voss' scope. They've still got that damned laser pointed at me."

The hits just keep coming.

...

"You hearing that?" Ryan asked. "I don't know if we can stay masked long enough."

Penny stole a glance at the chart projection by her knee, examining their options. "We can't," she agreed. "Soon as we pop up high enough to do them any good, we'll have made ourselves an easy target."

"But we're going anyway, aren't we?" As she nodded her assent, Ryan hit his mic switch. "Raiders; *Snoopy* is inbound."

"Bad idea," Quinn answered. "LZ is hot."

"We're coming anyway," Penny said. "I'm not waiting for you to call dust-off."

There was a long pause. "We could use a distraction. Stand by." It was hard to tell through the attenuating static, but he sounded relieved.

She zoomed the map closer in on Farside. "You won't be able to play door gunner, not if they have someone outside the complex. We can't risk it."

"Cabin would fill up with dust anyway," Ryan thought aloud. He began punching possible burn vectors into the flight computer. "Here's our plan. Check your PFD."

Penny smiled as she watched it play out on the map. "Beautiful." She returned to the radio. "Raiders, listen up: keep your heads down. Your distraction's on the way."

...

Snoopy II leapt into the black sky as its hovering thrusters flared to life. The module flew better already, having lost about two thousand kilos of mass with the TAC team gone. The rocket-propelled soup can was nimble, responsive to every control input, and would have been fun under other circumstances.

While scrambling to prepare the ship, they had listened in on the unfolding mess at Farside. One confirmed dead, Quinn pinned down in the open with a bad guy heading his way, and the rest unable to do anything about it without exposing themselves. Ryan's plan would have to alter the balance.

He had his faceplate open, searching for the complex with binoculars. "I think I've got it." He pointed straight ahead.

"Good plot, Ryan. I'll have to brag on you to Audrey."

"No thanks. She'll have me pulling shifts in the control center." There was a flash of light low ahead as sunlight reflected off the metal structures. He lifted the binoculars back to his eyes. "Tally ho…complex is intact…laser's not looking in our direction."

"Hope it stays that way," she said. "Pitch point's coming up." Penny's eyes danced between displays as she followed the count, her hands wrapped gently around the pitch and translation controls. "Pitchover!" she called out, and pulled both levers back until they reached their detents.

"Idle thrust."

Penny was already tipping them back. They flew slightly nose down, rocketing up into the sky under full thrust and now coasting through a steep parabola. They would come down almost on top of Farside, putting themselves and their ride home between the Marines and their target.

"Too bad we can't come in blasting *Ride of the Valkyries*," Ryan said, and began humming the familiar theme.

"Wondered how long it would take you to do that," she said. "Need your callouts real soon here."

"On it…five thousand, down at…wow, *forty*." They were falling like a rock.

"Surprised?" She was way too calm for his comfort. He knew that the cooler she sounded, the more freaked out she was.

"We're falling towards the friggin' Moon at…forty seven meters per second." Over one hundred miles per hour. "You'd be a little edgy too if you had to sit and watch."

She pulsed the engines gently to slow them. “This was your idea, bubba. Just keep the altitude calls coming. I’m trusting you more than the instruments.”

“You’re crazier than I thought, but I’ll take it as a compliment,” he said. “Three thousand, down at thirty.”

They continued falling silently, one minute until their lander would hit the surface. Ahead and below, they couldn’t see the turret ball swing up in their direction.

• • •

Still watching the video feed, Haggerty saw the laser begin to pivot. They were changing its aim point, taking its eye off of his position for a clear shot overhead. He looked up to see the lander falling out of the black sky on jets of blue flame.

He shut off the camera and scrambled upslope, settling back into his firing position. There was no time to think, only to shoot. He centered the scope’s video crosshairs on the turret’s glass emitter and exhaled, steadily increasing the pressure from his fingers around the trigger paddle. He hoped the heavily modified Barrett worked as advertised up here. Those dust covers and vacuum seals were a real pain in the ass to maintain...

Even through multiple layers of spacesuit, Haggerty felt the recoil pound into his shoulder when the trigger broke. He was rewarded with a fountain of shattered glass as the .50 caliber round found its target.

Guess it works.

• • •

“What the *hell*?”

Quinn’s suit was suddenly being buffeted from all sides amid an eruption of excited chatter. No one had heard from the lander since Stratton had warned them to keep their heads down, now they found themselves in the middle of something they’d never expected: a furious dust storm.

“Here comes the Air Wing,” someone exclaimed. “About damned time!” Haggerty, maybe? Quinn couldn’t blame the kid; he was cut off in a wholly unfamiliar environment that now seemed to be swallowing them whole.

The next voice was Hunter’s. “Everybody hates the Wing until we save your bacon. Raider Six, need your status.”

"Reverse slope of that ridge, southwest side of the control platform," Quinn said. "Where are you? I have zero vis."

"Look up."

Quinn lifted his head to see dust swirling across his visor and figured it was safe to at least roll over. He pushed off with one elbow and rolled onto his back, swiping the crud away. The glass was hazed from a thousand different micro-scratches, but he could plainly see torrents of dust playing out around him. A cluster of four bright blue flames hovered directly overhead.

Oh shit.

...

"*Snoopy*, wave off! You are coming down on my position! Repeat: wave off!"

Penny's blood ran cold. Barely a hundred meters above the surface, goosing the throttles to gain altitude would only make matters worse for him. "Tracking forward!" she said. "Ground opens up ahead."

"Do it!"

...

Quinn rolled back onto his stomach, digging deeper into the gray dust and realizing that if his suit hadn't been trashed before, it surely was now. The buffeting increased momentarily; thankfully his suit's thermal plates held up. He'd expected to start roasting like a chicken at any second. He could only imagine the earsplitting noise if there'd been any atmosphere to carry it. The dull roar transmitted through the ground to his suit was jarring enough.

A shadow passed overhead and the dust plumes followed. There was the lander, settling down nice and easy. The cloud didn't billow up and away, instead spraying through the vacuum in a uniform arc, thick as any Middle Eastern sand storm. Perfect cover, if you could see through it. Which they could.

"Go!" It was Haggerty, ordering somebody to do something. As he scrambled up from his makeshift hole, a Marine in a filthy EVA suit galloped towards him.

"You're clear, Gunny." A gloved hand reached down to help him up.

Quinn shook out the cobwebs and clumsily wiped at the grime on his visor. "What's our situation?"

"FUBAR as usual," Breedlow said. "Goode and Haggerty are chasing down our Lone Ranger. They're heading for the Altair lander." He poked a gloved finger at himself and Quinn. "That makes us the breaching team."

"Then let's get going," Quinn said. "We're both too ugly to live forever."

. . .

Haggerty approached the Altair as carefully as he could in the stiff vacuum suit, using the optical sight from his carbine to sweep the area ahead. The lander was an odd contraption, resembling a propane tank atop a flying drill platform. The thing looked dead; its interior lights were dark and the hatch was closed. Yet the tracks ended at the ship's egress ladder. It was impossible to see inside through its tiny windows without getting up close. Hopefully that worked in both directions.

He swept around back, clearing his blind spots, and began thinking about how to get inside the thing. There was no sense heading straight up the steps to the guy's front porch, so he'd have to get up through the back. He hooked a grappling line around a thruster support and pulled hard. It didn't give way, so he took advantage of the low gravity to high jump and use the line to pull himself the rest of the way. In the distance, he saw one of his teammates heading in his direction.

. . .

Inside *Altair*'s cabin, Hassani went through the launch checklist from memory, feeling through each switch setting in the darkened cockpit. Lights would only draw unwelcome attention from their visitors. He had no doubt there were men on their way, if they were not already outside at that moment.

Launch and rendezvous were ridiculously simple: synchronize the lander's flight computer with the master system aboard *Orion* and it would calculate the launch azimuth for him. Fortunately the ascent stage had enough propellant that timing wasn't a concern. He need only get to the proper orbit and adjust his phasing from there to catch up with the command module. It helped that he would be the only occupant in a craft designed to carry four, with no bothersome mass from rock samples and other nonsense.

There was a scraping noise from behind him. Startled, he swung about to face an empty bulkhead. Someone was out there.

It would not matter. He climbed into one of the acceleration couches in back of the cabin and waited.

...

Haggerty carefully worked his way around the lander, thankful that the upper stage was surrounded with EVA handholds. It was a long way down.

He pulled even with the hatch just as Goode approached; slow and methodic, his weapon at high ready. Haggerty admired his mastery of the stiff suit and low gravity, as his stride looked no different than if they were running an op back on Earth. Kneeling atop the lander's porch, he waved for his partner to take a covering position in front of the opening.

As he reached for the entry hatch, a cloud of incandescent gas erupted from the ascent stage.

30

Farside

Penny was absorbed in shutting down the lander when Ryan handed her the spare M55. "What am I going to do with this?"

"You'll figure it out," he shrugged. He kneeled in the side hatch with the other rifle, covering any likely avenues of approach while she finished securing the flight deck. She'd never seen him so hyper-focused, in an entirely different manner from flying. They must have really beat that infantry stuff into their heads at Quantico. Or he played army a lot as a kid.

There was a flash of light at the other end of the complex, accompanied by shouting over the radio. Drawn to the light, they saw *Altair*'s ascent stage racing into the black sky atop a radiant plume of rocket exhaust.

Ryan traced its path back down to the descent stage, its insulating blankets now scorched and tattered. Two dark gray EVA suits lay sprawled in the dust beside it. Without a word, he unplugged their shared umbilical and took off in a stumbling run.

...

Quinn and Breedlow had taken up positions on either side of an airlock at the reactor's service complex, a simple cylinder that looked to be adapted from one of the lunar ascent stages. It was free of the thrusters and guidance equipment used by the one that had just blasted off, which they'd have missed were it not for the screams over the radio net.

What was most troubling was the abrupt silence that followed. "Raiders, this is Six. Report!"

More silence.

"Raider One Three, comm check," Breedlow added. He looked at Quinn and shook his head solemnly.

A new voice broke in. "This is Hunter. I'm at their position now." It sounded like he was on the run, or whatever passed for running up here. "It doesn't look good."

Quinn looked for the landing zone and saw what was left of *Altair*'s descent stage. Cursing, he turned back to Breedlow and raised his fist in a "get ready" signal.

He brought his fist down on the emergency release and flung the hatch open. No air rushed out, so the 'lock had already been vented. Breedlow crept in first and crouched by the inner door, signaling that he'd take this one, and grasped the lever. As he turned it, the door exploded in a blast of ceramic and metal fragments, throwing him back through the airlock and into the dust. A grisly cloud of ice crystals and blood droplets spouted from the entry wound in his chest as his life support backpack exploded from the exiting round.

There were no medical corpsmen here. Quinn was forced to ignore his mortally wounded teammate and ran inside. He crouched low and sprang forward, leaping through the open portal and using the low gravity for a move that would have been impossible on Earth. He flew in slow motion across the top of the cabin, sweeping the room with his viewfinder, and came to rest on his feet near the opposite corner. He swung his muzzle about, clearing it once more of human targets.

Another empty hole? No, not empty. A machine-gun looking contraption sat atop a tripod in the center of the room, its trigger lashed to the inside latch by a simple pulley.

He approached it cautiously. It was about two meters long, with a barrel of brightly polished steel surrounded by what he thought were electromagnets. He followed the cables that hung from its bulky firing chamber to a separate battery pack. *Damn…so we know what they did with their railgun.*

Movement caught his eye. He almost lost his footing as he spun around to see an equipment locker crack open. Two thickly gloved hands emerged, followed by the rest of Kam Varza in a standard NASA spacesuit. Even through all of the latex and beta cloth that encased him, he appeared wobbly. His arms were raised in a gesture of surrender.

Quinn lunged across the room in two huge loping steps, shoved Varza back into the corner, and pressed their faceplates together: "Don't move!" He was aware that he'd somehow managed to not spit all over the inside of his helmet in rage. As he stepped back, he could see the idiot's mouth going as if he could still hear him.

He reached down to Varza's wrist controls to put them on the same frequency. "Works better this way," he said, keeping his muzzle pressed into a soft spot on Varza's suit beneath the chest pack. "Where are the others?" he demanded. "Your buddies all bail on you?"

"What do you mean?" Varza asked shakily. The radio gave his voice a tinny quality, which Quinn found appropriate for the little weasel. "Omar's the only one left. DeCarlo died on the surface," he stammered. "His suit was just meant for vacuum, it couldn't handle the dust."

"I'm guessing he wasn't aware of that," Quinn spat. "Looks like that's how you two deal with people once you've used them up."

"Joseph was necessary," Varza protested. "He understood the…"

Quinn interrupted by shoving the muzzle deeper into the suit. Hopefully the little prick could feel it now. "Doesn't matter," he said. "Your boy Omar just left with your ride home, and my whole team's gone. It's just you and me."

Varza stared at the gun mount. "Hassani set it up..."

Quinn shoved him back into the gear locker and slammed the door. "Shut your word hole, princess." He switched back to the open team frequency. "This is Quinn. Objective secure, one confirmed casualty. All hostiles accounted for."

"Two KIA's here," Hunter said. "Rocket blast and shrapnel."

"Copy that," he answered somberly. "I need you both here at the reactor control, ASAP." While he waited for them, he rooted through the station's repair kit and found something resembling a caulk gun. He began sealing that hole blasted into the door, the work clearing his mind as he considered what to do with their prisoner.

...

Penny and Ryan removed their helmets once Quinn had confirmed the compartment was holding pressure. "Keep those close," he warned. "You hear a whistling noise—"

"We know," Ryan said for them both.

"Time to meet our guest of honor." Quinn flung the locker open, yanking Varza out by his arm. He forced him into a webbed chair and tied his arms to it. That was when Ryan noticed Quinn had been careful to leave the man's sun visor down. In this light, he wouldn't have seen any of them standing there without helmets. This should be fun.

He began struggling when Quinn unlocked the helmet ring. As he tore it away from his head, Varza was screaming.

Quinn stood serenely with something resembling amusement on his face. Ryan thought it was the same look a delinquent grade schooler might give an ant as he pulled out his magnifying glass.

"Are you done?" Quinn asked calmly.

Varza was pale, his mouth trembling. His eyes darted about. "Who are these people?"

Penny answered for them. "We're the people who own the ship you stole. Friends of the people you killed."

"And you brought your own private army?"

"Marines, actually," Ryan said with a nod towards Quinn. "You've managed to piss off all of the wrong people, Doc."

"It wasn't supposed to be like this," Varza said. "Hassani thinks his allies can take advantage of it."

"Compared to what?" Penny demanded. "You were prepared to wipe out human civilization, remember?"

"You wouldn't understand…"

"Try us."

Varza pushed against his restraints; whatever resolve he might have left welled up within him. "We've fallen too far from the natural order," he explained, as if lecturing a class. "Technology has been turned into a tool for thwarting natural selection. There are too many of us. Too many diseased who should have died, too many elderly trapped in their own dementia, too many oafs dumping their waste indiscriminately. We've fouled our own nest. That comet," he argued, "has been part of this solar system for billions of years. Nature is greater than any of us and is long overdue for a rebalancing."

"So choosing to let nature wipe the slate clean even though we have the ability to stop it is somehow virtuous?" Quinn asked. "That's not just stupid, that's graduate-level stupid. That's stupid with sprinkles on top."

"You just proved my point by ignoring it," Varza sniffed. "It's already too late. The shard's trajectory can't be changed at this point. Even nuclear warheads aren't powerful enough to redirect it this close to impact. I suppose you could use them as brute force and just blow it up, but that won't appreciably change the mass. You'll just end up bombarding a few cities with debris."

"Shard?" Quinn asked. "What are you talking about?"

Varza's eyes widened. "You really don't...no, of course you wouldn't. We just discovered it yesterday."

Ryan kicked hard at his shin. "I have a three-year-old at home, so understand I watch a *lot* of educational TV. I never did like you, Varza. You're even more patronizing and obnoxious in person. So get to it and quit waiting for the next commercial break."

Wearing an odd smile, Varza pointed them to the telescope controls. Quinn opened up its screen and quickly found their observation log. "So your grand idea came up short. Good."

"Look closer."

Quinn scrolled through the last two days' sightings and stopped. "Is that what I think it is?"

"Our lucky winner," Varza said victoriously. "Though I doubt you're smart enough to understand what it really means."

Quinn was unmoved. "Probably not. But I know someone who is."

...

It didn't take Audrey long to work through the parameters that Quinn had transmitted. Within the hour, she had determined the newly liberated fragment's mass and its orbit. As she studied it further, she guessed it was almost a half a kilometer across and estimated its density to be around 1200 kilograms per cubic meter. Moving through space at about 50,000 kilometers an hour, at the current separation rate it would strike a glancing blow out of the south before the main nucleus swept by hours later, safely missing Earth.

Compared to the astronomers back on Earth who would soon be frantically revising their predictions, she probably had the single best data set. The rest would be depending on optical astrometry, as she suspected the fragment was at the resolution limit of ground based radar.

Estimating the impact area took considerably longer, but she settled on an ellipse roughly two hundred nautical miles long, centered at 30 degrees north latitude, 78 degrees west longitude. The Atlantic Ocean, due east of Melbourne.

Audrey fell back from her work, wide-eyed. She had to get this out through Denver, fast. This wouldn't affect just the Space Coast, the direction of impact would actually make it worse farther up the eastern seaboard.

She thought about the effect on people closer to home: if she were in Ryan's shoes, she'd be in a killing rage.

• • •

Ryan exploded across the room, grabbing Varza by the collar and dragging him into the airlock.

Quinn grabbed him roughly by the arm to pull him back. "No sir. Not yet." He turned to Varza. "What's Hassani's play?"

"Allah's final judgment has been put into motion through his faithful servants." Varza wore a vacant expression, as if he couldn't believe he was saying it.

"Meaning?"

"Meaning he's fulfilling prophecies that will bring forth the apocalypse. The Fourth Horseman incarnate."

"Let me guess," Penny said. "'The second angel sounded his trumpet, and a mountain, all ablaze, was thrown into the sea.'"

"Revelation," Quinn said. "Everyone's favorite guide to the end of the world."

Varza turned reflective. "I'd been quite upset when it first appeared our efforts had failed. But discovering that fragment, and learning where it would go?" he asked. "It was an epiphany. What I had once only believed, I now *know*." His tone became a warning. "Hassani was right, and it is right that he be the one to implement Allah's final will."

"You know how many Muslims live in Florida these days?" Quinn asked. "I suppose they're all just martyrs to the cause?"

"It will be their honor to die for the final reckoning, as the blessed prophet foretold," he intoned. "America will be badly hurt, and soon more will come. There will be no crusaders to the rescue, no escaping this decadent world's final judgment."

"Speak for yourself," Penny hissed. As a young woman, she'd piloted bombers that carried enough weaponry to turn a small country into molten slag. She knew exactly what would be coming. "All you've done is ensure the entire civilized world will finally unite against your death cult. I actually *fear* what we'll do in response."

"You should," he laughed. "It will be a self-fulfilling prophecy. Allah's enemies will be gathered in the desert and destroyed. Megiddo...your Armageddon. Have you ever questioned whose side you're actually on?"

"Not anymore," Penny said. "You just settled that argument for me."

"We can't both be right. Though we are all children of Abraham, yours followed the way of deception. You worship a false god."

"Isaac and Ishmael," she said.

"Ishmael was first born," Varza insisted, as if the point should be obvious. "His was the birthright of a nation."

"He was born out of a deception," she argued. The realization that it may not have happened by accident sent a chill up her spine. It was electrifying, as if she'd been struck by the long reach of history itself. She suddenly understood the full depth of the ruse that mankind had fallen under since the very beginning, and realized how weak she had been until now. Like Varza, she had believed but not known. "He will be a wild man; his hand will be against everyone, and everyone's hand against him, and he will make war on all his brothers," she whispered.

"Zionist propaganda," Varza scoffed. "Justification for the sins of your ancestors."

"What the hell are you talking about?" Ryan asked angrily. "This is not a good time to go all holy-roller on us, Penny."

Penny closed her eyes in a wan smile. One theological argument was enough for now. "That was a prophecy over Abraham's illegitimate son, Ishmael. The Muslims consider him the source of their lineage, whereas the Judeo-Christian lineage traces itself to Isaac. Draw your own conclusions."

"They all think they have the answers," Ryan said. "Maybe the solution is to just up and glass the whole continent. If they really want to live in the dark ages, we can arrange that."

"Typical alpha response," Varza sneered. "Bluster in the face of defeat."

Ryan threw him against the door and reached for his helmet. "That's it. I'm taking Kam here for a walk."

Quinn kept a firm hand on his shoulder. "Not like this, Captain. I have an idea."

31

Melbourne

Marcy was startled by the buzz at her side. Working in the back yard while Marshall played, she'd nearly forgotten the phone in her hip pocket. She stood to wipe her hands on her shorts and fished out the vibrating slate, hesitant to answer until she recognized the Denver phone number.

"Morning, Charlie," she answered cheerfully, hoping for some news from Ryan. "What's the good word?"

Grant was uncharacteristically evasive. "Ryan's okay," he blurted out, as if it were necessary to state that quickly. The silence that followed told her that while her husband might be okay, something was certainly not.

"Charlie?"

"Ryan's okay," he repeated.

"I think we've established that, hon." The jarring departure from his usual straightforwardness piqued her curiosity.

"Calls will be going out to all of our employees at the Cape, but I wanted to talk to you myself."

"Calls about *what*?" she asked impatiently. This was starting to feel too much like disaster-assistance protocol.

She heard Grant suck in his breath. "The news will be all over real soon, but for now you *cannot* repeat this." His tone carried a weight greater than his words. "They really stuck their necks out by slipping this to us."

Marcy's knees faltered as he explained what was happening on the far side of the Moon. She curled to the ground and clawed at a tuft of grass as if it would keep her from spinning away.

She must have been quiet for a long time, finally hearing Grant call her name. He continued slowly. "Listen to me very carefully: pack a bag for you and your son. Art's sending every spare bird in the fleet to get all of our people out of Florida before the mass panic starts. We'll text you with an ETA and showtime." He paused. "I need to know you understand what I just told you."

"Yes," she whispered shakily. "I understand." Marcy thumbed the phone off and slipped it back into her pocket with trembling hands. Fighting to gather her strength, she looked across their little inlet towards the Atlantic. Marshall stood at the edge of their yard and threw rocks into the estuary, probably imagining that he was protecting his mom from alligators.

"Come here, baby. We're going on a little adventure."

...

SS Grissom

"They've got real problems, Simon. That hop over the mountain shot their delta-v budget to hell."

He floated over to Audrey's side at an improvised chart table in the galley. "They can launch, right?"

"Sure, but they won't make orbit. Not even close. Even if they leave behind every gram of excess mass, they'll only get about half the velocity change they need."

"Half an orbit." They'd had to know that dust-off would've been one burn too many. He floated over to a nearby porthole and stared at the Moon outside, scratching at the beard he'd grown over the last couple of weeks. It was just heavy enough to have become really annoying. He turned back to Audrey. "We could do it."

"Do what?"

"Meet them halfway. Time our braking burn and their launch right, we can match our perilune to their apolune."

"Of course. I should've thought of that..."

"That's why we like having you back on the ground with time to think."

...

Melbourne

Marcy silently thanked God for the clear roads she'd encountered so far. Every highway had been shut down to all but northbound traffic, which was all anyone south of Tallahassee wanted anyway. The southbound lanes had been closed off to route more traffic north, out of the likely path of destruction. No one in his right mind was staying on the peninsula, but being Florida there were a surprising number of people not in their right minds. The roadsides were dotted with random pockets of eccentrics advocating every harebrained conspiracy theory they could think of. The full spectrum of crazy was on display.

If the whole blasted comet was about to hit the South Atlantic, she'd have been inclined to agree with the apocalyptic weirdos. It was the regular sight of pickup trucks sporting gun racks and rebel flag window banners, also headed north, that rattled her. Those guys were the last ones to give up ground. If the rednecks and good ol' boys were packing up and getting the hell out of Dodge, then maybe they really were looking at a catastrophe.

Eight lanes full of cars, all headed north at a surprisingly good clip. Beside her, Marshall was remarkably calm in his booster seat. She'd figured with everything else going to hell at once, she might as well give the kid a break and let him sit up front. He was just enjoying the view and the speed. *Lord help me but that boy's got his Daddy in him.*

She'd never seen anything like this, despite having ridden out a few hurricanes both here and back home in Charleston. Class 1 and 2 storms were no big deal, not for a town that was used to seeing flooded streets whenever afternoon thunderstorms happened to coincide with high tide.

This was different, of course. For the public to suddenly learn that a big chunk of the comet they'd been watching every night was headed for the ocean, just beyond the horizon? It was one thing to think you could outsmart Mother Nature and ride out a hurricane, but to know you'd be in sight of what promised to be the equivalent of a thermonuclear explosion? One that would guarantee a tsunami?

It must be an absolute madhouse down in Miami, she thought. There were stories of massive ocean liners filled to the railings with evacuees, all of them sailing west at full speed.

Marcy stole a glance overhead and saw dozens of contrails, all headed north. Beyond, her husband was up there somewhere with a front-row seat to this madness.

• • •

A half-mile ahead, an aging purple Honda minivan rolled along with the traffic. Suitcases and crates had been hastily lashed down across its cargo rack, as inside there was not a spare cubic inch of room left. A couple, mother-in-law, four children, a dog, and a cat had all been cramped inside after fighting the traffic out of south Florida hours ago.

A tired voice squeaked from the back. "Dad, I really have to go."

"I know you do," Dad answered. "I said we can't pull over."

"But I have to pee!"

"So does everyone else," Mom said in a strained voice. "You've got to hold it, dear. We can't pull over, we'll never get back on the highway."

"Here," Dad said, tossing an empty milk jug towards the back. "Use this. There's a funnel back there somewhere, one of your brothers can find it."

A chorus of offended voice piped up. *"Dad! Eww!"*

He pounded the steering wheel in frustration. "It's either that or pee in your seat, and we're going to be in here a long time. It's a solid day's drive up to your Aunt's place." In normal traffic, he didn't add. At this rate, getting all the way to New Jersey would take a full two days.

"Was that really necessary?" Grandma demanded. "Honestly, you can't so much as pull over and –"

"Look out the window!" he shot back. "Do you see anywhere for a five-year-old girl to cop a squat?"

"I won't allow it," Mom interjected. She'd not had much to do since daybreak but stare at the passing marshes, pine woods and palmetto scrubs. "Those woods are full of snakes." Their youngest daughter started crying at that.

"Would someone *please* find that funnel back in my tool kit?" Dad pleaded with their sons.

"Not me," the youngest said triumphantly. "I'm not allowed in your tool box."

"You're closer," oldest said, and punctuated it with a punch to younger's arm. "Wuss."

The van exploded in admonitions, curses, and corrections. As Dad turned around to shut everybody up, he didn't notice the sudden eruption of brake lights ahead. It didn't take much to turn a uniform mass of moving vehicles into a giant accordion, and the old purple Honda plowed into the rows of cars ahead.

. . .

The highway ahead turned into a sea of flashing taillights, and Marcy was suddenly grateful for the powerful brakes on Ryan's otherwise clunky old Jeep. The thing might ride like a school bus, but it did exactly what you wanted when you wanted it.

Her arm instinctively went up in front of Marshall and she watched him from the corner of her eye. It was when they came to a stop that she finally saw the column of oily black smoke snaking into the sky.

. . .

Denver

Grant put down the phone and sank into in his chair. "That was Marcy Hunter," he sighed. "They can't make it to the Cape. All the highways headed north were already full, and she said now there's one hellacious pileup on the Interstate." He switched a monitor to one of the news networks, which had been running a nonstop traffic map of Florida. "They haven't seen an evac like this since...well, ever."

"The whole state's pulling up stakes," Hammond grunted, staring at the same map. "There's an enormous boatlift picking up stragglers on the Gulf side. I don't see how she can make it over there."

"And if they can't get to the launch hub?"

"Then she won't be the only one," he said, finishing the thought. Marcy knew the direct lines into the control center, but how many other employee families were in the same predicament and just weren't calling in yet?

Probably quite a few. Within minutes of the news about Weatherby's wayward fragment, the whole East Coast had descended into pandemonium.

Phone lines began lighting up over in the customer service area. No doubt those were the rest of the stranded families, frantically calling in for other escape routes.

There would be none, not unless they could land a couple of 787's on the highway – a fallback option that Grant had already been forced to rule out by FEMA, which had immediately cordoned off large sections of highway for disaster airlift while denying similar requests from every other major airline.

Maybe it's time we just did it anyway, Hammond thought. It was easier to beg forgiveness than ask permission, after all. But landing a widebody unannounced onto a contingency airfield during a national emergency could create real problems beyond the usual pencil-pushers squawking about their authority. That was a good way to crash an airplane and shut off a vital flow of logistics.

His throat burned as if he'd swallowed hot coals. He coughed, swept a thumb around the waist of his trousers and straightened his tie, fighting to regain his composure. He leaned in quietly over Grant's shoulder and drew in a long breath. "We can't wait any longer," he said. "Launch everything. Get whoever we can the hell out of there. Whoever shows up, we take them."

Grant solemnly acknowledged the order. He began typing a departure alert that would immediately appear in the cockpits of every airliner and Clipper sitting at the Cape:

LAUNCH ON SCHEDULE…MULTIPLE PAX STRANDED//REPEAT//DELAY NOT AUTHORIZED//OFFLOAD PAX TO OTHER ACFT IF NECESSARY//GRANT

Hammond collapsed into the seat beside him and wiped at his eyes. "God help them."

32

Farside

The service module echoed with the drumbeat of Varza's frantic pummeling against the airlock hatch, occasionally interrupted by muffled screams for mercy as he pressed his face against the porthole.

"How long are you going to let him carry on like that?" Ryan asked sharply. "Because I didn't think it was possible for him to piss me off even more."

Quinn ignored him, staring impassively at Varza on the other side of the glass. He held a hand to one ear, mouthing "I can't hear you" for show. The shrieks intensified.

Penny watched silently as she paced the room, impatiently chewing a thumbnail. Quinn felt her piercing eyes but remained undaunted. He took one last look at the pressure gauge and turned back to them. "We'll let him go a bit longer," he said. "I know we've got a launch window to meet but it won't do us any good if we don't know where we're going."

Penny looked annoyed. "He can't tell us anything if he's dead, Quinn."

Quinn shook his head in disappointment. "I'm aware of that. I'm not an animal, Colonel. Did you notice the pressure differential?" He pointed at the gauge.

Ryan leaned in for a look and fell back in disbelief. "Half a millibar? That's all you dialed it down to?"

"Made his ears pop a couple times," Quinn explained, "but it got his attention. He's out there in his skivvies and I'm the only thing between him and a very ugly death. Me, and this outflow valve..." He slowly dialed down the differential a tad more. Varza's mouth opened in terror as the pressure in his sinuses spiked. Quinn pressed the intercom switch. "Oops. Might have overdone it there. You ready to talk now?"

"What more do you want?" Varza exclaimed. "I can't tell you what I don't know. I'm not a mind reader!"

"You two spent an awful lot of time together, Doctor. I'm guessing if you think hard enough, you'll come up with something." Quinn made a sad *tut-tut* expression and turned the oversized knob a few more clicks. He saw Penny recoil from the sudden screech, made all the more wrenching by the tinny speakers. "Relax, ma'am. He's more frightened than he is hurt."

"Once we get what we need I really don't care if you space him," she finally said. "But his caterwauling is breaking my concentration."

Quinn turned off the intercom. "Anything you need to share with the class?" he asked, turning her own line back at her.

"It took a lot of gas to hop across this crater and we'll have to be really creative to get off this rock. It may not be enough."

"Define 'creative,' please. Remember I'm a dumb grunt."

"We can't make it all the way back into orbit. Simon and Audrey are working out an intercept. If I can fly us into a suborbital parabola, they'll meet us in mid-flight at the top of the arc."

Quinn thought he understood. "Hitting a slow bullet with a fast bullet?"

"Worse," she explained. "Since we can't go fast enough to make orbit, they'll have to slow down to catch us. Once we're docked, we burn back uphill."

"Oh boy," Quinn whistled. He was beginning to miss old-fashioned earthbound spook work. "Will it help if we ditch any excess weight?"

Penny nodded as she stared through a porthole at their ship, which sat a hundred meters away. "Only way this can work. We have to lose every last gram of unnecessary mass."

Ryan tapped on the airlock hatch. "Speaking of unnecessary mass..." he said, twisting the big control dial. Through the thin metal door, an agonized howl pierced the air.

Quinn bounded across the room and shoved him aside. "Dammit, Hunter!" Through the window, he could see Varza's trembling hands pressed against his ears. "You trying to blow out his eardrums?"

Ryan was oddly unmoved. "Don't tell me you're going easy on him..."

"I don't give a damn about his comfort," Quinn argued, "but he can't tell us anything if he can't hear my questions!"

"I'm betting he'll be real chatty now." Ryan pressed the intercom switch. "Any pieces starting to come into place there, Doctor?"

"Maybe…" Varza said weakly. "Omar was obsessed with trajectory planning. He wasn't heading back to Earth…"

"So where he'd go?" Quinn demanded. "Gateway? You two already stripped it of everything useful."

Varza shook his head with a defiant smirk. "No."

"Oh God," Penny gasped. "I know where he went."

…

Washington

Abbot paced in front of his corner office's wall of windows, which offered an uninspiring view of the tops of every other office building clustered around the National Mall. Being closer would have been nice, but those prized addresses were saved for the museums and their nonstop flood of sweaty tourists.

He tapped his feet impatiently and contemplated the scrap of note paper in his hand. On it was the phone number of someone who Winston had presented as a trusted contact at the *Post*. The kid had gone to great pains to demonstrate his loyalty, not dropping any juicy tidbits without Abbot's express permission. But that channel had eventually closed off until the contact could be assured that he was getting solid information and not just spin from one more grasping functionary. The question *what can you do for me* was the glue of most friendships here.

It sickened him. Never very social himself, Abbot at least understood the value of competence. That, and the naturally strong work ethic of the people back in Houston, had satisfied most of his primal need for trusting relationships among equals. Not that he'd really ever considered any of them equals, but he did know who could be counted on when necessary. Here was different. There was a lot of truth in the old joke about Washington: if you want a friend in this town, get a dog.

"Is something wrong, Doctor Abbot?"

"You're sure about this? I'm taking a hell of a risk going to the press."

"Sometimes it's the only way to do the right thing, sir. We end up bound by rules and chains of command to the point that we can't think for ourselves." He pointed at the note in Abbot's hand. "Jared knows that. He's one of the *Post*'s best."

"Funny that I've not heard of him then."

Winston smiled knowingly. "The big name bylines hardly do any of their own work," he explained, "all the research and contacts come from people you've never heard of. He'll get the information you need out in just the right way." Which meant spin. "If the security lapses at Polaris are as bad as you say, and Hammond's manufacturing division is cutting corners..." Perhaps not by civilian standards, he thought, but that was the point. How could they possibly build a safe vehicle with development times that were a fraction of NASA's? There were good reasons this was such a complex endeavor, all of which seemed to be lost on yahoos like Art Hammond. And now the whole world was going to pay the price.

And still. The security situation meant his hands were tied. "That's all very good," Abbot finally said, "but there's been a media blackout, remember?"

Winston was unmoved. "Not for long, sir. This is a first-order fiasco. They have a way of breaking out at just the wrong time. Our task is to get ahead of it."

"Our task?"

Winston looked embarrassed. "What happens here is important, sir. I left EPA because I realized that NASA was actually doing the kind of work that will save our planet. All they do is regulate when what's really needed is bottom-up activism. The people will never let go of their comforts for a renewable future if they can't see the big picture: our planet is all that we have. The space agency allows them to see that."

Now the kid was getting tiresome. Abbot had mediated enough budget squabbles with grant-chasing doomsayers in the planetary science division that he harbored no illusions about their motivations. It was its own form of religious fanaticism, which he decided to play along with just to keep the kid focused. "I'm glad you think so," he said, "though I'm afraid our research and development is a relic of what it used to be. Knowing the problem exists is only half the battle, son. What matters is what we can do about it."

"Sir, once this present crisis has passed you'll be in an enviable bargaining position when the time comes for appropriations."

In other words, he could lean on Congress for more money. *Lots* more money. Like humans-to-Mars money. Saving the planet would give them unimaginable leverage. It made him wonder how much this kid really did know.

33

Farside

The three were fully suited up when they finally pulled Varza from the airlock. He trembled uncontrollably, whether it was from the cold or abject terror wasn't clear. To Ryan it didn't matter. He dragged their prisoner back into the service bay and sat him down roughly in a corner, then threw a Mylar emergency blanket at him. "Here you go. All the comforts of home."

Varza looked at them wide-eyed. "What are you talking about?" he asked. "I'm going with you, right?"

Ryan laughed bitterly. "You're the scientist, pal. We're just dumb pilots. You heard us: not an ounce of excess weight." He sized Varza up theatrically. "And you're approximately eighty kilos of wasted meat."

Varza began to rise angrily. "You can't do that!" he protested. "You can't—"

Quinn pushed him back down. "Yeah, we can. You've got a month's worth of air and rations in here." He nodded at a porthole. "I wouldn't recommend going outside, though. You might find the climate a bit disagreeable."

"What kind of people are you?" Varza demanded, clutching at his remaining shreds of self-control. "Do you really think you're any better?"

He might as well have stepped on a coiled snake. In one smooth burst of righteous fury, Ryan wheeled around to scoop Varza up by the collar and hurl him against the bulkhead. He pressed his forearm against the scientist's throat. "I know damned well we are!" he roared. "You were prepared to exterminate millions of people like cockroaches. For the sake of what? Your own delusions about saving the planet?"

"Short term thinking," Varza lectured him. "You and I define 'innocent' differently. I see too many who can't get beyond their own selfishness. A whole society that can never serve the greater good because they're too obsessed with protecting their own *stuff*." His voice was pungent with derision.

"That's because most people are just trying to take care of their families, which fools like you make that much harder." Ryan spat the words out. "All because you think you know better."

"Family," he sneered. "That's it. You work at the Cape, don't you? Which means your family must be in the impact zone." He shook his head mockingly. "How terrible for you."

Ryan took advantage of the low gravity to lift Varza off the floor, his feet kicking at the air. He quickly ran into Quinn's blocking forearm. "Not now, Captain," he said calmly. "Asshole's trying to trip you up."

Penny's expression was a mask of revulsion. "All Ryan did was get to him first. Can we take our leave of this puke once and for all? I'm tired of sharing oxygen with him."

"Gladly," Ryan said, his eyes fixed on Varza. "Faceplates down, people."

"No!" Varza's façade fell quickly, his voice rising with panic as they finished sealing their EVA suits. "*No!*" He turned away to plead with Penny. "You're going to let them do this? Is this what your merciful god teaches you?"

Penny stepped forward and stared him down like a cat regarding its prey. She jerked a thumb over her shoulder. "This was *my* idea. These two were going to vent you into open space."

He lunged at her with an anguished wail and was quickly met by the butt of Quinn's carbine. Blood sprayed from his mouth in slow motion as he crumpled to the floor in the low gravity. "Sunday school's over," Quinn said. "We didn't come to play God. We're just here to arrange the meeting."

...

Grissom

Audrey was furiously crunching numbers now, this being her last chance to polish their ad-hoc plan before it was time for Penny and Ryan to launch. "I'm still pissed about that relay sat," she said. "It'd be real handy to not be blacked out every time we're at opposition to them."

Simon hovered over the pilot's console, double-checking that each line of her burn sequence was correctly programmed. There would be no time for catching mistakes, much less fixing them, during their rendezvous on the next orbit. "You accounted for rotation, right?"

It was one of the easiest things to miss when in a hurry. The moon didn't sit still beneath them; as they orbited it continued to spin on its axis so they would not appear over the exact same spot the next time they rose above the local horizon.

"Once," she admitted tiredly. "Caught it when we almost missed comm with them on the last pass."

Simon grunted. "Thought so after we had to realign the antennas. Wasn't by much, but…"

"I know," she said, her frustration bubbling up. If that had happened during *Snoopy's* launch, there'd have been no time to recover before the lander fell back to the surface. "It's not going to happen again."

"Never suggested that it would," he said. "We're all we've got, Aud."

"You mean we're all *they've* got," she gently corrected him. She pushed off from her station and floated to the empty pilot's seat next to him. "Speaking of which, I'd better start getting my head around the front office," she said. "I may not be able to fly it, but I can sure read a checklist and throw switches when you tell me."

"Ryan would say that makes you the perfect copilot. Just don't touch anything until I tell you." Simon looked over and regarded Audrey appreciatively as she buckled in, now filled with a casual competence that helped to put him at ease. Her normally flowing auburn hair had been tied into a bun and the days spent in null gravity had softened her features, making her look even younger than she already was. Years of relying on her for support during his escapades in space had nurtured a professional fondness that made him feel unusually protective, Audrey being so far removed from her element. It was an unexpected delight to finally have her working alongside him, especially with the Moon passing silently overhead as they glided over its craggy surface.

She caught him staring. "What is it?"

"Sorry," he said self-consciously. "I was just thinking that spaceflight agrees with you."

Audrey flushed. "Are you hitting on me?"

Now he really was embarrassed. She wasn't that much older than his own daughters. "What? No! I just, well…damn. You really know how to throw me for a loop, you know that? Can't a guy compliment a lady without getting his balls handed back to him?"

She was having way too much fun at his expense. "Have I ever struck you as the type that would get all offended by men acting like orangutans? I work with pilots."

"True," he said, relaxing again. "What I meant was that we've all leaned on you pretty hard for a long time and it's good to finally get you up here. Kind of like when my girls learned to drive and didn't get themselves killed in the bargain."

Audrey smiled and looked over the copilot's station. It was deceptively simple, just some touch-screen monitors with a bank of hard-wired switches between them. She'd worked out so many procedures with them in the simulators that none of it felt foreign to her. "It's not like I don't understand this stuff," she said. "Flying an old Cessna is probably harder in some ways."

"It is for me," Simon agreed. "The big difference is that stuff happens unbelievably fast up here. If you're not thinking a good half-dozen maneuvers ahead, you've already lost. But you know all that."

"Sounds like you're trying to recruit me for flight crew. Houston was always so focused on fighter jocks and Ph.D.'s that I never considered it for myself. Guess that carried over here."

"Houston only recruited me because they were toying around with nuke plants." The program had of course been canned not long after he finished his training. "But that was then. Guarantee you Art doesn't think like Don Abbot. Damn flyboys," he added cynically.

"Seems like they always need rescuing, don't they?"

…

Snoopy II

The ship buzzed with the whine of fans and pumps as they followed Audrey's countdown checklist. She and Simon would soon be appearing over the eastern horizon, if their ships recognized each other at the correct time then *Snoopy* would launch soon after. If not, it would be another two hours spent recalibrating their plans and Ryan had no intention of missing this appointment. He turned away from his controls to check on their passenger.

"Hang on to your seat, Mr. Quinn. This is going to be a wild ride."

"I've got nothing else to do back here," Quinn said. "And I've probably had worse rides."

"We'll see about that," Penny said. "This is gonna be a first for me, too." She looked at the countdown timer on their center console's flight computer. "Thirty seconds. Getting close..."

She was interrupted by a burst of noise from the radio. "Ryan, Audrey; how copy?"

Right on time. Ryan flipped the microphone switch to voice-activated. "Five-by-five, Aud. Both FMCs are in ascent guidance mode, standing by for your time hack."

"T-minus twenty on my mark," Audrey said. "And...mark."

"Mark." Ryan punched a command into the keypad and synchronized their flight computers. "T-minus sixteen."

Audrey's voice became clearer as their ship rose higher above the gray horizon. "Acquisition radar is pinging your transponder. Good signal. T-minus eleven."

Penny moved to lock down her helmet. "Faceplates down."

"Ten." Audrey sounded unusually reassuring. It had better not be an act...

"Set V-NAV mode."

"Confirmed," Ryan said. "Target set."

"Eight..."

"RCS to main A?"

"RCS is charged," Ryan confirmed. "Main bus A."

"Six..."

"Tanks pressurized?"

"Pressurized. Volume thirty percent."

"Five..."

"This'll be close," Penny muttered. "Gimbal check."

"Four..."

There was a thumping sound beneath them as the liftoff thrusters swung through their mounts. “Positive directional control,” he said. The pump fans’ whining seemed to rise in pitch.

“Three…”

“Ignition sequence start.” Penny snapped open a red cover to expose a glowing switch. She pressed it down forcefully and moved her hand to the throttle levers.

“Two…”

The lander shuddered as its four thrusters came to life and quickly settled into an encouraging rumble. This might work.

“One.”

Ryan placed a gloved hand atop Penny’s and they moved the throttles forward together. It felt as if the floor was going to push right up through them as the lunar surface fell away in a cloud of dust.

“Liftoff!”

34

Grissom

Simon watched the horizon intently; they were already as low as he'd ever been and were about to head even lower. Dusty mountains seemed to reach up into the black as the surface swept beneath them, steadily growing closer as they descended. At these speeds, twenty kilometers didn't feel all that high anymore. Flying upside down and backwards made it worse.

From the corner of his eye, he snuck a peek at Audrey in the copilot's seat on his right. She was admirably focused on her own instrument scan when the temptation to steal a glimpse of the view outside was overwhelming. Very few humans had been to the Moon at all, much less flown this close to it. No doubt the epic proportions of what they were doing would hit her when it was all over and she had time to reflect – of course, that assumed they made it home.

Her eyes lit with excitement. "Got 'em!" she exclaimed. "Transponder's pinging. Bearing zero-zero-six, twenty clicks."

That's my girl. "Altitude?"

"Not as reliable," she cautioned. "It's not like the traffic avoidance gear on the Clippers." Having said that, he knew she'd figure it out anyway. "Signal's consistent, though. I'd say they're passing through four kilometers."

"About halfway there." Their long arc over the surface would top out at ten kilometers, a path carefully planned to both prolong their level flight and keep them clear of the terrain below.

"We're coming up on our pitch point," Audrey reminded him. As the other ship leveled off, he would fire their own thrusters in a final retro-burn to drop them down to the same semi-orbit, matching altitudes and velocities.

Assuming they timed it right: if Penny flew her ship too fast or he slowed theirs down too much, they'd zip past each other. Lunar rendezvous and docking in less than half an orbit, forty minutes of positioning themselves for a maneuver window that would be open for maybe five minutes. *Snoopy* would begin relentlessly losing speed and altitude, beyond the point where Simon could recover them using *Grissom*'s thrusters.

"We're go on your signal, Aud," he said, warming up the igniters. A low whine filled the cabin as blowdown fans stirred their propellant tanks. "Give me a ten-second count."

...

"Passing eight thousand meters." Penny was relieved to hear Ryan's "pilot voice" take over, a hint that he was steady and in control. "Lateral track's offset about half a degree."

She stayed fixed on the information projected in her window, gently caressing the control stick to keep the floating green crosshairs centered on their desired flight path. "Positive or negative?" she asked from habit.

"Positive," Ryan said, "not that it matters." They had burned their tanks dry just to get here and were left with nothing but maneuvering thrusters which couldn't do much more than maintain attitude.

Penny tapped some commands into her master display. "I can at least calibrate my HUD before we put everything on autopilot. It wasn't picking up that translation error. You're sure?"

Ryan nodded and pointed at the primary flight computer. "Aud saw it too. No sweat, they'll just adjust their intercept vector. They've got the gas for it – we don't."

She hated that he was right, because it meant they were just along for the ride now. She'd taken her gloves off for launch and ascent, she now slipped them back on and twisted the locks on each wrist ring before turning to check Ryan and Quinn. "Suit check," she ordered. "Everybody confirm pressure."

"Good seal," Ryan replied quickly. "Holding at six psi."

"Good to go," Quinn said. His voice was remarkably clear. Besides looking tough, those military spacesuits must have fantastic radios.

"Thanks boys," Penny said. She hesitated before turning what little control remained over to the automated system and floated to the back of the cabin, where Quinn waited by a coiled umbilical. His suit was buckled into a compact EMU, short for "extra-vehicular mobility unit" which was just government-speak for a jetpack contraption he called the "Buzz Lightyear" suit. He held out a d-ring, which she snapped onto her suit. She played out a few more meters of umbilical and handed it to Ryan, who did the same. Both were now lashed to Quinn and his rocket pack.

Matching orbits and docking two spacecraft was, at its essence, an exercise in matching velocities. Speed dictated the dimensions of an orbit, which in turn dictated when the two ships would meet at the same spot. A few meters per second's worth of errors would send them flying past each other, close enough to reach out and touch but without enough time to mate the two together. And if it came to that, Quinn was prepared to make up the difference.

• • •

The two ships raced silently above the smooth, dark plains of the moon's equatorial mare, the cooled remains of what had once been enormous seas of lava. They grew steadily closer, *Snoopy* slipping ahead of and beneath *Grissom* as it reached the top of its suborbital arc. Still flying backwards, Simon kept his eyes on their target like a wide receiver waiting for a deep pass. And like a football, Penny's ship was going where it was going; nothing could change that now. It was up to Simon to get in position to catch them.

"That thing looks a lot bigger from here," he said drily. "What's our separation?"

Audrey had become remarkably comfortable in her role as his ad-hoc navigator. "Three kilometers even, closing at two. Altitude ten-point-two kilometers, down at three hundred per minute." It was a nice, shallow fall that would steadily become much less so.

"What's our delta?" The increase in their rate of descent would determine how much time they really had.

"Point four per minute. That'll give us about eight minutes before we start getting terrain alarms."

Simon blew out a long breath and flexed his hands around the control sticks. “I’m an engineer, not a pilot,” he grumbled, nodding out the windows toward their rapidly approaching target. “Next time we make sure one of those two does the flying.”

“I’d just as soon there not be any ‘next time,’” Audrey said. “After this trip you guys will be lucky just to get me into an elevator.”

“That’s my girl. Stay positive.” He focused on the rapidly approaching lander and tried not to think of the steadily rising terrain that waited for them along the eastern border of Mare Tranquillitatis. The beginning of Mare Crisium, the “Sea of Crises,” was aptly named all right. Its rugged hillocks, pockmarked with ancient impact craters, would be sweeping by unnervingly close.

“I’ve got a Lidar lock on their docking target,” Audrey said, watching the two ship’s flight management computers synchronizing themselves. “FMC’s are synched, guidance platforms are talking to each other. You should be getting updates in your HUD now.”

A new icon appeared in the window ahead of him, centered on *Snoopy’s* forward docking hatch. Two crenellated circles danced about it, one attempting to merge with the other. “Got it.” He tapped the control stick in his right hand, gently pushing them to one side, then cancelled it with a tap in the opposite direction as the ship grew silently in their windows. The glowing rings began blinking steadily and *Grissom*’s own maneuvering jets began pulsing in sympathy, its computer keeping them centered in Simon’s display.

“Targets aligned,” he said, and pushed the translation controller in his left hand. “Thrusting forward.” With a mild kick in the backside from their own RCS jets, they quickly began closing the distance. “Not that hard, really.”

Audrey wasn’t as easily convinced. “So long as the computers work, all we have to do is point them in the right direction. We pay you guys the big bucks for when all that stuff breaks.”

“I was just showing off.” Simon had become qualified as a civilian pilot with NASA, and had of course been checked out in Hammond’s moonliners, but that was the extent of his flying. These were completely different machines than the suborbital Clippers that were the company's workhorses. Those things required actual flying.

She brought their attention back to the lander, which was quickly filling the windows. "Closing at three, nearing blackout. Let's back off a bit."

He smiled to himself as her flight director's persona emerged. Without a word he tapped back on the translation controller, rattling the cabin as the nose thrusters fired to slow them down. "On speed, on target," he said as the symbols and numbers in his HUD screen settled.

"Concur," she said coolly. "We're in blackout." They were separated by less than two ship's lengths and could not make any more control adjustments without risking damage to either lander.

This was the part that knotted Simon's gut: two ships, each about ten meters long and massing several kilotons, irreversibly heading for an intentional collision as they fell steadily towards the lunar surface. He purposefully avoided looking at the altitude and velocity displays, in fact he'd intentionally removed them from his HUD projection after they'd been established on trajectory. If the ships couldn't rendezvous, none of it would matter: Penny, Ryan, and the enigmatic Quinn would be doomed to crash back to the surface. What they didn't know was that he and Audrey had decided to ride this all the way down with them – whatever happened, they would not give up on getting their people safely aboard. Whether that occurred too late for him to bring them all back to orbit seemed irrelevant at the time. Now, with their sister ship looming large outside, he wondered if that had been foolishly bold.

Then again, he could at least see outside. It hadn't always been so. "Aud, when this is over remind me to tell you a story about the Sea of Okhotsk," he said absent-mindedly.

"Okay," she said tentatively, wondering what his point might be. Their forward windows were filled with *Grissom*'s metallic bulk. "Ten meters. Closing at point five."

"Twenty seconds, then. Coming in a little hot," Simon warned. "We're gonna feel it."

They did. The two ships met, the shock absorbers in their docking collars absorbing some of the impact but not enough. Each bounced away from the other, suddenly opening up the distance between them. An alarm sounded as the flight computers lost alignment.

"Damn!" Simon angrily thumbed the mic switch. "Penny, you see that?"

"Sure did feel it. I might've lost a filling. Don't worry, we've got this."

"You've got the propellant?"

"Not really," she said, "but I won't need much. Just keep it tight on your end. I'm synching our guidance platforms now."

• • •

Quinn had been holding on to the handrail above the pilot's stations and had nearly face-planted into the console between them. "You sure about this? Because I'm ready to take us over there."

"Just hold your horses," Stratton said brusquely, not taking her eyes off the docking target outside. Hovering just a few meters away, the gap between ships was steadily growing. "Don't take this the wrong way, but I really don't want to try that stunt."

"I have," Hunter chimed in, "and you're right to feel that way. I sure don't want to try it again."

"Thanks for the vote of confidence." Quinn actually looked disappointed.

"You don't strike me as the type to take things personally." Her tone was distracted, mechanical; she was thinking aloud and not realizing it. With slight but very precise movements she was gently pulsing the translation controller while keeping them centered with the RCS jets. Her concentration was so intense it was surprising that she managed to say anything.

He noticed the same from Hunter; his eyes were locked on a single control panel that he'd swiveled in front of his seat. All Quinn could see were a variety of colored lines tracing angles across a circle as a torrent of numbers cascaded down either side of the screen. No doubt they conveyed vital data but to him it might as well have been Egyptian hieroglyphics. The crosstalk between them was clipped and just as impenetrable:

"Alpha steady at point-two. Watch your pitch trim."

"Yeah, I saw that. Switch us to attitude mode, please."

"ATT mode," Hunter said. "They're still locked on."

"RCS level?"

"Stand by…fourteen percent."

She reacted with a subtle flinch that made him wonder if that would be enough. Quinn had decided it best to shut up and let them work – he may not have been able to interpret the dizzying array of information they were using but he could certainly judge relative motion. And he could read a fuel gauge: they had to make this work, or their separation rate would be beyond his EMU pack's ability to recover if they had to bail out.

"We're gaining on them," Hunter said. "Twenty meters, closing at point three. Down at ten."

"I'm keeping it that way," Stratton said, still tense. "We can't do this again."

It was then that Quinn looked beyond the lander hovering just outside their windows to the moon beyond – the surface was slipping past rapidly, and seemed noticeably closer. Everything about it looked bigger. He decided since both pilots had been silent for a few seconds, it was safe to ask a question.

"What's our altitude?"

Hunter didn't turn away from his instruments. "Nothing worth mentioning," he said ominously. "Down at twelve," he added, meant for Stratton.

Quinn had been hoping for an actual number he could understand but decided not to press his luck. It would work, or it wouldn't.

"Almost there," she whispered, then reached for the mic switch. "Simon, we're gonna have to turn and burn as soon as we both see a hard dock. There won't be time to transfer full control to either ship, so we'll have to do this together."

"Got it," he answered. "I'll pitch nose up, you nose down. We'll light our mains as soon we get positive alpha."

"Good man," she said. "Let's keep it to one-second pulses; I'll call 'em."

"You're the pilot. Almost there…"

From Quinn's spot, they were so close it looked like they were already mated. There was a disquieting *thud* as the docking rings connected, he noticed a prominent center console light turn amber as the cabin shuddered.

"Contact!" Hunter exclaimed. There was a quick series of metallic rattles as clamps around each ring slammed shut. The amber light turned green. "Capture!"

"Hard dock!" Stratton shouted. It was perhaps the most excited he'd seen her. "Simon, pitch up on my mark. Ready…now!"

Quinn bounced off the floor as the ship rotated around him; he scrambled for the nearest handhold and cursed himself for not staying buckled in. Outside, the Moon wheeled past.

"Pitching through ninety degrees," Stratton called. The horizon reappeared overhead, now upside-down as they swapped ends. "Get ready to null rates on my mark. Three…two…one…*mark*." As she tapped the control stick back, he saw the other ship's control jets pulse in sympathy.

"Pitch angle passing through zero," Hunter said, this time turning to face him. "Hang on, Marcus."

Quinn threw on the shoulder harness just as *Snoopy's* main engine lit. A bloom of incandescent gas erupted from its tail and a rumble shuddered through the joined spacecraft. Through the exhaust plume, he could see the lunar surface steadily falling away. Stratton sank into her seat, closed her eyes and rolled her neck. He assumed that meant they weren't about to die.

"Positive rate," Hunter exhaled, relief evident in his tired voice. "Passing through two thousand meters, delta-v one hundred per second."

Two kilometers? "We were that close?"

"Closer. We just climbed back *up* through two grand."

…

The combined ships steadily rose up out of the moon's shallow gravity well in a long spiral which would end at Gateway and its precious stores of methane and oxygen.

"We're almost out of gas," Penny said. "I can get us close, but we'll need to use a lot of RCS prop to actually get into position for tanking."

"I don't see that we have a choice," Simon agreed. He was floating behind her in the "captain's chair" and poring through a copy of the station's operating manual. "Fortunately it's just cold gas. We can possibly divert some of their nitrogen, if I can find the fittings." Their primary fuel and oxidizer tanks had common filler ports, thanks to the Clippers servicing NASA's old space station.

"Might not be too good for the seals," she said, "but it ought to work in the short term."

"Short term is all we've got right now." Simon jerked his head back to where Ryan floated in the cupola. He'd become a near-permanent fixture there after Penny had the entire stack back under control and they'd been safely established in orbit again.

Simon stole a glance at the countdown timer on his watch and turned away. No one had wanted to put a constant reminder of the inevitable on any of the ship's displays.

The immense distances in space had the effect of making everything appear deceptively slow. When two objects orbited in close proximity to each other their relative motion seemed leisurely, like birds wheeling about in a rising thermal. But when their motions weren't in such close synchronization, when their directions and relative velocities became at odds, that was when the illusion fell away.

Weatherby burned white against the black void, from out here now frighteningly close to Earth as it was maybe thirteen hours from its nearest pass. That meant its fragment, recently labeled "Weatherby-1A" was ahead and now indistinguishable against Earth's blue disc. It was like a four-dimensional billiard game, a bank shot that not only counted on hitting the ball just right but on the bumper actually appearing in the right place at the right time. Any number of dangerous objects frequently crossed their home planet's path; the question was when Earth itself would be in the same spot at that particular point in time. It wouldn't be long until a new sun would briefly flare in the ocean off Florida.

35

Melbourne

The traffic had been piling up steadily for hours. Emergency vehicles had been maddeningly slow to arrive, which she knew was out of their control but it was no less frustrating. Everything was being moved inland until after the "event" (as it was being referred to officially); coastal residents had been told in no uncertain terms that they were on their own now.

She had fought to tamp down her own fear, if only for Marshall's sake. The little guy couldn't see Mommy start to freak out, not when everything around him was quickly turning full-on crazy. She knew their only way out of here was to try and make it to the spaceport before the last plane left – and judging by Charlie's message, that would be very soon.

"Look, Mommy!" he shrieked, pointing to the sky above. "One of Daddy's planes!" Sure enough, the unmistakable triangular shape of a Clipper thundered overhead in a wide climbing turn, trailing fiery exhaust as it sped away towards the low afternoon sun. "Was that our special ride?" he asked worriedly. "Did we miss it?"

"No, baby," she said quietly. They were supposed to be on one of the jets bound for Denver; she knew the Clippers were being evacuated to the maintenance and test center up at Moses Lake, Washington. The one that just launched would probably be there in the next half hour.

Time was running out. She tapped the steering wheel impatiently and considered her options. Nothing was moving; even with clear roads she was a good half an hour from the launch terminal. The last plane was going to leave soon, before the impact.

They were stuck, and sitting here on a jammed highway was suicide. The crowd had been remarkably well behaved but cracks were beginning to show. Horns had started to blare and a few arguments had erupted among the cars around her. Several people milling about on the shoulder were becoming visibly agitated, and appeared to be formulating some kind of half-baked plan. To accomplish what, who knew?

They'd luckily been in the left lane when everything came to a stop. She reached down for the shifter and dropped the Jeep into four-wheel drive, suddenly thankful for Ryan's absurd off-roading beast. As Marcy turned onto the grass median and gunned the engine, she promised herself to never make fun of this thing again.

Marshall jostled in his seat as they bounced across the rough ground, going against the flow of stopped cars. "Where are we going?"

"Home." As they made their way back, her eyes were drawn to the southeast. In the low afternoon light, Weatherby's brilliant white coma hung menacingly in the sky.

• • •

"Where are we going?" Marshall asked again in a quivering voice as Marcy hurried him along. It was the first thing he'd said since they'd left the madness of the interstate behind them. She scooped him up in her arms and ran for the back door, and very nearly kicked a foot through the sliding glass pane before the stubborn panel finally gave way.

"Outside," she said brusquely. She hated being short with the little guy but there was no time left for niceties. He clung tightly to her neck as she ran towards the garden shed. Thankfully, the lock was open. "Wait here. Don't move," she commanded, in the firm way mothers do when they need their children to know they mean business.

Marshall stood motionless, though he'd barely heard her. He was too enthralled by the brilliant flash that suddenly burst on the horizon. Like a sunrise, but it couldn't be: the sun was over there, in the other direction, on its way down for the day. The sky, already fading to orange in the late afternoon, was ablaze with new light. As his mind tried to process this sudden appearance of dawn and dusk, he stumbled as the ground began to shake and the air filled with noise. Farther out over the ocean, an ominous white ring appeared in the sky where the flash had appeared: a wall of clouds was heading their way, and it was moving really fast.

And the tide was receding, withdrawing much faster – and farther out – than his young memory could recall. The canal along their backyard had quickly drained with it, a fact punctuated by his father's boat that now rested in mud by the dock. Fiddler crabs skittered atop the muck, scrambling for their hidey-holes along the shore. To his young eyes, it was as if God Himself had just opened the world's bathtub drain. "Mommy?" he asked nervously.

"Yes, hon," Marcy answered, rushing out of the shed with an extension ladder and a coil of nylon rope. She motioned for him to follow her.

"What's going on?" Something was very, very wrong.

Marcy hesitated. "We're going on a little adventure," she said, propping the ladder against their house as she silently hoped two stories would be enough. "Remember when you tried to climb on top of the house to help Daddy fix the satellite dish?" Even if he didn't, she'd certainly never forget it. Her heart had nearly leapt out of her chest when she'd seen him trying to step out onto the roof, unknown to his father working just a few feet away. That they'd both remained calm enough to keep from startling him into a certain fall had been a miracle.

"I remember," he said. "You were mad."

"I was scared."

"But you're not scared anymore?"

Oh Lord. More than I've ever been. Being stranded with Ryan on that sabotaged Clipper years back seemed like a vacation by comparison. She finally decided honesty was the best policy. "It's a whole different kind of scared, baby."

He thought about that. "I'm afraid of the sky," he confessed with the singular understanding of a young child. Maybe it would make his Mom feel better.

Marcy swallowed, her throat suddenly bone dry. "So am I, hon. Come on now, up the ladder. Fast as you can, baby."

As he eagerly scrambled upward, she kept a worried eye on the approaching barrage. They'd said the fragment would strike a couple of hundred miles offshore, which sounded farther away than it really was. The shock wave would hit them about ten minutes later, but she was more afraid of the tsunami, which was expected to arrive about an hour after impact.

Soon.

She turned at what sounded for all the world like an approaching freight train. A menacing gray shadow appeared along the horizon, like a cliff growing out of the sea. Marcy fought past sweaty palms and trembling knees, struggling keep a grip on the ladder as she coaxed her son upward.

"Hurry, baby. Keep climbing."

...

Grissom

Ryan's grip tightened around the handholds in the observation dome, ignoring the pain as his fingernails dug into his palms.

Though a quarter-million miles away, he could still see the flash. A halo of white exploded outward from the center of impact, roiling foam in the otherwise sapphire-blue Atlantic. It was a ring of clouds forming behind the supersonic shock wave; it reminded him of pictures from Jupiter when it had suffered the same punishment from a fragmented comet decades earlier. But that had been interesting, whereas this was horrifying. It was a ring of destruction, rapidly moving across the south Atlantic and consuming everything in its path. Millions of people were down there, trapped on the giant peninsula that was Florida, and who knew how many were left down in the islands or farther up the coast.

It would be a matter of minutes. Minutes until devastation was visited on humanity in a way not experienced in centuries. Certainly not in modern times; maybe Krakatoa or that awful Indonesian tsunami came close. Lifetimes of human toil, of family histories, were about to be swept away by one freak act of nature.

Not an act of nature. An act of *men*. Barbarians, fanatics of their own twisted religions. Ryan didn't much care at this point whether Varza would've scoffed at the characterization, the little prick had whatever was left of his miserable life to think that one over. He'd so badly wanted humanity to be freed of its dependence on artificial technology, we'll see how he likes the idea now that his own survival depends on it. It would eventually run out and there wouldn't be a damn thing he could do about it except watch the gauges slowly drain to zero.

Hassani, on the other hand, was just another in a too-damned-long line of Islamist maniacs who'd gotten his hands on way too much firepower for everyone else's good.

It was the curse of the modern era: too many people had fooled themselves for too long that peace was something other than temporary, not a condition that could only be earned through the total destruction of one's enemies. Heartless as that sounded, history's single lesson was that global politics worked by the same rules as grade school playgrounds: there would always be bullies, and the only way to protect yourself was to confront them swiftly and without remorse. Ryan's throat tightened, he felt the bile welling up inside as despair threatened to overwhelm him.

No. Despair was for the helpless, and though he couldn't do a thing to save his family he sure as hell had the means to go after the one who did this.

...

Melbourne

Marcy kept a close eye on Marshall as she gingerly stepped off the ladder and onto the roof, sat them down on the most level spot she could find, and held him tightly in her lap.

They turned to the sound of a distant rumble. The gray wall was closer, moving fast over the drained beaches as the noise attacked them from all sides. Flecks of seawater fell against her skin, like the first drops of an approaching storm.

Any second now.

She pulled him in close and pressed herself flat, placing her body between her son and the rapidly approaching wave. She swallowed hard against the icy lump that stabbed at her throat and hugged Marshall ever tighter, both of them curling into a fetal position.

The wave swept ashore, across the canals and over the causeways, and swept down their street. The house trembled beneath them.

"Hang on, baby."

...

What had at first rumbled like a distant freight train now roared like one had crashed into their neighborhood, the wall of water coursing up streets and exploding through canals and over causeways as it came for them. Marcy was dumbstruck as entire blocks were swept away in its path. The sky burned a dozen shades of orange in the low sun, an angry palette reflected in a mushroom cloud of vaporized seawater towering in the distance.

The surge came, bearing with it the remnants of countless lives. Some she'd known, most she hadn't. Up the street she could see a friend's home torn apart, set at ground level like so many of the newer builds. They didn't stand a chance against the onslaught of countless millions of gallons of seawater.

That was when she noticed that not all of the homes were buckling – the ones built largely above ground on piers, the ones intended to handle hurricane-borne tidal surges, were still standing. Not all of them, but most…

Thank God they had wanted an older home to fix up. She'd had no problem with the old-fashioned "house on stilts" look; it had reminded her of beach houses back in Charleston.

When the ocean arrived at their doorstep, her capacity for fear had been long since drained. No time for that. It was time to act. But how? A thirty-something suburban mom with her toddler son, clinging to each other on their rooftop against the end of the world? They didn't stand a chance.

It was then that she heard a whine above the deafening surge: Marshall, head buried in her chest with a death grip around her neck and wailing against nature's onslaught.

Like hell. She grit her teeth. *Not today.* "Hang on baby," was all she could say, over and over again, even if it did nothing other than calm a child by the sound of his mother's voice.

His grip tightened as the water rose. The house shuddered with the passing surge. Water crashed beneath the house, buffeting its piers and still rising. She reefed in the length of climbing rope and looped the excess around their chimney. Hopefully it would hold when everything else gave way.

The house groaned until it was wrenched free with a bone-shaking *snap* as the piers buckled. She felt the roof rise and fall, like a raft on the crest of a wave.

...

Coastal towns farther north fared worse due to the glancing blow. Most of Weatherby-1A's destructive energy was directed northwest, at the Carolinas and coastal Virginia.

Along the fragile Outer Banks, vacation homes were battered by an invisible wall of air as the shock wave hit with the force of a sudden hurricane. Decades of efforts at halting coastal erosion were wiped clean in a matter of minutes as the ocean swept over the dunes. The Cape Hatteras lighthouse, which had withstood countless tempests from the sea, finally collapsed as the wave surged past.

Virginia Beach and Norfolk suffered much the same fate. Those left behind in the evacuation's chaos scrambled to the tops of hotels along the beaches, others tried to move inland and quickly found out they'd have been better off in the beachfront high-rises. Had they known the fate of the unfortunate souls still trapped on the Bay Bridge, they would have thanked their good fortune.

The sea continued its sweep inland, remorselessly seeking the path of least resistance. The surge rolled across the Chesapeake Bay, coursing up the Potomac before finally spending itself along the banks of Annapolis and Washington.

...

Melbourne

The roof came unmoored as the foundation gave up their house to the water. They found themselves clinging to a raft of lumber and ceramic, hurtling down once-familiar streets and surrounded by the detritus of what a few minutes earlier had been their neighborhood. The tidal surge had become encrusted with trash, the debris of ruined homes and businesses riding atop the invading sea as it flowed across the peninsula towards the Indian River. From there, no doubt the waters would merge and eventually flow back to sea.

Back to sea. Marcy shuddered at the thought, now truly and deeply afraid. Bad as this was, she thought they'd survive so long as the roof held together. The water had to recede at some point, and heading for a large open river meant fewer things to run into that held the potential to wreck their makeshift lifeboat.

Soaked through, yet her mouth was bone dry. The fear was palpable now, a living thing she could almost touch. And at this moment, the paralysis it threatened in her was more dangerous than the chaos surrounding them.

She dug her nails into her thigh, the pain forcing her to focus. *Out to sea*, she thought. That's what waves did after they rushed ashore; the water was drawn back out to sea. And this was just a wave, after all, albeit a terrifyingly big one. This water and most everything with it would soon rush right back out into the Atlantic where it belonged.

And they didn't belong. She still remembered that awful Indonesian tsunami decades ago; as a young girl she'd been morbidly fascinated by it and had even organized a charity drive for the region at her parent's church. And she recalled that a large percentage of the more than a quarter-million deaths were of people who had been caught up in the surge and swept out to sea. Decomposed bodies had reportedly washed ashore for months afterward, sometimes hundreds of miles from where they'd been taken. And now it was happening to them.

No. They were not going to survive this perverse whitewater ride only to be swept out to sea atop what was left of their own home.

She unwound the climbing rope from around the remains of the chimney and began searching frantically for something to lash themselves against. Light poles and gas station signs appeared almost randomly. She ignored them, assuming anything manmade could be uprooted just as easily as she and Marshall had been.

Uprooted. Amazingly, the older deciduous trees had mostly held firm through the onslaught. So many palms and conifers, with their weaker root systems, were being torn from the ground and swept away by the deluge. But not the big hardwoods...

She prayed for trees. Big beautiful live oaks, some hundreds of years old, with root systems that she imagined were so strong and so deep that they inspired Tolkienesque fantasies. *Maybe we'll get lucky and find one that can just walk us out of here*, she thought with a laugh.

It felt strange to laugh now, as inappropriate a time as she could've imagined. The rushing water became turbulent ahead, signaling that something was close to the surface. Out of place in this temporary river, what appeared to be an island or sandbar appeared in the distance.

No, not an island. Impossible. She looked around to get her bearings and realized they were being carried toward a golf course, the one she passed every week while running errands. Never having the patience for golf, she'd still admired the gorgeous landscaping…

Trees. Live oaks, looming ahead.

Marcy grabbed her son firmly by the shoulders and leaned in close so as not to raise her voice above the roaring flood: "Stay close baby. Mommy's going to stand up now. Okay?" Marshall nodded back nervously.

She took up the trailing end of the rope and tied it around a loose brick from the chimney. Marcy stood carefully on wobbly legs, swaying through every crest and trough as she focused on the largest tree. She focused on the thickest branch she could find and began swinging the rope in a circle over her head.

Her mind had become a telephoto lens, zooming in on her target at the exclusion of all else. Even the sound of her son's voice fell into the background, barely noticeable above the tsunami's roar. She recognized the tunnel vision effect for what it was, embracing the intensity it gave her. Beyond this stand of massive hardwoods lay the Indian River; normally tranquil, it was already well past flood stage and rapidly becoming one with the invading sea.

Her mind wandered a split second, recalling Genesis and its story of the Tree of Life – that was as good a name as any for the fast-approaching tangle of limbs. She estimated they were doing at least thirty miles an hour. This was going to hurt.

With all the strength she had left, Marcy flung the rope ahead, screaming with the effort. As the water swept them past, she watched their line snag a thick limb. The sudden recoil snapped back the rope's weighted end and wrapped it around the limb. She looked down at her feet to see the slack quickly begin to run out. Praying the rope didn't wrench her off of their makeshift raft before she could reach him, she turned to grab Marshall.

He was gone.

As children did, when her back was turned he had moved just out of reach to cling to the rubble of their chimney. The rope played out quickly behind, threatening to pull her free any second and leaving her son behind. "Marshall!" she shouted over the roaring water. "Run to me!"

Marcy let him move first, afraid it would frighten him even more when she jumped. She lunged forward, leaping across the remaining distance to wrap him up as the rope went taut behind her. He yelped as she fell on top of him, both crying as they were pulled roughly away from the remains of their home. The water was shockingly cold.

36

Grissom

The debate about how to catch Hassani had not been nearly as lively as the one about what he might be doing at Weatherby.

"He can use *Orion* as a thruster, nose the docking port up against the surface," Penny said. "The main engines would probably have enough impulse to move it into a different orbit."

"Not enough to hit Earth, though," Quinn said. "It's twelve hours from closest approach. Not even the nukes could do that."

Audrey had stayed out of it until now, choosing instead to immerse herself in trajectory planning. In her mind, this was all academic if they couldn't catch up to him in the first place. She looked up from her work. "No, but he could keyhole it."

Quinn's head was swimming now. "Say what?"

"They didn't put nukes on Gateway to blow up rocks," she pointed out. "Well, maybe the little stuff, but you can do a lot with a few well-timed detonations. A few kicks in the right direction now would put it on an intercept with Earth when it whips back around the sun."

"Hit us on the back side..."

"So another six months?" Ryan surmised. "It's a long shot. He's got to know we'd be able to put something up to stop it."

"He probably knows we can't," Quinn interjected. "The entirety of our planetary defenses are under Hassani's control right now. We were the only country with the necessary hardware laying around. DARPA can't put together another weapons battery in enough time to do any good."

"Moving it out of our way in six months means they'd have to be able to launch something *this* month," Audrey agreed. "Gateway and Farside were crash programs and they still took almost two years to deploy. If Hassani can change its orbit now—"

"It seals our fate," Ryan said bitterly. "Plus he has a nice little defense in place: you don't dare go after him or he'll unleash one of his nukes." He looked to Penny, the only one with any experience on the Orion program. "I'm guessing he's going to be shepherding that comet all the way around?"

"He won't have any choice," she said. "He's already used a lot of prop just to break orbit. He'll have to use even more to rendezvous with Weatherby. The model he's flying has the extended-duration service module, so he can sit it out."

Alone in something the size of a minivan for half a year...not that Hassani would care. The ringleaders rarely had the nerve to actually sign up for the suicide runs, but he was on a divine mission unparalleled in history. Six months of mind-numbing isolation was a small price to be the man with his finger on Allah's very own "smite" button. In fact it was probably a necessity, Ryan thought.

Hassani was a "Twelver," a sect that believed in fomenting maximum chaos to enable the return of a savior they called the Mahdi, or Twelfth Imam. By Penny's account, it sounded like their messiah was our antichrist. Or hers, he wasn't that sure himself and had frankly started to glaze over whenever she talked about it. In his mind it was all subject to interpretation.

But she had been on to something: this comet could bring devastation on a Biblical scale, something not seen since Noah's flood if you believed in that sort of thing. Penny obviously did, and no doubt had come to some sort of religious epiphany via the cold equations of orbital mechanics. Hassani must have had the same realization a long time ago but with completely different intentions. The juxtaposition of such sharply opposing actions from similar motivations defied his sense of morality. At least to him the motivations were similar.

Maybe there was something to Penny's newfound piousness but he could work through that later. There was too much to do now. "We're the only ones who can catch him," Ryan said, laying bare an idea that they'd hoped to avoid. "It'll take a lot of delta-v, maybe everything we have. We're talking a one-way trip."

Audrey smiled. "Maybe not."

• • •

Johnson Space Center
Houston, TX

"Flight, CAPCOM."

"Go CAPCOM."

"Flight, we've got an...*unusual* request on the secure freq."

Over the years Ronnie Bledsoe had become resigned to his fate of managing the decline of the International Space Station. The orbiting complex had been kept in service well past its predicted useful life and was showing all of the usual signs of a machine long in the tooth: they liked to think that failure wasn't an option, but it was sure as hell turning into a daily occurrence. Bledsoe made a quick check of the station's plan of the day and saw nothing that would lead one of their astronauts to call home on the scrambled channel. So, another surprise in a job that had already become full of them. "What's the nature of the request?"

The astronaut working as CapCom pulled off his headset and stepped over to Bledsoe's console. He reached across and switched the comm line so Bledsoe could speak to whoever it was directly. "SS *Grissom*, you're on with flight director Bledsoe."

Grissom? *Wait a minute...*

"Good morning, Ronnie," a female voice called. While distorted by the encrypted signal, it sounded awfully familiar...

"Audrey?"

There was a two-second delay as the signal traveled a good half-million kilometers each way. Finally, there was the familiar *beep* just before she came back.

"That's my name, don't wear it out."

Definitely her. That line had been a running joke between them back when she'd been one of his more promising young flight controllers. "Where are you?" An obvious question, but still...

Beep. "Gateway Station. L2."

That explained where the scrambled signal came from. He looked down the line at the comm station and double-checked his own status board to make certain he was the only one on this channel. "What the hell are you doing up there?" He'd heard some disquieting rumors about the complex going silent…

Beep. "Good, so at least you know about it. That'll make the rest easier."

"You didn't answer my question." The rumors had started a few days after Polaris had that moonliner go missing. He'd wondered if Aud had been sitting at Flight then.

Beep. "It's a long story," she said, "but I'm up here with Simon if that helps."

"I'm not sure that helps at all," he said. "What did you two get yourselves into?" The Air Force had been in a big enough hurry to get those old ISS modules launched...

Beep. "Again, long story. We're in kind of a jam and need your help. Can you send us the specs on the structural nodes you guys used to build Gateway?"

"I'm afraid to ask why." Not that the Air Force had been very forthcoming about it.

Beep. "We wouldn't be able to tell you anyway, not without landing ourselves in a whole lot of trouble."

That she was calling at all told him they were already in a lot of trouble. "Understood, Aud. But can you be more specific?"

Beep. "Affirmative, Flight. Stand by." Back to standard radio phraseology, which meant the small talk was over. "We need the design longitudinal load and torque limits for the multi-purpose logistics module and the common docking node. Emphasize design limits, not operational limits. Over."

Design limits, she'd said. The actual maximum capability of each component to bear twisting loads; not the self-imposed limits they used for mission rules. That would take some time. "Copy all," he replied. "What's your timeframe?"

Beep. "ASAP. We have to skip town in thirty-six hours and there's a lot to do in the meantime."

• • •

Grissom

Simon had been fiddling with the navigation system for the past hour, picking apart Audrey's predictions for their different orbits while he scratched at his beard. Ryan and Quinn busied themselves with the propellant transfer while bringing *Grissom's* systems back to life.

He could sense Penny staring at his back, no doubt trying to figure out what he was thinking. He finally broke their mutual silence. "You helped put those spacecraft into service," he said. "How can we disable it, absent ramming the thing?"

"Wondered when you might ask me that," she said. "I've been giving it some thought." She floated over to him and pulled up a diagram of *Orion* on an open monitor. "Couple of options. We could either disable the flight controls or jam his propellant feeds." Its main engine used hypergolic fuels, excitable chemicals that spontaneously ignited upon contact with each other. They were as reliable as they were dangerous: a simple plumbing and valve system was all it needed to work. Just don't get any of it on you. Ever. "The service module has access panels for each that can be manipulated by suited astronauts. Disconnect either one and he's dead in the water."

Simon didn't have to think about it long. "I'm leaning towards the prop valves. It seems like a more permanent solution."

"It is," she agreed, and zoomed in on a schematic of the fuel system. "First we disconnect the solenoids, then the manual backup linkage. They're in the same area, and we can use Gateway's tool kit."

"Then that'll be our plan A," he decided. "Downside risks?"

"He'll probably be expecting us. Couple of bursts from a maneuvering thruster in the right location..."

An unpleasant thought. It would be far too easy to blast a spacewalker with rocket exhaust. "Probably," he agreed. "So how do we get the drop on him?"

Penny studied their projected orbit. "He's going to have his hands full," she said. "Between babysitting systems and constantly adjusting his intercept vectors, he won't have much time to look out the windows."

He looked at their own ring of portholes and tried to picture what Hassani might be able to see. "Can't imagine they have much field of view anyway." Two forward with one on each side and a small porthole in the entry hatch. "What about countermeasures? Does that thing have any kind of sensor array?"

"Just the docking radar," she said, "unidirectional and nose forward, where you'd be pointed for prox-ops. He'd only pick us up if he was looking in the right place to begin with. So we have stay in his blind spots during our approach, then roll in hard on his six."

Simon was easing into a slightly different line of thought. "If he's planned this far ahead, then he's also got a plan for clearing his baffles," he said, referring to the sub driver's technique of periodically turning their boats to listen for areas otherwise masked by their own propeller noise. "Hassani's already had to think through each move just to get there. He figures he knows what we'll do next."

"And he'd probably be right," Penny said, again studying their potential orbits and the limited choices available. "So what do we do?"

"We play to his assumptions, of course." Simon's eyes brightened as his tired face opened up with a devious grin. "But you're thinking like a fighter jock in a dogfight. This is submarine warfare."

37

Orion

Hassani felt strangely beholden to his latest acquisition, marveling at how Allah's master plan was falling into place. For all the frustrations of human interference, it was quite simple for a faithful warrior to defeat them: be patient, mind your surroundings, and follow the path laid out before you.

His years of training had certainly reaped an unexpected bounty. Hassani's education in the workings of Allah's majestic universe would have made him a prime astronaut candidate all on his own, had the Caliphate been interested in pursuing an actual space program instead of sending him to study under aliases in the United States.

And so his spiritual awakening had begun just as his education was approaching its apex. He'd been comfortable to remain among the quiet faithful as a young man, but something about living in the pit of Western decadence had lit a fire within his soul. They were fallen, corrupt, lost… and therefore primed for divine retribution. This depraved world would only be saved by a thorough purge of its infidels. If that meant entire continents, entire societies, were swept away, then so be it. The *hadith* taught that ultimate transformation could only happen after a purifying cataclysm.

But they – he – had not yet achieved their primary mission: shifting the comet's orbit enough to make it impact the North American continent. Instead, they were left with a sizeable chunk headed for the Atlantic coast. The anger he felt at his own miscalculations were tempered by the fact that it would still bring unprecedented devastation, something the privileged Americans had not yet experienced.

In the meantime he still had to complete the divine task he'd been assigned, revealed to him years ago when he'd been one of a select few to learn of this threatening comet. A strange excitement had quickly turned to inexplicable rage when he'd learned soon after of the plans to change its orbit.

Farside and Gateway had been part of an enormous "black project" that had only seen NASA brought in after the Pentagon had reluctantly determined that they couldn't do it on their own. Hassani had to admit the Americans had been wise to take this upon themselves. From their point of view, the project had been too important to afford the inherent security risks of international cooperation, not to mention the inevitable snags that came from trying to coordinate engineering projects with both the Russians and the Europeans. One could be guaranteed to stall at critical junctures in a bid for cash while the other would be certain to bureaucratize it into stagnation, not to mention it guaranteed the true purpose wouldn't remain secret any longer than it took to sign the agreements. The program they called FIREWALL was perhaps the one area in which the Americans still excelled: for all of their waste and bloat, when it really mattered they could move with remarkable speed and focus.

He floated up to the upper left pilot's seat and strapped in. The second correction burn he'd programmed would be coming up soon. This would cut his transit time by a few more hours and place his intercept directly in front of Weatherby's path, exactly where he wanted to be and without the risk of crossing its tail. Nose first, he expected to be able to impart enough delta-v to slow the comet down and shorten the radius of its orbit. It wouldn't be much, only a few hundred meters per second. Hardly perceptible on a cosmic scale, yet enough to turn a near miss into a glancing blow that promised to devastate most of the continent and throw the rest of the world into chaos.

Would it be an extinction-level event, as some had feared? Only if the "nuclear winter" hypothesis held true, and of that he remained deeply skeptical. It had been a popular notion when he was a child, which had also been precisely why he'd rejected it later as an adult: it had smacked of conventional wisdom. And as it had turned out, opportunities to test the hypothesis had been presented by both man and nature and had fallen short. He vividly recalled the dire predictions of Saddam's oil fires as a child in Qatar, memories all the more vivid for the manner in which so many apocalyptic predictions had been soundly refuted.

Yet modern humans had never experienced anything on this scale. It was certain to render at least a third of Earth's surface uninhabitable, thus fulfilling a popular end-times prophecy while hastening the appearance of the Mahdi, the *true* Messiah. Unspeakable devastation and turmoil would precede his triumphant arrival, just as it had been prophesied centuries ago.

So the delusional Christians had at least gotten it half right, though he'd expected no better as their weak excuse for faith was itself rooted in deceit. Their book of "revelation" could have only been the work of a deranged hermit under the influence of Satan himself. The filthy Jews, for all their faults, at least had the sense to turn their backs on such grand deceptions. Yet it had prepared the way for the billion or so wayward souls who believed all of that rot. He laughed to himself: they were *expecting* to travel down this road, just not to the final destination that was in store for them.

A warning chime pulled Hassani from his reverie to focus on the guidance panel as the computers began their next countdown. As the main engine roared to life he began crying rapturously, reveling in the elegance of physics and its gift of divine understanding.

...

Grissom

"Penny will fly while Aud navigates," Simon explained to the group. "Our two jarheads here will be the assault team," he said, nodding to Hunter and Quinn. "But we'll have to break orbit ASAP and work out the details along the way."

"Figured as much," Quinn said with a nod in Audrey's direction. "Guarantee you don't want me doing Red's job, or we'll end up planted in a crater down there somewhere."

Audrey smiled modestly. "Hassani would've had to go equatorial," she said, ignoring the backhanded compliment. "Orion wouldn't have enough delta-v to go direct, not if he wants to keep enough propellant to shift orbits later."

Ryan looked over her shoulder at the capsule specs they'd received from Houston. "So that high parabola sets him up for a slingshot around the front end and takes the scenic route to save prop. He'll have to do a plane change at some point, right?"

"He will," Audrey agreed. "And it'll have to be a minimum-energy maneuver. Again, it's safe to assume he's conserving propellant."

Simon stared at the diagrams, trying to tease answers from the swirl of circles representing their respective paths among the Earth-Moon system. He turned back to Audrey. "Shouldn't be too hard for you to figure out when he'll have to do some course corrections, right?"

Audrey shrugged her shoulders. "Sure. Easy math."

"Then that's how we catch him." Simon tapped at a screen, making a show of checking their propellant levels. "Energy is our hole card. We fly a transfer orbit that will get us in close while minimizing our exposure. Something that would keep us out of his likely field of view until the last minute, give us the tactical advantage."

"Maybe a retrograde burn?" Ryan asked. "We've got a lot more options dropping out of a Lagrange point." It would reverse their orbit, sending them around the moon in the opposite direction to intercept. "It'll burn more gas but we'd surprise the hell out of him."

"I think we can do it even cheaper," Audrey said. She traced a path that curved out from Gateway, nearly touching the Moon before continuing to Weatherby. "It's more delta-v than the Hohmann transfer he's on, but not nearly as much as a retrograde orbit."

"Like a slingshot?" Quinn asked, lifting an eyebrow.

"It's called the Oberth Effect," Audrey explained for his benefit. "We drop out of Gateway with enough of a push to fall around the Moon and then burn full-throttle at our closest approach. You end up with almost twice the velocity change for half the fuel, but it'll require some serious piloting," she said and swiped at the screen again. A curved green line swept past the Moon and came uncomfortably close to touching it; as she zoomed in closer a football-shaped bubble appeared around their path. "This is our 'uncertainty zone,' where all of the potential errors come together. Right now, the bottom of that zone scrapes the surface."

He didn't like the idea of "scraping the surface" at twenty-some thousand miles an hour. "So we could crash?"

"I can't make the pencil any sharper right now. Once we start burning it's a two-day fall from here, so we'll have more to work with."

"Planning is just that – a plan," Penny reassured him, "flying is where we make it work. Aud gets us pointed in the right direction, we'll take care of the rest. You ever have an op go as planned?"

"Point taken," Quinn admitted. He stared at the plot, trying to visualize what she'd just described. "But I'm confused. Won't this put the comet between us and him?"

Simon nodded. "Precisely."

...

Melbourne

"I'm cold."

Marcy massaged her son's back and pulled him closer to her. "Me too, baby. It's because our clothes are still wet. Just stay close." The sun had long since gone down, quickly taking its warmth with it. She doubted their clothing would dry out before morning. It would be a long night.

They were nestled against the old oak in the crook of the biggest branch they could find. She had lashed them to its trunk with the climbing rope, looping it beneath their armpits and around their waists. It was the only way they'd get any sleep without falling off.

The floodwaters had partially receded, leaving a horrific mess in its wake. Everything along the coast had been uprooted and thrown into a churning cauldron of debris, including wildlife she preferred to give a wide berth. They'd seen enough gators and snakes gliding past that Marshall had been just fine with her decision to stay up in this tree.

In the moonlight, she looked out over the wrecked buildings and knew they would find no safety down there. All were flooded; those that still stood were no doubt gutted and filled with mud. Crumpled shadows were strewn randomly and at odd angles; she knew those would be the dead.

The living were of greater concern to her: desperation could quickly make otherwise normal people unpredictable and dangerous. She had seen it firsthand in evacuation drills at the airlines: a cabin filled with two hundred volunteers, easygoing and jovial right up until the smoke was turned on. It was then that they panicked, not having been warned. In a controlled environment they still stampeded for the exits, shoving each other aside to leap for the escape slides. While excellent training for the flight attendants, it had also taught her some unforgettable lessons about human nature.

Were there any survivors? She had yet to see or hear anyone. Most had hightailed it north up I-95 and A1A. How many had stubbornly stayed put on the highways, crawling along and hoping against hope to get out, only realizing the futility of it when the sky blazed with fire and the wall of water came? She recalled how the town, how their neighborhood, had felt deserted when they returned just before the cataclysm. *Someone* had to have stayed behind, right? There were always the random old cranks who refused to leave. She and Marshall couldn't be the only people left alive in all of Melbourne.

She reached into her hip pocket, habitually checking the little .22 magnum revolver Ryan had given her several years ago. Diminutive but surprisingly effective, she'd rarely left the house without it. They had never seen eye-to-eye on exposing Marshall to it – Ryan had wanted to train the boy on its proper use and thus remove the mystery, while she'd been steadfast that he not even know it was in their house. As she kept careful watch for predators of both the four- and two-legged kind, she began to wonder if her husband had been right. He'd never let up if she ever admitted that possibility.

It was then that she looked up at the sky and wondered if she'd ever get that chance. Somewhere between the Moon and that comet – now alarmingly large in the southeastern sky – flew her husband and their closest friends. With someone else who undoubtedly, she now realized, had played a role in the destruction just visited upon them. She noticed her grip tightening around the pistol as her anger simmered.

Go get 'em, hon.

38

Grissom

Snoopy I and *II* were now mated to opposite ends of Gateway's multipurpose logistics module, it being the only remaining structure that could bear the loads two fully fueled ships were about to exert. Originally built as extra storage for the space station, it had been reequipped and sent on a spiraling orbit out to L2 to become the core of Gateway. Now liberated from that duty, what had once been the center of Earth's first planetary defense system was now the core of what had to be the most slapdash spaceship ever conceived. It was a fifty-meter daisy chain of metal cylinders connected through two separate docking nodes. With both flight module's engine bells protruding from either end, the stack resembled a couple of flashlights bolted to a soda can.

Inside the core module, Audrey and Quinn transferred the last of the stores from *Grissom*'s lockers. Once they pushed it out of L1, it would be left behind on a long orbit that would take it farther than Hammond could've imagined. Audrey had made sure its telemetry was left running, wiring the transmitters directly to the ship's backup electrical bus and extending its dedicated solar panels. The power it would receive was inversely proportional to its distance from the sun; she'd figured it would be sending data for a least a year before it was too far gone. It would be fun to watch from the control center back in Denver, an interesting distraction from the daily grind. She could already envision a company-wide guessing game of "Where's Gus?"

The thought made her smile, until she considered the likelihood of being there to follow the fun herself. A sigh escaped her.

Quinn touched her arm. "What's the matter?"

"Nothing," she said, knowing deflection wouldn't work.

"Awfully sour face for nothing," he said. "If there's something bothering you, now's the time."

She wished he'd quit looking at her. "Nothing that hasn't already been keeping me up," she said, trying to remember if she'd had any sleep in the last three days. She debated whether to keep going before finally drawing in a breath. "You know we may not make it back," she said flatly, pulling away imperceptibly.

"Always a possibility in my line of work, Red," he said. She didn't find that as obnoxiously macho as she should have; it was simply a statement of fact. "Yours too, I suspect."

"We normally don't have people actively trying to kill us," she pointed out. "First time for everything."

"More than you know." His eyes were tired; Audrey suddenly perceived the world-weariness behind them. "Something like this was bound to happen. There aren't many opportunities for mischief with the taxis SpaceX and Boeing are running for NASA. Until one of them starts selling tickets to the public, you guys are the only game in town. That's made Polaris a hijacking target since the first Clipper started flying."

"More than *you* know," she rejoined. "You know how I ended up here, don't you?" It was more a statement than a question; he'd thoroughly investigated everyone involved with this expedition.

Quinn's knowing look would've irritated the hell out of her if it hadn't given her a slight flutter. "Good work on that one, by the way. Hunter never would've been able to do that without you backing him up."

She glanced up into the tunnel, where the others were prepping the flight module. "I didn't know him back then but I'm betting he'd have tried anyway. Simon was the one who surprised me. I'd always taken him for a by-the-book commander."

A chime from the intercom demanded their attention. "Oh, I've no doubt that he is," he smiled. "The good ones just know when it's time to throw the book out."

Audrey held his gaze. "Yes, the good ones do."

• • •

Simon thumbed the mic again to get their attention. "Aud, this is your two-minute warning. We need both of you forward and buckled up." He was once again strapped into the "captain's chair" behind the pilot stations, following Penny and Ryan as they worked through the deorbit countdown. There was little for him to do at this point other than help to keep them from missing a critical step.

He checked his watch against the onboard chronometer. "Ninety seconds...hack."

"Hack," Ryan said as he did the same. "Ships are talking to each other. Big Al's engine controls are slaved to my station." He would control their jury-rigged booster stage from the copilot's seat while Penny flew the combined stack.

"This kludge had better work," Simon muttered as Quinn and Audrey glided through the hatch and grabbed their seats. "No offense, Aud." Combining the ships had been her idea, after all.

"None taken," she said, focused on ensuring Quinn was strapped in before she floated across to her own seat.

Simon arched an eyebrow, stifling the urge to ask off-putting questions. *Later, on the ground.* "Sixty seconds," he announced. He glanced at the tablet in his hands, searching for the next item in their cockpit flow. "Confirm RCS pressurized."

"RCS pressurized," Penny answered, "and auto-dampening is active." With every burst of their control jets having to eventually be countered by an equal burst in the opposite direction, the automatic dampening would calibrate the thrusters to smooth out their ride and (it was thought) improve their accuracy. No self-respecting spacecraft pilot had actually used it yet as the thing tended to waste propellant. Penny was willing to take every possible advantage as they prepared to skim over the Moon one last time, faster than anyone had ever flown.

"Forty seconds. GNC check?"

She depressed a switch on the center console. "Inertial platforms aligned, engaging NAV mode."

"Thirty seconds. How's your aim?"

"I stayed off the coffee this morning, if that's your point," Penny said. "We're on pitch, steady as a rock."

"Never doubted you. Twenty seconds. Booster?"

"Go," Ryan said. "Tanks are stirred." There was a muffled hum as blowdown fans kept the liquefied methane and oxygen pressurized in their reservoirs.

"Ten seconds. Igniters charged?"

"Charged," Ryan said, and ceremoniously lifted his hands away from the controls. "Ignition sequence is slaved." The engines would light themselves at the exact moment commanded by the flight computer; all they had to do was watch it happen as the master chronometer counted down to a point in time and space where they would be in the optimal relationship between the Moon and comet Weatherby.

They were silent as *Snoopy I* roared to life, pushing the stack clear of Gateway for the last time and accelerating it toward the Moon's limb.

...

The Moon grew at an alarming rate, a stark reminder of their speed and harrowingly close approach. The flyby would take them within a few kilometers of the surface – no closer than they'd already been, but now at velocities that would give them no time to correct any mistakes.

To Ryan, it brought to mind the difference between loping along at five hundred feet in an old Cessna versus keeping the same altitude while supersonic in an F/A-18. A moment's inattention in the former might be forgivable, whereas the latter promised to turn you into a smoking hole with no time to even realize how badly you'd screwed up. Hitting the ground at eighty knots or eight hundred left you just as dead.

Audrey's voice disturbed his introspection. He wanted to blame it on a lack of sleep, forcing himself to ignore the thoughts of what might be happening to his wife and son at this moment.

"Updating your HUDs," she said. "New trajectory cues coming up."

The attitude and velocity targets blinked in their windshields, while the seemingly endless string of ellipses projecting their flight path shifted almost imperceptibly. It had also gotten noticeably smaller.

"Feeling optimistic?" Already threading a needle, Audrey had just made it smaller.

"Just sharpening my pencil after that last correction. Got a better idea of where we really are."

"It had better be pretty sharp," Penny said as the countdown clock reset itself. She turned to Ryan. "Stay frosty. Perilune burn is coming up real quick here."

...

"Three..."

Ryan's hand tensed around the throttle levers as Penny counted down calmly. He ignored the Moon outside, which filled their windows as it rushed by at a speed his brain couldn't process.

"...two..."

It was a lot like flying a jet through heavy weather: ignore the outside visual cues and focus on the instruments. No matter what your guts and inner ear were trying to tell you, know that they'd get you killed.

"...one."

And in this case, they were once again flying backwards relative to their direction. As he pushed the throttles to their forward stops, they were punished by the unpleasant sensation of being pulled out of their seats as *Snoopy's* main engines burned furiously. The "eyeballs-out" negative gees shoved them up against their harnesses as the acceleration mounted, the straps digging into their shoulders and stomachs.

"Full thrust," he grunted. "Chamber pressure at one hundred percent, both engines." The moonliner's twin engines were meant for redundancy and so were typically not run at full power simultaneously.

"Keep an eye on the nozzle temps," Penny said. "They can redline for about forty seconds before we have to roll back power."

"Umm...I wouldn't recommend it," Audrey interjected. "Run them hot that long, they could start chuffing." She didn't need to explain further. Excessive heat threatened to create waves of backpressure that could make the engines run rough. An uneven burn this close to the surface could send them careening into the dust at over thirty thousand kilometers an hour.

Ryan chewed his lip. Both engines had to run for at least three minutes, so they'd damned well better not redline. Outside, the lunar surface passed by ever faster. He pulled down another monitor and set it up for every conceivable engine parameter. "Just keep us from hitting the ground. I'll keep us from blowing up."

...

"Escape velocity," Audrey reported with a tinge of sadness as the Moon fell away again. The experience felt lonely, as if they had just abandoned their own race. Which they had, in a sense – their stacked spacecraft was moving sufficiently fast that it was beyond the influence of Earth's gravity well. They were now in orbit around the sun just like Weatherby, making their little ship one with the untold millions of asteroids that moved undetected around the solar system.

"Here there be dragons," Simon intoned solemnly, echoing her feelings. "Seems like there should be some kind of ceremony, like when you cross the equator."

Penny rolled her eyes. "Holy crap, Simon. Does the Navy have a friggin' ceremony for *everything*?"

"Yes," Hunter and Quinn chimed in emphatically.

Simon ignored the barbs. "Time to intercept?"

Audrey held up a finger as she finished accounting for their final velocity change. "Thirty-eight hours, seven minutes. About four hours before Hassani gets there."

Quinn whistled. "He had almost two day's head start and we're still beating him to it? Impressive little ship you've built here."

"It's actually not that complicated…" Audrey began.

"Yes it is," Ryan said tiredly. "Quit selling yourself short, Aud."

She shrugged him off with an exasperated sigh. "What I meant was that we have more fuel and more efficient engines than that capsule he's flying." Her cheeks bloomed in a self-conscious blush. "And I guess it did help having someone who knew how to take advantage of that."

Quinn nodded his understanding. "It'll be a long trip home, won't it?"

"It will be," she agreed. "We'll have to do a braking burn at Weatherby, then another injection burn to put us back in Earth orbit when it's all over. And the farther away we are, the longer that'll take. It'll easily be a month before we're in position for a Clipper to pick us up."

"First things first," Simon counseled them. "I want everyone rested. I'll take first watch up here, the rest of you get some rack time." There were no protests, as none of them had slept for the last two days. Without argument, the four unbuckled and pushed off one by one through the tunnel and into their sleeping berths.

39

Denver

From the safety of his office, Art Hammond watched in dismay as throngs of protesters pressed against the security fence. *Don't these people ever go home?*

Being on airport property and thus under strict police observation had been the only thing that kept them from crashing the gates. He wondered how long that would hold them back as the full scope of the catastrophe along the Eastern Seaboard became known. No mob could be kept at bay by a chain link fence and a few cops for very long if they really believed the end of the world was upon them. The torches and pitchforks were guaranteed to come out once the mob had decided it was all his fault.

And true to form, that was a notion the jackass news outlets were more than happy to perpetuate. All it took was one well-placed rumor from a "reliable source" to craft a narrative plausible enough to render a complicated story understandable. A nation of luddites, fearful of technology they didn't understand. Hell, too many people didn't even have the *capacity* to understand this stuff. All of them being whipped into a frenzy by politicians and professional agitators who maybe knew better but didn't care – they only needed to control the flow of information in order to stampede the public into whatever direction served their needs. Aided and abetted by an ignorant press, nominally independent but which had long ago taken sides and served as willing shepherds of the flock.

It was like blaming 9/11 on Boeing. This was somehow all his fault for opening up space to the public, even though the Feds had let a known Caliphate sympathizer slip through the cracks. Hijacking one of his ships to take over their own top-secret space station would've been deliciously ironic in any other context. The politicians and bureaucrats might've found a way to weasel out of the recriminations had it not resulted in Biblical-level destruction on our own soil. No, Washington rules meant that *someone* had to be fingered as the bad guy and this one was just too big to keep inside the beltway. And that turd blossom Abbot had finally found a way to take down everything he'd built with nothing but half-truths and carefully placed leaks. No doubt he'd angle to shut down the whole operation – or worse, engineer a government takeover in the name of "public interest" and slap big NASA meatballs on the whole fleet. Amtrak in space.

Hammond rubbed his jaw roughly, working out the aches from the tension. He felt like he'd been walking around with his teeth clenched for two weeks straight.

Checking on his companies' financial performance didn't help. Polaris stocks had tanked along with ticket sales while the manufacturing arm, Hammond Aerospace, wasn't far behind. He'd been maneuvered into a hostile buyout once before and would be damned if he allowed it to happen again.

It was all about public perception. If everything he'd built was going to be tarred as a threat to humanity, the only way to turn that around would have to be through something just as dramatic. And there was precious little about that he could do himself.

He heard a *thud* in the distance, followed by a sharper report close by. That was when the building went dark.

...

Melbourne

The morning sun burned through the trees, dripping-wet leaves of oak and citrus sparkling in its yellow light. A dense fog had settled in overnight as the already muggy air became saturated by the incursion of so much seawater. As it burned off, the clear sky held the promise of another day of punishing heat and humidity.

Marcy rolled her neck, trying to work out a painful crick. Sleeping upright, tied with her son to the branches of an oak tree, had been decidedly bad for her joints. She made a mental note to never try camping with Ryan again, no matter how many comforts he tried to bring along for her.

She looked out through the branches, for the first time able to see solid ground. The town was wrecked; those buildings still left standing had been under several feet of water and were now left covered in muck. Smoke curled up into the sky in several places, no doubt electrical or gas-line fires still burning themselves out.

Around the park, debris was strewn about the swampy ground. Tree limbs and lamp posts were half-buried in the nasty muck, holding the occasional pile of random detritus built from the lives of families swept away by the deluge. Thank God they'd not yet seen any bodies, at least not close enough for Marshall to notice…and that was when her heart sank. It was just a small pink tricycle, hanging from a nearby branch. One of those cartoon princess toys, like the little girl next door had. The one Marshall was sweet on, as much as a three-year-old can be. She thought of the two children sitting next to each other at the end of their backyard dock, kicking their toes in the water while tossing out bread crumbs to the ducks that somehow always knew to make their way over when those two came out.

Marcy felt a catch in her throat as a croaking sob burst out. She'd been oblivious to the thrumming noise that had become steadily louder, causing Marshall to become increasingly restless. His voice finally broke through, barely audible above the roar that suddenly enveloped them.

There was an impatient tug against her arm. "Mommy!"

She stared at him blankly. What could he be going on about? What horror did she miss that was now getting his attention?

"Look!"

Marshall pointed excitedly towards the complex of ball fields in the center of the park. The oak trembled beneath them, its branches swaying and leaves buffeting in the wind. She shook her head, once and for all clearing out her own mental fog. A dark green mass settled into the clearing, clattering beneath its twin rotors. She immediately recognized it as Army, and stared wide-eyed as the old Chinook gingerly lowered a pallet of perforated metal plates onto the muck below. Once its cargo was released, the big chopper continued hovering while a dozen men in camouflage fast-roped down the final twenty or so feet. Safely clear, the helicopter sped away as the men began to hurriedly unpack its cargo, which resembled sections of a massive Erector set. Airfield matting, maybe?

Two men broke away from the group and headed for a nearby utility shed. One unslung a bulky pack and began erecting antennas atop the building while his partner began connecting radios. Whatever kind of recovery operation they were putting together, it looked like this was going to be the command post.

Marcy went slack and collapsed against the crook of the tree. Marshall, on the other hand, couldn't get untied fast enough to go see the "army men." He began tugging at her once more.

"Why are you crying?"

...

Denver

Posey called from his cellphone, sounding like he was on the move somewhere. There was a thrum of helicopters in the background; no doubt the police choppers Hammond could see orbiting the field. "They took out the transformers, Art. Police found a couple of witnesses. Sounds like it might have been an RPG."

"Rocket propelled grenades!?" Hammond exclaimed. "Are you shitting me?"

"I wish," Posey said. "More than one at that. One went after our main supply while the other went after the backup generators."

That explained the two explosions he'd heard. "What about the backup, then?" The power had been intermittent and phone lines were completely gone.

"Blew the hell out of the shelter and took out one generator. The other two are running but that means essential needs only." Everything but the hangar and control center would be blacked out until this was fixed. "A third Haji went after the comm lines also, that's why the phones are out."

"What about data?" Hammond asked anxiously. They could have all the power in the world, but if their network went down the fleet would grind to a halt.

"He couldn't finish the job," Posey said triumphantly.

"You caught one?"

"Sort of. We think at least two more are still on the loose. Airport cops called in Denver PD for backup, they're creating a perimeter around the airport but that's a lot of real estate for the Hajis to hide in."

"Why do you keep calling them that?"

"It's kind of a collective term we use for Islamic terrorists."

This was getting to be too much. "Gotta ask, Tony. How do you know that?"

"Process of elimination," he explained. "He was screaming 'Allahu Akbar' when I shot his ass."

40

Snoopy II
Flight Day Twenty

Simon was unquestionably in his element, savoring the role of a wily ship's captain on the hunt. "Remember ladies, there's only two kinds of boats: subs and targets."

"Which one are we again?" Audrey muttered. She had tuned their own docking system to *Orion*'s radar, which allowed her to follow the other ship. Though they couldn't see him – nor he them – the receiver showed that his radar had been on constantly. Hopefully, they would appear as just another part of the comet's background clutter.

Audrey had noticed the already faint signal had been fading in and out regularly. If it had been audible, it would've been comparable to the rise and fall in pitch of a passing car. It appeared at the top of each hour, as if the spacecraft was rotating in a regular pattern. Just as Simon had predicted, Hassani was periodically checking the space behind his ship.

"There's that same Doppler shift," Audrey said. She checked her watch. "He just turned, right on schedule."

Simon's face broke in a crooked smile. "This guy's a creature of habit," he said. "Predictable."

"Makes sense," Penny said. "That ship's designed to be flown single-pilot, but that doesn't mean he has time to be unpredictable."

Simon tugged at his beard, which had grown far too unruly over the last couple of weeks. "Good. Omar needs to be right where we expect him when we come out on the other side."

"Judging by the Doppler shifts, he's facing aft and is roughly abeam us right now," Audrey said. "Another retro burn will drop us a few hundred meters behind him while we're transiting the tail. Three seconds from the dorsal quads should do it."

Penny swiveled her seat to face them both. "Been thinking about that transit," she said. "The only vehicles to ever fly through a comet's tail were designed for the purpose. We don't know what kind of particulates are in there, and the relative velocities mean anything bigger than a grain of sand could blow a hole right through us. It's an awful lot of risk."

"Agreed. But I don't see how else we can surprise him."

"Likewise agreed," Penny said. "Going through the tail and rolling up on his six may be too obvious. There's a better way to do it," she continued, and explained her idea.

Simon's eyes darted back and forth as he thought it over. "Good plan," he finally decided. "Make it so."

"You're enjoying this *far* too much, Simon."

"That's why I joined the Navy in the first place," he said. "Starfleet wasn't hiring."

• • •

Orion

Hassani floated freely in the cabin – already spacious enough, having it all to himself was a luxury after being so close to so many unpleasant people. He was meditating, forcing his body and mind into a state of serenity that danced along the thin boundary between exhaustion and unconsciousness. As he had no time for actual sleep, this resting state would be the most he could allow himself.

He'd struggled most with the incessant mental gymnastics that this ad hoc mission demanded of him. He'd had no intention of going this far, but events had forced his hand. It would have been so much easier to shatter the comet's nucleus and let it rain random chaos upon the world while he took *Orion* into Earth orbit to provide carefully targeted nuclear chaos.

But now they would be waiting for him. He knew the Americans still kept some air-launched antisatellite missiles, and the Russians and Chinese were even more ambitious. Unleashing his weapons quickly would have eliminated that risk: by the time they'd figured out where he was, the bombs would already be falling. New York, Washington, Tel Aviv, Moscow, Beijing…he'd planned to target the sixth "special delivery" for London but considered it best to keep one of the warheads close. No need to program its burns or reentry phasing, just keep it in reserve to discourage anyone who might be foolish enough to follow him. He was certain they would try.

It was difficult to put the target programming out of his mind. He'd calculated, recalculated, and practiced it countless times in the elaborate simulator they'd constructed in Tehran. But all of that had been from a polar orbit, where the targeting solutions were comparatively straightforward. Now he'd had to do it from close proximity to a passing comet, literally "on the fly" as the Americans might joke. It was most fortunate that he'd foreseen this eventuality and had at least practiced it once on the ground.

Hassani understood it was from nothing he'd done on his own, and rebuked himself for his ego. *Allah is with me, I am an instrument of his perfect will.* He looked once more at the Earth and found the eastern Mediterranean, his desired target. Perhaps he'd have enough delta-v left to shift the nucleus onto a more precise path. How wonderful it would be to strike the Zionists directly with the full force of Allah's magnificent creation.

He cursed, losing track of time while contemplating a world about to be thrown into an apocalyptic cataclysm. What a blessing to be here, to be the instrument of divine will. But it was past time to turn the ship and check his blind spots once more. The Americans were sure to be after him. They had the resources, but did they have the time? He grasped the control stick and gently tapped it forward, pitching over in the opposite direction.

...

Snoopy II

The damage inflicted on the outer hull had been severe. Passing through Weatherby's ionization tail had created enough electronic chaos to make it nearly impossible to judge. There were no signs of atmosphere leaking out, but it would never carry passengers again.

"Static's clearing up," Penny said as the interference from Weatherby's ionization tail passed. Her screens had been rendered nearly useless during the entire transit, and piloting the ship visually was impossible with no clear references. Like so much else, maneuvering in space had relied more on careful timing of rocket motor pulses than traditional piloting skills. "I think we're clear."

Simon looked to Audrey for confirmation. "Nothing I can see to indicate otherwise," she agreed. "This is about when I expected to see all that electromagnetic fluff dissipate. And I'm seeing another Doppler shift."

"He's swapping ends again," Simon decided. He turned to Penny. "Could our docking radar trip anything in his cockpit?"

"Depends on how he configured the system," she said after a moment's thought. "If he's set up for close proximity ops, the sensors will alert him if they detect any transponder pings. Like the traffic advisories in an airliner."

"Then we should assume he did."

...

Orion

Hassani meticulously searched the black sky from each window, moving from one porthole to the next only after he was satisfied that nothing was out of place. It was an acquired skill. The stars were so numerous out here, even more than the darkest nights in the deserts, that it was difficult to recognize all but the brightest constellations. Nevertheless, his relative motion to the distant points of light was such that he'd been able to quickly identify new patterns. It had become easy: pitch over every hour, thus clearing his blind spots.

Moving to the port window, he searched up and down the length of Weatherby's tail. It really was magnificent up close. The coma had grown to almost completely shroud the rocky nucleus in gas, which streamed away down-sun like some luminescent bridal veil. From this distance it was possible for him to faintly detect motion within its glowing curtain.

Motion.

Hassani sucked in his breath, startled by a sudden change in the tail: a shadow emerged from inside the halo of ionized dust. His mind scrambled for a natural explanation. What sort of phenomenon could it be? It was comparatively small and would've been barely discernible had the background not become so familiar. Perhaps it was a chunk of rock or ice, another fragment from their prior work with the laser?

No. The object was moving at a tangent to the comet's direction, and just beginning to resolve itself inside the shimmering tail. Like a distant ship emerging from a thick morning fog, it slowly began to take shape. He lifted a pair of range finding binoculars from behind the pilot's station.

That was it: a ship. A shining metallic cylinder, somewhat worse for wear, with a conical nose at one end and a cluster of fuel tanks and engine bells at its rear. The other Polaris moonliner, about five kilometers away.

I see you.

There could be no doubt that Allah's will was at work. Providence had once again guided his hands. He pushed across the cabin for the screen he'd set up as a fire control station and activated the reserve warhead's batteries. The hypergolic propellants in its simple booster would ignite the moment he opened their ignition valves, only requiring a short pulse to cover the distance. All that remained was to keep the directional control jets aligned with their target, which at this range was a simple altitude/azimuth problem. The guidance system would make easy work of it. It didn't even have to be that accurate, though the detonation would be uncomfortably close.

Satisfied with the targeting solution, he released the missile and quickly moved to pitch his nose away from the coming blast.

...

Snoopy II

"He's turning," Audrey said. There was a sharp edge to her voice. "Stand by...just picked up a second radar. Doppler's shifting fast in our direction."

Simon and Penny traded anxious looks as they reached down to tighten their harnesses. She quickly moved to point their tail towards the expected detonation while he punched the intercom for Ryan and Quinn in back: "Incoming, close aboard! Secure the cabin and buckle up."

"Time to impact?" Ryan asked.

"Unknown. Depends on his—"

The cabin was filled with a searing flash of light, as if a new sun had been born.

...

Denver

An instant message flashed in the corner of a monitor on Charlie Grant's desk, quickly followed by a shaky voice over the flight control net.

"Charlie…"

"Go ahead, Liz."

"We just lost telemetry."

"Wouldn't be the first time," he sighed. The power had been intermittent, even with the backup generators running.

"This is different. Everything got really weird and then dumped, like they just turned out the lights."

That didn't sound good. "Describe 'weird.'"

"Three second retro burn from the mains, followed by a few seconds of translation pulses from the starboard RCS quads. Not long after that we picked up a lot of funky static, almost like reentry ionization."

Or perhaps passing through the tail of a comet... "How long?"

"About a half-hour of that until everything cleared up normal. Not long after that we saw a big spike across the whole EM spectrum coupled with a surge in skin temps."

"How big?"

"Fifteen hundred."

"Okay, that *is* weird," he said cautiously, "but not completely unheard of." A string of buggy sensors could account for that. With no atmosphere to distribute heat, spacecraft were built to tolerate fierce temperature swings. "Fahrenheit or Centigrade?"

"Kelvin." The term hung like an accusation. The little ship had suddenly been heated to well over two thousand degrees Fahrenheit.

Grant sank his head into his hands. There was a shrill ring from the credenza behind his desk: the encrypted phone they'd been issued by NORAD.

…

Orion

Hassani's world went dark. The sensation of freefall quickly overwhelmed his senses in the darkness, as if his spacecraft had simply evaporated to leave him naked in the void. His mind improbably raced to a distant memory of Milton's *Paradise Lost* and its depiction of Satan's fall through Chaos after his expulsion from Paradise.

No. Not falling, or rather not in an earthly sense. He began tumbling as he flailed about for purchase, his limbs seeking anything to grab hold of in the black. Soon his foot contacted what might have been a seat frame, whipping him forward until his head struck something smooth and cold. Pain shot through his temples and he swore. He stretched out his arms and brushed a handhold. He grabbed for it desperately, searching with his feet to find the seat railing again.

Finally stabilized, he took a deep breath and settled into his new surroundings. With his free hand, he reached out and found what felt like one of the touchscreen control panels: flat glass, with a frame of recessed buttons. He walked his fingers left, expecting to find the adjacent panel right...*there.* Primary and secondary MFD's on the left, center handhold...he gingerly reached up and his fingers brushed over a collection of pushbuttons and protected switches – the main control panel.

That meant he was dead center in the spacecraft, oriented heads-up. Carefully rotating backward, so as not to further confuse his inner ear, he reached up for what should have been the main hatch. He was rewarded with the sensation of cold metal, what felt like a maze of aluminum tubing and latches. In its center would be a small porthole. A few inches up, he felt the hard plastic of its sunshield and yanked it open.

He was rewarded with a blaze of unfiltered sunshine, harshly spotlighting the cabin and finally allowing him to see. Hassani next rushed about the cabin, uncovering the other windows in a wave of relief. He basked in the warm glow, grateful that his task had not been cut short. Not yet.

His revelry would be short lived. Every light, panel, and switch in the cabin had gone dark when the warhead detonated. Almost certainly from electromagnetic pulse, but how could that happen in space? EMP was an earthly phenomenon, propagating through excited air molecules that interacted with Earth's magnetic field. It couldn't happen in space for the same reason there'd been no sound or blast wave: there was atmosphere to transmit it.

Clearly that didn't explain everything. A nuclear explosion released tremendous amounts of X-ray and Gamma radiation. They would penetrate the outer hull and try to find their way through, accumulating current on the skin. The ship's radiation shielding would have protected him, and its electronics were already hardened against cosmic rays. They shouldn't have been overwhelmed by a nuclear weapon, even one going off just a few kilometers away.

Yet everything had died as if someone had thrown a switch...

He felt around in the equipment bay and snapped a flashlight out of its clamp, then floated up to the circuit breaker panel. As he'd suspected, the masters for both main buses had tripped, completely shutting off the flow of electricity to every component aboard the ship. And that was when he realized what had happened.

Solar panels were fragile by nature. They must have been overloaded by the close burst of energy. The sudden accumulation of electrons would've behaved almost like water, the new current naturally following the path of least resistance. It would have flowed straight to the solar cell transmission system, immediately overloading it and tripping breakers.

Like throwing a switch.

It was of little consolation. His main power source may well have been damaged beyond repair, leaving him with a backup battery system that might last twelve hours. It would have to be enough.

He moved to one of the forward windows to see where the Polaris ship had been and rejoiced. The last obstacle had been removed. What had once been a billion-dollar spacecraft was now an expanding cloud of incandescent gas.

• • •

Denver

Art Hammond collapsed into his chair. With trembling hands, he removed a handkerchief from his back pocket and wiped at his brow. Grant paced behind him as Kruger stood before them both, waiting perhaps too patiently. After a long silence, Hammond's eyes burned with accusation as he choked out the words: "I want to make sure I heard you correctly. Our ship was *nuked*?"

"Regretfully correct, Mr. Hammond. We can appreciate the severe impact the loss of your vehicles represents."

Hammond's strength returned quickly. He slammed a fist on the desk, scattering notes and folders to the floor. "To hell with that!" he thundered, rising up to face Kruger. "I really don't know which one is the bigger sociopath: the suicide-cult hijacker or the cold-blooded bureaucrat," he said. "You'll never get it: I don't give a damn about the machines at this point. They're insured. We'll build more." Grant warily stepped over beside them, praying he wouldn't have to intervene. "Our best pilots were on that ship. We're missing even more people in Florida, and our Canaveral hub is *gone*."

For his part, Kruger remained impassive; not even acknowledging Hammond's rebuke. "About that," he continued carefully. "Kennedy Spaceport represents a tremendous loss of national capability. If it becomes necessary to launch some kind of interceptor at what's left of Weatherby..."

"With Kennedy's pads under water, that leaves the government with roughly jack shit for lift," Hammond said. "Good thing those Clippers just need a really big runway, right?"

"It's a contingency the Secretary was prepared for," Kruger confirmed. "Though you must understand how seriously we take nationalizing a private concern."

Hammond had suspected as much. High stakes confrontations had an annoying tendency to come out of nowhere. He glared at Kruger as a grim smile crossed his face. "Nationalize Polaris? Your boss is going to commandeer my whole company? Hell, why not just contract for the extra lift like the Air Force does?"

"We wouldn't require the entire spaceline," Kruger explained, as if that might salve the wound. "You'd retain the suborbital routes and your subsidiary feeder airline. The orbital operation would be spun off into a government-sponsored corporation under NASA oversight."

That drew a derisive laugh from Grant. "Amtrak in space. You called it, Art."

Hammond turned back to Kruger. "It won't happen. I'll ground the whole damned fleet first. Sell 'em to museums, like the Concorde."

Kruger remained infuriatingly unaffected. "And a platoon of Justice Department lawyers will be on your doorstep with injunctions before the ink's dry on the first lease, Mr. Hammond. You must understand that national security takes precedence."

"National security my pasty bald ass," he said. "This begins and ends with Don Abbot, son. If you think otherwise then you're more naïve than I imagined."

Kruger took his leave with the cold smile of a victorious functionary. "Naïveté is a matter of perspective, Mr. Hammond. The Secretary will be in touch."

41

Snoopy II

Weatherby's nucleus revealed more details as they drifted near, its features a strange concoction of sandy crust and basaltic rock like one might find on the volcanic islands of the Pacific. Alien terrain, in the truest sense.

It was so close now that the coma formed a translucent haze. Occasional breaks drifted past, allowing clear glimpses down to the surface. It was not unlike scraping along thin overcast in a small plane while looking for a "sucker hole" to dive through.

"Is that igneous rock down there?" Audrey wondered aloud. She had hijacked the observation dome almost immediately, crowding into the small compartment with Simon after Penny and Ryan had stabilized them above the nucleus. "It *can't* be volcanic, can it?"

She'd apparently directed that at Simon, who'd become unusually taciturn after sacrificing *Snoopy I* as a diversion. It was one of those decisions that had been easy to make but painful to execute, particularly for the man who'd commanded its first cruise. A "plank owner" scuttling his own ship was like a father killing his firstborn.

"It's not big enough," Penny said for him. Audrey was too enamored of the spectacle outside to have noticed Simon's brooding silence. "Remember, you're looking at one of the solar system's building blocks. It's literally older than dirt. Maybe it was once part of something bigger."

To her right, Ryan floated in the copilot's seat. He had likewise been stubbornly quiet ever since they had evaded Hassani by sending the spare flight module through the dust tail. An occasional twitch in his tightened jaw signaled that his mind still worked feverishly behind the dark expression he wore.

Penny knew the look, had once seen it in herself long ago. Now that they were stable with Weatherby and safely hidden from Hassani, the rage that been smoldering within him finally had room to burn. She reached over to grip his hand tightly. His eyes shifted to meet hers, which she answered with a deliberate nod. He gave her hand a reassuring squeeze in return. "I'm still here," he said in a dry whisper.

"You certain about that?"

"Does it matter?" he asked testily. "You're doing all the flying from here on. I won't even be aboard."

"That's why I ask," she scolded him. "Quinn's going to need your head on straight out there, and it's my job to make sure it's not firmly planted up your ass."

He winced at her rebuke. "That bad?"

"Not bad," she said. "Just normal. I do know what you're going through, my dear." She let the thought hang.

"I suppose you do." His shoulders sagged. "But did it make a difference actually being there? Seeing the finality of it right in front of you?"

She turned away, thinking it over while pretending to study the dirty ice hovering in their windows. "Hard to say. Maybe it did. I knew Dan was gone, and the public affairs officer knew better than to even try his shtick with me. It barely worked on the civilian wives."

Ryan arched an eyebrow. "I'd have loved to have been a fly on the wall for *that* visit. So did he leave on his own or did they have to call an ambulance?"

"Little bit of both," she said. "Listen, I know it looks really bad down there but I'm not giving up hope. You shouldn't either. That's one tough chick you married."

"Don't I know it. Think she'll ever let me fly again?"

It was good to hear him talk as if Marcy was still alive. She went to punch his arm, then stopped herself short. Screw it, he's family. She instead leaned over and planted a motherly kiss on his forehead.

"I still haven't decided if *I* will."

• • •

As they glided above the nucleus, the cabin rattled with the dull thud of directional jets. Penny had managed to keep them at what they hoped was a safe distance from the coma and its unknown mixture of gas and dust. Its glow washed out most of the star field save for the very brightest, which made the important part easier: as they slowly circled the heart of Weatherby, the visible stars were easily tracked as they slid across the windows.

After hours of deliberate maneuvering, a new point of light emerged from the comet's haze. Different from the rest, this one twinkled randomly as if it were reflecting light rather than producing it. The occasional puff of gas gave *Orion* away.

Simon unconsciously tightened his seat harness and wished like hell that photon torpedoes were real. "This is the part where I'd normally holler 'match bearings and shoot.' Think he saw us?"

"His clearing maneuver is a little late," Audrey said. "We'll have to keep an eye on him, see if he does anything stupid."

"I'm more concerned about him doing something *smart*," Penny said.

"Precisely. Go ahead and move us in closer." She had been careful to position them up-sun, using the glare to hide their approach. Simon thumbed the microphone switch by his waist. "Mister Hunter, is our boarding party ready?"

• • •

Ryan's gloved hand had been resting on the hatch, anticipating the order to head out. "Underway on your signal."

"Very well," Simon replied. "Prepare to board. Radio silence begins now. Good luck, gentlemen." The static from his channel cut off with finality. The spacewalkers each tuned their radios to the encrypted frequency.

"Damnation," Quinn said as Hunter drifted out. "It does sound like we're back on the boat." The comet's glow filled the airlock tunnel with ghostly blue light. "Good Lord," he whispered as he emerged into open space. An immense wall of gas and dust shimmered just a few kilometers away and seemed to stretch all the way back to the Moon. Ahead, it terminated abruptly at Weatherby's nucleus. Right about where Hassani waited inside of that spacecraft.

Ryan floated up close behind. "Doesn't look much like a boat from here, does it?"

"Begging your pardon, sir," Quinn said as he secured their safety tethers to the hull. "But this ain't much like spacediving, either. Never had much of a chance to look around, especially being this close to something I'd only seen through a telescope."

"Believe me, I understand," Ryan said. "Hell of a week, isn't it? Walk on the Moon one day, fly by a comet the next."

Quinn nodded behind his faceplate. "My fun meter is just about pegged." He paused. "We never discussed what to do with that sumbitch after we secure his ship," he said as they prepared to leap across the void.

"I don't recall seeing instructions about handling prisoners in your op order. Guess they didn't plan on us taking any," Ryan said coldly.

Each man braced along opposite sides of the hatch and pushed off.

...

Simon had settled into the observation dome and waved for Penny's binoculars. She sent them sailing across the cabin and they connected dead center in his free hand. He turned down the cabin lights, cutting glare and filling the control deck with the comet's natural glow.

"Spacecraft looks to be in good shape," he said, pushing the binoculars back towards Penny. "Have a look."

She caught the binoculars in midair and flew up into the dome next to him. Relative to its position in space they were below *Orion*, safely in Hassani's blind spot. "From what I can see, it's functional," she said. "Even the MMU's are still in place on the starboard equipment rack." MMU's – Manned Mobility Units – allowed astronauts to zip around in open space without the need for a safety tether.

"The port rack looks good too." That was the service bay that now held five rocket-propelled, self-guided nuclear warheads. Simon chewed his bottom lip as he considered their options. "Think you can maintain position if he moves again?"

"We'll have to keep an eye on his RCS quads. Soon as we see them squirt gas, I'll back us off. When he pitches the nose, we'll translate forward. All depends on which way he turns." The tricky part would be timing: they couldn't move until Ryan and Quinn had reached *Orion* and detached their tethers.

...

Orion

Hassani checked his life-support panel to ensure the cabin had completely depressurized and gave another prayer of thanks for being allowed to evade his pursuers. Until they had so dramatically emerged from within Weatherby, he'd halfway expected to hear the impact of depleted uranium slugs tearing through his ship at any moment. Being freed of that fear had been a welcome blessing.

Which, by his cautious nature, was why he'd become suspicious. It had only been one of the Cycler's flight modules without its bulky habitation module. They'd have needed it for what was sure to be a long flight; he knew it held most of their water and air. The flight modules were purely functional, good for no more than a few days on their own. Mostly control systems and propellant tanks...

Propellant. Of course. They couldn't possibly have made it up from the surface and all the way out here. So they had made it back to Gateway and refueled. It was the only way they could have caught up to him. But would that have been enough?

He considered what it had taken to get this capsule out here: a considerable velocity change, leaving him barely enough to finish his task at Weatherby. By his math, *Orion* could impart the necessary velocity change against Weatherby to move its orbit back into Earth's path. He was confident the tough little capsule could absorb the load.

By contrast, Hammond's ships were made to stay in orbit and were thus much lighter. Hassani recalled that they had more efficient engines, thus getting more "mileage" from the same amount of fuel. So yes, they could have made it out here after a stop at Gateway's fuel farm.

What about getting back? These were Americans after all – tenacious, unpredictable, but not known for gallivanting off on suicide missions. They'd have needed two stages: one for the trip out here, another for the trip home.

It had been an empty stage, then. His mounting anger was blunted by his appreciation of their tactics: giving up their spent mass had caused him to use his only defensive weapon. The others were already committed, programmed along a precise sequence of carefully timed burns that would deliver them to their targets over the next several weeks. Something so small, arriving from the immensity of deep space, would be undetectable. Major cities would disappear while the rest of the world awaited destruction beyond comprehension. The final cleansing fire would yet come from the sky, just as foretold.

An unnatural calm swept over him. Yes, his adversaries were still out there and he had wasted his shot. They were still hiding, no doubt watching him right now. Perhaps they were training whatever weapons they had on his ship and were simply waiting for the opportunity to shoot. That they hadn't led him to one of two conclusions; they either had no weaponry, or they needed this ship intact. Which meant they would be trying to either board or sabotage the spacecraft. Perhaps both?

He frantically searched the cabin for anything that might be used as a weapon. Simple repair tools, all useless. Embedded in one corner were compact yellow cases full of survival equipment: Desert, Arctic, all just as worthless. When he opened the case marked "Tropic," Hassani gave fervent thanks for the divine blessing he'd just received.

...

Ryan approached the spacecraft with outstretched hands to absorb the impact and hoped it would be enough to avoid announcing their presence. He let his body fall gently against the service module and grabbed one of several handrails that girded the hull. Ahead, near the base of the command module, sat the two MMU's.

"Those would've been nice to have about five minutes ago," Quinn observed as he fell into place alongside Ryan.

"Maybe we'll take them with us," Ryan said, only half joking. He pointed down the side of the spacecraft. "Access bay is right over there, along the bottom of the service module."

Both men quickly made their way towards the engine, hand-over-hand along the yellow railing. "Looks easy enough from here," Ryan said. An oversized latch was recessed into the panel, sized for space-suited astronauts working with stiff gloves.

"Never say 'easy,'" Quinn admonished him. "You'll jinx us."

Ryan slipped his boots into footholds below the panel and grabbed the lever. It turned in his hand and the panel opened slowly. He lifted his sun visor to answer Quinn with a sly grin as he held out a hand. "Torque wrench, please."

Quinn lifted what looked like a large cordless drill from the pouch on his side. A touch-screen controller above its grip gave it away as something more elaborate than what he might have used for a weekend project at home.

Ryan turned on the headlamp atop his helmet and leaned into the cavity they'd just opened. "Lots of plumbing," he mumbled as he searched for the engine's manual control valves, a last resort for astronauts who might have otherwise been left stranded by malfunctioning electronics. He traced the maze of foil-wrapped tubes and wiring to a junction near the base of the compartment. "There it is." As he began to fit the tool's business end over the valve stem, the spacecraft lurched to one side, knocking the wrench from his hand.

...

"What the hell was that?" Audrey exclaimed as they watched a flurry of vapor suddenly erupt around *Orion*. The spacecraft lurched back and forth, rolling and pitching violently around all three axes.

"The jig's up," Penny said grimly. "He's trying to shake them loose."

"Should we move in closer?" Audrey asked. "In case they need our help?"

Simon hesitated, then cursed under his breath. "Negative. Too much of a collision risk. We maintain our distance."

...

The labyrinth of plumbing rushed up at them as the ship twisted violently. Ryan was left flailing at the open hatch as he was tossed out of the access bay, before grasping the safety tether that led back to *Snoopy*. Clouds of exhaust burst at random from thruster quads as the ship lurched about.

Quinn barked in his headset. "Get back in!" he exclaimed. "He's trying to shake us loose."

"Then it's working," Ryan grunted as he bounced against the hull. He glanced back at Quinn, who'd looped an arm around an antenna mast. "Stay close and hang on!"

"Roger that," Quinn said as he let go of the mast and began to pull himself back towards the access bay, legs flailing behind him. As he hand-walked along the hull, another burst from a nearby thruster scored a direct hit on the knot of safety lines behind them. The tethers blistered in the exhaust plume and were tossed about like windblown vines, pulling Quinn away from the ship.

He scrambled for a handhold that was suddenly just beyond reach. As the spacecraft pitched back again, the hull smashed against his feet and sent him tumbling away. The remains of his weakened tether snapped effortlessly as his mass pulled against it, barely slowing him down as he spun away into space.

Quinn's howl of pain over the radio made Ryan look up from his own struggle. "*Marcus!*"

"Stay put, Captain," he said with a groan. "Mission first."

"But I can reach you!" If he jumped now, he'd have enough safety line left.

"Negative, sir. Disable that spacecraft."

Ryan looked along the length of his own tether, which appeared to be in just as poor a shape after being flash-broiled by the hydrazine thrusters. He reluctantly returned to the open compartment.

...

"Three o' clock, low!" Penny shouted, her face pressed against the window above her station. Amid the volcanic ripples of erupting thrusters, there appeared to be a body tumbling away from the ship. "Is that what I think it is?"

Simon put the binoculars back to his eyes and swore when they came into focus. "God help them." He continued searching. "There's movement." He adjusted the focus. "That's a military suit. It's Quinn."

"Is he alive?" Audrey asked, voice rising. "What can we do?"

"We're going after him," Penny said. "Any objections?"

"Not yet!" Simon barked, still scanning their target. It had suddenly stopped its violent gyration and was directly facing them. "I've lost sight of Ryan. His tether's still bunched up around the tail...oh hell." Out on *Orion's* command module, its hatch opened and a figure emerged in a white NASA spacesuit. He carried something in his right hand...

Good God, was that a *sword*?

42

Orion

Penny's frantic call of *"Danger close, forward!"* had shocked him as much as the warning itself. If she was calling over an open frequency, it was bad.

Forward, she'd said. It was hard enough to get your bearings in zero-g, much less after being tossed around like laundry in a dryer. Forward...he searched for any reference markings inside the compartment – every spacecraft had them in some form or another – and found what he was looking for. He spun about, careful to stay inside the service bay. No sense letting Hassani know they were on to him. He reached down and punched the "vox" selector on his microphone. "Does he have any weapons?"

"No guns that we can see," Simon answered. "Umm...he's carrying some kind of sword."

"OK, out," was the only reply Ryan could muster. What fresh insanity was this? He frantically searched through the tools, anything to counter a long blade.

In zero gravity. Wearing a fabric suit.

Ryan frantically searched his memory – what was the first rule of Space Fight Club?

He doesn't know I'm on to him.

...

Hassani calmly looped his umbilical outside of the ship, keeping a wide berth from anything that might snag his supply of air and coolant. It was remarkably easy to lose control of one's own momentum out here. There was too much space (he smiled at the irony) with no sense of bearing. Nothing like pushing oneself about inside of a ship or loping about on the lunar surface. He'd have to be certain of his footing, needing both arms free to manipulate the only weapon he'd brought up here.

Hassani slipped his boots into one of the outside footholds, flexed his knees, and twisted his waist. Satisfied that he understood the suit's limited range of motion, he practiced a few cautious slashes and jabs with the machete and prayed whoever was down there had not brought one of those zero-g rifles. Arrogant as they could be, the Americans were right about one thing: never bring a knife to a gunfight.

The one still floating away out there in the void appeared to be in a military suit. That meant whoever was left would probably be civilian. Unprepared, certainly unarmed.

He pulled himself down and peered over the capsule's base, looking down the service module's cylindrical hull. He spotted the open service bay and glimpsed a white EVA suit moving inside.

Of course, he thought. *The main engines*. They could indeed do great harm from there. Very well, then. He carefully slipped the curved blade back in its sheath, pulled his boots free of the foothold, and walked himself down the handrail towards the engine.

• • •

"Heads up. Omar's making his way towards you, about halfway there. He's been practicing his swing."

"Great." Ryan wedged himself deeper inside the bay and tightened his grip around the wrench. He would use himself as bait, drawing Hassani into the cramped space where he'd have precious little room to swing that blade around.

Or so he hoped. Unarmed combat training had been a long time ago, and it sure as hell hadn't been in anything like this. The cold mud of Quantico suddenly seemed like an inviting place in comparison.

• • •

Hassani cursed as his prey wormed deeper down into the service bay. His back was facing him, suggesting that whoever was inside remained blissfully unaware of his presence. Was he even aware his partner had been thrown into oblivion? His friends apparently did as their ship had started backing off in a cloud of thruster gas. It quickly fell away, opening the distance enough for a brief kick from one of its engines.

Whoever was down there had been left on his own, so they did know when to make sacrifices. The kill would be that much more satisfying. He stopped less than a meter from the open bay and slipped one boot into a foothold, keeping his other free to pivot. He carefully slid the weapon free of its scabbard, its blade gleaming like a jewel in the blazing sunlight.

...

Ryan saw a flash against the open hatch, as if reflected from a mirror. Or polished metal.

He checked the oxygen gauge on his wrist: maybe three minutes left in his emergency bottle. He grasped struts on either side and pushed himself against the compartment floor, carefully placing his feet against his disconnected PLSS backpack. He nudged it up against the opening.

...

A bulky white contraption emerged: a life-support pack. An easy target. Hassani leaned forward and slashed his blade across the nearest hose and was enveloped in an eruption of ice crystals. The backpack tumbled out of the compartment, spiraling up in a cloud of frozen vapor.

...

Screw it. I'm not waiting.

Ryan launched himself out of the bay, free of his pack and swinging the long wrench. He barely missed Hassani's lifeline. Hassani countered, slashing down across Ryan's tether to cut it cleanly in two.

He grabbed the nearby antenna mast with his free hand and kicked against Hassani's body, knocking him free of the foothold. Ryan spun about the mast as Hassani tumbled away, then lunged for the umbilical hose and wrapped it around his arm. Satisfied he wasn't going anywhere, he pulled hard against the foil-wrapped lifeline as they both floated away.

Hassani was whipped around as the slack ran out and flew back towards Ryan. He reached out with the spanner and swung at Hassani's faceplate. It was a glancing blow, getting more helmet than glass. There was a glint of light and a sharp *clang* inside his suit as the machete rebounded off of his helmet.

It was by accident that the blade managed to connect with anything at all; Hassani was now spinning at the end of his line and thoroughly disoriented. But an unhinged nutcase floundering about with a machete was only slightly less dangerous than one swinging it with purpose. As

Ryan fought to keep his own bearings, he felt a cold stab of fear: could a stainless-steel blade make a dent in a composite space helmet?

It wouldn't matter in another minute anyway as that was about all he had left in the emergency bottle. Soon he'd be rebreathing old air and slowly suffocating from his own exhaled carbon dioxide.

He looped Hassani's umbilical around his free arm and yanked hard, whipping them back towards each other. Ryan reached out with the spanner and swung hard as Hassani flew past, finally connecting with his faceplate. Ryan wasn't sure what he'd done, but the impact rang through his forearm.

They snapped around to face each other as the slack ran out. Hassani still held the machete in one hand but was pawing wildly at his helmet, its visor now a web of fractured glass. Ryan reefed the line back in, pulling Hassani straight to him. He let go of the line and floated free as an alarm began beeping steadily in his ear – his emergency air, gone.

Ryan instinctively drew into a wrestler's crouch and wrapped himself around Hassani as they collided. Riding his back like a bucking horse, he raised the wrench and brought it down hard on Hassani's forearm and broke his grip on the makeshift sword. As it tumbled away, the spinning blade slashed across his arm.

He closed his eyes and waited for the remaining oxygen to escape. Coolant sprayed out of the cut, but there was no rush of air behind it. The status lights in his helmet showed the suit was still holding pressure. He found the outer shell laid open with a severed coolant tube beneath it. The inner layer was untouched.

Surprised that he wasn't dead yet, Ryan reached for the combat knife Quinn had given him. The Ka-Bar was still there, taped to his utility belt. He tightened his grip around the hilt and narrowed his focus on Hassani's tangled lifeline, undulating about them like a tentacle searching for something to grab. *Enough of this.*

He slashed its blade across the umbilical, stabbing at it until he was rewarded with a fountain of ice crystals. Ryan seized the live hose; it was his only chance of getting aboard.

Hassani drifted away, grasping in vain for his severed lifeline as he tumbled into the black. Ryan looked down at the blade still in his hand, the spacecraft below him, and the radiant comet beyond. "*Yes!*" he exulted, waving the knife over his head and pumping his fists. "That's right – enjoy your seventy-two virgins!"

A shadow crept over him. What now? He turned to see *Snoopy* rise up from behind, eclipsing the sun. Quinn floated in the airlock. "That is so cliché, Mister Hunter. I've heard better from boot privates."

"Fresh out of snappy one-liners, Gunny. I got nothing."

"Ah well," he said, watching Hassani's limp figure spin away. "Nobody ever promised him they'd all be women."

• • •

Ryan pulled himself along the umbilical and into the open capsule as a subtle but annoying alarm sounded in his ears. He didn't need reminding that it would be a really good idea to find fresh air *now*. He hastily reefed in the remaining line and yanked the hatch shut. He scrambled to find the life support panel, fighting a swelling headache to remember what little he knew about the capsule's systems. Carbon dioxide poisoning had begun insidiously the moment he'd started rebreathing his own air.

Ryan pulled himself up to the center pilot seat in front of the instrument panel. These things were generally laid out the same way: primary flight controls, guidance, propulsion...which meant life support would be...there. The pressurization controls were just one more touch screen panel surrounded by menu buttons. He kept looking for something simpler – no time to figure out their menu logic – and found an old-fashioned differential control dial. He tried to read the values inscribed on it but everything had turned blurry. Was it his breath fogging up the glass, or was it something worse? The pounding headache made it hard to think. He cranked the dial over to what he hoped would be a safe level and punched it. A nearby scale glowed red. He guessed that was the "idiot light" that would tell him when it was safe to crack open his helmet.

The light turned amber. Okay, that was a good sign. Probably.

He blinked against the thickening fog to grab a handhold and locked his eyes on the scale. Amber could be such a stubborn color.

It felt like someone was shoving an icepick into his skull. He screwed his eyes shut against the mounting pain.

Ryan?

Ryan!

Who was calling him now? Leave me alone, I've got work here.

When he opened his eyes, Ryan thought he saw a green light through the haze.

Answer me!

He twisted the safety lock along his neck ring. There was a hiss of escaping air as the seal vented. He slid the rings apart and tore the helmet away. His body wheezed reflexively in a long, sucking breath, before his conscious mind could even form a command to breathe. The stabbing headache disappeared as his vision cleared. So it hadn't entirely been the faceplate fogging up. The thought of completely losing control over his own body was terrifying. What if—

"Ryan!"

What?

There was a tinny voice in the air on his right. *Oh yeah – the radio.* He turned his head and found the earpiece floating a few inches from his face. It must have been torn loose when he yanked the helmet free. He placed it back in his ear and thumbed the microphone by his throat.

Another deep, luxurious breath. "I'm here," he croaked. "Don't get your undies in a twist."

"That's good news," Penny answered. Damn, but she actually sounded sincere. "We were really getting worried."

"What, that I was having all the fun?" he asked with a sigh. "Geez, what a day."

"Try not to break anything, slacker. We need that spacecraft."

. . .

Ryan was left with nothing but time on his hands. Time to contemplate what had happened in the last twenty-four hours and what needed to happen in the next twelve. He tried not to think about his family.

They had run out of options. Catching the spacecraft which he now occupied had taken a sizeable fraction of propellant, and going after Quinn had spent too much of what little reserves remained. There wouldn't be enough to correct their own trajectory, not after they used the mains to ram Weatherby with enough delta-v to move it safely out of Earth's way. They and their ship would be doomed to remain on the same path, zooming past Earth in a long parabola that would take it to the outer reaches of the Solar System in a few hundred years.

Sorry, Art. Maybe you'll be able to come out here and find us someday.

• • •

Denver

"That's going to be a really high speed reentry," Grant warned, "almost as if they were coming back from Mars."

Hammond snorted cynically. "Maybe we should tell Abbot 'you're welcome.' Seeing as how we're flight testing the Ares mission profile for him."

"Bledsoe's seriously worried, Art. You know the heat gradients go up exponentially with velocity. Orion's shield might be designed for that kind of entry profile but it hasn't been flight tested."

"I don't see how they get home otherwise," Hammond said. "Long braking burns aren't an option anymore. They'll use too much prop redirecting that damned flying iceberg and we're still looking at almost six months before they intersect Earth orbit again." The combined supplies of both ships wouldn't stretch that far. "What's Ronnie's play?"

"Split the difference. Leave the crew capsule docked to *Snoopy* but ditch the external stores while they're still synchronous with Weatherby. Houston will take over remotely."

Hammond followed the logic right away. "So the nukes stay in orbit?"

"They're working up an incremental detonation sequence to nudge the trajectory. In the meantime, our people get clear and start burning for home. It'll take a few weeks."

"Loopers?" Hammond asked, though he knew the answer. They would slow down just enough to be captured by Earth's gravity and bleed off their remaining velocity over a series of long orbits that would eventually bring them to the edge of the atmosphere. "How are they set for consumables?"

"Our own stash plus whatever they took from Gateway. Simon figures seven weeks' worth of food and four weeks of fresh air and water. After that they have to recycle everything through the Sabatier reactor.

Best wag on an ETA is forty-four days from now, so reserves are adequate." If nothing else happened, he didn't add.

Hammond grimaced. "If you call breathing their own farts and drinking their own piss 'adequate.' Remind me to give them extra fat bonuses next Christmas."

43

Washington

The VH-92's executive interior was remarkably good at dampening the racket that would have otherwise dominated the big Sikorsky's cabin. Active noise cancelling no doubt contributed to the uncomfortable silence that now dominated the well-appointed helicopter. The President rested her chin in one hand as she brooded over the spectacle of flooded coastal Virginia. Don Abbot faced her in the opposite seat, looking at the same view but not seeing. A mask of civility hid the contempt in which he held her and so many other politicians.

"After the Coast Guard captured the crew of that spy trawler off the Cape, it didn't take long for CIA to connect the dots," she began, as if picking up an old conversation. "Their missiles came from an Iranian tanker that we tracked all the way back to its home port, which unsurprisingly turned out to be their naval base at Bandar Abbas. The Straits of Hormuz are still rather important, so we keep a couple of fast-attack subs on patrol there. You know how big one of those supertankers is, Don?"

He was vaguely familiar, but shook his head "no" anyway.

"*Big*," she said. "Bigger than our aircraft carriers, if you can believe that. Over a quarter mile long. Nearly half a million metric tons empty. I can't remember the draft, but it makes a hell of a mess when one gets broken in half right at the entrance to your biggest port. It'll keep their navy bottled up for a long time."

Abbot grunted and nodded again, as if appreciating her point.

"The intel analysts tell me that the hardest part of unraveling a black operation is figuring out one exists in the first place. But once you can identify a couple of players, you just keep pulling the thread. We yanked on quite a few."

Relief welled up inside. Maybe there was still a way to dodge this bullet. "So we don't think it was someone inside my agency?" he asked guardedly.

"I didn't say that," the President replied. "Getting the specs for a couple of unclassified spacecraft is one thing. Finding out the location and capabilities of a codeword-secret weapons platform is entirely different."

He stared at her quizzically.

"Your aide has been arrested," she said, getting right to it. "I'm told he's been rather chatty even after he lawyered up. I don't think he realized he was feeding information to the Caliphate. Apparently he was okay with engineering mass destruction if it was for *his* cause and not that icky religious stuff. He's still terrified that we'll send him to Gitmo," she chuckled, as if he'd committed some kind of social gaffe. "I don't think he realizes how much better off he'd be down there than at a SuperMax prison."

The wave of relief he'd felt washed away just as quickly. "So what happens now?"

She faced him with ice cold eyes. "You hand in your resignation, effective immediately."

Abbot began stammering in protest. "There is no way I'll—"

"There's no *what*, exactly?" she demanded. "This came out of *your* shop, Don. Your executive assistant used his access to convey extremely sensitive information to an enemy who used it facilitate the most devastating attack our nation has ever suffered." She stabbed a finger at the window. "Look outside! It'll take weeks just to assess the damage and take a body count. Markets are probably closed for the next month, so businesses that weren't even directly harmed are taking it in the shorts. Supply chains are already shutting down because they can't sell product to factories that no longer exist. Nobody really knows how bad this is going to get."

"We'll rebuild," he said lamely, "make things better than before."

"Taking advantage of a crisis?" she asked in a voice brimming with contempt. "The 'broken window' fallacy? You might be a whiz of a rocket scientist but you're a piss-poor economist. Money spent on rebuilding old things is not the same as money spent on creating new things." She pursed her lips as she considered her next words. "What you don't yet know is that we very nearly ended up with a jihadist insurgency. The protest organizers we rounded up in Denver were supposed to be the first wave. There were dozens of cells just waiting for the 'go' order to take advantage of the carnage they'd been promised was coming."

"This isn't NASA's failure," he argued. "If anything, it's Homeland Security. DHS is a clown show and you know it."

"I do," she said, "which is why I'll be asking Congress to shut it down and return its agencies to their original homes. But how many families are gone? How many funerals will we have to attend for entire towns?" She let the thought hang, settling back into her seat as she stared him down. "There is no way you get out of this clean, Don. I want your resignation on my desk by the end of the day."

Save for the discordant thrum of rotors, the flight aboard Marine One continued on in silence.

...

Denver

Hammond had expected his final meeting with Kruger to be tense and the agent didn't disappoint: the man's practiced calm belied the great satisfaction he took in laying out the details of the all-but-inevitable government takeover of Polaris' orbital launch service. It was chillingly well thought out for being dropped in their laps so quickly. A phalanx of industrious busybodies in the national security establishment had no doubt been planning this for some time, just waiting for a convincing pretext.

Hammond had limited the attendees to Grant and Posey: one for his operational expertise, the other to keep him from launching across the desk and throttling the DHS official. His mind raced between multiple depressing scenarios for their business as Kruger droned on, so it was no real surprise that he was startled when his desk phone rang.

Kruger wore a contented smirk. "Something wrong, Arthur?"

Hammond glared back silently as he picked up the receiver. "I distinctly remember telling you no calls." A chatter of rushed explanations caused him to raise his eyebrows suspiciously. "The Secretary of Defense? Yes, absolutely that's worth the interruption. Thank you. I'll hold."

He kept an eye trained on Kruger as he waited for the line to switch over. "Hal? Art...Yes, Abigail's fine, thanks. What can I do for you?"

He listened quietly, his body language giving away nothing. "You're serious...I mean, she's serious? They've already whipped enough votes?" He chuckled at something the Secretary said. "No, the lady doesn't move on anything until she's certain of the outcome. That's very good news, Hal. You be sure to stop by next time you're out this way. Glad your family's safe."

Genuinely smiling for the first time in a long while, Hammond set down the phone. "I'm not in a polite mood, so I'll just get to it: corral your goon squad and get the hell off of this property."

"I'm afraid that's not up to you," Kruger sniffed. "You and your company are still subjects of an investigation."

"Then come back with a warrant," Hammond said, stepping around the desk. Posey stayed close behind.

"You don't seem to understand," Kruger said sternly. "A Federal takeover is the only way you get to stay in business at this point."

"Hal Horner says otherwise. By this time next week your department won't even exist. I'm sure your superiors will explain it all in due course."

Kruger tipped his chin defensively, a thin crack showing in his composure. The buzzing phone on his belt was no doubt informing him of the sudden change in relationships. "What are you talking about?"

"We just saved the world, that's what. Tony here will show you out. I recommend you do as he says."

44

Snoopy II
Flight Day Sixty-Two

To call it a long seven weeks would have been a gross understatement. Despite having both vehicles at their disposal, the Orion and Cycler modules together had about the same interior volume as a small RV. The five crewmates remained judiciously respectful of each other's personal space, in fact the NASA module had been turned into a de facto "girls' dorm" for the two women. And while all of it was new to Audrey, for Penny it was the most personal space she'd ever had on a long-duration flight.

Audrey had devoted most of her off-duty time tending to Quinn, who'd broken a foot against *Orion*'s hull. With limited medical supplies and even less training, she'd spent a great deal of time on video conferences with doctors back on Earth. Most of the conversations had felt decidedly one-way, as her gaps in knowledge were amplified by the transmission delays across almost a million miles of space.

Ryan had been the one they were most concerned about. He'd gone about sharing his piloting duties with Simon and Penny almost robotically, with no trace of the easygoing wit they were used to from him. The more time that passed without contact from loved ones, the more distant and aloof he'd become.

For his part, he had tried to remain optimistic in spite of his doubts. Each passing day had only added to the burden, and during their final hours in orbit the weight of it threatened to crush him as Earth loomed ever larger. The southern coast had been swamped, with Florida and Georgia faring the worst. Millions had been successfully evacuated inland, but tens of thousands were still missing. Most were presumed dead. Entire towns had been swept away, though occasional miracle stories still appeared in the most unexpected ways. Hundreds had been picked up at sea after being found riding atop the roofs of their homes. One couple, unable (some believed unwilling) to leave, had been so well-prepared that they'd offered beers to the National Guard helicopter crew that had found them aboard their makeshift houseboat.

Pockets of survivors were still being found in some unlikely places, but as time went on the stories coming out of the southeast U.S. turned grim. After their original stories became part of the background noise, the news outlets largely failed to report on the bodies that continued to wash up along beaches from Miami to Maryland. Recovery crews were scrambling to keep up, finally having to accept the ugly truth that rebuilding now took priority over continued searching.

Ryan assumed most of the survivors were simply out of contact. Entire networks had been destroyed and the mobile cell towers being rushed into service were presently committed to the recovery teams. There were no doubt hundreds of thousands of people – *refugees*, he admitted reluctantly – who might otherwise be fine but had no way to let anyone know. With all avenues of communication down, the country was suddenly faced with a family-notification challenge on a scale not seen since World War II. Judging by the news, any speculation that the comet strike had been meant as the opening shot of the next World War was being painstakingly discouraged.

And despite his role in averting the apocalypse, Ryan remained strangely ambivalent about it all. Perhaps it would have been better to force a final confrontation, otherwise the savages were certain to return as they always did. The bastards couldn't take anything more from him, so why not?

That dark thought pushed its way to the fore whenever Earth filled the windows, as it did now. As he arrived for his final shift in the pilot's chair, Penny somersaulted out of it and hovered behind him. Simon stayed put in the adjacent seat, grinning like an idiot and no doubt happy as a pig in slop to finally be going home. He'd been up here longer than any of them, but that didn't make it any less annoying.

He eyeballed Simon curiously. "What?"

Simon ignored him and thumbed the headset mic. "Denver, we are transferring pilot duties to Mr. Hunter now. Stratton will be moving over to *Orion* for transfer of re-entry control to Houston."

"Copy that," a tinny voice replied a second later, attenuated by the hundred thousand kilometers that still remained between their ship and home. "Please have him check in ASAP."

"They need your comm check," Simon advised curtly.

"It's SOP," Ryan said with a tinge of irritation as he robotically set up his instruments. "Tell Denver to keep their shorts on."

Still hovering above him, Penny looked amused. "Just do it, hot dog."

They were both too damned giddy for their own good. Ryan plugged in his headset and switched the radios to his panel. "This is Hunter, taking over command pilot's station at 1800Z. Comm check."

There was the usual time delay, then: "Denver copies, but voice channel is like nails on a chalkboard. Switch high gain to Bravo."

Ryan tapped a selector on screen and waited for the new frequency to bounce back from Denver. "We're back up on Bravo. How copy now?"

The delay was a little longer than usual but the grating static had mercifully cleared. They must have switched to voice-activated comm, judging by the shuffling noises and muffled conversations in the background. A new voice answered, different and decidedly higher-pitched:

"Hi, Daddy."

Epilogue

Waxhaw, North Carolina

Penny parked the rental car in front of an old steel hangar, making it a point to keep it in the shade. Seasonal changes were really more of a suggestion in the southeast, as September could still get quite toasty. She hoped the clear "Carolina Blue" morning held the promise of an equally agreeable day, as she expected to spend much of it either in that steel building or outside.

As she stepped out of the car she turned to the roar of a high-wing airplane passing overhead. The Maule taildragger had just finished its takeoff run, leaping into the sky after maybe three hundred feet of ground roll. Its tires were cartoonishly large, enabling it work off almost any terrain. It had been a while, but as a new missionary pilot she'd have to master those short field techniques quickly. It promised to be a lot different than guiding hypersonic planes back from orbit. She smiled and lifted her overnight bag from the back seat.

Walking around to the front of the hangar she saw a collection of men under the cowling of another airplane, this one a larger turboprop version of the plane she'd just watched taking off. Probably not a one of them was under forty, yet they looked like teenagers milling under the hood of a buddy's car.

"Sorry I'm late," she announced. Her voice echoed inside the steel cavern. She ambled up to the man who appeared to be overseeing the group. "GPS sent me on a wild goose chase through Charlotte. You must be Buck," she said, pointing out the name stenciled to his shirt.

"I am," he said, "and it'll do that." He wiped his hands on a rag from his back pocket before shaking hers. "My fault – should've warned you."

"Didn't help that I had to drop my husband off first so he could start moving us in," she said, and nodded towards the ongoing work behind him. "You weren't kidding about being a jack of all trades."

"Only way to be when you're out in the bush," Buck said. "That's a couple hundred pounds' worth of mechanic we don't have to carry around."

"But you still have your own here, right?"

"Not as many as we used to," he sighed, wiping his brow on his sleeve. "About half of our staff are at the regional support bases down in Augusta and Gainesville. First time we've ever had that many ops and maintenance people clustered in one place. It's like running an airline hub. Not something we're used to."

"Which is where I come in."

The wrinkles in Buck's weathered face disappeared in his grin. "Tell you what, I'm looking forward to handing those logistics off to somebody who knows what they're doing. Helps that you know your way around an airplane, too."

She looked appreciatively at the few remaining high-wing bush planes parked outside. Almost everything they flew had been recalled from missionary flying in South America for this new relief work in their own backyard, helping with the cleanup and reconstruction of the devastated East Coast. "It's good for me to be less reliant on technology. It can become a crutch."

He waved away her concern. "That all comes back soon enough. You're not the first ex-astronaut who's had to learn how to fly with steam gauges again."

"If Hoot could do it, I certainly can," she smiled. "So where do we start?"

• • •

Denver

Audrey sat cross-legged on the floor of the living room in her townhouse, absently tossing a ball down the hallway for her dachshund to chase. The little guy had missed their playtime while she'd been gone.

It was therapeutic for her as well. The months since they'd splashed down off of Catalina Island had begun as a whirlwind of activity, largely focused on painstaking debrief sessions with every conceivable intelligence agency (and a few she hadn't conceived of). After that, she and Simon had quickly gone to work refining the layout for Art's next generation of moonships. As she understood it, their insurance hadn't covered "war risk" and there was no doubt Arthur had played that hand well in Washington. Judging by the magnitude of resources being thrown at building new Cyclers, it must have been a pretty juicy payout.

She welcomed the distractions, because sitting at home was nearly unbearable and sleep had become elusive in a way she'd never known. Of the many stories she'd heard from her days at NASA, the one that had intrigued her the most was how the astronauts had coped with comparatively mundane lives back home. The sad fact was that too many of them hadn't – once you've stood on the Moon and looked back at Earth, what comes next? What could you possibly do for an encore, especially when the Mars missions they'd expected never materialized? Many of them had taken comfort in alcohol or something harder, to the point where years were lost in a haze of artificial quietude. Some came home to find their marriages ruined by years of absenteeism. Others just got weird.

Audrey was determined to not get weird.

So why do I talk to my dog?

Lots of people do, she rationalized. She knew it was time to become more social and less introverted, but she felt even less in common with "normal" people than she had *before* going farther than anyone ever in the history of spaceflight, before orbiting the moon and flying alongside a comet and helping prevent an extinction-level event. Before being so close to such unhinged violence.

What comes next? How do you top that?

The doorbell combined with her dog's frantic barking snapped her back to the present. She picked up Wernher to calm him down and pulled the door open enough to peek outside. It was dark, and she'd forgotten to change out the porch bulb that had burned out in her absence. Her heart raced as she spied a figure move in the shadows.

Audrey hurriedly shut the door as a familiar voice called out.

"Is that how you always treat company, Red?"

She flung the door back open. *Marcus?*

"Evening," he said, and offered a bottle of wine as he leaned against a cane. "I don't know what you like, but figured since I was stopping by unannounced..."

"No kidding," she said. "Not that I mind—I mean it's okay. I mean I just don't get a lot of company. What are you doing out here? Didn't you go back east?"

"I did," he said, "long enough for them to give me transfer orders. Mind if I come in?"

She stepped aside to set Wernher down. "Sorry."

"For what?" The pup began busily sniffing his feet and licking his hand. "I like dogs."

"Sorry for being rude. I've kind of been keeping to myself lately." She led him inside and gestured toward the sofa.

Marcus Quinn picked a corner and set the wine bottle down. "So I've heard."

"Heard what? Who have you been talking to?"

He held his hands up defensively. "Calm down, Red. I'm not spying on you. Not really."

"Not really?"

"Meaning I stopped by your office and caught up with Simon. He introduced me to Mr. Hammond. Got to meet Charlie Grant as well. They all think very highly of you."

She didn't understand. "They sent you out here?"

He smiled. "No, this was my idea. They just gave me your address. I'm going to be in the area for a while and it'd be nice to have a friend nearby."

"How's that?"

"They've transferred me to Colorado Springs to train military EVA specialists, since that's kind of a thing now." He tapped the cane against his leg. "Those who can't do, teach."

She felt her heart race again. "That's not very far."

He smiled again, throwing her off balance. She really wished he'd stop that. "They've put me up in visitor's quarters but I'll need to find a place in short order. I'd appreciate it if you could show me around."

"That's funny," she said, "because I don't get out very much, except for running. Not very social, I guess."

"Then we can go explore together. It'll do you good to get out." He held up the wine bottle. "Want to talk over what to do next?"

"Let me get some glasses from the kitchen." Audrey slipped away, hoping she didn't look as flushed as she felt. Wernher trotted up beside her, wagging his tail vigorously. She stared down at him and sighed. "I know you like him," she whispered. "So do I. Quit looking at me like that."

...

"It's cold out here."

"It is," Ryan agreed, and reached down to his son's coat. "Stay zipped up, pal. It cools down quick after the sun sets."

"Because of the mountains?" He'd noticed how they hid the sun before it really wanted to go away for the night.

"Sort of. Air's thinner way up high like we are. And yes, the mountains make it dark earlier. But they sure are pretty." Ryan had grown up in Virginia's Blue Ridge and was quite happy to be living near real mountains. The beach was nice while it lasted but he'd been eager to break out his climbing gear again. Even Marcy, who'd spent most of her life on the coast, hadn't hesitated when Art had offered him the chief pilot's job after Penny's early retirement. They were all finished with being near large bodies of water.

Marshall kicked impatiently at the dirt. "Is your telsco ready yet?"

He laughed. "My *telescope* is ready, pal. I'm just waiting for the sky to be ready."

Marshall processed that with his four-year-olds' mind. "Oh." As stars materialized out of the gathering darkness, a pale yellow-orange dot appeared among them. "What's that one?"

"Pretty sure that's Mars." Ryan looked up the star chart on his phone. "Yep, that's it. Mars."

"What's Mars?"

He wondered how to explain. "It's a planet, kind of like ours. Not as big, though." He searched for a better way to describe it to a young child. "You know how the Moon is kind of a giant ball of dirt? Like that." He knew differently but would save that conversation for later. Much later.

"It looks really small."

"It's a long way away. It just looks smaller." Ryan tapped on the planet's icon and handed the phone to his son. "See for yourself."

Marshall studied the image, looked into the eyepiece, then returned to spinning and zooming virtual Mars with a finger. “Can I go there?”

Ryan smiled. “Not tonight,” he said. “Too close to bedtime. Sorry.”

Marshall knew his Dad was teasing again. “I know that!” he protested. “When I’m big, like you. Like the way you went to the Moon.”

Ryan stared silently at the red planet’s brightening disk as the sky seemed to open wide around them, promising to swallow him whole with his fears and anxieties. *Yes*, he decided. *But not like that. Never like that.*

“Of course, pal. Except you’ll do it better.”

Author's Notes

"Asteroids are nature's way of asking, 'How's that space program coming along?'"

-Attributed to Neil deGrasse Tyson

First, my thanks to those who helped make this book possible:

To Leona, for your guidance and enthusiasm. You're a great friend and editor.

To Winchell Chung and his invaluable Atomic Rockets website.

To Melissa and our boys, for putting up with and protecting me from the distractions. We're all figuring this out together, and I'd be lost were it not for you guys.

...

None of the concepts in FARSIDE are made up. Let's clarify that: they were made up by *somebody*, it just wasn't me. I'm happy to take full credit for everything else.

The inspiration for this story came from a commercial lunar voyage being put together by the Russians, which would mate an expanded Soyuz capsule to an upper stage with enough impulse to get the vehicle onto a free-return Lunar trajectory. The tourism agency that brokers Soyuz passenger seats to the International Space Station says they've collected deposits for two passengers (the third seat would be the pilot's). This struck me as eminently possible, since that was what Soyuz was originally intended for. The only thing that will hold up this flight is Russian politics.

Add that idea to the progress being made with inflatable space habitats, and now you've got a business proposition. What could possibly go wrong? After all, that's where the stories live. You'd never want to read a story about everything being just wonderful, right? Something like Apollo 13 seemed way too obvious and real life would've beat the pants off of anything I could come up with. Around the same time, I'd begun reading about ideas for deflecting earthbound asteroids. One concept involved a network of defensive satellites, controlled from a service station in orbit behind the Moon at L2. And thus Gateway was born.

And of course my devious mind immediately wondered how someone might get their hands on that technology. How would they even get there? It's not like they could just hijack a Soyuz or something...or maybe they could.

FARSIDE wasn't conceived as a military thriller, but given the stakes involved that was the only place it could go. There are a lot of veterans in the aviation world, so it didn't seem out of place to have Penny and Ryan in the middle of the action. And while I'm clearly biased towards the Marine Corps, they have in fact studied the use of suborbital spacecraft to drop troops anywhere in the world on very short notice. SUSTAIN (Small Unit Space Transportation and Insertion) is a capability I wish they'd had when I was a young Marine. Even now, the necessary vehicles elude them (I was tempted to add "as far as we know," which is a nice thought but I'm not completely naïve).

The lunar exploration architecture described in this book has been studied extensively by both NASA and private enterprise, each with varying degrees of enthusiasm. The Snoopy vehicles were inspired by a proposal to modify a Centaur upper stage into a reusable lunar lander. One of many great ideas that has yet to make it into real life, the least I could do was to help it along a bit. The framework of this story is the space transportation architecture we need to see: cheaper access to Earth orbit, a propellant depot at one of the Earth-Moon Lagrange points, and a network of spacecraft in permanent orbit between the two. We have the ability to do this now. All that remains is the will.

On a far more serious note, close calls with comets and asteroids have been gaining popular attention. I partially attribute this to comet Shoemaker-Levy 9's impact with Jupiter some twenty years ago, inescapable evidence of exactly how dangerous our neighborhood can be. More recently and much closer to home, the explosion of a Near Earth Object (NEO) above Chelyabinsk, Russia was captured by a number of dashboard and security cameras. And by "explosion," understand that it let go with a force equivalent to 500 kilotons of TNT. Destructive as that was, a minor change in trajectory would have been devastating. Instead of detonating almost twenty miles above Chelyabinsk, imagine if it had happened at just two miles: the equivalent of a half-megaton nuclear airburst.

It's almost like somebody's trying to tell us something: Yes folks, it can happen here. So what do we do about it?

There have been a number of studies to investigate how we might divert an inbound comet or asteroid. Perhaps the most serious player in this effort is the B612 Foundation, whose "Sentinel" space telescope will identify and catalog NEOs large enough to pose a serious threat. Which is kind of the first rule of marksmanship: you can't shoot what you can't see.

That begs the question: what could we do about it? The answer depends on reaction time. The available solutions become a lot less dramatic when we have plenty of time, which I hope came across in descriptions of the fictional Comet Weatherby. Three years is not much on a cosmic scale, and so would require a lot of force applied over a short time. Nuking it (or rather, setting off nukes in close proximity) is an obvious brute force solution, though it stands to reason that high-energy lasers of the type described in FARSIDE would be more effective on objects containing a lot of frozen volatiles (like comets). And if we have several years to respond, a sturdy satellite with enough propellant could simply push a pesky NEO out of the way. That's time the Sentinel space telescope is intended to provide us.

Access to space used to be a lot more complicated than it is today. As a species, we owe it to ourselves to take the obvious next steps to protect our home.

Coming Soon

July 2015

As the decades passed, men would hotly debate whether the chance encounter had been one of divine providence or blind luck. After nine years of sailing across the solar system, faster than any other object humans had previously flung from Earth's gravity well, the nuclear-powered probe *New Horizons* had finally entered Pluto's fragile sphere of influence. It was to be a fleeting encounter: despite carrying the hopes and expectations of so many, the event amounted to not much more than a cosmic one-night-stand.

That was the cynic's view. After a whirlwind round of begging and pleading, a small but determined group of scientists and engineers had prevailed upon the politicians to fund their little mission before it was too late. Finally convincing them that Pluto's tenuous atmosphere—which they could barely detect from Earth—would collapse onto the tiny planet's surface within the next decade, frozen into crystals by their host planet's unstoppable migration away from the Sun.

"How long until it reappears?" one Senator had asked.

"Two hundred years," the planetary geologist had replied. Because he was a geologist, of course the Senator had to ask the physicist seated next to him, who in turn had to produce a meteorologist that would verify their assumptions. Despite his protests of not knowing a single thing about extra-planetary atmospherics, the meteorologist agreed that, yes, the thin envelope of gases would indeed turn to ice and fall to Pluto's surface. And no, it would not reappear for another two centuries. When he cited sophomore-level physics to support his reasoning, it had finally been enough to satisfy the gathered politicos.

And so, New Horizons had been put together largely from off-the-shelf components meant for other (cancelled) missions. It resembled nothing so much as an ambitious grade-schooler's concept of what a space probe might be: about the size (and shape) of a grand piano, but covered in gold foil and sporting a radioisotope generator from one end with a dish antenna from the other.

After a quick pass by Jupiter to steal the energy from some of that giant planet's gravity (it wasn't going to miss it, after all), the little probe went into hibernation until awakened by its masters back on Earth. That it would be in position to capture such amazing images and data, after such a long sleep, so far from home, was amazing enough in itself. That it was further able to capture the image that had set so many men to arguing was indescribable. Some had called it miraculous. Others, carefully adhering to their image of detached objectivity, simply marveled at the luck and explained it with mathematics. But in private, they whispered amongst themselves that it was stunning, phenomenal, and extraordinary.

That the gold-wrapped piano, the first to encounter the solar system's farthest planet (or at least it was still called a planet back in 2006), swinging by at nearly forty-thousand miles an hour, would be in a position to see what it did (and that what it saw was in a position to be seen to begin with) was difficult to describe as anything other than, well, miraculous.

In the game of cosmic billiards, it was a blindfolded double-reverse bank shot. When the masters had removed the blindfold, what they saw was beyond anyone's ability to describe: there was Pluto, its prime moon Charon, and the two minor moons discovered along the way. All of them appeared in full color, high-definition detail, imagery of a depth and quality that the probe's masters could scarcely have hoped for.

Yet as with any exploration, it was those things which they didn't expect to find that were the most breathtaking. In this case, it had at first appeared as an unexpected trace of gamma radiation in orbit around Pluto. That was most odd, because it would have normally been associated with some kind of high-energy source: a faraway supernova, maybe a black hole. In Earthly terms, it would've only manifested itself in the violent fusion reaction of a nuclear bomb.

This only became noticeable in the final weeks of New Horizon's approach, and was assumed to be the result of instruments which were in dire need of recalibration after being asleep for six years. The radiation trace eventually disappeared as the probe was two weeks away from its closest approach.

Surprisingly, it reappeared the day before New Horizons made its closest flyby. As the tiny probe swept past its long-awaited target, its cameras were trained on the point in space where the gamma emissions appeared to be concentrated. The first image showed a pinprick of visible light, reflected from the distant Sun. It corresponded to the weak radiation and even weaker thermal signature.

Energetic and warm—not what anyone had expected from a tiny moonlet orbiting a minor planet. Some wondered if it was volcanic, like Io, though the lack of Jupiter-sized tidal forces ruled that out.

No matter, others said: we'd been convinced that Mars was devoid of water for decades, remember? The atmosphere was just too thin to keep it from evaporating, until we discovered a naturally-occurring antifreeze below the surface.

The next day's imagery simply caused more arguments among the masters. The little point of light had grown larger as the object came closer to their probe while it followed its own orbit. This time the light had taken on a more definitive shape: irregular, yet roughly symmetrical. One commented that it looked like a dragonfly.

And while the second day had created turmoil, the third day had uniformly shut them up. The dragonfly had resolved itself into something completely unexpected: faded green, with metallic highlights randomly dotting the surface and ungainly ebony protuberances clustered around one end. It was startlingly familiar: there was no mistaking it for a natural object. To a chorus of groans, one wag down in engineering had nailed it: that's no moon. It's a space station.

It was the markings that surprised them more than anything else:

CCCP. The Cyrillic acronym for the defunct Union of Soviet Socialist Republics.

. . .

Even in spring, Moscow was cold. Low clouds scudding across the sky gave a monochrome pallor to the equally gray, equally dismal apartment blocks that seemed to march forever across the cityscape. The architectural style had been called "brutalism." Leftovers from the country's long, abusive relationship with collective economics, they were nonetheless left standing simply because all those people had needed to live somewhere. The fall of communism and subsequent rise of an imperial kleptocracy had not done much to create incentives to build anything else. Large populations were simply easier to manage if they were all clustered in one place.

Architecture revealed a culture's character, and the deeper Owen Harriman wandered into this canyon of towering concrete the more he longed to get the hell out of it. He wasn't sure what spooked him more: the vaguely threatening air of an unfamiliar neighborhood in a country they were just barely civil with, or the realization that the same overpowering tendencies could just as easily be found in America's seat of government. Random scraps of loose garbage tossed about by the wind only heightened his anxiety. He realized the only thing missing was the sound of a dog howling in the distance.

He shook off the chill as a welcoming splash of sunlight opened up along the face of the next building. As luck would have it, the block number matched the one on the Post-It note tucked in his pocket. Owen decided to take that as a sign of encouragement. He had to admit the place looked a little more tended to than the warren of dirty cement he'd just come through to get here. Maybe that was a way of protecting certain people.

Fortunately, the man's apartment was only one floor up – he guessed a ground-floor entry was too inviting for burglars – and not that far of a walk. Owen's facility with Russian was perfunctory, just enough to manage what little reliance they still maintained on their launch systems, and he hoped it would be good enough to at least start a conversation on friendly terms.

He knocked on the door, trying to make it sound as non-threatening as possible despite realizing how ridiculous the effort was.

As expected, there was no answer. He tried again. After a moment, a faint shuffling noise as a shadow moved behind the threshold. Owen unconsciously sucked in his breath with nervous anticipation. He mentally ran through his rehearsed greeting as the door creaked open. A wizened old man, hunched by time, regarded him skeptically.

"Doctor Rhyzov?"

The little man just stared, dark eyes darting beneath brows like overgrown hedgerows.

"Anatoly Rhyzov?"

Without a word, he began to shuffle away and pull the door shut behind him. Owen leaned in and tried one last time, perhaps a little too loudly:

"Arkangel."

The door stopped moving, then inched open after a moment. The old man still didn't speak.

"Doctor?"

"I am Rhyzov," he sighed in a voice turned gravelly by the years. "What is it you want, *Americanski*?"

"How would you know I'm an American?"

"You are rude. Noisy too. I heard you coming up the stairs and down the hall. No hoodlum makes such racket. That is why they are dangerous whereas you are simply annoying."

Owen smiled in a way he hoped was disarming enough to keep the conversation moving. "Please accept my apologies if I come across as rude, Doctor. But if this neighborhood is as dangerous as you say, then may I come in before somebody creeps out of a dark corner to mug me?"

The little man grunted. "Only because he would then move straight past you into my open home," he said. "Very well, then. Inside."

"Thank you," Owen said as he slipped past. Round one was over, at least a tie if not an outright win. After months of background research, he was finally standing in Anatoly Rhyzov's living room. It was small and tidy, painstakingly cared for and decorated with what had to be several generations' worth of family heirlooms. In one corner was an open study which was much more cluttered: an old computer sat atop an older desk, surrounded by floor-to-ceiling shelves stuffed full of mathematical texts and loose notebooks. Scattered among the academic detritus were the hallmarks of a life spent in the Russian space program: plaques, paintings, models, even bits of equipment that must have been pulled from old Soyuz capsules. Owen noted that they appeared remarkably heavy to have ever been used on a spacecraft. The rocket equation didn't discriminate between competing ideologies: weight was the enemy which stalked every mission, no matter whose flag it flew.

"So," Rhyzov grunted as he studied Owen. "You come a long way, Mister..."

"Harriman. Sorry," he said, and extended his hand. "Owen Harriman. I'm with NASA."

"Is not surprising. What do you do for your space agency, Mr. Harriman?"

"I'm a mission manager in the operations directorate," he replied, hopefully appealing to the Russian sense of authority. "I'm in charge of something called the Nautilus project."

"Ah. I have heard of this. Deep space exploration vehicle, correct? I hope for your sake it is not rabbit hole."

"Excuse me?"

"I may be old, but I am not foolish. Neither am I naïve. You appear an earnest young man, Mr. Harriman. Your agency has wasted many such men on grandiose projects that never left the drawing board. Tell me, does that frighten you? The prospect of devoting perhaps your entire life to a goal that may elude your grasp?"

The old fart was cantankerous in a very Russian way. Owen realized he wasn't in the clear just yet. "That is a risk in any scientific pursuit, Dr. Rhyzov."

A grin cracked his weathered face. "That is the difference in our programs, Mr. Harriman. Spaceflight is engineering, not 'rocket science,'" he said, wagging a finger. "You know this. I know this. Yet your superiors pretend it is somehow about science. The research is secondary – because what does it matter if you cannot get there in the first place?"

Owen was taken aback. Rhyzov was right, and there was the difference in cultures laid bare.

"You are very quiet for one who has traveled so far. Yet you come asking of Arkangel."

"I'm not sure it was a question, to be perfectly honest. But here we are. So may we speak?"

"We are speaking now."

Holy God but this guy liked the wordplay. He must not get many visitors. Time to cut the crap. "Doctor..." Owen began, unconsciously catching his breath while ceremoniously pulling a manila envelope from his inside pocket. "We've found it."

The surprise in Rhyzov's eyes said it all. His hands shook as he took the proffered envelope. "This is certain?" he stammered. "How did you even know where to look?"

"We didn't," Owen said. "It was a chance encounter. Your derelict spacecraft was at western elongation during our probe's closest approach last summer. Truth be told, we probably wouldn't even have noticed that without the radiation signature. Even after thirty years, that pusher plate's pretty hot."

Rhyzov glared up at him from beneath those unruly eyebrows. "You deduced our drive system?"

Owen laughed. "Are you joking? What else could it be? And I must say, that's one hell of a lot of nukes to absorb without it all glowing like a neon light."

"It was long ago, as you said yourself. Please, Mr. Harriman of NASA, we have bantered enough for today," Rhyzov said as he shuffled towards the study, waving Owen along. "Come, we have much to talk about."

***

Glossary

ALPHA (α): Angle of Attack, the angle between an aircraft and the oncoming air. It's rather important.

BIG AL and GUS: Nicknames for Mercury astronauts Alan Shepard and Gus Grissom, for whom the first Cyclers are named.

CAPCOM: Capsule Communicator. At NASA, this is an astronaut who acts as Mission Control's voice link to spacecraft in flight.

CISLUNAR: The region of space between Earth and the Moon's orbit.

CYCLER ORBIT (aka ALDRIN CYCLER): Astronaut Buzz Aldrin proposed orbits for spacecraft that could permanently transit between the Earth and Moon, or the Earth and Mars. The long-period orbits would be timed to always sweep past each body at either end of its cycle, thus the name. A "cycler" spacecraft would thus be in constant use, taking on new crew and supplies each time it swung by either body.

DARPA: Defense Advanced Research Project Agency, the Pentagon's department of really cool stuff.

DELTA-V (or ΔV): Change in Velocity, perhaps the single most important parameter in spaceflight. A spacecraft's performance is measured in terms of Delta-V because that determines how much propellant is needed to get where you're going, do things when you get there, and come home. Unlike with aircraft, there is no taking advantage of tailwinds or throttling back to stretch your range. Go somewhere without enough ΔV to get home and you're stuck.

DSN: Deep Space Network. NASA's network of radio telescopes that allow constant communications with space probes beyond Earth's influence.

ECCENTRICITY: The degree to which a body's orbit deviates from a perfect circle (i.e., an ellipse).

EVA: Extra-Vehicular Activity, aka "spacewalk."

EOC: Emergency Operations Center. Every airline has one, and we all hope they never get used.

FACSFAC: Fleet Area Control and Surveillance Facility.

FLIGHT: Flight Director. The Boss of Mission Control.

FIDO: Flight Dynamics Officer. The mission control engineer that evaluates a spacecraft's trajectory and delta-v state.

FMS: Flight Management System, a very sophisticated autopilot and navigation computer.

FOX THREE (TWO, ONE, etc.): Military aviation radio code for an air-to-air missile launch. The number announces the type of missile fired, not its sequence.

g ("gee"): A reference to the force of gravity at Earth's surface, 9.8 meters (or 32.2 feet) per second squared. Commonly used to describe levels of acceleration (two gees, three gees, etc.).

GUIDO: Guidance Officer. Closely related to FIDO.

JPL: Jet Propulsion Lab at Caltech. Runs the DSN spaceflight operations center.

J-SPOC: Joint Space Operations Center, the U.S. military's command and control center for spaceflight operations.

LAGRANGE POINTS (also LIBRATION POINTS): Positions within the orbital configuration of two bodies where a third object can remain in a stable position relative to them. Put simply, they are points in space where the combined gravitational pull of the two large bodies can almost be thought of as cancelling each other out. There are five such points, labeled L1 to L5, all in the orbital plane of the two large bodies. This holds true for Earth and Sun, Earth and Moon, Sun and Jupiter, and so on.

LOX (O2): Liquid Oxygen.

MARSOC: Marine Corps Special Operations Command. Marine special ops units go by the name "Raiders," originated in WWII and just recently put back into use.

MAX-Q: Maximum dynamic pressure ("Q" being engineering shorthand for dynamic pressure, which is the pressure air exerts as it moves around a vehicle).

MECO: Main Engine Cutoff.

NORAD: North American Air Defense Command.

OMS: Orbital Maneuvering System, a collection of rocket motors powerful enough to change a ship's orbit.

ORBIT: The curved path described by a satellite around a celestial body, such as Earth.

PLSS: Personal Life Support System, typically fitted into a spacesuit's backpack.

RCS: Reaction Control System, a collection of smaller rockets that are used to change a ship's orientation or to make minor directional changes. Less powerful than OMS.

SAM: Surface-to-Air Missile.

SOCOM: Special Operations Command. All service branch Special Operations units report through SOCOM.

S2, G2: Military shorthand for staff officer functions. S2 is a unit's Intelligence section (G2 is the equivalent in a General's staff).

S3, G3: Same as above. S3/G3 is the Operations section.

TEI: Trans-Earth Injection.

TLI: Trans-Lunar Injection.

TLE: Two-Line Element. A standard method for cataloging the six essential mathematical elements of a satellite's orbit.

T-MINUS: "Time Minus." The countdown to a specific event that must occur at a specific time.

VAB: Vehicle Assembly Building. A massive black-and-white slab rising more than 500 feet above the marshes around Kennedy Space Center, this is where the Saturn rockets and Space Shuttles were assembled for launch. Mecca for rocket nerds.

"ZERO G": Zero gravity. Actually a colloquialism for what is more accurately termed "Micro gravity" or "Freefall." Zero-g is what popular culture is used to hearing, and it sounds cooler.

About The Author

Patrick Chiles has been fascinated by airplanes, rockets, and spaceflight ever since he was a little kid growing up in South Carolina. Fascination morphed into obsession when he witnessed the final Apollo/Saturn launches in person. How he ended up as an English major in college is still a mystery, though he managed to overcome this self-inflicted handicap to pursue a career in aviation.

He is a graduate of The Citadel military college, a Marine Corps veteran, and is licensed as a private pilot and airline dispatcher. In addition to his novels, he has written for aviation magazines including Smithsonian's Air & Space. He reluctantly lives in Ohio as an expatriate Southerner with his wife and sons, two lethargic dachshunds, and a bovine cat.

CPSIA information can be obtained
at www.ICGtesting.com
Printed in the USA
LVHW021622170423
744539LV00003B/21

9 781518 837418